Black
Current

Also by Karen Keskinen

Blood Orange

Black
Current

KAREN KESKINEN

MINOTAUR BOOKS ·
A THOMAS DUNNE BOOK
NEW YORK

A THOMAS DUNNE BOOK FOR MINOTAUR BOOKS.
An imprint of St. Martin's Publishing Group.

BLACK CURRENT. Copyright © 2014 by Karen Keskinen. All rights reserved. Printed in the United States of America. For information, address St. Martin's Press, 175 Fifth Avenue, New York, N.Y. 10010.

www.thomasdunnebooks.com
www.minotaurbooks.com

Designed by Omar Chapa

Library of Congress Cataloging-in-Publication Data

Keskinen, Karen
    Black current: a mystery / Karen Keskinen.—First edition.
        p. cm.
    "A Thomas Dunne book."
    ISBN 978-1-250-01271-5 (hardcover)
    ISBN 978-1-250-02834-1 (e-book)
    1. Women private investigators—Fiction. 2. Teenage boys—Crimes against—Fiction. 3. Drowning victims—Fiction. 4. Brothers—Death—Fiction. I. Title.
    PS3611.E834B57 2014
    813'.6—dc23

                                                                    2014008160

First Edition: June 2014

10 9 8 7 6 5 4 3 2 1

For Thor,
now and always

Acknowledgments

This story rose to the surface in a hard and painful time in my life, and was carried to shore on the blackest of currents. I am grateful to all my family and friends for their caring support through the course of the voyage. I especially want to thank Kat Brzozowski, my talented, skilled, and buoyant editor; Becca Stumpf, my wise and generous agent; Doug Reich, the good doc in the Bronx, NYC; and De Anna Dellabarca, steady center of the whirlwinds. Thanks as well to Jan Luc and to Diana Kennett, for their staunch friendship.

I also wish to thank Sea Center Manager Richard Smalldon for guiding me on a tour of our aquarium in Santa Barbara. Rich is an agreeable guy who most certainly bears no resemblance to any character in this book! My gratitude to Shelly Lowenkopf for his discerning critique of the manuscript at a critical stage, and to Corinne Contreras for her perceptive comments and advice. Thanks also to Clare Reich, bright young woman-about-town; Margot Reich, kid-wrangler and mystery maven; and Phuong-Cac Nguyen, for her warm introduction to *Mission & State*.

Most of all, I want to acknowledge those who rode through the storm with me: my partner, Salvi Dellabarca, and Casey

Dellabarca, our son. To you both, as always, my deepest thanks and love.

A portion of the proceeds from the sale of *Black Current* will be donated to Mission & State, the brave new investigative news service Santa Barbara so sorely needs—and all big little cities deserve. Visit then at www.missionandstate.org.

THE PIÑATA SONG

Dale, dale, dale,
No pierdas el tino,
Porque si lo pierdes
Pierdes el camino.

Isla Vista: February 1970

The four are dressed in black from head to toe. Though the night is warm, they wear balaclavas. Overkill, Rachel thinks, too dramatic. Like being an actor in some kind of ancient Japanese play. They glide past a lush front garden and she smells something blooming in the night: sweet, tropical. What in God's name is she doing here?

Aragorn carries two Molotovs, one in each hand. Frodo declined to carry one at the last minute, claiming an allegiance to nonviolence. And that's fine by her, but Rachel guesses he's just afraid.

The names—it's ridiculous, the names Aragorn insists on using. In case they're overheard, he says, because everyone knows there are spies in the movement. Aragorn, Frodo, Galadriel. She's supposed to be Arwen. It's from *The Lord of the Rings*, that book all the guys are reading these days.

Aragorn's in charge, there's never been any question of that. Following his orders, the women each carry a bottle of wine. They are handmaidens: reverting to a traditional role. Rachel's been reading about something lately, women's lib they're calling it . . . it's exciting, *real*. Not like this little boys' game.

"Step back!" Aragorn hisses. They do as he says, pressing

against a dust-choked hedge. Up ahead, a patrol car slides across the street on the prowl.

"The pigs are crawling all over Isla Vista," Frodo mutters. "Because of last night."

"Yeah." Galadriel smiles. "They didn't like seeing a bank getting burned."

Aragorn sets the Molotovs down at his feet, and sticks out a hand. "Arwen. Give me a swig."

Rachel obeys, handing him the half-full bottle. He tips back his head and drinks, and when he leans down to kiss her, she tastes the sour red wine on his lips.

They are lovers, and she returns his kiss readily, smelling and tasting him in the dark. They'll make love after, in her cramped room on Sabado Tarde. For the first time she wonders, is that why she's here?

Aragorn steps back out on the road, and the others follow. Maybe, Rachel thinks, maybe he isn't worth it. Because this whole charade is beginning to feel stupid and wrong. Dangerous, too. Even so, she remains by his side.

They move through the streets, then halt a few doors down from the La Playa Rental Agency office. The blinds are all closed, the narrow two-story building is empty and dark. They'd scouted it earlier in the day. Everything's going as planned.

"OK, remember. You women watch out for us, here in the street. Frodo, you stand guard at the side of the building. I'll toss the Molotovs from the back. When you see me come out, everybody scatters. We run in four different directions. Got it?"

Rachel senses the anticipation, the exhilaration of the hunt in Aragorn's voice.

Aragorn and Frodo take off. In less than a minute, Rachel hears the shattering of windows. The sound is muffled, not as loud as she'd expected. And then the two men reappear around the side, Frodo in front, both running hard. Aragorn waves everyone on, and they split.

Rachel walks away quickly, not wanting to run in case somebody notices her. Just before she turns the corner, she looks back. Already, the window at the front of the building glows a wavering orange.

Rachel doesn't hear the screams of the one trapped inside. She doesn't hear a thing.

Chapter One

It was early, just past seven, and I was the first tenant to arrive at the bungalow court at 101 West Mission. I wheeled my bike over the curb and up the steps, glancing at the seagull-spattered plaque near the bottom of the board. JAYMIE ZARLIN, SANTA BARBARA INVESTIGATIONS—SUITE D. Yep, that was me.

A giant fern frond patted my cheek with dew as I pushed my way down the path. Next time I'd need to bring a machete. The courtyard was a jungle these days, the giant bird-of-paradise plants towering over the huddle of stucco offices. The landlord had fired the gardener, informing the tenants it was that or raise the rent, take your pick.

Suite D, be it ever so humble, was down at the back. I wheeled my old Schwinn to the steps and reached into my pocket for the key to the cable looped to the banister. And halted in my tracks.

An elegant rose, poised like a ballerina with her toes in a bell jar, stood on the top step. The soft pink was pristine, the petals flared. A little white tag on a string dangled from the stem.

Mike Dawson.

My heart hip-hopped like a rabbit. The rose could only be from Mike. He'd stopped being mad at me for nearly skipping town.

There were two men in my life, and sending roses just wasn't Zave's thing. Zave was about as romantic as a coyote, and besides, we were just friends. Other than Zave and Mike, there was nobody.

So it had to be Mike, who was dating another woman now, who was, as he'd put it himself, "moving on." At one point, in anger, I'd told him that moving on was just fine by me.

Standing there alone in the courtyard, gazing down at the late-summer rose, I admitted the truth: it wasn't fine by me, not at all. I missed the guy, missed the way he talked and laughed and rocked back on his feet.

Hell. I even missed the way he ignored me half the time, obsessed over sports on TV, and worked himself up to a low rolling boil for reasons that escaped me.

I cabled the bike to the banister and floated up the steps—if you can float in jeans and a T-shirt—unlocked the door, then bent down and picked up the jar. I carried it inside and placed it on the desk.

I opened the shades, the windows, and the door to the kitchenette at the back. Only then did I allow myself to bend down to the rose and take a deep breath. A sweet perfume teased my brain. I held the tag between thumb and forefinger, and read:

Por Gabi—"Friendship"

Por Gabi? What the! Right then and there, the Mike Dawson daydream popped like a big overblown bubble.

Since when did my assistant have a suitor? As far as Gabi Gutierrez was concerned, the male of the species was no-good, downlow, nothing but trouble. I shifted the jar to the center of the desk blotter. Gabi's blotter, her desk. My station was the kitchen table in the back room, which was where I was now headed. Not to waste my time daydreaming, but to get some work done.

In fact I'd been busy since the conclusion of the Solstice Murders, busy with the sort of work I preferred. I'd located two children abducted by parents involved in custody squabbles, one a four-year-old being used as a pawn. And I'd tracked down and recovered a developmentally disabled young woman who'd been lured into a cross-country road trip by a pair of abusive teenagers. The punks had narrowly escaped kidnapping charges.

Now I began to sort through the stacks of paper, clearing the table and my mind, so I could focus on what mattered.

"Hola!" Gabi banged open the door at eight on the dot. In spite of my lingering chagrin, I was gratified to notice a Rosarita Bakery bag peeking out from her giant purse.

"Morning." I watched as she went to her desk.

Gabi noticed the rose all right—who wouldn't, the flower practically purred for attention—but she parked her purse on the chair, removed the paper bag, and walked on into the kitchenette.

"Buenos días, Miss Jaymie. How about a croissant today? We gotta fatten you up, maybe I should get you two every morning, huh?"

My, wasn't she sweet. And now that I thought about it, Gabi had been uncharacteristically agreeable for over a week now.

No doubt about it, something was up.

I continued to observe my personal assistant (her choice of title, not mine) as she opened the cupboard over the sink, took down a pair of pink Fiesta ware plates, and positioned a paper doily on each.

"Gabi." I couldn't stand it anymore. "What's with the rose?"

"Huh?" Her expression remained serene.

"Come on. Don't say 'huh.' And don't say, 'what rose.'"

"I did not say 'what rose.'" She ripped open the bakery bag. I'd skipped breakfast, and the sight of the pastries almost made me pant.

She filled the carafe at the sink, then started the coffeemaker. "I see the rose, OK? I just don't have no time to *look* at it yet."

"Well, I had time. I read the tag, and it says it's for you." The heavy rich aroma of God's great gift to humankind, coffee, filled my nose. "But it doesn't say who it's from."

"No?" She arched an eyebrow. "Maybe it's a secret. Private. Did you think about that, Miss Jaymie?" Gabi sat down opposite me, clearing a space in the paper chaos for her cup and plate.

"All I'm asking is—"

She smiled sweetly, then put a thumb and forefinger to her lips and turned a pretend key.

At 5:15 that afternoon, Skye Rasmussen wanted the waves so bad it was almost an ache. Three texts from his buds had jumped into his phone: *wind's picked up and changed to a sundowner, the surf off Leadbetter's running strong,* and *where the f are you bro?* He could almost feel the sting of the salt spray and the heat of the sun on his skin.

But first, Skye had to take care of Cruella. She was his project, his baby. He alone was responsible for the pale blue jellyfish with the lethal nine-foot-long tentacles. And baby would be getting hungry just about now.

So Skye jammed the logbook and pen in a pocket of his baggy shorts, chained his board to the rack on his pickup, and headed out for the aquarium. Dealing with the man killer shouldn't take long.

He parked out on Cabrillo where it was free, answered one of the texts, then tossed his cell in the glove box and hopped out of the truck. The wind had picked up for real, and as Skye jogged down the planks of the wharf he heard the waves slap against the pilings. Excitement rippled through him. This was going to be an awesome afternoon, maybe the best all summer.

He slowed to a walk, then stopped at the rail behind the aquarium. His gaze drifted along the golden curve of East Beach. Skye was thinking about calling Taryn and asking her to meet him at Leadbetter.

He wanted her with him today, out on the water. She was still nervous about them being seen in public together, but they had to do it sooner or later. Skye looked down, into the churning surf.

He'd fucked up with her, big time. But it wouldn't happen again. Now he knew what mattered. Taryn mattered. He was getting a second chance with her, and he would make it good.

Skye felt a smile spread across his face. Yeah. Having Taryn with him this afternoon would be just about perfect. When he finished with the jellyfish and got back to the truck, he'd give her a call.

He turned away from the rail, walked over to the blank service door of the aquarium and punched in the code. The door popped open. Skye stepped inside and pulled it shut. Then he hurried down the corridor and into the kitchen, where the live fish destined to be food swam in small tanks. He netted six flailing mackerel and dumped them into a white bucket. "Sorry, guys. At least you don't have a clue about what's gonna happen."

The aquarium had closed to the public at 4:30. By now the staff members and volunteers would have cleaned up the facility and shut it down for the day. That was good—he was in a hurry, and the last thing he wanted was to get drawn into some long conversation.

Skye left the kitchen and walked through the darkened halls to the room housing Cruella's two-story-high tank. Before climbing to the mezzanine, he stopped to admire his charge.

Supremely elegant as always, today Cruella looked irritated, somehow. Her long trailing ribbons twitched with agitation, and her big box-shaped head glowed like an alien's.

Skye selected a small bronze key from the collection on his ring, and unlocked the door in the mural wall. He raced up the steel stairs two at a time, then opened the lid to the tank and balanced the pail on the rim. "Sorry, guys," he murmured again to the shimmering fish.

Delighted to be released back to their element, the mackerel dove.

Casually, the big jellyfish stretched out an arm.

Mesmerized as always by the drama, Skye didn't take his eyes off the tank as he tugged the notebook and pen from his shorts pocket.

A minute later he heard the click of the door below, and the sound of footsteps on the steel stairs. But still he kept his eyes riveted on the jellyfish and her delicate death dance. Skye saw the embrace, the frantic struggle, and knew it was useless. He knew.

My cell woke me. I'd turned off the ringer but not the vibrator, and the damn thing buzzed on the nightstand like some giant beetle.

I peered at the red-eyed clock across the room: 5:23 in the A.M. Old worries and habitual fears surfaced in my sleep-drunk brain. Brodie? Had something happened to Brod? The question jerked me awake.

Brodie . . . but he was gone. No, not gone . . . I made myself say the words aloud in the dark: dead. *My brother is dead.*

There would be no more urgent calls in the night concerning Brodie. And the thing was, much as I'd feared them, I'd give anything for those calls to return.

Anyway, no good news arrived at this hour of the morning. I burrowed under the covers, and after a few seconds the cursed thing shut up. My heart had just started to slow when the groaning vibrations started up again.

I snatched up the phone and punched it on. ZAVE, the screen proclaimed in caps. Zave Carbonel.

"Zave? What—is something wrong?"

"Not with you and me, Jaymie, not ever," his sweet smoky voice growled.

I fell back in the bed. "Mmm . . . so what is it . . . at five-thirty in the morning you just had to hear the sound of my voice?"

"Not exactly, sweetness." Zave paused. "Just had a call, from a friend of a friend. Jaymie, you want a job?"

"Sure." I rolled over on my back and let my eyelids ease down. "Maybe in a few hours or so . . ."

"Jaymie? It's now or never. They mentioned a figure: a grand."

Times were tough, and this month, I recalled, we were struggling to make rent. I shoved back the covers and staggered out of bed.

5:43. I rolled my bike out of the breezeway, then stopped for a moment to tug the zip on my sweat jacket up to my chin. The sea fog was dense. In between blasts from the foghorn, I could hear the moisture drip like rain off the fronds of the big palm on the hillside above me.

I hopped on the Schwinn, pointed her nose down the drive, and angled into El Balcon. I needed to hurry, Zave had explained. I cut a sharp left through the fog onto Cliff Drive, then curved down Loma Alta.

Now I couldn't see a damn thing. The fog absorbed the light from the streetlamps and diffused it into a yellow glow. I listened hard for traffic as I neared Cabrillo.

The car must have been a hybrid, because I didn't hear it until it was nearly on top of me. I swerved right, caught the curb, and found myself upended in a patch of agaves at the side of the road. The big leathery leaves cushioned my fall, but a sharp spine dug into the left side of my face. I put a hand to my cheek, pulled it away: my palm was smeared with blood.

But I was fine, nothing broken. I clambered to my feet and stood there for a moment, blotting the mess with my sweatshirt and pressing hard to stop the bleed. Then I dragged the bike out of the gutter. Like me, it was no worse for wear.

I rode on, hugging the curb. The bicycle made a new sound now, a sulky clank-clunk. A sea lion bellowed not far off shore. Waves hissed on the sand.

A few minutes more and I was bouncing along the rough square timbers of the wharf. The Santa Barbara Aquarium, built on a spur pier, loomed out of the shadows on my left. Funny, I'd expected to see lights blazing, but the big two-story wooden structure was dark.

I pedaled slowly around to the back. There was the service-entrance door Zave had mentioned, illuminated by a single yellow bulb. "They'll be waiting for you," he'd said. "Knock twice, pause, then three times. Somebody will let you in."

Then, he'd said something else. "Prepare yourself, Jaymie. The guy who called me didn't spell it out, but I got the idea you're going to see something bad."

Something bad. Well, I'd seen bad things, I thought as I dismounted and leaned the bike against the building. I'd seen chilled bodies in the morgue, one of them the body of my own brother. Nothing could be worse than that.

Feeling like an actor in a 1930s detective flick, I knocked in code. After a minute or so the door inched open, and an eye peered through the gap. Then the door opened further. A man holding an unlit flashlight peered out at me. He was skinny and tall, slightly stooped. His pale, thinning hair was tied back in a scraggly ponytail.

"Who are you?" he said in an oddly pleasant voice. Odd because the voice didn't fit him: it made him sound more self-confident than he looked.

"Jaymie Zarlin. I believe I'm expected."

He stepped aside for me to enter, then shut the door after me. We stood facing each other in a short corridor illuminated by recessed ceiling lights. The space was empty, except for several lockers mounted to the wall.

The guy studied me uncertainly. His hair was actually light red, salted with white. He wasn't young—somewhere in his mid-sixties. "So . . . what were you told?"

"Not much. How about if we start with *your* name? I'd like to know who I'm working for."

"Not for me," he said quickly. Then he shrugged. "I'm Neil

Thompson. Aquarium director. Look, he told me they were sending someone discreet." He glanced at my bloody cheek and frowned, as if I looked anything but.

"Discreet? I can be that." I felt an edge of annoyance: this was like pulling teeth. "So, who is this 'he'?"

"Do you have any idea what—" Then he shook his head, too many times. "Listen. There's a young man in the other room. He's dead . . . drowned. You'll find a camera, I left it just inside the door on a chair. Take pictures of . . . of the boy. Take pictures of everything, anything you think's important. Take your time, look around. Look for . . ." His voice faded.

"For what?"

"For—I don't know—*clues*."

"Clues. Clues to the boy's death?" What the hell was going on? Thompson looked scared as a four-year-old.

"Yes. He wants you to have a good look. Before the police arrive."

There it was, that "he" again. "So they've been called? The city cops, or the county sheriff? Because if they have—"

"They haven't. Not yet." He switched on his flashlight. "He'll call them when you finish your job."

I nodded, trying to understand what was going on under the scant words. "OK. But I need to meet the guy who's paying me."

"He'll talk to you when you're done. Now, no more questions." Neil Thompson had stiffened his face and dropped his melodious voice, apparently trying to look and sound firm. It was a move that didn't work on the mild-mannered guy.

But I shrugged in agreement, reminding myself of the thousand bucks Zave had mentioned. "Whatever you say."

I followed the lanky guy out of the hall, keeping my eyes on the beam of his flashlight. Apparently he didn't want to turn on the lights, most likely didn't want to attract any attention from outside. What was all this about? Calling me in before they called the police—somebody didn't trust the cops. That, or somebody had something to hide.

We moved into the gloom of the foyer, past the main desk and the entrance to the gift shop. From a side room marked *Staff* I heard quiet sobbing behind a partly closed door.

Thompson held open one of a pair of big swing doors and motioned me in with the flashlight. I stepped into the narrow room, and he followed after.

The space was lined with tanks glowing like neon. Iridescent fish darted through the bubbling sea water, and purple-red starfish sucked on the glass walls.

"It's in there. You'll . . . you'll see." Thompson pointed to an opening at the far end of the hall-like room. The gap was covered with a heavy drape that resembled a theater curtain. "Go on through. After, he'll be waiting for you back at the main desk. You'll give him the camera and make your notes in his presence."

It was in there? A young man had died, and Thompson was already calling him 'it'? "How about loaning me your flashlight?"

"You won't need it. The tank is lit." He turned and walked back to the foyer.

I looked at the drape. Yellow light seeped around the edges. A boy was dead in there. Drowned in a tank. And yet, nobody wanted to look. In fact, they didn't want to look *so much* that they'd actually hired a stranger to do the looking.

Well, I was an investigator, wasn't I? I'd been offered a princely sum to take a few pictures, poke around for a few clues, and keep my mouth shut. No problem, I could do those things. I reached into my pocket, pulled out a pair of latex gloves, and tugged them on.

Then I pushed back the curtain, lifted my eyes, and let out a sharp cry.

The water in the two-story-high cylindrical tank glowed with a soft yellow light. A single huge translucent jellyfish, tinged pale blue, hovered close beside the figure of a beautiful young man of seventeen or eighteen. The creature's twitching tentacles, maybe eight feet in length, wrapped the boy's torso in an embrace.

The boy wore shorts and no top. His body was slight yet strong. There was a slight current in the tank, and his arms and legs moved rhythmically, as if he were dancing.

But the most terrible thing was his face.

The neck was twisted slightly, so that he looked straight at me. And the expression—*dear God*.

The boy's face was contorted in a terrible grimace of torment. His eyes were open wide, anguished. His lips were pulled back, exposing his teeth.

I moved around the tank to view the body from another angle. I could not look into those eyes for long.

The young man had been in the water for many hours. And yet, you could see how handsome he'd been. His hair was brown and gold, twisted in dreadlocks, bleached by the sun. He was tanned, and a single flip-flop dangled lazily from his toe. A surfer, most likely. A beautiful boy.

I noticed a labeled sign, and gratefully moved further around to read it.

> *Chironex fleckeri*—*Box Jellyfish*.
> *Native to Australia. Sting can be fatal.*
> *Also called* Wasp of the Sea.

I made myself look again. The creature shifted several of its bluish tentacles, exposing angry red stripes on the victim's torso.

The boy had been stung to death. From the look on his face, he'd screamed till he'd died from the agonizing pain.

"Do your job," I muttered aloud.

I retrieved the camera, examined it for a moment, then put

my eye to the viewfinder. But how could I do it? How could I peer at the victim, stare at him through a keyhole, make him into an object? I dropped my arm.

He's gone. There's nothing you can do about that. But maybe you'll see something—or the lens will see something. Some clue to what happened here.

I lifted the camera and shot several times. Then I edged around the tank and shot more, from different angles. What I was doing still felt obscene. I was making a kind of exhibit of the boy's terrible suffering.

To break the brooding silence, I spoke aloud. "First things first. How did he end up in the water?"

I tipped back my head. At the top of the open tank was a wide catwalk, almost a mezzanine, surrounding perhaps a third of the tank's circumference. But how could I get there?

Behind the tank was a blue wall painted with fish and other sea creatures. The wall appeared solid at first glance. But when I stepped closer I saw a door mounted flush in the stucco. A keyhole was cleverly set in a sea horse's eye.

I ran a latexed finger down the door seam, and to my surprise, the unlocked door gave way.

Still carrying the camera, I stepped into a tight column-shaped space, just large enough to hold a steep circular staircase. Behind me the door, which was mounted with a spring, clicked shut. Now I wished I'd insisted on borrowing Thompson's flashlight.

I inched my way over to the stair and grabbed the handrail. The steel steps beneath my feet were sturdy, corrugated, and I had no trouble climbing up.

At the top, I could see again. The soft light from the tank illuminated the platform. I noticed a light switch on the wall and pressed it. Abruptly the platform was starkly lit. Keeping my eyes averted from the tank interior, I set about examining the scene.

The wall of the tank rose some three to four feet above the

platform floor, which was wood, probably mahogany, thickly coated in marine varnish. The tank itself, some fifteen feet in diameter, was partially covered with a folding lid. But what caught my attention were the objects resting on the platform.

A long-handled scoop net lay beside an upright lidded plastic pail. I lifted the lid: the inside was wet, but the pail was empty. I bent down and sniffed: it smelled of fish. Beads of water glimmered like pearls on the varnished floor.

The matching flip-flop, red with a black sole, lay close by the tank. Several feet away lay a black ring binder, open flat, and a ballpoint pen. Except for the flip-flop, the objects seemed organized, in their right places.

I shot photos: of the pail, the net, the rubber sandal, the pen and the binder. Then I knelt to read the open page. It wasn't much. A nine-week-long record of feedings of the jellyfish, a few brief observations. All noted with dates and times. I photographed the pages from the beginning, flipping them over one by one.

Then I drew in a breath and moved closer to the tank. In my head I repeated a mantra: *It's a job, just a job.*

The lid was folded back on itself. It was aluminum, lightweight, constructed in sections and hinged. A few gleaming fish swam back and forth, oblivious to their impending doom. I forced my eyes to focus on the boy.

He was directly under me, swaying slightly. Clasped in the translucent arms, securely embraced. The creature seemed to be brooding, sullen. Unwilling to release its prey.

I stood frozen for a moment. Then I made myself actually *see* the young man. He was so close I could make out the golden hairs on his forearms.

Had he jumped into the water? Not likely, if he knew anything about the so-called wasp of the sea. Even if he'd decided to kill himself, this was too painful and ghastly a way to go about it. Besides, that flip-flop still dangling from his toe: if he'd entered the tank purposefully, he'd most likely have left both sandals behind.

He could have had an accident, though. Tripped, fallen over the raised edge. The surface of the water was some five feet below the rim. It would have been nearly impossible for the boy to have climbed out quickly. How much time had elapsed before the lethal jellyfish attacked?

But . . . tripped? I studied the boy's body. The kid wasn't especially tall, but he'd been athletic, strong. I doubted he was so clumsy as to have fallen in.

On the other hand, he could have been shoved.

Yes. A surprise push. And then, in a flash, he was in the jellyfish's arms and stunned with its powerful neurotoxin. I watched a few unattached streamers, ruched like a girl's hair ribbons, drift to and fro.

Certain things didn't add up. Why hadn't the police been called immediately? I pulled my cell from my pocket again, and snapped a dozen more shots, as a record. A recording of the truth.

"Are you finished?" a strong male voice called out. The voice was filled with anguish, yet firm. Used to command.

I looked past the railing and down, into the room below. A tall, well-built man stood just inside the door. In the gloom, I couldn't make out his face. "Who are you?"

"I hired you. Come down and we'll talk."

Chapter Two

By the time I'd descended the stair and reentered the room, the man had stepped out again. I turned back to the tank and looked one last time at the boy suspended in his agonized world. I said a quick prayer, then pushed through the drape.

The guy stood halfway along the narrow space, hands shoved in the pockets of his khakis. In spite of the hour and the circumstance, his navy button-down shirt was freshly pressed, his silver hair combed in waves. But even in the gloom, his handsome face revealed his suffering: his mouth was bitter, his blue eyes dark and staring.

He looked familiar, somehow. And then it hit me: he looked like the boy. The boy in the tank.

"You're Jaymie Zarlin?"

"Yes. And you?"

"Dr. Steinbach. I'll take the camera." He held out his hand, and I gave it to him. It was his, after all.

"You want to know what I observed." I pulled off the gloves and stuffed them into my pocket. "Shall I tell you now?"

"No." He hesitated. "Look . . . come to my office."

I followed him into the entry foyer and around the main desk. The sobbing in the staff room had ceased. I could hear voices behind the now-closed door.

At the end of a short hall was another door, bearing a brass plate reading DR. ROD STEINBACH. The plate looked shiny and new.

Steinbach unlocked the door, entered, and motioned me in. The small windowless room was lined with floor-to-ceiling bookshelves, which made it claustrophobic. "Here." He nudged an office chair with his toe.

He walked around the desk and dropped heavily into his own chair, then stared down at a sheaf of papers. He didn't seem to be reading, just staring.

"Dr. Steinbach?" I said after a full minute had passed.

"What?" He looked up sharply, then swallowed. "Oh. I want you to jot down some details. What you noticed, what seemed . . . I don't know. Out of place." I heard a current of pain beneath the unemotional words.

"All right." I hesitated. "Dr. Steinbach, I have to ask. What I've just witnessed, it's truly terrible. Who was the young man?"

"I don't see why that—" Then he broke off. "You'll hear all about it anyway." He opened his hands and stared at them, first the backs, then the palms. "My grandson. Skye Rasmussen. My *grandson* . . ." I could see the effort he exerted, to stop himself from breaking into tears.

"I'm so sorry. I'll help in any way I can." I searched for words. "Maybe we should just talk, you know? I can tell you what I observed."

He raised a hand, let it fall to the desktop. "Go ahead."

"All right. I'm assuming your grandson was stung to death, or stung shortly before he drowned. By the jellyfish. The sign said, 'Wasp of the Sea.'"

"*Chironex fleckeri.* The sting is often fatal. They say—it's excruciating. If the neurotoxin doesn't kill you, the pain's so strong it makes you pass out—and even after you've passed out, before you drown you continue to . . . scream."

I was silent then. I couldn't think of a single thing to say that would ease the horror.

"I needed someone to come because I—I just can't go up there. I needed someone to be my eyes. Because I can't even be in the same room—"

"I understand, Dr. Steinbach. But what I don't understand is why you haven't called the police."

He frowned and looked past me. Then he got up, walked around the desk, and closed the door.

"I'll phone them when we're done. It's just that . . ." Dr. Steinbach returned to his chair. He gazed at his desktop as if he couldn't recall what it was there for. "I don't trust them, that's all."

I watched as his hands picked at the upholstered arms of his chair. "Are you saying you don't trust the cops to get it right?"

"For one thing, yes. And . . . I don't trust them in general." He shot me a glance. "Never mind, you wouldn't understand. Let's just say I don't want them poking around in my—my *family's* affairs."

"As a matter of fact, I do understand. But in a case like this you have to call them, Dr. Steinbach. Right away."

"I'll do it when I'm ready. Now, just tell me what you saw."

"I can tell you there's not much up on the top level. A three-ring binder—the notes seem to be about tending to the jellyfish over the past eight or nine weeks. A pen. A net with a long handle, and a white plastic bucket with a flip lid. By the way, the bucket was knocked over at some point, then turned upright again. I think it held fish. It smells of fish, and there are several swimming in the tank."

Steinbach nodded his head slowly, as if these sparse facts could somehow help him make sense of it all. "Any conclusions?"

"I don't have enough evidence to draw a conclusion." I spoke carefully, not sure how far I should go. "I assume your grandson was feeding the jellyfish?"

"Yes. That was part of his study project." Steinbach shut

his eyes for a moment and gripped the bridge of his nose. "I'd given Skye the code to the back door, so he could come in after hours."

"It's possible your grandson tripped, fell in accidently. And I suppose . . ."

"Yes?"

"It's possible he jumped."

"Suicide?" Steinbach's head snapped up. "That's nonsense."

"It's far-fetched, I agree. But I wouldn't call it nonsense. If your grandson knew about the box jellyfish, then he knew their stings could be fatal."

"Skye knew all about *Chironex fleckeri*. He'd applied for a small grant to study the species. That was one of the things that got him accepted at Stanford—he was starting there this fall. And no, Skye would never—*never* have done something so stupid as kill himself."

"OK."

"So it was an accident," Dr. Steinbach said with finality. "Anything else?"

"The door leading to the stairs was shut but unlocked, which is what you'd expect. I'm no expert, but I'd say the body has been in the water for eight to ten hours. Your grandson's body still wears one sandal—the other is up there on the deck. By the way, I'd recommend you drain the tank, sift through the contents at the bottom with a fine mesh. But the police will do that, anyway."

"Who knows what the hell the police will do. Bunglers. Idiots."

His vehemence surprised me. But I knew all the man's emotions must be overwrought.

"Dr. Steinbach, I have a question. Who found the body?"

"Who—oh, Delia Foley. She runs the snack bar here in the aquarium. Delia comes in early and gets everything set up and running." He waved his hand dismissively. "She's in the other room with Neil, crying her eyes out."

"Would you like me to interview her?"

"No. Delia is very upset. I'll talk with her myself."

"And Skye's parents, have they been notified?"

"My family is not your concern. Now, anything else?"

Rod Steinbach had to be in control, I realized. Had to. Maybe this was his way of dealing with the monstrosity of it all. "Does the aquarium have security cameras mounted at the doors?"

"There are no cameras out here on the wharf." He shook his head as if disgusted. "There's a security system of sorts, but it's hopelessly outdated. One of the many things I plan to change, now that I'm here."

"So you've just recently taken up your position with the Santa Barbara Aquarium. What is it you do?"

"I'm a consultant. Hired to whip the organization into shape. I wish to God I'd never agreed to take the position! If I hadn't, Skye would never . . ." He broke off, and lifted himself to his feet. I watched as he struggled to pull himself together. "All right. Anything else?"

I stood too, facing him. There was plenty I wanted to ask Rod Steinbach, but apparently he'd decided our conversation had come to an end.

"I should emphasize again that you need to call the police right away. If there's any chance of foul play, they'll need to move quickly."

"Foul play?" He scowled. "Did you see any evidence of that?"

"No. But it's possible your grandson was pushed."

"Skye was very popular," he snapped. "Why would anyone want to shove him into that tank?"

I had the sense Dr. Steinbach was testing me, though I'd no idea why. "I can't say. But I think it's too early to close the door on—"

"Thank you, Ms. Zarlin. You've fulfilled your purpose, and you may go. No, wait. I'll pay you now."

"No need. You can mail me a check."

"I want to close it off now." He stood, pulled out a money clip from his pants pocket, and peeled off ten one-hundred-dollar bills. Then he added an eleventh. "Here."

"Thank you. That's generous."

He slipped his money clip back in his khakis and walked around the desk to the door. "It's generous, yes. Understand I'm buying your discretion. I don't want you jabbering about what you've seen to the police."

"I don't jabber, Dr. Steinbach." I folded the bills and wedged them into my jeans pocket. "I have a request along the same lines."

"Oh?"

"Don't mention to the cops that I was here. It would only cause problems for both of us. And please ask Dr. Thompson not to say anything either."

"Fine. We're agreed."

As I pedaled around the arm blocking the vehicle entrance to the wharf, a Crown Vic purred past the dolphin statue. I sped up.

"Stop. Stop right there, Zarlin."

The words were bold, but the voice cheeped like a chicken, weakening the effect. I thought about continuing on, but the woman was a plainclothes detective. A cop.

"Deirdre. Lovely morning."

She pouted like a bad-tempered cherub. "What are you doing here, Zarlin? As if I didn't know."

Quickly, I weighed the options: the truth, or a lie? Deirdre Krause wouldn't believe the lie, of course. But if I told the truth, she just might have the big male cop riding shotgun arrest me. I decided freedom looked good.

"Riding my bike. Greeting the dawn." I smiled brightly. "Is there a new law against that?"

"There's blood on your face. Been in a fight?"

"No. But the day is still young."

Deirdre rapped her lacquered nails on the car door. I noticed she'd cut them square, leaving sharp corners.

"Listen, I don't need an amateur like you messing with my cases. And by the way, Zarlin, there is a law against interfering with an investigation. There's a law against tampering with a crime scene. There's a law against—"

"And there are laws against harassment and detainment. So if you—" I closed my mouth. The big cop had opened his door and was hefting his bulk out of the vehicle.

"Troy, don't bother," Deirdre snapped. "I don't have time to mess with her."

"Am I free to go, Detective?"

"Sure, why not." She gave me her dimpled baby doll smile. "I know where to find you—in that decrepit hovel you call an office. Or I can always drop by the other hovel you call your home."

"Make sure you phone first."

"By the way," Deirdre said as the car began to roll, "I saw Mike the other day. With Mandy Blaine. Know what? She was wearing a ring."

The car pulled away. I stood there straddling my bicycle, feeling as if I'd been socked in the stomach. But it was bullshit, I assured myself. Just Deirdre Krause messing with me. Mike wouldn't allow me to be blindsided like that. He'd let me know.

I stopped at the dolphin fountain and splashed cold water on my scratches to wash off the blood, then dabbed my face dry with the hem of my sweatshirt. After a moment I crossed Cabrillo, and rode on up State Street.

The fog, as usual, hugged the shoreline. Before I'd pedaled four blocks, the gloom thinned and the air turned deliciously clear. I should have felt great, yet how was that possible? I couldn't get Skye Rasmussen out of my mind.

I thought about stopping at Jeannine's for a bite of breakfast, but I wasn't hungry. I just wanted to den up in the office, maybe sip some of Gabi's strong brew. I biked on, heading up-town through the empty streets.

Why, I wondered, had Rod Steinbach called me in before he'd contacted the police? Of course, he hadn't called *me* in, ex-actly. He'd phoned a friend who'd phoned Zave. Still, the ques-tion remained.

Steinbach disliked the cops, didn't trust them. Plus he had to be in control. So that was it, wasn't it? He'd used me to garner information, to observe what he couldn't bear to see with his own eyes.

Fine. Except it wasn't fine, not for me. That lithe young body, clenched in those pale blue straps . . . and the horror imprinted forever on Skye Rasmussen's face. No, I couldn't let it go.

Gabi turned from the kitchenette counter and stared at me. "Miss Jaymie, did you get in a fight with a cat? If you did, I think the cat won."

"No, the fight was with an agave." I leaned back in my chair.

"Those scratches can get infected." Gabi lifted two pink cups and saucers down from the shelf. "At home I got some special ointment from my curandera. I'll go at lunch and get it for you."

"No thanks. Soap and water will do."

"You don't know what's good for you." She handed me a cup of aromatic brew. "So why did you get here so early this morn-ing? You beat me, two days in a row."

"Yesterday Dexter woke me up early. The raccoons were having a party up on my roof. Today . . . today I had to go out on a case." I didn't feel like talking about Skye Rasmussen, not even to Gabi. Not yet.

"A case, so early?" She paused with a pastry halfway to her mouth.

I decided to try and distract her. "Sorry about yesterday, Gabi. You're right, we shouldn't pry into each other's personal affairs."

Bingo: her face lit up. "It's OK, you can pry. I thought about it, and you're my friend, not just my boss." She examined her freshly lacquered nails. "See, I met a nice man. We went out to dinner. Then we went out to lunch."

I was impressed, maybe even a little shocked. I'd never known Gabi to speak positively about any man, let alone go out on a date.

"That *is* news. What's his name?"

"If I tell you will you keep quiet?" She pointed a stubby finger at me. "I don't need my family to know. One dinner and one lunch? My sisters will go to Paseo Nuevo today, to buy outfits for the wedding."

"Don't worry, I promise."

"An-hel. That's what I call him and that's his name."

"How old is—"

"Miss Jaymie? Here's what I'm gonna tell you. He's kinda short, like me. He's young, three years older than me. He's not really handsome, but that's OK, I'm not really beautiful. Angel is from Mexico and he's got no papers, thank God. He—"

"Wait a minute. What's good about that?" I talked around a mouthful of pastry. "If he had papers, then you could get papers if you two got married. I'd say—"

"See?" She tilted her chin disdainfully. "You don't get it, do you? Even though I already told you what I think. If Angel has papers, then how do I know if I really like him?"

Oh boy. "Uh, yeah. I guess you want to be sure you like him for himself."

"That's it. Besides, you don't want a man to think he's got something you really want. You should remember that, Miss Jaymie."

"Me? What for?" I felt myself flush. There was Zave, if having great sex with a good friend counted. And of course, there *wasn't* Mike. Gabi knew all about both. "I'm not involved with anybody," I said in a small voice.

"Sure you're not!" Gabi sounded triumphant, probably because she'd succeeded in turning the conversation into something about me.

I rapped my fingers on the tabletop. "Can we change the subject?"

"If you want. I got the same question for you I already asked. What case made you get up so early? Something new I don't know about?"

The smile slid from my face. "Gabi, I don't know if I want to talk about it just yet."

"I help you solve cases, that's one of my jobs."

"I know. But right now, a shoulder to cry on is more what I need."

Gabi reached across the pile of papers and patted my hand. "I got one of those for you too."

"OK." I centered the cup in its saucer. "I've got some pictures to show you. Prepare yourself."

"I'm prepared already, don't worry about me."

But she drew in a sharp gasp as she peered at the first photo on my phone. "Dios mío! What happened to him?"

Late that afternoon I pedaled up Cliff, then dismounted and walked my bike up El Balcon. The air was gauzy and hushed, as if time was taking a siesta. A gold mist hung over the Pacific, and only one dreamy island, Santa Cruz, was visible on the horizon.

When I reached the bottom of my drive, Dexter hopped partway down to me. As usual, he was beside himself with airheaded joy. Ever since he'd lost a leg, the little cow dog hadn't been able to negotiate the steepness of El Balcon. He was forced to wait at home like a bored house-spouse, pining for my return.

"Hey boy, what's for dinner tonight?"

"I'm asking you," he barked back.

I left the Schwinn in the breezeway between the house and the studio. Dex gave me a loving nip on the heel as I unlocked the front door of my humble abode and passed through to the kitchen. I would get no peace until His Lordship got what he asked for, so I measured kibble into his bowl, then added his favorite topping from a can in the fridge. I spoiled him these days, and Dex took full advantage of my weakness.

When the cow dog had scarfed down the lot, which took about fifteen seconds, he and I went back outside and over to the studio. This was our nightly ritual.

I unlocked the door to Brodie's place. As always, my brother's presence—his spirit, I sometimes believed—rose to meet me. "Hi, Brodie," I murmured.

Dexter shot past me and clambered onto the bed, his customary spot. Mine was the Papasan chair facing the window.

Brodie's remains rested in a carved wooden box I kept in my bedroom, on the dresser. But this is where he truly resided, here in the studio, with all his boyhood things. Lately, though, I'd felt my brother had a roommate: Danny Armenta, the boy who'd stayed here before he was murdered. Danny's baseball cap, *Santa Barbara Dons*, hung from a hook on the wall.

"Brod, it was rough today." I leaned back in the chair, tucked up my feet, and closed my eyes. "This kid Skye—he really suffered. I can't get it out of my mind." I let myself picture the young man, his slumped form wrapped in the long translucent tentacles, his dreadlocks floating like golden cords around his head.

Brodie never answered me. But he listened, somehow. He listened and accepted whatever I said . . . as long as it was true.

My brother was thirty-two when he died: mentally ill, homeless, and alone in the Santa Barbara city jail. I blamed myself. I'd ignored Brodie's overtures for years, convinced he was just using me for money to buy weed. His phone calls were pleas for help, but I was too closed-off and self-absorbed to comprehend.

Finally, his desperation was so apparent that even I understood. I moved down to Santa Barbara, bought 12 El Balcon, and filled the studio with my brother's childhood belongings in an effort to get him to join me. Somehow, I was too late.

Brodie had visited one day, stuck his head in the door and taken a look. He'd smiled wistfully and thanked me—but he never moved in.

"Did you stop trusting me, Brod? Was that it? Can't say I blame you."

My brother was in and out of jail by that time, pushing the well-oiled revolving door between homelessness and incarceration. My efforts to help him were either too forceful and strident, or too weak and off the mark. I never seemed to get it right. And in the end, love wasn't enough. My beloved brother hanged himself in his cell.

I must have dozed. After all, I'd been up since five. When I woke, the sun had rolled over the horizon, and every object in the room had turned to soft ash.

Chapter Three

The next morning, just before coffee time, Gabi poked her head in through the kitchenette doorway. Her face wore a solemn expression. "Miss Jaymie. There's a man here to see you."

My mind had sunk so deep in the hog's wallow of paperwork that I hadn't heard the door open, hadn't heard a thing. I set down my pen and pushed back the chair. "Who is it?"

"His name is Steven Steinbach."

"Steinbach?" I frowned. Three days had passed since I'd witnessed Skye Rasmussen in his watery grave, and I'd only been comforted by the fact that I would have nothing more to do with the matter. Now it looked as if I might be wrong.

I stepped through into the main room. "Mr. Steinbach?"

"Steven Steinbach."

The man had left the door open, and his figure was illuminated from behind while his face was in shadow. He wore gray slacks and a tight cranberry-red polo shirt. I couldn't see him very well, but one thing was certain: this person was kin to Skye. His body was lithe and strong, the planes of his face proportioned, handsome.

"Jaymie Zarlin." I stepped forward and extended my hand. After a moment's hesitation, he did the same.

Steven Steinbach looked very much like Skye, though he had straight black hair and folded eyelids. He didn't share Skye's last name, but still, the resemblance was uncanny, and I felt I should ask. "Are you Skye's father, Mr. Steinbach?"

He frowned. "Uncle. *Was*, of course. Past tense. Melanie's my sister."

The emphatic "was" surprised me. It seemed harsh. I knew from experience that relatives use the present tense for some time when they speak of the deceased, before they are ready to let them go. But Uncle Steve was ahead of the curve.

"I'm so sorry for what happened to your nephew."

"Yeah, it was"—he frowned again, with a quick knit of his brows—"it was bad."

"Did you—go to the aquarium?"

"No. None of us went, except Dad. He handled it his own way, as usual." He shrugged. "'Handling it' is my father's term for running the show."

I remained silent. Just what did Steven Steinbach want from me?

"Miss Jaymie?" Gabi jumped into the lull. "Why don't you sit in my desk chair. Mr. Steinbach can sit in the hot—I mean, in the visitor's chair. I got some work to do in the kitchen."

She'd nearly offered the man the hot seat. I smiled to myself. Then I shot her a warning glance, which meant: *don't you dare organize my papers.*

Gabi smiled knowingly in reply, walked through and pulled the door shut.

"Mr. Steinbach, please sit down. Tell me, how can I help you?"

He looked down at the chair, as if resisting an urge to brush it off. But he restrained himself and sat, draping one long leg over the other. "I'm here for my sister Melanie, and for Dave, her husband. Skye's parents." He started to say something more, then stopped.

I pulled Gabi's chair around from behind the desk, and sat facing him. "This has to be difficult," I tried again.

"It's harder than it should be, because as usual, Dad's standing in the way. What exactly did you do for my father?"

Rod Steinbach had just paid me eleven hundred bucks to keep quiet. As far as I knew, that included not talking to his family. "Not much. I think he just wanted an unprejudiced eye to look at the scene. It was extremely difficult for him, you know. Seeing his grandson like that."

"Yes, I guess it was." He shrugged, then glanced over at me. "Look. I have my own take on things, obviously. But Dad loved Skye. I'm sure it was hard."

I nodded and said nothing. The family's dynamics were none of my business, and I didn't want to get drawn in.

"But this is much worse for my sister and brother-in-law," Steven continued. "Melanie can't think straight. Dave's slightly better, not much." He shifted his leg and examined his charcoal sock.

"You know, the police found Skye's cell in his truck. He sent a text to a friend at 5:17, saying he'd be at the beach around six."

"Steven, I don't want to cut you off. But why are you telling me this? Your dad hired me and paid me. End of story."

"Like I said, I'm here for my sister." He raised his manicured hands, let them fall on the arms of the chair. "Dad has decided Skye's death was an accident. And now the police are agreeing with him. But Skye was an athlete, right? A top-notch surfer, plus he pretty much played every sport the school had to offer. Dave and Melanie find it hard to believe Skye fell accidentally into that tank."

I'd promised myself I'd keep my distance. But I now began to break that pledge. "Do you think it's possible your nephew committed suicide?"

"What—did Skye *kill* himself?" He shook his head. "I can't imagine why. He was everybody's favorite. A real golden boy, you know? Not perfect, but a pretty decent kid. And let me tell you, he was *never* depressed. Never."

"If it wasn't an accident and it wasn't suicide, that leaves foul play."

"I don't have any answers." He swung his tasseled loafer off his knee and got to his feet. "I'm just the errand boy. Dave and Mel wanted me to ask if you'd come to the funeral tomorrow. Ten o'clock at Muller's."

"I don't want to sound cold." I stood too, facing him. "But why would they want me there?"

"To just—I don't know. Come and observe."

"Your father paid me, Mr. Steinbach. My part's done."

"Your part is done as far as *he's* concerned, maybe. Look, it's not for me to say, but I think Dave and Melanie want to hire you."

"Hire me? To do what?"

"To find out what really happened." There it was again, that quick automatic frown. "You saw the—the body. Already, you know things."

"I'm not sure I—" Then the image of Skye, wrapped in those punishing arms, flashed in my brain.

"All right. I'll come to the funeral, for his parents' sake. But I can't help them, Mr. Steinbach. Please let them know. This matter rests with the police."

"You tell that to my sister. It needs to come from you." He folded his arms across his chest. "I've been here for nearly a week now. After the funeral, I'm going home."

"You live out of town?"

"San Francisco. I came down for Melanie's birthday party, her fortieth. Since my parents moved back here to Santa Barbara, I don't come down much anymore."

"Do you mean Skye died on her birthday?"

"Yes. She'll never celebrate it again."

When Steven Steinbach had gone, I nudged open the door to the kitchen. "Gabi, you can come out now."

Gabi peeped around the door like a bright-eyed squirrel. "What did he say?"

"He asked me to go to his nephew's funeral. But I know you heard every word."

"Yes, you would know. 'Cause you're the one that sits in here and listens all the time."

I ignored that. "What did you think of him?"

Gabi walked into the room, shook her head at the location of the desk chair, and pushed it back into place. "I don't think nothing about him. You are the investigator, not me. But I saw his hands were too clean, they don't do no work. I like a man who gets his hands dirty. And then washes them," she added.

"Mm-hm. Somebody like Angel."

"An-hel, you mean. Yes, that's what I like."

I gazed out the front window. A single giant bird-of-paradise leaf shaded the pane like an awning. The green leaf glowed like stained glass. "The service is tomorrow. I said I'd go."

Gabi looked over the top of her new rhinestone cheaters. "Miss Jaymie? Are you one hundred percent sure about this?"

"About twenty percent sure. Maybe not even that."

It *would* have to be Muller's Funeral Home, I thought as I chained my bike to a stucco pillar the following morning. Muller's had received my brother's body from the coroner, and so this was where I'd held the memorial service I'd put together for Brodie. Our parents hadn't wanted that burden.

I brushed off my best black jeans and tightened the band on my ponytail, then stepped into the vestibule. I could see through the double glass doors into the large chapel. The service was about to begin, and the room was packed to the rafters.

As I headed toward the chapel, I noticed the visitors' book lying open on a podium.

One thing I'm sure of: a detective is a voyeur. Maybe that's why I prefer to think of myself as an investigator.

Anyway, who's kidding herself? I picked up the book without a qualm and walked down a short hall and around the corner, to where I remembered there was a ladies' room.

When I pushed through the door, I discovered I wasn't alone. A young woman of about seventeen was huddled in a corner of the bathroom, weeping. Her curly dark hair was tied back with a purple ribbon, but a frizzy halo stood up around her pretty round face. She looked up at me, and I saw the grief in her eyes.

"Hi," I said. "The service is about to start."

"I—I can't go in."

"Are you sure? Maybe you can, even if you just stand at the back. Believe me, it will be better in the long run if you do. Better for you later on, I mean."

I'd told the girl the truth, but my comments were also self-serving. I wanted to open the guest book right away, so I could return it to the podium before it was missed. I needed her to leave.

She nodded, and dabbed at her cheeks with the paper towel I offered. Then she glanced at the book I held clutched against my chest. "Is that—the guest book?"

"Ah—yes. Yes, it is." I couldn't think of a single plausible explanation as to why I'd carried the book into the restroom. But she didn't seem to care about that.

"I'd like to sign." She fumbled in her purse and came up with a pen. "I wasn't brave enough to do it before, with all the people out in the hall."

I placed the book on the counter and watched as she slowly turned the pages, scanning the signatures. Then she signed at the end, and stared for a moment at the page.

"I'm glad I did that," she said in a small voice. "Thanks."

The instant the door swung shut behind her, I flipped back to the first page. I grabbed my cell, aimed and shot. Each page held a dozen names. Many people had signed in as couples, or families. Skye Rasmussen had been well liked: I estimated nearly three hundred people were in attendance.

But why in God's name was I doing this, I asked myself as I slipped back down the hall to the foyer. I'd no intention of taking the case. Then that image of Skye, wrapped forever in his agony, silenced my thoughts.

I laid the book down on the podium, opening it to the last page.

Only a few people turned to look as I eased into the back of the chapel. It was standing room only, and it took me a minute to spot an empty niche, halfway down the side of the room. An opening hymn struck up, and I was able to move to the location without attracting attention.

I studied the crowded chapel. All ages were present, from babies in arms to the elderly. Most of the mourners, though, were young men and women, high-school kids. The mood was heavy in the room. When the organ stopped, I heard sobbing.

The open coffin stood at the front. Behind it was the altar, and behind the altar the soaring glass windows looking out to the steep terra-cotta mountains sheltering the city. You could make out a faint haze of green on the live oaks which had survived the Stonecroft Fire.

The family sat in the front pews. On the right hand, closest to me, were Skye's distraught parents. Steven Steinbach sat beside them. Across the aisle was Rod Steinbach and an attractive Asian woman with silver-white hair. She must be Rod's wife, I realized. Skye's grandmother.

The service dragged on like a wounded animal, tormented. At last the parents approached the coffin.

And then we heard it, what we knew was coming: the most anguished cry on earth, the sound of a mother mourning the death of her child.

Melanie's cry tore through the room, split open the air.

I was unlocking my bike from the pillar when Skye's father approached me.

"Miss Zarlin? I'm Dave Rasmussen."

He was well into middle age, an ordinary-looking guy who'd married into a handsome family. His light brown hair was receding, and he carried a small paunch. Dark circles hung under his eyes.

"Mr. Rasmussen. I'm sorry about Skye. So very sorry for your loss." Useless words, but I uttered them anyway. I knew there were no words to comfort a parent who was mourning the death of a child. My words only functioned as sounds, really, sounds that I trusted would somehow convey sympathy.

"Thank you." He nodded once. "I can't—can't talk now. But thank you for coming. I wanted to meet you before we decided. . . ." He shrugged, gave up. "Tomorrow. Will you come and talk to Mel and me?"

"Mr. Rasmussen, I'm not sure that I—"

"Please, don't say no." He looked away. "We'll come to your office. Yes, maybe that's better. We'll come to you."

I gave in. How could I say no at that moment? "All right. That would be fine." I pulled a card from my pocket and handed it to him.

"We'll be there after the . . . cremation. At eleven."

I bowed my head. "Yes," I repeated, "that would be fine."

I argued with myself as I pedaled down Anacapa. Should I take the case on the Rasmussens' behalf? Part of me said no, I needed to stay away from murder, and stick with what I saw as my calling: investigating the disappearances of the living, finding those who were lost.

But another part of me, my ego, I suppose, muttered something else. *Take the case, solve it, show what you can do. Once and for all, prove you're no flash in the pan.*

I could do with advice, and not just any advice. I needed the therapeutic advice that only my old mentor and pal Charlie could give.

So instead of riding straight to the office, I decided to cruise the beachfront parking lots in search of Charlie's VW van. I turned on Carrillo, circled TV Hill, then glided down through City College to Leadbetter Beach, Charlie's customary daytime location.

A big black Explorer filled Charlie's usual parking spot, the spot he'd occupied for decades. I wove up and down the aisles, just in case he'd parked somewhere else. But there was no white van inscribed from fender to fender with Charlie's version of the Great American Novel.

I worked my way east along the waterfront, checking more lots plus the vehicles lining Cabrillo Boulevard. The marina, West Beach, the wharf, East Beach: nada. Charlie's van always stuck out like a sore thumb. If I wasn't seeing it, it wasn't around.

What the hell had happened to the guy? The old varmint had never vanished like this. As I pedaled back up Cabrillo, I wondered if I should mount a serious search. Problem was, I knew Charlie wouldn't appreciate me prying into his business.

Anyway, for the time being I'd just have to devise my own therapy. I chained my bike to a post at the yacht club, rolled up my jeans and removed my sneakers, then jogged across the hot sand.

The seawater was deliciously cool on my feet. Wavelets tickled my ankles like soft little tongues. Damn, I needed to keep a swimsuit in my messenger bag. I was dying for a swim.

I really shouldn't be here, I reminded myself. I needed to go to the office, get some work done. If you weren't watchful, Santa Barbara could lure you away from what mattered.

Of course, one could argue that *this* was what mattered: hot sand, cool surf, brisk breezes teasing your hair. I shut my eyes and wiggled my toes in sheer pleasure.

I'm no masochist. In the end, I decided to forget about the fact that I was fully dressed. I waded farther out and dove into a translucent green wave.

The water, colder than I anticipated, sent a shock wave through my body. My hair swirled about my head in a flowing corona. I stayed down, held my breath till my lungs ached, then shot to the surface. For a moment I thought, *Life is beautiful, and good.*

The following morning I watched the Rasmussens make their way up the walk to the office. Moving as a single unit of grief, they clung together. It was difficult to tell if Melanie and Dave were supporting each other, or weighing each other down.

I opened the door and stepped to one side. "Please, come in."

Today I was on my own. Gabi was out operating her other business, Sparkleberry Cleaning Service, of which she was, once again, both owner and sole employee. Good help—the kind that would do precisely what Gabi spelled out and never complain— was tough to find.

The Rasmussens entered and stood side by side in the small room, gazing at me. They had just witnessed their son's cremation, and they looked empty, drained.

"Miss Zarlin, this is my wife, Melanie."

Melanie Rasmussen was every bit as good-looking as her brother. She'd inherited their father's height, and in her plain black pumps, she was taller than her husband. She was more attractive than Dave, too, and some might have said she could've done better. But as I watched her cling to his arm, I saw how she needed him.

I motioned to the Craigslist couch against the wall and pulled the hot seat around for myself, facing the couch. "Can I get you some coffee?"

"No, thank you," Dave said automatically. But Melanie answered, "Maybe . . . a glass of water?"

I wasn't sure she really wanted water. I guessed she only wanted what she couldn't have: her son.

"Sure. Be right back." I was glad of the moment alone. I turned on the tap, let it run, and took the best glass from the cupboard. Then I filled the glass and stood there staring at it.

I was wrong, I thought: Melanie did want something from me. And so did Dave. They wanted me to tell them what had happened to Skye.

"I'm sorry, we don't have ice," I said as I handed the glass to Melanie. I perched on the edge of the chair. As she sipped at the water a silence unraveled, fuzzy, confused.

Dave cleared his throat. "We—we—" Then he stopped midsentence and waved his hand in the air.

It was Melanie who filled the gap. "We want you to find out what happened. The truth."

"I understand. But the police are the ones to talk to. They have the resources, the expertise—"

"No." Melanie shook her head, from side to side. "Dad took control. He told the police what to think. He's always doing something like that. But this time he's not going to get away with it." Her dark eyes burned. "Skye is *our son*."

"The police have decided your son died in an accident, Mrs. Rasmussen. Your father thinks the same thing. But that doesn't mean they're following his orders." My heart ached for her. I'd been there with Brodie: I knew how she felt.

Her head drooped. She raised her hands to her face and began to weep softly.

"I'm so sorry, I didn't mean to be—"

"It's all right," Dave said heavily. "It's not you. It's just all so—so unbelievable to us." He pressed his handkerchief into his wife's hands.

Melanie dabbed at her eyes, then looked up at me. "Our son is an athlete. A graceful, beautiful boy . . . do you really think he fell into that tank?"

She had me there. Because I didn't believe he'd fallen in. In fact, I suspected Skye Rasmussen had had an assist. But this business about the truth—I needed to be certain they meant it. Because as I knew from experience, the truth was often ugly—and cruel.

"Mrs. Rasmussen, forgive me. But I'm not the only private investigator in town. I have to be frank: this isn't the sort of case I normally do. I guess what I'm asking is, why me?"

"You found out who killed that poor girl, Lili Molina, and the Armenta boy. Everybody else gave up, and you didn't." Melanie twisted the handkerchief into a tight ball. "We know you'll get at the truth, Ms. Zarlin. That's all we want."

"But are you sure that's what you want? Because it might be terribly painful."

"Melanie, she's not going to help us." Dave stood. "Honey, we need to—"

"*No. Wait.*" Melanie leaned forward. Her eyes bored into mine. "Do you think the truth could be any more painful than what we're going through right now? Skye was our son. Our son! I will not let this go."

"Mrs. Rasmussen—"

"Stop. Just stop." She lifted a shaky finger and pointed at me. "You don't believe what the police are saying, I can tell you don't." Her voice rose. "So why won't you help us? Why!"

The outburst clanged like a bell in the room. Even after the woman had finished, the air seemed to ring with her words.

And abruptly I was angry, deeply angry with myself. This *was* my job, after all: to help those in distress.

"You're right. I don't believe it. I think someone else was up on that platform with Skye. I don't know if your son was pushed. But I don't think he was alone."

Melanie moaned as she fell back against the couch. "Skye, Skye—"

Then I heard myself say exactly what I'd tried to avoid: "I'll take the case. And I promise, I'll find out what happened to your son."

Chapter Four

The Sea Horse Snack Bar was located on the second level of the Santa Barbara Aquarium. I sat at the counter and watched Delia Foley as she rearranged a snack display, then snatched up a dishcloth and wiped down the stainless counter. The attractive woman was somewhere in her early forties, but her thin, youthful figure made her look younger.

"Gabi Gutierrez said to say hi," I began again. My first attempt to connect with Delia had met with a quick scowl. "She's my office manager." Of course, Gabi insisted on "personal assistant," but she wasn't here to object.

"Gabi?" Delia Foley halted, cloth poised. "Is that somebody I should know?"

"She's your cousin."

Delia tipped up her chin imperiously. "My mother's side, probably. I've got so many cousins on that side, I don't bother to keep track of them all."

Whoa. That was something I would not be passing on to my office manager. "Well, Gabi knows who *you* are."

Delia shrugged. "Maybe I do know her. Is she the kinda fat one with the big mouth, the one that never got married?"

Now I really was not liking this woman. "No. I'm talking

about the kindhearted one, the one who would probably give you the shirt off her back if you asked."

Delia tossed the rag onto the counter. "Just what do you want from me? I've got work to do."

I thought of Melanie and Dave. And decided to try again, a third time. "Look, Delia. I'm not here to harass you. I'm only here because of the Rasmussens. They've asked for my help. You're the one who found their son's body, and that's the only reason I want to talk."

Behind all the makeup, in spite of her sharp features, Delia Foley seemed to soften. "Let's go outside. I've got a few minutes before I have to open."

She had forty-five minutes, but I didn't press the point. "Thanks."

I followed Delia through a pair of large sliders to an outside deck. She sat down at one of three round tables and flicked a lighter several times, then touched the flame to the tip of a menthol cigarette.

"I liked him. Skye." She looked out to sea. "Everybody did, as far as I know. I just don't want to think about it. Or picture it, all right? I need to wipe it out of my mind."

"It must have been a terrible shock, coming on it all by yourself."

She nodded, took a long drag. "It was a shock, all right. I called Neil, and he came right away."

"And Neil called Dr. Steinbach?"

"I guess so. I wasn't paying all that much attention by then. I couldn't stop crying."

Everything with Delia, I figured, would always come back to the almighty "I." Still, that was fine by me. I was here for info, not friendship. "So Skye got along with everybody here, all the staff?"

"As far as I know. There's not a lot of staff. Volunteers, mainly. But Cheryl Kerr, she runs the gift shop, I saw her talking with him once or twice. Cheryl comes in at nine—you can catch her this morning, if you want."

"I will."

"And a couple of Skye's high-school friends are volunteers. I don't know what their names are, but I heard he got them their positions. For senior-year community service, you know?"

"Right." I steered her back on track. "Dr. Thompson, did he like Skye?"

"Neil? Of course he did." Her expression grew guarded. "Why are you asking me all this stuff?"

"We're not sure what actually happened. And the Rasmussens need to know." I watched as Delia got up and walked over to the rail, then tossed her cigarette butt over the side. A big seagull sitting on a post lifted his wings as if to dive after it, then decided to stay put.

I joined her at the rail. "What about Rod Steinbach? I understand he hasn't been here very long."

"Dr. Steinbach?" She pursed her lips and drew her thin white cardigan close around her. "I don't really know him," she said in a flat tone. "I've only talked to him a couple of times."

I knew a retreat when I heard one. How was I going to get this woman to open up? "Do you have kids, Delia?"

"Two, a boy and a girl." Sure enough, her expression relaxed.

"How old?"

"My son is seven and my daughter's almost ten. That's why I work, really, to buy them nice things. My daughter already loves clothes, you know? And Alex, my boy, likes video games. You know how expensive they are."

"I do. And I'm sure you'd do anything for your kids. You probably understand how the Rasmussens feel right now, especially Melanie."

"Yes." Delia hesitated. "I heard her at the funeral, when she screamed. It was horrible."

I nodded, let the silence expand. "Can you think of anything else you can tell me that might help them?"

"Not really." She twisted her mouth into a knot, and studied the varnished deck.

"One more question, then I'll let you go. Who knows the combination to the service-entrance door?"

Her head jerked up. She rubbed at her cheek.

"There's me . . . and Cheryl." I saw she was working to control her voice now, to keep it casual. "Neil—Dr. Thompson, I mean—and Dr. Steinbach, of course. I think that's about it."

I was pretty sure that wasn't "it." But I'd pushed as far as I could, short of calling Delia a liar. "Thanks. I'll let you get back to work now. If you think of something, anything at all, here's my card."

I was outside on the dock below, waiting to ambush the gift-shop manager, when Delia pushed open the service door ten minutes later. She paused, then walked on over.

"Look, I thought of something. I probably shouldn't say this. So if I tell you, will you promise to keep quiet about where you heard it?"

I was itching to say, "I promise." But I'd learned it was best to be straight. "I'll do everything I can to keep it quiet."

"I guess that's OK." Delia stepped closer and dropped her voice. "It's about Dr. Steinbach. See, he's been driving all of us crazy. The board only hired him to be a consultant, you know. But he's on everybody's case, all the time. Even Neil's."

The big gull swooped down from the deck above and landed on a table a few feet away from us. I stared at the bloodred spot on his beak. "Everybody's case? What about?"

"What about? Nothing. Everything!" She planted her hands on her hips. "Nobody measures up. According to him, we all deserve to get fired."

"Is that why they hired him? To clean house?"

"Delia?" Neil Thompson stood in the service doorway. A thin strand of hair hung down the side of his face.

She spun around. "Oh, Neil—"

"Ms. Zarlin? What are you doing here?"

"Chatting with Delia, Dr. Thompson. How about you—do you have time to talk?"

"No. I'm sorry, but I need to speak with Dee—with Ms. Foley. And we have to get ready to open up." He bent his tall frame as he took a step backward, in through the door.

When a potential informant takes a step away from me, I can't help it—I take a step forward. Or two or three. "I understand you're busy. Can we set up an appointment?"

He retreated further inside, like a crab backing into a shell. "About what? Rod—Dr. Steinbach—said your job was done."

"I'm not working for Dr. Steinbach now. My clients are the Rasmussens." I walked right up to the doorway. Delia was behind me, waiting to go in.

"Melanie and Dave want me to find out what happened to their son. They'd appreciate it if you'd set aside some time to talk."

"Ah. Well, if you put it that way." He frowned and looked away. "But phone me, Ms. Zarlin, if you don't mind."

"Excuse me." Delia stepped around me. As she pushed past Neil Thompson, I noticed how her hip brushed against his thigh.

There was no surprise in that—the space was tight. But she didn't apologize, and neither of them shrank from the touch.

The door closed. I walked back to the edge of the dock, stared down into the water, and thought about what Delia had told me. So Skye's grandfather had been riding the staff hard. I wondered: had someone taken exception to that?

Cheryl Kerr was late. Frazzled, she bustled past me, her heart-shaped face pink behind her big owlish glasses.

I caught up with her just as she was beginning to punch in the combination on the door lock. "Hi, Ms. Kerr."

She turned to me with an alarmed look. "Yes?" A fine beading of sweat shone on her upper lip.

"I realize you're in a hurry. But do you have a minute?"

"Not—not really." She tugged her peach-colored nylon top down over her wrinkled linen pants. "What's it about?"

I handed her my card. "My name's Jaymie Zarlin. I'm assisting the Rasmussens."

She looked at the card, and blanched. There really was no other good word for it: the woman turned white as a marshmallow. To steady herself, she placed a hand on the door.

I took her by the arm and led her to a plank bench bolted to the back wall of the aquarium. "I'm sorry if I took you by surprise. May I call you Cheryl?"

She nodded, then gulped. "Terrible," she finally murmured. "A terrible thing."

"Yes. Yes, it is."

Cheryl smoothed her graying hair. She wore it in a long pageboy, held back off her face with a faded headband.

"I'd just like to ask you a few questions. I'm sorry to put you through this, but the family would appreciate your help."

"I—I really do only have a minute. I have to open the gift shop."

"This won't take long. Tell me, what time did you leave work last Friday?"

"Oh. At ten past five, the same time as always. I'm paid to five, so I work right up till then. Then I take ten minutes to get ready to go, on my own time. I think that's fair."

"Ten minutes? What do you usually do in that time?"

"Oh, clean up my counter. Use the restroom, I guess. And I go talk to Legs, tell her good night." Cheryl smiled. "I'm her favorite, actually."

"Legs?"

"Our two-spotted octopus. Octopi are very intelligent, you know? About as smart as cats."

"I didn't realize that. Tell me, did you know Skye?"

"Just a little. I don't really talk to the volunteers much." She stared down at her hands, knitted together in her lap. "But he seemed . . . he seemed nice."

"Did everybody get along with him?"

"I think so. I really don't know. You should ask somebody else. I'm stuck over in the gift shop all day, I don't see much of what's going on."

I wasn't sure interviewing Cheryl Kerr was worth the effort. But I reminded myself that you never knew where a clue might rear its tricky little head. "How about the Rasmussen family, and the Steinbachs? Do you know them?"

"No. Why, should I?"

My ears pricked up. Unless I was mistaken, a tiny tinge of rebellion had sounded. I decided to give a further prod.

"But you do know Skye's grandfather, right? The new consultant, Rod Steinbach."

She sat up straight. "Dr. Steinbach. Of course I know who he is."

Ah. I'd put my finger on the sore spot. "Do you—"

"Excuse me. I don't like to be late. I almost never am." Cheryl glanced over, and her pale blue eyes met mine. She almost seemed to be pleading.

"Of course. Sorry if I've kept you."

She stood and shouldered her handbag. "Our director, Neil Thompson? That's who you should be talking to. I'm just the gift-shop lady. Now please—I need to go."

For the second time in a week, a fresh rose graced the office steps. This one was bouncy and bright, yellow as sunshine. I picked up the plastic water bottle and read the tag: *Buttercup*. Oh, great. Happy days were here to stay.

I unlocked the door, set Buttercup on the desk beside Friendship. Was it time to discard the somewhat tired Friendship, and establish the new rose in its place? I would leave that up to the beloved.

Why was I feeling sour, with all these roses raining down on us? Maybe because they were raining down on Gabi, not *us*. And that was selfish of me.

I snapped up the window blinds and raised the sashes. Summertime, mocking my mood, rumbaed into the room.

I plopped down on the couch and stared at Gabi's roses. Something was nagging me, all right. Something about love, and hot August nights. Love—and what lurked behind love. Namely, *desire*.

Skye Rasmussen, with his athletic skills, winning personality, and good looks, would have attracted more than his share of admirers. *More* than his share—which meant that female competition for Skye would have been sharp, if not fierce.

Fierce competition. Bruised teenaged egos. A motive for murder? A long shot, maybe, but one that needed looking into.

Delia had said that two of the aquarium volunteers were friends of Skye. I needed to find out something about them. And the girl hiding in the restroom at the mortuary—who was she?

It was time to have a more probing chat with Skye's parents. I picked up the phone.

The Rasmussens lived in a renovated 1950s tract home in San Roque, near the Earl Warren show grounds. The landscaping had recently been redone, in the politically correct California native plant style. The house was painted a stylish gray-green, and the tangerine front door was mounted with brushed stainless hardware. Either Dave or Melanie kept up with the taste of the times. My bet was on Mel.

I lifted the door knocker, let it fall. When no one answered, I rang the bell. The minute I pushed it and heard a loud *bringgg* inside the house, I felt I'd transgressed. This house was in mourning, and should be left in peace.

I expected Dave or Melanie to open the door. But it was Mrs. Steinbach who faced me. Her straight silver hair was fashioned into a sleek geometric cut, and her sleeveless black cotton shift revealed a gym-toned body. She studied me for a moment, then spoke. "You must be Ms. Zarlin."

"Yes. Melanie's expecting me."

"I'm Alice Steinbach, Melanie's mother." She inclined her head, and her vintage copper earrings swung out in an arc. She didn't extend her hand.

"Mrs. Steinbach, I'm so sorry for your loss." Again, that dratted empty phrase. It had just popped out, apparently having a life of its own.

"Thank you." She was silent for a moment. "I suppose you should come in. Melanie's in the kitchen."

I followed the slight, rigidly upright woman down a hall and into a large kitchen fitted out with an array of appliances. Probably top-of-the-line, but since I barely know how to switch on anything other than a microwave, I couldn't be sure.

Melanie stood at the kitchen island. She was up to her elbows in flour, rolling out dough on a marble slab. Her face was a blank. But when her eyes met mine, they filled with tears.

Just seeing me made her remember, I realized. Remember what she was trying so hard to forget: that her son was dead.

"Hi, Melanie. What are you making?" I smiled and tried to strike the right note—encouraging, but not gleeful. It would be a long, long time before glee was OK in this house.

"Individual lemon-apricot compotes. Ninety-six of them." She turned and rinsed her hands at the sink, reached for a towel.

"My daughter owns a catering service," Alice explained. "For select customers."

"Not all that select." Melanie managed a smile. "Mom's always trying to make me sound better than I am."

"That's what mothers are for," I responded. But then I added a silent corollary: *That's what they're for, but some moms don't ever get it.*

"Actually," Melanie continued, "Mom's the impressive one. She's sixty-six, and she works out at the gym every single day. Right, Mom? Two o'clock on the dot."

"Oh, you go to the Y?" I asked, by way of polite conversation.

"No, I prefer Hard Body." Alice turned to her daughter. "You'll do that too when you get to my age, Mellie. It's that or seize up and—" Alice fell silent. Even so, the completed phrase hung in the air: *seize up and die.*

Melanie walked over to a rattan lounge set in the far corner of the open kitchen. She and Alice sat on the couch, and I took one of the chairs opposite them.

"With Skye it's different." Melanie seemed compelled to keep talking. "I've never had to make him look good. He's smart and athletic. Popular, too. That's just the way he is. Right, Mom?"

Alice folded her hands in her lap. "Yes. Skye was exceptional. We were all so proud of him."

"Mom, you said 'was.' Please, don't say 'was.'" Melanie began to weep, and her mother placed her hand on her daughter's shoulder.

After a moment, I spoke. "I can come back another time."

"Yes, that would be best." Alice's chin trembled, but she held herself firm, her lips pressed together. "In a few weeks, perhaps."

"*No.*" Melanie sat upright and looked hard at me. Flour now dusted her left cheek. "You said you needed more information. And I want to help."

Alice Steinbach frowned, but said nothing.

"OK." I pulled out my phone and punched the Notes button. "I'd like to know more about Skye's friends. I understand he helped get volunteer positions for two of them at the aquarium."

"Yes. Porter and Vanessa. Porter, well, Skye's known him since preschool. And Vannie—I think Skye and Vannie started hanging out together in middle school. Maybe eighth grade."

"Can you give me their full names?"

"Porter Logsdon and Vanessa Hoague."

I tapped in the names, trying to avoid making eye contact with the glaring Alice. "Were Skye and Vanessa ever romantically involved?"

"Honestly," Alice hissed.

"It's all right, Mom." Melanie smiled a little. "Vanessa always has had a crush on Skye. Really, though, they're just friends. She wasn't his—" Her face fell. "His type," she finished in a near-whisper.

I sensed an opening, and took it. "Who was his type? I'm sure a boy like Skye never lacked for a girlfriend."

But I'd said something wrong. Melanie's features were dissolving.

"He hasn't—hasn't had a girlfriend for—for a while."

"Melanie. This is not a good idea." Alice turned to me, her eyes black and hard.

"Miss Zarlin, what is the point of all this? My grandson had a terrible accident. You seem to be taking advantage of my daughter's vulnerability, creating an issue where one doesn't exist. Perhaps you need the cash?"

My mouth fell open. I looked from mother to daughter and back again. "Mrs. Steinbach, I'm only here because Dave and Melanie asked me to look into Skye's death."

Melanie grasped her mother by the elbow. "We're doing this, Mom. It's our decision, Dave's and mine. We're going to find out what happened to Skye."

"But we know what happened, dear. Your father and the police agree. It was an accident. You and Dave don't need to—"

"Stop!" Melanie jumped to her feet. "I don't want to hear about what Dad thinks. I don't trust him with this. He always—"

Alice rose from the couch. She was seven or eight inches shorter than her daughter, slight as a stalk of bamboo. Yet somehow she was the stronger of the two. "Don't air family matters in front of a stranger, Melanie." She turned to me. "Ms. Zarlin, I really don't think—"

"Mom, I *want* her here, don't you understand? Jaymie's going to help us. She needs information, that's all." Melanie turned to me, pleading. "Explain to my mother. Tell her."

This wasn't going to work. Melanie seemed to be at a breaking point, and her mother was making it worse.

"We can talk in a day or two. Maybe your mom's right, it's all too soon." I stood too. I wanted to walk over to the distraught woman and give her a hug, but Alice was in the middle, blocking me. "I'll phone you tomorrow."

Melanie was sobbing hard.

"Please don't come back," Alice Steinbach said as she shepherded me to the front door. "You can see how you upset her. And to what purpose? We all know Skye had an accident."

"I'm not so sure it was an accident, Mrs. Steinbach."

"Nonsense! Tell me the truth. Why are you stirring the pot?"

I halted just inside the open doorway, and turned to face her. "I think the question is this—why are you holding down the lid?"

"Excuse me?" Alice Steinbach scowled. "My husband and I feel we know what's best for our family. Certainly we know better than you."

"Just what do you think you're doing, harassing my family at a time like this?"

I shifted the office phone to my other ear. "Dr. Steinbach, I haven't harassed anyone. Melanie and Dave—"

"They're overwrought, and you're taking advantage of them. I paid you, your involvement is done. Now I'm telling you, leave my family alone."

I rolled my eyes at Gabi and took a deep breath. "Dr. Steinbach, your daughter—"

Silence. The line had gone dead.

I handed the phone back to Gabi. "Just another one of my fans."

"He don't sound like a fan to me." Gabi folded her arms over her chest and fixed a pair of mascaraed eyes on me. "Miss Jaymie, you sure you should take that job?"

"Why, don't you think I can handle it?"

"Huh? Sure, I think you can handle it. I just don't like to see people be mean to you. This case, I think it's gonna get nasty."

"That's why I have you, Gabi. To kick butt."

"I know you are joking, Miss Jaymie. But I do protect you, you just don't know it."

Gabi was dressed to kill. I'd never seen her like this before: lipstick, sparkly blush, mascara, and something improbably blue painted on her eyelids. Black toreador pants and a pink crocheted top completed the look.

"You seem kinda—dressed up," I observed.

"Sorry, I know this is a bad outfit for the office. Not professional. But Angel's picking me up right at five."

"I see. Where are you and lover boy going?"

"First to dinner. And then we're going out to dance. Salsa, meringue, even tango. Leopoldo's downtown, they have Latin dancing every Thursday night."

"Hm. So when do I get to meet this Angel from heaven?"

She raised a sharply penciled brow. "Miss Jaymie? I don't like to say this. But you sound kinda jealous."

"What?" My voice squeaked as it slid up an octave. "I don't need a man to make me happy. And that, I might add, was your lifelong attitude, up until a few weeks ago."

"Things change. You just gotta meet the right man."

"You sure about that?" I decided to pick up the gauntlet.

"This Angel character is pretty slick. He tosses a few roses at you, and you fall at his feet."

"You got him all wrong." Gabi shook her head and smiled. "Angel, he is no slick guy. He's a rosarian. That's a expert on roses, in case you don't know. The ladies he works for, they all grow roses. Know what, I'm gonna introduce him to you. Then you'll see." She nodded sagely. "You should maybe think about being more nice to Mike, know what I mean?"

So Gabi was now the Ann Landers of love. "Mike's gone, past history. He's with another woman now—you know that. And somebody told me she's wearing a ring."

Ouch. Saying it out loud didn't feel so good.

"Ring. Pft." Gabi waved a dismissive hand in the air and got to her feet. "Some other woman? Don't worry about that. Mike's just a man, he's gotta be with somebody, right?" She headed for the kitchenette.

"But don't wait too long, Miss Jaymie," she called through the open door. "Things happen. Luz Montez, she wanted to marry a guy named Aurelio Sanchez, but he was just fooling around. Know what she did? She took a needle and made little holes in his, you know, his condoms." Gabi pointed a dramatic finger at me. "You know what happened next?"

"I can guess."

"Excuse me, you can't. Yes Luz got pregnant, but so did this other girl too. And that Aurelio, he couldn't marry both of them, could he. So what he did was—"

"Gabi? I've got to go. I'm meeting those two kids in twenty minutes, at McConnell's."

"And that's another thing, Miss Jaymie, you need a car. Investigators don't ride around on old bikes, it looks like—"

"Enjoy your rosebuds while ye may," I called as I went out the door.

Chapter Five

I was still pining for Blue Boy, the El Camino I'd inherited from my brother. Last year, in a funk I didn't like to recall, I'd donated the car to the local homeless shelter. They'd quickly sold it on to a collector down in LA, a well-off boomer who rechristened Blue Boy *Dudette*.

Since then I'd rented vehicles a few times, testing the waters, but nothing measured up. Still, as I pedaled down De La Vina in the late-August heat wave, wishing I'd worn shorts instead of black jeans, I did find myself considering the undeniable virtues of the automobile. Any automobile.

By the time I turned into McConnell's parking lot, I was more interested in their Meyer-lemon ice cream than in my two potential interviewees, Porter Logsdon and Vanessa Hoague.

Vanessa and Porter were ready and waiting, though, seated at a table on McConnell's tiny patio. Each held an ice-cream cone. The heat was melting the ice cream faster than they could lick.

The two watched me as they lapped like sleek satisfied cats. I rolled my bike into the stand, pasted a smile on my face, and approached them.

"Hi. Vanessa, Porter?"

The young woman, a blonde with hazel eyes, blinked slowly

and continued to lick away with her pointy tongue. The boy blinked at me. "Nope."

Then they both laughed. "Who else?" Porter Logsdon asked. He had a Midwestern look, muscled and fair. The thickness of his shoulders and neck suggested supplements.

Vanessa Hoague, on the other hand, seemed observant and quick. She wasn't beautiful, but she was quite pretty. The combination of her bottle-blond hair and bright hazel eyes made her compelling to look at. She inserted the tip of her tongue into the cone and came up with a curl of chocolate ice cream. Porter turned away from me and watched Vanessa with fascination.

"Right, who else. I'm Jaymie Zarlin." That was the trouble with this job, I thought with annoyance. Too often, you had to be nice to people who you wanted to send to a time-out chair.

"You sure?" Porter crunched his cone between perfect square teeth. "You don't look like a detective."

Enough of this bullshit. Time to bring these two toddlers to task.

"Like I said on the phone, I'm here to talk about the death of Skye Rasmussen."

To their credit, they now seemed distressed. Porter frowned, and Vanessa dropped her head and stared at the ground.

"Where were you on the evening of August sixteenth, between five and ten P.M.? Porter?"

"Is that—the night he—died?"

"Yes. It was a Friday."

"I was at a party up on Camino Cielo. Vannie was too. Lots of kids were there."

"The party started at five? That's unusual."

He looked over at Vanessa. "What time did it start?"

"Around nine, Port." Vanessa turned to me. "Yes, I was at that party. Before that I was at home with my mom and my sister, and before that I was shopping downtown with a girlfriend."

"How about you, Porter? Where were you before the party?"

"Surfing. At Leadbetter, with some buds," he added. "Like usual, it was flat. I stayed out there for a couple of hours, then I went home and got cleaned up. After that I drove up to the party."

The two beamed at me, pleased with themselves. Apparently they didn't realize their alibis were as porous as sponges. "OK?" Vanessa challenged.

"For now. Tell me, did Skye have enemies? Anyone who might have wanted revenge?"

"Revenge? No way." Vanessa tossed her head. "Skye was like maybe the most popular guy in school."

"Porter, any ideas?"

"Naw." He looked away. "Dude was too cool."

"Now, I want to ask you about the aquarium. I understand you both volunteer there, and it was Skye who got you the positions. Is that right?"

Vanessa nodded. "Skye's grampa is real important."

Bless teenagers today. The way she said "grampa" made her sound abut five. I looked over at Porter. "So the three of you were close friends?"

"Yeah, we knew each other like forever. Right, Vannie?"

"Uh-huh. I moved here in seventh grade." She turned to me. "Skye was my friend right away, you know? And in high school I was a cheerleader, and Skye and Port were both on the varsity football and basketball teams. So we were like, traveling to all the away games together." She stopped and looked at Porter. "Wait. You were on the football team but not the basketball team, at least not till this year. Skye was on both all the way through."

Porter gave a short nod. "Yeah. He was on both all the way through."

"So did the three of you always get along? Or did you have the occasional fight?"

Porter picked up a napkin and swiped at a smear of ice cream on the glass tabletop. "Sure, we got along. Why not?" The kid smoked a lot of weed: the thumb and index finger of his right hand were stained a dark yellowish brown.

I looked over at Vanessa. "Yeah, sure." She shrugged.

"You two don't look so sure."

They both tensed. I let the silence expand.

"Why—why are you asking this stuff?" Vanessa picked at the corner of her mouth.

"I thought I explained on the phone. Skye's parents have asked me to look into his death. There are some unanswered questions."

"So you really *are* a detective." Porter looked as if he still couldn't believe it.

"An investigator." I handed each of them a card.

"Of course she's for real, dummy." Vanessa frowned at him. "Don't you know she's the one who figured out who killed that Mexican girl at Solstice?" She turned to me. "What was her name?"

"Lili Molina. And a boy named Danny Armenta was murdered, too."

"Wow." Porter flicked the card with a chewed fingernail. "That's cool. What else do you want to know?" It was hard to tell if he was being sarcastic or serious.

"I want to know what you're hiding from me."

Their mouths flopped open like the jaws on a pair of ventriloquist's dummies. "Nothing," they echoed each other, a little too late.

"Mm-hm. Tell me something. Did Skye have a girlfriend?"

Porter shrugged, but Vanessa flushed scarlet. Good. Pay dirt at last.

"Yeah, he did," Porter said. "Did, as in months ago, but not anymore. As a matter of fact—"

"Porter," Vanessa squeaked. "I think you should probably shut up now."

Suddenly, it was as if I wasn't there.

"Why? The whole school knows."

"Yeah, but do his parents know?"

"His parents? So what. The dude's—"

"Porter! Shut up!"

He leaned back in the resin chair and spread his hands in surrender.

"Listen," I said. "I know all about it, of course. But I want to hear how you guys see it."

Porter looked over at Vanessa. "Go ahead," she muttered after a moment.

"Dude got the girl pregnant, that's all. Big effing deal. Taryn what's her name. They broke up, and she got an abortion. No surprise."

"They never were really together," Vanessa added. "She wasn't his type."

"Whatever," Porter said. "Actually, she's kinda hot."

"Hot?" Vanessa made a face. "It's pretty much like Porter says, though. Taryn used to hang around Skye. And if a girl throws herself at a guy, she gets what she asks for, right?" She lifted her chin and tucked a lock of hair behind her ear. "*Of course* she got an abortion—Skye wasn't really her boyfriend! It was all in her head."

That evening I carried my laptop and a glass of chilled wine out to the concrete patio at the back of my house. Santa Cruz and Anacapa loomed purple-black in the twilight, guarding the channel as they had for thousands of years. The other islands, Santa Rosa, San Nicolas, San Miguel, were lost in the velvety dark.

I'd planned to mull over the case. But the night seemed filled with romance, and Mike Dawson slipped into my mind. I was better off without him, I reminded myself for the sixty-third time. Sixty-three times, because in one way or another, I told myself this every single day. And it had been over two months now since he'd started up with somebody new.

No matter what Gabi was feeling at the moment, relationships weren't simple. Anything but.

I thought about the girl named Taryn. According to Vanessa and Porter, she was pregnant with Skye's baby, then had an abortion after he jilted her. If this was true, Taryn could be a person with motive.

I switched on the laptop and expanded the photos I'd taken of the mortuary guest book. Starting at the beginning, I scanned through the pages. Many signatures were hard to decipher, so the going was slow. I was coming up empty-handed—till I got to the end.

Dex pushed at my free hand with his muzzle, seeking a pat. I ignored him and stared at the screen.

I should have guessed that the last signature would be Taryn's. The girl in the restroom: I recalled her pretty face, dark eyes swimming in tears. This was my prime suspect? Please, no.

I peered at her last name. I couldn't quite figure it out. The letters were clear, written in a round girlish hand. But what they spelled was "Tactacquin"—not a name I'd heard before. I googled and got a few hits. Tagalog—a Filipino surname.

I needed to speak to Taryn Tactacquin again. My intuition protested she was no killer—but my intuition had failed me before, and besides, in my line of work you deal in facts. I would locate her in the morning. With a name like hers, it wouldn't be hard.

I closed the laptop, and the moonless night turned black and opaque. The vinegar tang of the ocean, tinged with the natural seepage of oil out in the channel, filled my nostrils.

Suddenly, I felt alone. "Brodie," I murmured. "Brodie, come back."

Usually my brother's spirit, or whatever it was that lingered with me, was comforting. But tonight I felt nothing. "Don't leave, brother. Please, not yet."

When someone you love kills himself, you want to reason with him. You want to turn back the clock, persuade him not to do it. Convince him life is worth living. I'd been having that argument with my brother for nearly three years now.

I heard a slight scuffling on the steep bank below, then smelled a few puffs of skunk. The animal was warning me it was time for humans to go inside, to shut their doors and leave the night world to the creatures who owned it.

But I didn't leave. What was inside for me but four blank walls? Better to be out in the dark, swept up and carried away in the black current flowing up from the channel.

"Thanks for seeing me on your lunch hour, Taryn." I pointed to a bench at the end of the bluff. "Shall we sit over there?"

"Sure." She cinched her navy terrycloth wrap more tightly across her chest. "It's not an hour, though. I only get thirty minutes."

"I'll try to keep it short, so you have a chance to eat something. Working with kids takes stamina."

She nodded. "They keep you running, that's for sure. But I like it, teaching them to surf. The program's for disadvantaged children, you know? They live in Santa Barbara, but some of them have hardly ever been in the ocean."

"They must love it, then. So you're a surfer?"

"Not really. I'm a beginner. Skye taught me—" She stopped, and her face twisted.

"Taryn, I'm sorry."

We sat down side by side. It was better that way. We could look out to sea while we talked, instead of staring at each other.

"What you just said, that you're sorry?" Distracted, she wrung the water out of her ponytail. "Nobody else has said that to me."

I patted her arm. I wanted to give the girl a hug, but I was afraid she'd burst into tears if I did. Besides, I reminded myself, Taryn Tactacquin was a suspect.

"I can see how much you cared about Skye."

"More . . . more than that. I loved him. Now I know that for sure."

I watched as a clutch of small sailboats bobbed past the point like baby waterfowl. "Before, you weren't sure?"

"For a while I thought I hated him. When we—" She stopped and picked at a white thread caught in the terrycloth. "I suppose you already know."

"I've been told you were pregnant. You know how it is: that kind of news travels."

"Yeah. Yeah, it does."

Taryn was quiet for so long that I thought she'd decided not to talk. But then she drew in a deep breath and let it out slowly, as if she were letting go.

"When I got pregnant, I didn't know who to tell. I knew my dad would be really mad, and my mom—well, things aren't so good in my family these days. My brother, Kenny—" She shrugged.

"Your brother?" I encouraged her.

"Kenny does drugs. The really bad stuff. He's in prison right now, up in Avenal. When Kenny comes out next month, Mom wants him to live at home, but Dad says no way. My parents fight about it all the time, you know?"

Boy, didn't I know. "That kind of thing can put a lot of pressure on a family."

"Yeah. Anyway, Skye and me, we didn't know what to do, not at first. We talked about abortion. I'm not against it. But we were *together*, you know? We were close. We started thinking about the baby, and we made some plans. We wouldn't have done it unless—" A sullen tone entered her voice.

"Unless?"

"Unless that—that grandfather of his hadn't gotten involved."

"Rod Steinbach?" I looked at her in surprise. Taryn's face was turned away from me, but I could see the tension in the set of her jaw.

"Yes. Dr. Steinbach. I hate him!"

"What did he do?"

"He told Skye his whole future was at stake. I don't know what all he said, but in the end Skye was convinced. He told me to get an abortion. I didn't want to, but with him not wanting the baby . . . and after I did it, it was too hard for us to be together. We kind of drifted apart."

"So you split up. That must have been tough."

"It was. It felt bad when we were together and then it felt bad when we were apart. The thing was—I don't know, I felt like Skye had sided with his grandfather against me." She bit her lower lip. "He did, at least for a while."

"What do you mean, for a while?"

"Nobody else knows this. But in February we got back together. Skye told me he was sorry." She turned and met my gaze. "It didn't feel the same as before, I'm not saying it did. But it was . . . it was all right."

"Are you sure nobody knew you and Skye got back together? How about his friends?"

"I don't see how they would. We never met here in SB. We'd go to Summerland or Carp, to the beaches down there." Her expression relaxed and she smiled. "It was cold in February, but we didn't care. The beach is great in the winter, you have to cuddle, and no one's around."

I returned her smile. The kid was hard not to like, but I had a job to do. "There's something else I need to ask you."

"OK. But then I do need to go eat my lunch. I'm taking the beginners out at twelve-thirty."

"The evening Skye died. Where were you, between five and nine?" I didn't take my eyes from her as I waited for the answer.

But Taryn didn't hesitate. "Babysitting at the Kleins' in Sycamore Canyon. I do it every Friday, four-thirty to midnight. Mr. Klein runs the Laugh Track Comedy Club, and his wife helps him out on Friday nights. You can call them if you want."

"Thanks. Now, I guess you'd better go. I'll walk you down to the beach."

We descended single-file down the narrow asphalt path leading to Leadbetter. "Since we've got a minute, there's something else I'd like to ask. Did any of Skye's friends resent him? He had it all, didn't he—looks, smarts, athletic ability. Personality, too. Some people would have been jealous."

Taryn stopped so quickly I bumped into her, then caught her elbow to keep her from falling.

"Nobody said anything like that. But sometimes I thought . . ."

"Yes?" I realized I was still gripping the girl's elbow, and let go.

"It's silly, but there was this triangle. There's a girl named Vanessa Hoague. She's had a crush on Skye like forever. And then there's Porter, Porter Logsdon. Port likes Vanessa, but Vanessa likes Skye. And Port is supposedly Skye's best friend. At least, he used to be." She turned and continued on down the path, and I followed.

"I know who they are," I said to her back. "Skye got them their volunteer positions at the aquarium, right?"

"Yeah, he told me about that. You know, my dad goes to the aquarium a couple of times a week, for work. Usually he goes in real early, before the aquarium opens. But sometimes he's there later, after it closes. One time he saw Porter throw a starfish real hard against the wall. Dad said he was showing off for Vanessa."

"Oh, very cute." My ears had pricked up. "You said your father goes there?"

"Mm-hm. Dad's got a food distributorship. He stocks the snack bar."

We stepped off the path, onto the sand. "Taryn, just now you said Porter used to be Skye's best friend. Did something happen between them?"

"I'm pretty sure it did. Skye wouldn't talk about it. But I think—"

Just then a flock of kids raced up like sandpipers from the water's edge. "It's time! Taryn, can we go in now?" they clamored.

She smiled as several of the kids grabbed her by the arms and pulled her toward the water.

"Two minutes, guys. While you're waiting for me, brush off the sand like I showed you, and help each other into your wetsuits." She turned back to me.

"I think something bad happened, something connected to Vanessa and Porter. It was before Skye and me got back together. But I really don't have a clue what it was."

"So you took the guy up on the one-night stand."

"I did." I switched the phone to my other ear. "Thanks for the rec, Zave."

"Anything for you, Princess."

"Don't call me princess, it's sexist."

"Oh, it's sexy all right. Especially if you're wearing that blue satin nightie I—"

"Zave? I'm at the office."

"Then I stand corrected. Standing up now, for your information. What are you wearin' under those old jeans of yours?"

"I'm going to hang up now."

"Go right ahead. But then you won't hear what I have to say." Playtime was over. Zave's tone had switched to all business.

"I'm listening."

"What I hear is, you're rubbing the cat the wrong way. Causing sparks, and some hissing."

"Let me guess. Would that be Dr. Steinbach you're talking about?"

"You'd know better than me. Point is, the attorney who called in the first place, the one who gave you the job? He's not happy with you. Said his client wants you to take a hike."

"Maybe his client would like to pay me a very large sum of money to take that hike."

"Jaymie? I'm not so sure this is a joke."

"You're right, it's not. The victim's parents have asked me to take on the case. They don't trust the PD's conclusions, which for some reason coincide with Rod Steinbach's. And neither do I."

"Steinbach's an eminent biologist, Jaymie. A member of the National Academy of Sciences. You're not talking about some crook here."

I hee-hawed into the phone. "You're the guy who trusts nobody."

"Trust is overrated. But listen, girl. You're stepping into the middle of a family feud. What's in it for you?"

"What's in it for me?" I pushed away from the kitchen table and walked to the back window. The dark pink curtain of bougainvillea draping the block wall filled my view. "Respect, for one thing. I solved the Solstice Murders, but people are saying that was just luck. And . . ."

"And?"

"Zave, listen. Skye Rasmussen's death was no accident. I'm pretty damn sure of it."

"How so?"

"He was young, strong, and athletic. Somehow I doubt he tripped over his own feet and tumbled into that tank."

"Hm." Zave was quiet for a moment. "Jaymie, I think I need to massage some sense into you. My place at eight?"

I closed my eyes. I could almost feel Zave's charcoal satin sheets caress my skin, and taste that smooth dry sherry he liked to sip in bed.

"Don't try to distract me, Zave. I know all your tricks. When I'm good and ready, I'll give you a call."

Someone had left the irrigation running throughout the night, and the courtyard was warm and wet as a glasshouse. A snail, late to bed, glided down a big Ensete banana leaf on a glistening trail of slime. Another hot day was in store.

Two objects awaited me outside the office. One was a lustrous apricot rose slipped into a soda bottle. I lifted it to my nose. Spicy, sweet. The tag read, *Tango for Two*. So, the temperature was rising.

The other object was an ordinary white envelope, the kind you'd buy at a grocery store. It was wedged into the slit where the screen door met the frame.

Holding the rose in one hand, I stuck the corner of the envelope between my teeth, held back the screen door with a shoulder, and unlocked the door with my free hand. Inside, the office was still warm with the heat of the previous day. I set the rose on Gabi's desk and dropped the envelope down beside it.

I was about to walk away to open the windows. But my eyes skipped back to the letter.

It was corny, almost. Comical. The letters of my name, J Zarlin, were glued in the lower right-hand corner of the envelope. They'd been cut from a magazine. I flipped the envelope over: the back was sealed shut.

When I'd first picked it up, I'd assumed it was from the landlord. A notice about termites, blocked drains, or deadlines for rent. But now something told me I was looking at bad news.

I sat down in Gabi's chair, rummaged around in her top drawer and located a letter opener.

The single sheet of paper was cream-colored. Thick and textured, it was of better quality than the envelope. I unfolded it. And for several seconds, I couldn't breathe.

> Your brother did not kill himself.
> What are you going to do about it?

The words were hand-printed with a black pen. I stared at them, stunned. Who—and why—

My mind went blank. Then a river of rage flooded my brain.

I shoved the chair back and it crashed to the floor. "Brodie," I cried out. "What did they do to you?"

Chapter Six

I stuffed the note in my jeans pocket and rushed outside, unlocked my bike with fumbling hands, and pushed my way through the courtyard to the street.

Then I rode like a bat out of hell. I headed for the downtown jail, where Brodie had died. Where he'd supposedly committed suicide nearly three years ago. I raced through intersections, pushing the old Schwinn to its limits.

But then, winded, I slowed. Rational thoughts crept into my shell-shocked brain. What would I do once I got there? Brandish the note? Storm in and demand to see the head jailer? I'd be hustled straight out to the street. And worse than that: someone would learn that I knew the truth, and be alerted to cover his tracks. I would tip my hand.

I glided to a stop in front of the county courthouse and argued myself down. If I burst into the jail, I'd never find out what happened to Brodie. My hands tightened into fists. I'd never get what I now wanted, more than anything in the world: *revenge*.

So I turned around and headed back up Anacapa, bending over my handlebars and pumping hard. I stair-stepped the blocks and pedaled through the stately old homes of the upper East.

It was possible the note was bogus, I realized. The brainchild of some supremely bored person who wanted to have a little fun with me, to see Jaymie jump. Fury and despair flipped back and forth through my brain, sparking a battle of conflicting thoughts.

I approached the Santa Barbara Mission, glowing soft pink and white in the early-morning sun. Just once, I thought fiercely as I pounded past the old lavandería and the figure of a forgiving Christ, just once in this town I'd like something to be exactly what it appeared to be.

I rode on up the hill through centuries-old oaks to Mission Canyon. The bike slowed on the incline but my legs kept going, grinding away at the pedals. Grinding away my painful emotions. Trying to obliterate whatever had happened to my brother.

In spite of the coolness of the morning air, I was bathed in sweat. I tasted acid, welcomed the exhaustion. Pushed on. Then, somewhere near the top of Mission Canyon, the front tire blew. I was riding on a steel rim.

I got off my bike, wheeled the crippled thing over to a large sandstone boulder, and laid it to rest. I sat there for a while, waiting as my raspy breath slowed. A locust struck up a shrill lament in the singed August grass.

I could walk on down, and drive up later in the day in Gabi's station wagon for the bike. Or I could just phone somebody for help. Zave, for instance. Zave wouldn't come himself—time was money, after all—but he'd send somebody, double quick.

But I realized it wasn't Zave I needed. I tugged my phone from my jeans pocket.

"Mike." My voice sounded cracked. "Mike, I have to ask you a question. Are you and Mandy engaged?"

"Jaymie? Where the hell did you get that idea?"

"Deirdre Krause."

"Deirdre's messing with you. Hell, I thought you were too sharp to fall for her tricks."

"I—just thought I'd check."

He laughed. "So what's up?"

"I—I could use a little help." Now I felt foolish. "I'm stuck up the top of Mission Canyon with a flat bike tire."

"Uh—sure. You need a lift." Mike sounded surprised, as well he might. I never asked him for any kind of assistance. Not since Mandy Blaine had twirled into his life, and I'd slunk out like a whipped cur.

"I'll be there." Now his voice was flat, noncommittal. "Just do me a favor, will you? Stay put."

I hung up and stared dully at a mob of glittering ants dismembering a small blue butterfly. Why the hell had I called Mike? Was it just automatic, reverting back to old memory pathways? Or worse, had I reverted to some kind of girlish dependency? On the other hand, did everything have to have a god-damned reason?

I stomped back into the brush, pulled down my pants, and peed. Wasn't till I stood back up that I noticed the brush was poison oak.

I heard Mike's big pickup growling up the hill before it came into view. He pulled up on the opposite side of the road, switched off the engine, and climbed out. Instead of his uniform he was wearing ranch clothes, blue jeans and a work shirt.

"So what the hell are you doing up here?"

I was in no mood to take any lip. "Never mind. If you want to help me, great. If not, go away."

"Same old Jaymie." He laughed. "You're the one who called *me*." He was rubbing it in, making the most of the situation.

"All right, I did call you. And if you think that means—" But then, I stopped. It was just as if you pricked a balloon with a needle: all the air went out of me, and I sat down in the dry grass.

Mike crossed the road and stood there for a moment, gazing down at me. I'd forgotten how big he was. And I'd forgotten how stern he could look, when his eyes narrowed.

"Jaymie—" Then he waved a hand, as if it wasn't worth talking about. He picked up my heavy steel bike like it was a kid's toy, carried it across the road, and hoisted it into the bed of the pickup without bothering to open the tailgate.

"Coming?"

For two seconds I actually thought about staying. Then I scampered across the road like a rabbit and hopped into the cab.

Mike jammed the key into the ignition and the truck rumbled to life. "Look, I'm not going to ask." The hint of a smile tugged at the corners of his lips.

"There's a reason."

"Course there's a reason you're way up here with a flat tire at eight in the morning. Sure there is."

What did it? Being in the cab with him? Feeling safe, safe enough to think about the note in my pocket? The minute the truck began to roll, I started to cry.

"Aw, shit." Mike slammed on the brakes, shoved the truck into park and switched off the engine. The only sound was me, blubbering.

After a while he put a hand on my shoulder. Then he pulled me close.

"Sorry," I managed to say into his chest. "I know you can't stand it when—"

"Never mind. I didn't think you called me about a flat. What's going on?"

I couldn't say it out loud. I'd quit bawling and didn't want to start up all over again. Besides, Mike smelled just the way I remembered: like saddle soap, burnt grass, sun. I didn't want him to let me go.

I arched my back, reached into my pocket and pulled out the folded note. It was damp with sweat. I handed it to him. "I found this when I got to the office."

Mike smoothed open the note. He read it, turned it over to look at the back of the paper, then read it again. "Where was this exactly?" His voice had turned angry and tight.

I moved out of his arms. "Front door. Stuck in between the screen and the frame. Mike—" I was quiet for a moment, fighting tears. "What if somebody did kill Brodie?"

I looked over at him and our eyes met. His were black and cold, the way they got when he didn't like what he was hearing.

"It's just a note, Jaymie. You already know what happened. Somebody's yanking your chain."

"Maybe. Or telling the truth."

"No. Somebody's messing with you. A real sick joke."

"I thought about that. But Brodie died three years ago. Why go to all this fuss for a laugh, why now?"

He scowled. "Tell me something. What're you working on? Anything dicey?"

"You could call it that. Skye Rasmussen, the boy who died in the aquarium? His parents have asked me to look into his death."

Mike ran an index finger along the edge of his broken tooth. "Heard about that business. Hell of a way to go. But I thought it was ruled an accident."

"It was. A rush to judgment, I'd call it."

"So you've been poking around."

"A little," I admitted.

"A little? You've been jabbing a snake with a stick." He handed the note back to me, turned the key, and started the engine.

"OK, but who is the snake?"

"Come on, Jaymie. You're pretty much telling the PD they've got it all wrong—again."

The big pickup straddled the center line as it powered on down the mountain road. Why was it, I wondered, that Deputy Dawson always seemed to be telling me to back off, pull in my horns, go with the status quo?

"No. I don't buy it, Mike. What could Skye Rasmussen's death have to do with this note?"

"Probably nothing. All I'm saying is, somebody at the PD could have sent you that note to sidetrack you. To get you to back off the aquarium case. The last thing they want is for Jaymie Zarlin to go poking her nose in their business."

I stared out the window as we whisked by the mission. A cowled Franciscan monk was now out in front, sweeping the tiled steps with a kitchen broom.

"Seems far-fetched. They don't take me seriously—I'm just a pesky gnat. Anyway, I'm going to look into this letter. You know I can't let it go."

"I'm telling you, it's bullshit. You'd be playing into somebody's hands." He looked over and cocked an eyebrow. "And that's not like you."

After several minutes of silence, Mike pulled up at the curb. "Let me have another look at that note, will you?"

When I handed it over to him he stared at it for a moment, then rubbed the piece of paper between his fingers and thumb. "Know what? I think I was right the first time. This is a joke. Just a nasty sick joke." His voice had taken on the mean-deputy edge I heard every once in a while, the one he probably used with meth dealers and cattle rustlers.

Mike's anger was different from mine. It was slow and hot, and came from somewhere deep inside. Once it started to burn, it was nearly impossible to put it out.

"A joke. But why?"

"Who knows? Run it through the shredder. Want me to do it for you?"

"No. I'll do my own shredding, thanks." I gave him a questioning look, but he just handed the note back, pulled onto the road, and stepped on the gas.

I was silent as we drove down into the town, bound up in my own thoughts—my own *selfish* thoughts. Thank goodness I remembered Bill Dawson as Mike angled into a parking spot near my office.

"Mike, how's your dad? Is the cancer still in remission?"

"No." He cut the engine. His hands dropped into his lap. "Dad still looks pretty good. But we heard from the doc last week. The cancer's spreading."

"Oh—I'm so sorry! I wish—wish I could do something."

"You're still one of his favorites. He always asks after you."

"Not in front of Mandy, I hope." And I meant that. Mandy Blaine was nice, actually. Nicer than me.

Mike tapped the steering wheel. "Mandy . . . hasn't met him."

"Why not?"

He looked out the window. "Dad thinks . . . well, he thinks you're still in the picture."

"What?" I stared at him. "I'm still in the picture but I haven't bothered to come up and see him? How dare you let him think that."

"I was going to tell him." Mike looked away. "But lately . . . I don't feel like handing him any more disappointments."

"Where is Bill? Is he still at your sister's in San Luis Obispo?"

"Trudy moved him back up to the ranch for the summer. That's where Dad wants to be. She's up there with him, her and the kids."

"Mike? You tell Bill he's getting a visitor, soon. And I might as well warn you, I'm not playing along with your game. If I have to, I'll tell him the truth about us."

I slammed my way out of the pickup. Mike got out to help me, but I'd already dropped the tailgate and wrestled the injured bike to the ground.

It wasn't till an hour later, when I was ensconced at my table in the kitchenette, that I realized what I'd done. Too embarrassed to talk, I texted Mike: *Sorry. Easy for me to say how things should be done when it's not my own family.*

I closed my eyes and thought about the note. I didn't buy Mike's conclusion that it was nothing more than a joke, not after three years. But it was possible his other idea was right: somebody down at the PD was trying to distract me, to get me to back off the Rasmussen case. And under any other circumstances, that was something I wouldn't have allowed.

Yet this was different, personal. After all, distraction or not, it was possible the note told the truth.

I needed to focus my efforts on discovering what had happened to Brodie. My brother came first. So, it was decided. I'd have to phone the Rasmussens in the morning, and tell them I couldn't take on the case.

I stared blindly at the papers strewn across the tabletop. Had my brother been murdered? If so—if it took me a lifetime—the killer would pay.

Just look at me, I thought. I'm opposed to the death penalty. Convinced it makes barbarians of us all. But if you handed me my brother's killer, I swear to God: I'd return his head to you on a plate.

"Miss Jaymie? What's going on?" Gabi tapped on the kitchenette door. I seldom shut it, and she probably guessed something was up.

"What do you want?"

"Please, open the door. I got something to tell you."

"Just say it."

"OK." I heard Gabi give a loud sigh. "A girl called. She wants to see you."

"What girl? Did she have a name?"

"Miss Jaymie, even a dog has a name. The girl, her name is Taryn. Her last name, I couldn't get. It's like the noise a woodpecker—"

"Taryn Tactacquin." I got to my feet and pushed back my chair. "I'll phone her. I'm not taking the Rasmussen case, so there's no reason for her to come by."

I heard a sharp tsk through the door. "If you say so. 'Cause who cares if we never find out who killed that boy? Or maybe the police will figure it out. Yes I think so, just like they figured out who killed Lili Molina."

I opened my mouth to reply, then closed it. I wasn't taking the bait.

"Anyway," she continued, "it's too late. She's on the way over."

"Great." I got up, went to the door and opened it. "Now I get to tell her to her face."

"Miss Jaymie?" Gabi peered into the room. "What are you doing in here?"

I picked up the cream-colored sheet of writing paper from the table and held it out to her. "Read this."

"'Your brother did not'—" Gabi frowned, then started again. "'Your brother did not kill himself. What are you going to do about it?'

"*Dios mío.*" She stared at me, then pressed a hand to her mouth.

You could see Gabi approved of Taryn Tactacquin. She'd ushered the girl to the couch, not the hot seat, and now she fussed over her. "How about a Coke, mija? Diet. I got some cold in the fridge."

"Thanks, Ms. Gutierrez. That would be great. It's getting hot out there."

"Call me Gabi. Yes, it's terrible. The climate is changing, you know? They said on the radio it's gonna be hot like this every summer for the rest of our life." Gabi disappeared into the kitchenette and reemerged with a frosty Coke can. "Do you want a glass?"

"No, thanks. What a pretty rose."

Gabi puffed up a little. "My boyfriend, he's a rosarian. Almost every day I get a new rose. That one, it's called 'Baby Talk.'"

"*Baby talk,*" I muttered. "Love is blind."

Gabi looked over at me and frowned. "Miss Jaymie? What can I get you, something with a little sugar in it?"

Taryn giggled, then covered her mouth with her hand.

"I'm fine," I declared. "Taryn, how can I help you?"

"I thought of something." Her smile faded. "Something about Skye and Vanessa and Porter, about why they stopped being friends."

"I'm sorry, but there's something I need to tell you." It was time to speak up. "I'm not going to take the case."

"What?" She looked bewildered. "I thought you were—already doing it."

"I haven't taken a retainer from the Rasmussens, or signed a contract. And now I won't be."

Gabi was pretending to work on her computer. She let out a loud *huff*.

"But who's going to do it now? Somebody said the police decided Skye had an accident. Was it an accident? Is that why you're going to quit?"

The word "quit" stung me. But it was accurate, I supposed. "Please understand, Taryn. My decision is based on something personal that's come up."

She shook her head. "I don't understand, not really. But I'm going to tell you this anyway, OK? I don't want to keep it to myself."

And I didn't want to hear it, whatever it was. But I couldn't think of a way to cut her off, short of insulting the girl. "All right, I'm listening."

"I think Skye and Vanessa and Porter had some kind of a fight. At that stupid party club."

"Party club?"

"The Piñata Party Club—that's what they call it. I don't really know why—it sounds kind of lame. You have to be invited to go, and of course I never got invited. They started it last fall, after Skye and I broke up."

In spite of my decision to back off, my curiosity reared its crafty head. "Piñata Party Club? Sounds like something for children. What's it all about?"

"I don't have a clue. Skye wouldn't tell me. Anyway, he quit it in January, I know that for sure. Right before we got back together."

"So you think something went wrong there. Any idea where this party club is?"

"No. But I don't think it's in a house. And it might be wild, *really* wild. That's one reason I didn't tell you about it before. I didn't want to say anything bad about Skye." She flushed. "He was a really good person, you know? But he could be—" She stopped.

"Kind of rowdy?"

"Actually, more than kind of." She shrugged. "I'm not. We had a lot in common, but we were different that way."

"Maybe that's one reason you two were a good match."

"Yeah. Yeah, it was." Taryn's eyes welled with tears.

Gabi jumped up, glared at me, then carried the box of tissues from the desk to the couch. "I'm sorry, mija. So sorry about your boyfriend."

I stepped over to the side window. The repo woman's parrot, tethered to its perch outside the office next door, caught sight of me and shrieked its usual mantra: "Deadbeat, deadbeat!"

So, what was it going to be? Was I going to spend my time searching for a person who might or might not have killed my brother three years ago? Or was I going to find out who had shoved Skye Rasmussen into a tank holding a lethal jellyfish? I stared at Deadbeat's black scimitar of a beak.

In a way, I supposed, it amounted to this: would I find a way to exact revenge—or to catch an avenger? I turned away from the bird and back to the room.

Right then and there, I made up my mind. Somehow, I was going to do both.

I studied the buffet in the Rasmussens' dining room. It was crammed with pictures of Skye. Sports photos, graduation portraits, snaps of him with family and friends.

"We asked you here because there's something Melanie and I need to tell you." Dave Rasmussen rested his elbows on the dining table and pressed his fingertips together, forming a steeple.

Beside him, Melanie tensed. "Skye was a wonderful son." Her voice trembled. "He wasn't perfect, that's all."

"A normal teenager," Dave agreed. "Skye had a good heart. And raging hormones, the usual stuff."

I nodded and waited for what was coming.

"There was a girl," Dave continued after a pause. "She got pregnant." He cleared his throat, then rubbed at a water-ring stain on the tabletop. Melanie looked at the floor.

"Taryn Tactacquin," I said. "I've talked with her. She seems nice. But I want to hear what you have to say."

"So you already know who she is." Dave met my eyes. "Maybe she is nice, we don't really know. But her father isn't. John Tactacquin's a thug. He came over here, throwing his weight around—"

"He threatened us." Melanie leaned forward in her chair. "He came in this house and made threats."

"He threatened you? How?"

"No, Mel." Dave held up a hand. "We have to be accurate here. The man was aggressive and rude, he called Skye some bad names. But he didn't actually threaten us."

"He might as well have. His attitude was intimidating." Melanie shook her head. "Thank God Skye wasn't home at the time."

I didn't want to upset the Rasmussens if I didn't have to. I thought about the best way to proceed. "Here's what I'd like to know. Did Taryn's father show up *after* Skye told her to get an abortion?"

"*What?*" Melanie sat bolt-upright. Her dark eyes showed shock.

"Skye didn't—you've got it all wrong." Dave shook his head from side to side. His sallow complexion had reddened. "Our son was ready to do the right thing!"

"Is that what she told you?" Melanie's voice rose. "She was the one who wanted the abortion!"

"Melanie, I don't want to upset you. But if I were in your position, I'd want to know the truth."

"What are you talking about?"

"Do you realize your father intervened?"

"Christ," Dave growled. Melanie jumped to her feet and wrapped her arms around her middle, as if she'd been punched.

"Are you saying Dad had something to do with—" Melanie looked at her husband. "He did, of course he did! Why can't you ever stand up to him?"

"Mel, come on. You know what Rod's like!"

"Of course I know." Melanie sounded despairing. "I'm the one who lived under his thumb for so many years."

"Then you should understand," Dave pleaded.

I looked out the window at the Rasmussens' pretty garden. Dwarf fruit trees: an apricot and a plum, a lemon and an orange. Raised boxes filled with lush tomato plants, here and there a hint of red peeking through. It looked peaceful out there, and I caught myself scanning for the door.

Dave seemed to read my mind. "Let's take this slow. Shall we go sit outside?"

He led the way, opening the French doors to the patio. "Ms. Zarlin, would you like a cold drink?"

"Jaymie," I corrected. "Yes, that would be nice."

"There's some iced tea in the refrigerator," Melanie said in a dispirited tone. She sat down at the patio table and Dave went back inside, to the kitchen. "That's my husband for you. Always sweeping things under the rug."

"Maybe it's better than the opposite."

"Is it? Is it better?" She rubbed her eyes, then looked over at me. "Tell me, Jaymie. What exactly did my father do?"

"It seems he persuaded Skye to press Taryn to get an abortion. He told your son his future was at stake."

"He had no right to do that. No right at all."

"Your father is a strong-willed man."

"Oh, yes. Control is what Dad is all about. We did fine, Dave and I, until my parents moved back here a year ago. I saw it coming. I knew they'd retire to Santa Barbara, and I knew Dad would run our lives from the day he arrived."

"But now you've taken a stand against him, haven't you? By deciding to keep asking questions."

Melanie ran a finger under her watch strap and nodded. "Yeah, I guess we have. But see . . . see what it took to make us stand up to him."

Dave came through the doorway, tray in hand. He unloaded three tall glasses of iced tea, each decorated with a lemon wedge, and three berry tarts. "I thought you might enjoy these, Jaymie. Mel's baking. I pulled them out of the freezer."

"Olalaberry tarts. Skye's favorite," Melanie said.

We ate in silence. Birds chirped and sang, but underneath you could hear the muted growl of the freeway.

"Delicious." I dabbed my mouth with the napkin, folded it, and set it beside the plate. "Look, I'm sorry. I have to return to the subject of your father, Melanie."

"Whatever you need to do."

"Rod seems to be blocking me from speaking with Neil Thompson. What can I do about that?"

"You could talk to Alice, Mel," Dave suggested. "Maybe your mom can convince him to back off."

"Maybe." Melanie shrugged. "Mom pretty much does what Dad wants. But I'll try."

"One other thing," I said. "There's the subject of Steven."

"Steven?" Melanie's tone sharpened. "What do you want with my brother?"

"I'd like to speak with him, that's all. I'm going to be touching base with everyone over the next few weeks." I hoped my own tone was soothing, offhand. "It's a matter of piecing together a patchwork, you know?"

"But it sounds like you think Steven might know something," Mel said, her voice rising. "And that's nonsense. Just so you understand, he's very important to me."

"Mel. You're being defensive." Dave looked over and gave me an almost imperceptible nod. "I wouldn't worry about Steven, Jaymie. He's always been on Mel's side."

Dave walked me out a few minutes later, closing the front door behind us. "I'll text you my brother-in-law's cell number," he said. "But please, don't tell Melanie I've passed it on."

Chapter Seven

"Yeah!" a voice yelped inside my office. "Yeah, you fuckah, I got you!"

I locked my bike to the railing, ascended the steps, and opened the door.

A four-foot-ten figure, weighing approximately ninety pounds, lay stretched along the couch. Dirty basketball shoes kicked at the couch arm as the fourteen-year-old punched and swiped at her phone. "Hey, Jaymie," she called without looking up.

I glanced over at Gabi. She was staring hard at the computer screen, her hands curled like cat's claws over the keyboard. When she looked up at me I could see the effort it was taking for her to keep quiet. She opened her mouth in an "O" and let out what looked like a silent scream.

Gabi and Claudia Molina are dead opposites, that's all there is to it. They'd bonded after the death of Claudia's sister, Lili . . . for a time. Gabi still tried with the kid, but I could see her supply of goodwill was about to run dry.

"Claudia," I said. "Kill them all, so we can talk."

She nodded without looking up, but continued to grunt and yelp. I raised a hand to Gabi, advising patience. Then I went on into the kitchen for coffee.

When I returned, the girl was still obsessing away. I knew it was a bad idea to give in to little Claudia, so I put the coffee down on the desk, walked over, and plucked the device out of her hands. "Sorry. I asked you here on business, remember?"

"Hey! Gimme my phone!"

"After. First, we talk. You seem to have picked up a habit."

"Huh? I gotta do something all day, while people are talking shit."

"Excuse me." Gabi scowled. "This is a place of—"

"Yeah, yeah. This is a place of busy-ness."

The kid bounced up from the couch and lunged for the phone. I was ready for her, and slipped the device into my pocket. "You'll get it back when we're done."

The police had returned Claudia's Smith & Wesson knife, and I was reasonably sure she was packing it in her baggy basketball shorts. But the girl knew better than to take me on.

"Fuh. Whadda ya want, anyway? I only came 'cause your message said something about a job. What kinda job?"

"Do you like fish?"

"Huh? Naw, fish make me puke."

Gabi made a disgusted sound.

"Not to eat, Claudia. To look at. To admire."

"Yeah. Yeah, I like to sit around all day and admire the fuck outta fish. You gonna pay me for that?"

I grinned at the kid. "As a matter of fact, I might." I sat down in the hot seat. "I'm offering you a job working undercover, at the Santa Barbara Aquarium."

That caught her interest, all right. I saw her trying to come up with a smart remark, and failing.

"Whadda I gotta do?"

"For starters, change your hair. Maybe undo the ponytail and let it down to cover up that shaved part underneath."

"Nope. No fuckin' way." She folded her skinny arms across her chest and glared at me. "That way I'd look like some girl."

Gabi snorted.

"What?" Claudia snapped at her with a high yip.

"That's it, Miss Jaymie, I'm going." Gabi rose with dignity from her chair and picked up her new bag, which was the size and general shape of a folding chair. "I got errands to run."

"We'll be done in fifteen."

"I'll be back in one hour, just in case." She glared at Claudia as she walked around the desk to the door. I could see the truce was about to end.

"Claudia, here." I tossed back the phone. "Let's get down to it."

"So far all I got is you wanna pay me to watch fish. Yeah, I can do that. You want me to count them too? That'll cost more."

"You'll be an aquarium volunteer. I'll arrange it. There are a couple of other kids volunteering who I want you to keep an eye on. Their names are Vanessa Hoague and Porter Logsdon. They volunteer after school, and you will, too."

I could see I'd caught the kid's interest. She smoothed her baggy white wife beater over her purple shorts. "Never heard of 'em. What am I trying to find out?"

"You know about Skye Rasmussen, right?"

She frowned. "I heard he got killed by a jellyfish, man. Fell into a tank."

"The thing is, Claudia, Skye didn't fall. He was probably pushed."

"Some asshole *pushed* him?"

I nodded. "So you need to be careful. All I'm asking you to do is hang out at the aquarium and keep an eye on Logsdon and Hoague. Nothing spectacular, got it?"

"Sure. Those two—are they suspects?"

"Possibly. Vanessa and Porter were close friends of Skye's until something happened. A fight, maybe, or something else. Your job is to get info about why he split up with them."

"Got it. Anything else?"

"Just keep your ears open. The falling-out could have to do with something called the Piñata Party Club."

"Piñata Party Club? That's weird. Sounds like something we did in second grade. *Dale, dale, dale. No pierdas el tino.*"

"What does that mean?"

"It's the piñata song, what you sing before the kid whacks it. Hit it, hit it, hit it. Don't lose your aim."

"Well, these are no second graders, believe me. I want you to be careful. Now, about your disguise."

"I gotta wear a disguise?"

I was trying to be as diplomatic as possible. "So to speak. You'll be working undercover, Claudia. The idea is you're going to get in good with these two."

"What're you saying?"

Diplomacy be damned. "Like I said, do something about the hair. Lose the basketball shorts and the wife beater. Also, the lingo. Try to fit in."

She tipped back her head and stared at me, along the line of her nose. "You tellin' me to fit in with a couple a lame-ass white kids who go around whacking piñatas? Next thing you're gonna tell me to wear a fuckin' dress."

"You don't have to go that far. Though a touch of makeup might not be a bad idea."

I'd said this to rile her, and I expected Claudia to shriek with indignation. But instead, after a tense moment the corners of her mouth turned up in a sly little smile.

"I get it, you want them to like me. Don't worry, they'll love me. Trust me, I'll figure it out."

I pedaled past the dry dock on my way down to the marina. I got a warm fuzzy pat-myself-on-the-back feeling, just seeing the sleek *Icarus* mounted high and dry on a lift. The pleasure yacht's owner, Sutton Frayne, was currently also high and dry in Soledad Prison, and I was the one who'd put him there.

Today I was headed for a part of the marina that held the berths of working-class boats, rusty buckets loaded down with frayed ropes, stained plastic pails, and lobster traps. The kind of boats that were held together by barnacles and stunk of fish guts. I rode along the breakwater, looking for Neil Thompson and his *Lindy Sue*.

I was all the way out to the end before I spotted the guy. His pale red and white hair, tied back in a scraggly ponytail, was the giveaway. Dr. Thompson was bent over a snarl of nets piled on the deck of a small aging fishing boat. *Lindy Sue, Santa Barbara CA* was painted across the stern.

"Ahoy there," I shouted across. "Could you unlock the gate?"

Neil Thompson straightened up and stared across at me. After a minute he gave a small wave, and bridged the gap between the boat and the dock with his gangly legs. I pedaled back down the breakwater, dodging the errant waves crashing over the wall.

My timing was off, though. Just as I reached the end of the breakwater, I was doused. The cold wave actually felt good, as the morning air was heating up. But the result, wet T-shirt and jeans plastered to my skin, was not a look I wanted just then.

"Got caught, huh?" Neil Thompson's smile seemed welcoming as he held open the steel gate. I was taken by surprise, since his recent behavior to me hadn't been so friendly.

"Thought I'd cool off." I wheeled my bike through, and Neil pulled the gate shut with a clang.

"By the way," he said, "you've got dead man's fingers on your sleeve."

"What?"

He pointed to a sprig of seaweed on my T-shirt. "Scientific name, *Codium fragile*."

"Don't think I've ever met someone who can name a seaweed before."

"It's an alga, in fact."

I followed Neil Thompson along the dock, leaned my bike against a post, and took a leap after him onto the *Lindy Sue*.

"As a matter of fact, seaweeds are my specialty. They're humble but critically important." He pointed at an ice chest. "Like a root beer? All I've got."

"Sure. So what do you do, go out in this boat to collect seaweed?"

"That, and fish for my dinner." He tossed me a can. "I spend a lot of time on this tub. I'm pretty much here whenever I'm not working at the aquarium."

"Your wife must be understanding."

"My wife?" He looked puzzled for a moment, then glanced at his hand. "Oh. You noticed my ring."

"Was I wrong?" I popped the can.

"Not exactly. I'm married. But Linda and I, we don't live together. Haven't for nearly twenty years. She's down in Summerland." He grinned. "That's how we've stayed married for so long."

"Got it. So, the *Lindy Sue* is named after your wife."

"Yeah. I named her decades ago. Just never got around to changing it."

"If it ain't broke, I suppose." I balanced the can on a box. "Dr. Thompson, thanks for agreeing to talk to me."

"Sorry I was kind of evasive before. Rod—Dr. Steinbach— he was against us talking to you. I couldn't see the harm in it, but Skye was his grandson, after all."

"Has Dr. Steinbach changed his opinion, then? About the staff talking to me."

"Not really." Neil squatted down and gathered up the nets. "But his daughter—Melanie? She phoned yesterday and asked me to help you out. Begged me, as a matter of fact." He shrugged. "Rod might not like it, but I can't see how it hurts."

"Great. The thing is, I'd like to talk with Delia and Cheryl again too. All I'm going to do is ask them some basic questions, go by the book."

"I'll tell the girls they're free to talk to you." Neil sat down on an overturned bucket and picked up a net. "Of course, it's up to them. But I think they'll both want to help."

I watched as Thompson picked at a snarl in the nylon cording. His efforts weren't very productive.

"How about you, Neil? Where were you on Friday evening, between the hours of five and ten?"

Startled, he looked up, rocked back on the bucket and tipped over to the deck. I couldn't help it, I laughed. It was such a classic Hollywood guilty reaction.

"Me?" He struggled to his feet. His face was red. "I was with a friend."

"Oh?" Delia, I guessed, remembering what I'd observed at the aquarium. "This friend, does she have a name?"

"Of course she has a name." He frowned, and a stubborn look settled on his face. "But I won't be giving it to you. She wouldn't want that."

"Fair enough. But would this person back you up, if push came to shove?"

"Yes." He righted the bucket and sat down again. "But why should it come to that?"

"No reason. Like I said, I'll be asking everyone the same questions." I looked him square in the eye. "Including Delia Foley."

"So . . . you know." His face fell. "Please, don't say anything to anyone. She's—she's got a husband, a mean sonofabitch."

"I don't see any reason for me to gab about her personal life." I polished off the root beer and tossed the empty into a wastebasket half full of recyclables. "Just one more question, and I'll leave you in peace. Did Skye Rasmussen know about you and Delia?"

"Did he . . . Now look here! Just what are you suggesting?"

I'd made the guy angry at last. "Did he?"

"No, he didn't. Nobody knows." Neil looked upset, a mix of

shame and defiance playing across his face. "Say, maybe Rod's right about you, maybe you *are* trouble."

"Only for the guilty." I smiled and shrugged. "If you want to help the Rasmussen family, you'll let me do my job."

"Jaymie, baby, you know the rules of the game. Call me at bedtime and you're gonna get sweet-an'-hot-talk."

I sipped my glass of white wine and studied the nearly full moon, trapped in a palm tree. The fronds dug into the moon's flesh like the teeth of a shark.

"I need to come and see you, Zave. It's important—about Brodie."

"Brodie?" His voice sobered. "When do you want to come by?"

"Tomorrow morning."

"Tomorrow I've got an appointment, at ten. Can you come by first thing?"

"When's that?"

"Before I get out of bed."

In spite of my bleak mood, he'd made me laugh. "Just can't help yourself, can you."

"Baby, when you get low like this, I'll say or do anything to cheer you up. See you round about eight."

That night I didn't sleep well. Dexter woke me at five, barking at the door to get out. I didn't get up. I figured he'd smelled a skunk or a raccoon, and I didn't need the little cow dog tangling with either of those critters.

From five till six I lay wide awake, thinking about Brodie. The coroner's report had stated he'd hanged himself in his cell. I'd never questioned that—why should I? Instead I'd taken it as God's truth, and agonized for three years over the reason for my brother's suicide. Had my own persistent in-your-face attitude toward the cops caused them to harass Brodie, to the point where he just couldn't take it anymore?

More than that, I'd blamed myself for having ignored his pleas for help for so many months. Months? Make that years.

Dawn splashed the bedroom with light. I flipped onto my back and stared at the cracked plaster ceiling.

Now it seemed I'd got it all wrong. Suddenly, I was drenched in sweat.

Somebody knew something. Somebody knew Brodie's death wasn't suicide. And that made it murder.

I threw back the sheet and jumped out of bed. Zave would help. That's what I needed: breakfast with Zave.

It was 6:30 A.M. on a Saturday, and the Lower West Side was still nestled in sleep. I circled around a broken beer bottle, looked up and saw a lone runner cross the road in the distance. The guy was jogging along in sweats in spite of the warm sun, shadow-punching the air like a boxer.

I drew in a deep breath. The mild air was laden with the perfume of the stately magnolias lining the street. Farther along the enticing aroma of simmering chili nearly lured me into the courtyard of an apartment house. I hoped Zave planned to ply me with breakfast.

I thought about Zave as I pedaled along. He was a complex guy. There was Zave the arrogant attorney, master puppeteer who pulled more strings than anyone in town. There was down-home Zave, who liked to pretend he'd clawed his way out of a ghetto. And there was flirty Zave, who could make you yank off your top with the heat of a sultry look. But there was also Zave my good friend, who'd never let me down. That was the guy I was looking for now.

The road meandered up Carrillo Hill. The sidewalks disappeared, and the small Spanish-style houses, built in the 1920s and '30s, sank into their overgrown gardens. I turned into the rutted alleyway that led to La Casa de la Boca del Cañón, Zave's home.

As I pedaled along I heard creatures rustling in the mountains of ivy growing on either side of the track. Most likely rats.
And sure enough, around another bend I came across one former
denizen, recently deceased, being gutted by a glossy crow.

Another turn, and I arrived at the spiked gate. I pulled up at
the keypad and was about to punch in a call when the gate swung
silently open. I pedaled on through.

Zave was waiting for me at the top of the old sandstone steps.
His hands were plunged in the pockets of his crimson robe. I
knew that robe. It was made of a terry cloth so fine it felt like
velvet. And I knew how the robe smelled: musky, sweet.

"Still no four wheels?" Zave shook his head as I dismounted
and climbed the steps. "You could lease one, you know."

"I like getting exercise."

"Oh, I know you do." Zave smiled and ran a hand down my
arm. "But there's got to be an occasion or two where you want to
show up nice and fresh."

I cocked an eyebrow. "Is there a problem?"

"Nothing a shower between us won't fix."

Usually, Zave's heavy-handed flirting made me laugh. But
this time the most I could manage was a lopsided smile.

"Sorry, Jaymie. You said this is about Brodie." He opened
the carved oak door and stood to one side. "Let's go in and talk."

The interior of the thick-walled Spanish home was cool and
dark. We passed through the shuttered living room to the
kitchen. Like all the rooms, the kitchen had white plaster walls,
a dark redwood-beamed ceiling, and brick-colored saltillo tiles
on the floor.

"Mm—what's for breakfast?" I edged toward a pan on the
stove.

"French toast with pralines. Egg casserole, Cajun style." Zave
smiled at me. "And you brought the dessert."

"I didn't—oh. I get it." This time I managed a real smile.

"But business before pleasure. Let's talk first." Zave led me out to the deck off the kitchen. The platform was surrounded on three sides by tropical plants: big-leafed bananas, fishtail palms, and a tall frangipani. I sat down at the round teak table, under a striped umbrella.

Zave sat opposite me, in the shade. The shadow of the umbrella cut across his face, masking his eyes. "Now tell me. What's come up?"

I opened the side pack I'd attached to my belt, and withdrew the cream-colored note. "This." I held it out to him.

Zave unfolded the sheet of paper and read it, examined the back, then read it again. He met my eyes as he handed it back to me. "Where did you get this?"

"It was stuck in my office screen door."

He leaned back, folded his hands, and pressed his index fingers to his lips. "'Your brother did not kill himself.' What do you make of it?"

"I suppose it could mean Brodie had an accident." I picked up an ivory-colored frangipani blossom from the tabletop and crushed it between my fingers. "Or it could mean . . . Well. It could mean he was murdered."

"The note—why now? Your brother's been dead for two years."

"Three, almost. I asked myself that. Mike Dawson thinks"— I saw the corner of Zave's lip curl—"he thinks it's just a mean joke. But he also wondered if it had something to do with the job I'm working on. The aquarium murders. Somebody, maybe the cops, could be trying to distract me. To get me to drop the case."

"That's a long shot. Still, I suppose the hayseed could be right. Law of averages: it's bound to happen now and then."

No love was lost between Zave and Mike. Mike saw Zave as a manipulative shyster of a lawyer, and Zave saw Mike as a redneck and a plod. And I knew they each saw the other as a rival. I didn't see it that way, though. Never had.

"Anyway, I've decided I'm not dropping the case. And I'm

going to uncover the truth about Brodie." I ran my fingers over the soft gray teak of the tabletop. "So what do you think I should do?"

"Do? I know you, Jaymie. It doesn't matter what I say." He leaned forward and his eyes burned into mine. "Just stay as cool and discreet as you can. Somebody's got an axe to grind. Don't play into their hands."

I trailed after Zave as he returned to the kitchen and completed the preps. Then we sat down together and devoured the food. We finished up with strong black coffee laced with thick cream.

"Got all your energy back?" Zave pulled me down to his lap as I got up to clear the table. "How about a kiss for the cook?" He tasted of raspberries, cayenne, and coffee.

"Mm. Yeah, I'd say I'm revitalized."

"Good, 'cause you owe me for that meal. And this restaurant don't take cash."

He led me off to his iridescent tiled shower. Perfumed, lukewarm, we soaped up in a downpour.

"I have a request," I said thirty minutes later, when I'd regained my rational mind. We lay stretched out side by side on the satin sheets.

"Guess what," Zave mumbled, half asleep. "You've caught me in a good mood."

"Figured I had." I trailed my fingertips over his shut eyelids. His lashes were beautiful, long and curved. "Remember Claudia Molina?"

"The juvie brat?"

"She's a good kid, Zave. The thing is, I need to get her a volunteer position at the aquarium."

He opened his eyes and looked at me. "You're going to use her for undercover? Sure that's safe?"

"She'll be under strict orders to work only at the aquarium, nowhere else, and only during scheduled hours. Any chance you could make it happen? Maybe through Rod Steinbach, I thought."

"I told you, that man is not sweet on you. A few more complaints arrived on my desk. Steinbach thinks you're an interfering stirrer."

I looked through the gauzy curtains at the flawless blue sky. "And you, I trust, replied that I'm nothing of the kind."

He rolled over on his side to face me. "I told my connection you are one hot little—"

"Zave?" Our eyes were inches apart. "I'm dead serious."

"Fine. We'll keep your name out of it." He pressed his nose to mine. "Consider it done."

I took a seat in the Sea Horse Snack Bar and watched Delia Foley at work behind the counter. Efficient and only as friendly as she needed to be, Delia dispatched each customer with a minimum of fuss. She liked her job, I realized. Here, she ruled her domain.

When the line had cleared, Delia walked around the counter and approached my table. "Did you want something?"

"I have a few more questions. Is this a good time?"

She shrugged. "The customers come in waves. There won't be anybody for thirty minutes, then you'll look up and there'll be ten people standing in line. I can talk, I suppose, but there's nobody here to help me. If I get a customer, I'll have to go."

"No problem." I studied Delia. She looked nice, very put-together with her black hair arranged on top of her sleek head. It wasn't hard to understand what Neil saw in her. But there was also an off-putting tension in the woman, a tension that never quite left her. She seemed almost hyper alert.

"Anyway, Neil—I mean Dr. Thompson—he told me it's OK to talk to you now." Delia flicked a loose thread off the sleeve of her crisp yellow button-down blouse. "Because Dr. Steinbach told him it was all right, I suppose."

There it was again, that tinge of resentment I'd heard the other day. "You don't especially like Rod Steinbach, do you, Delia."

"I like my job, OK? So I like Dr. Steinbach just fine."

"No, you don't. He's overbearing with the staff, am I right?"

She folded her arms across her chest. "Maybe."

"Delia, come on. Give me a break."

"Yeah, well. It's not like it's a secret." She shrugged. "Actually, nobody can stand him."

"Especially not you. Steinbach tells Neil what to do, even though Neil's the director, and perfectly capable. You must hate that."

"Like I said, nobody likes the way Dr. Steinbach behaves."

"Especially not you," I repeated, "since Neil's your lover."

Delia's mouth gaped open. It took a moment for her to recover. "How do you know that?"

"You try to hide it, but I can see you're a pair. Anyway, Neil and I discussed your relationship."

"What? Why would he tell *you!*"

At last, I had Delia's full attention. "Why? Because you're his alibi. Neil told me you were together on the Friday evening Skye was murdered." Of course, Neil had only reluctantly admitted it. But if I could drive a wedge between the two, I figured Delia would be more likely to talk.

"I can't believe Neil said that." Her shoulders slumped. "But it's true. My husband thinks I go to a cooking class at adult ed on Friday nights. Please, you need to keep it quiet. If Russ ever found out, he'd kill me. I mean it."

I recognized the real fear in her eyes, a fear I'd seen before in some women. "Delia, it's none of my business. But have you thought about leaving your husband?"

"I think about it all the time. But Russ can be trouble. If I asked for a divorce, he'd take the kids just to hurt me. They're everything to me, you know?"

"It's complicated—I understand. I'm sorry." And I was. Delia was managing the best she could in a tough situation.

"Yeah, well. I need a smoke." She got up and walked over to the entrance, pulled across a nautical rope, and hung a CLOSED sign on the post. She motioned to me, and I followed her outside to the deck.

Delia took a series of drags on her cigarette before she spoke. "Here's the thing: I can't lose this job. It keeps me going. All day I'm near Neil. At night I can go home and do what I have to do, to survive."

"Neil seems like a good man."

"He is. He's good to me. And everything was fine, you know? Perfect. Until Dr. Steinbach showed up."

"Sounds like he's ruined things around here."

"Oh, he has! Like you said, he tells Neil what to do all the time. And Neil just does it. It's like he's under a spell or something."

I looked along East Beach. There was a chop on the water, and the little waves reflected the sun like thousands of mirrors. "What exactly does Steinbach do for the aquarium? I understand the board hired him as a consultant. But he seems to be running the show."

"He got hired to clean things up. Make everything more *efficient*," she sneered. "I *am* efficient. But when I went in for my job review, Dr. Steinbach said I needed to sharpen up. Sharpen up—me!"

"Review?" I turned from the rail. "Do you know if Steinbach reviewed anyone else?"

"Cheryl Kerr. He really raked her over the coals. She's been working here for twenty years, ever since the aquarium opened. Her mom lives with her, and Cheryl has to go home every day on her lunch hour, then rush home again after work. She doesn't need that crap. And John Tactacquin, the guy who delivers our food supplies? For no reason, Dr. Steinbach told him he might lose his contract."

"Did he, now. Anyone else?"

"I heard he was even rough on the volunteers. Some of them are kids, temporary, they don't really care. But the permanent ones are retirees. Why should they come here if they aren't appreciated? Three people quit, just like that. And we need the volunteers, that's how the aquarium keeps going on such a tight budget."

"Sounds like people have reason to resent the guy."

"Oh, we all hate him." She stubbed out her cigarette on the rail, then bent down and blew the ash into the sea. "Not the board members though, or the donors. They all think he walks on water."

Delia was opening up with me, and I decided to take advantage of the thaw. "How about Skye? People seem to have liked him. I guess he was nothing like his grandfather?"

"You know, I thought he would be. I kept my distance at first. But actually, he wasn't like that at all. To be honest, Skye Rasmussen was a sweet kid." She straightened her back, and smoothed her hair off her forehead.

"Well. I can't talk all day. I've got to open back up."

"Sure." I followed her to the door. "Just one more question before I go, Delia. You said you thought only four of you know the combination to the service door, right?"

Delia was changeable. That sharp defensive look had returned. "I already told you. Me and Cheryl, Neil, and Dr. Steinbach."

"But Skye knew the combo, too. That's how he got in after hours that night."

"He did?" She shrugged. "The volunteers are only supposed to come in when the aquarium's open. Maybe Dr. Steinbach gave the combo to Skye."

"And there could be others, couldn't there?"

She tucked her shirt into her trim camel-colored slacks. "I suppose."

"It's just that I'm wondering about someone, Delia. The guy you just mentioned, John Tactacquin. I've heard he comes in early, before the aquarium's open. How does he get in, do you think?"

"I have no idea." Her voice had tightened. "Look, I've got to get back to work. Besides, I've told you everything I know."

Chapter Eight

The gift shop on the ground floor was empty of customers. Cheryl Kerr was seated on a chair behind the counter, nibbling on something. She ducked her head when she saw me.

"Hi, Cheryl, how are you?" I stopped to examine a collection of cuddly plush sea creatures, to give her time.

"Oh—hi." She dabbed at the corners of her mouth with her fingers. "Can I help you?"

"Maybe. I was talking with Delia upstairs, and thought I'd stop in for a quick chat with you, too."

Cheryl's eyes were large behind her big glasses. Her pale lashes were sparse, the lids swollen and red. "Oh—OK. Yes, I guess it's all right."

"I want to talk with you about Skye's murder. To help his family."

"M—murder?" Her eyes grew rounder. "I thought the boy—I thought he just, you know—fell in."

"No, we don't think that's what happened. Mind if I ask you a question or two?"

"Of course I don't mind." She fiddled with the top button of her pale pink cardigan. "Is there any reason I would?"

"John Tactacquin, then. What do you think of him?"

"Think of him?" She blinked several times before she answered. "I don't really think about him at all. He's OK, I guess. Sometimes he drops off candies for the gift shop, like those PEZ containers over there. Usually he comes in before I get here, and just leaves the stock on the counter."

"So he knows the security code for the back door?"

"I don't know. I guess so." Cheryl lifted her glasses and rubbed the bridge of her nose. "You need to ask Delia that, she'd know for sure. Mainly he's here for the café."

I nodded. Cheryl was relaxing a little, and it was time to broach a less comfortable topic. "Delia told me Dr. Steinbach's been raking everyone over the coals. Job reviews, he's calling it. How about you?"

"Me?" Cheryl flushed. Her skin was so pale I could see the blood rise like mercury in a thermometer.

"I understand he was rough on you."

"Um, I guess so. . . ." She picked up a pen and made some scribbles on a pad.

"Look, Cheryl. I know you're concerned about your job. Who wouldn't be? But I'll be discreet about anything you tell me."

"There's nothing to tell. Dr. Steinbach—he—"

"Yes?" I put an encouraging smile on my face. Anything to make this canary sing.

"Oh, I don't know, he just said . . ." Abruptly, her defenses fell. It was as if a wall came tumbling down. "He said I was over-weight, sloppy! Too—too ill-groomed. 'Not the image the aquar-ium wants to project.'" Her voice quavered in anger.

"I don't blame you for being mad."

"I always look neat, I'm always clean. I don't have fancy clothes because they don't pay me anything. And I told him that, I said how dare he, how dare he talk to me that way!"

"Steinbach shouldn't have said those things, Cheryl. If they were to fire you, you'd have ammunition for a lawsuit."

"He'd just deny it. Dr. Steinbach is slippery. And oh, so full of himself! Cock of the walk, you know?" Cheryl gripped the pen. I noticed her knuckles were white.

"Not anymore," I reminded her. "Not since his grandson died."

"No." Just like that, the fire went out of her.

"No, that's true. Not anymore."

A man knelt on my office step. I saw him lean back to admire his handiwork: a pristine white rose slipped into a water bottle. He got to his feet and caught sight of me.

"Miss Jaymie?" Angel was short, compactly built, with a worn brown face and gnarled hands. He wore brown work clothes. Everything about Angel was brown—of the good earth.

"Yep, that's me. You must be Angel?" He was rather plain-looking, this angel, but his smile was positively beatific. Gabi, I thought, you lucky girl.

"An-hel," he corrected as he stuffed a carpenter's pencil in his work belt. He reached out his hand and I extended my own. His skin was rough and dry as a gardening glove.

"An-hel, of course." I smiled back at him. "The roses—they're so beautiful."

He bobbed his head, somewhere between a nod and a bow. "The rose, she is the queen of the flowers."

"I can't argue with that. Did you want to see Gabi today? You usually bring her rose first thing in the morning, don't you? Before she arrives."

He shifted the work belt around his ample middle. Loaded down with a trowel, a weeding tool, and three or four different types of clippers, it must have weighed fifteen pounds. "Yes. I wanted to talk to her. But I guess she's not here."

"Today's her cleaning day. Sparkleberry, you know? She comes and goes."

Again he nodded, that curious little bob. "I have to go to

work now. Very nice to meet you, Miss Jaymie. Gabi, she talks about you all the time."

"Nice to meet *you*, Angel. Gabi's so happy these days."

"We are both happy. But . . ." He frowned and rested a hand on his work belt.

"But?"

"I am worried."

"You don't have anything to worry about. Gabi is lucky to have met you, and believe me, she knows it."

He bit his lip and looked at the ground. "But that is because . . . she don't know."

Uh-oh. So Angel was too good to be true, after all.

Suddenly I didn't want to hear any more, didn't want to know. "Look, I've got to get to work now too, it was nice—"

"Please." He raised a tentative hand. "You know Gabi, you know her so good. I want to ask you, what I should do?"

Angel was dragging me smack-dab into the middle of something. His eyes had moistened. "What's wrong?" I felt my common sense slipping away.

"My mother, she took me back to Guadalajara when I was four. I lived there most of my life." Angel opened his mouth to speak, closed it, opened it again. "But . . . I was born in Los Angeles."

"So you are a—" The word stuck in my throat.

"A citizen. Yes, I am a citizen of the United States."

"And of course, Gabi doesn't know."

"No." Angel sighed. "Right when I met her she told me, she don't want no boyfriend who is a citizen. So I said nothing. I thought maybe later I would tell her . . . but now it would be worse, you know? Because I waited so long."

"I understand. But sooner or later, you're going to have to confess. Maybe sooner would be better." I put a reassuring smile on my face. "She really cares about you, Angel. I'm sure she'll accept it."

"Do you think so?" A smile brightened his countenance. "I'm glad I told you, Miss Jaymie. Thank you for the good advice."

I set to work in the kitchenette. First I located my roll of blue painter's tape and a marker, then broke open a fresh pack of index cards. I was ready to construct a rogues' gallery of suspects.

One by one I taped names to the wall. One card per suspect. When I was done, I perched on the edge of the table and considered them.

Delia Foley. Neil Thompson. Cheryl Kerr. Each of these aquarium employees had shaky alibis for the time period in question. No motives, though. Delia and Cheryl hated Rod, but that animosity hadn't seemed to extend to his grandson. And none of the three seemed like killers—though I knew better than to trust *that* observation.

My eyes moved on to Skye's so-called friends: Porter Logsdon and Vanessa Hoague. Their alibis needed a closer look. Unlike the employees, both Vanessa and Porter just might have had motives for murder. I was hoping Claudia would come up with something, because those two weren't about to open up to someone of my advanced years.

Then there was Taryn Tactacquin. I'd checked into her alibi. She'd babysat for the Kleins on the evening of Skye's death, just as she'd said. What's more, the Klein kids had been allowed to have a friend around, and the little boy's mom had stopped by the house to check up. I shifted Taryn's card to the edge of the wall: she was pretty much out of the picture.

Then I turned to the members of Skye's family.

Rod Steinbach could be aggressive and, even at his age, possessed a considerable drive for power. But his grandson's death had hit Steinbach hard. It was extremely unlikely he'd have harmed Skye. Even so, I left his card in place.

Melanie and Dave Rasmussen were even less likely to have

killed their son. Stranger things had happened, but I moved their cards to the margin.

Steven Steinbach, on the other hand, I wasn't so sure of. He loved his sister, that was clear. But Rod had favored Skye over Steven. I wondered: how had Steven felt about that?

I needed to have a talk with Steven Steinbach. Conversations on the phone never worked, at least not for me. I had to see people's expressions, observe their hesitations and sideways glances. But Steven had left for home right after he'd spoken with me. And home was San Francisco, four hundred miles to the north. I would give it some thought.

My attention shifted to the card I'd saved for last: *John Tactacquin*. Taryn was a good kid, but that wasn't going to stop me from focusing in on her dad. Motive and opportunity: the man had it all.

Yeah, Steven Steinbach could cool his heels up in SF, at least for now. Tactacquin was the guy in my crosshairs.

I shoved up the window at the back of the kitchen and parked my butt on the sill, the better to plan my attack. Just as my mind began to move forward, the front door banged open.

"Hola!" Gabi trilled as she breezed into the office. I winced. The woman was so relentlessly upbeat these days.

She appeared in the kitchen doorway, a big smile on her face. "And how are *you* today, Miss Jaymie? Very good I hope?"

"I'm OK."

"OK? That's not good enough. Look at this beautiful day. You should be—"

"Sex is great, isn't it? Especially when you haven't had it for a very, very long time."

Gabi tsked. "You shouldn't talk like that, Miss Jaymie. Me and Angel, it's not about sex. I'm just so happy, that's all. I'm sorry you're grouchy, but maybe you'll get more happy just being around me." She beamed and returned to the front office. I heard her begin to hum a little tune.

"I *was* perfectly happy," I called, "until a person who is way *too* happy, who overdoes this happiness thing, walked in. By the way, I met your boyfriend this morning."

I thought the term "boyfriend" would cause her to bridle. In the not-so-long-ago past, it would have. But not now.

"Oh, did you?" Gabi called back. "Good. I wanted Angel to meet you, and I wanted you to meet him. He's nice, huh?"

"He is. Maybe too nice for you?"

"You know, Miss Jaymie, in the beginning that's what I thought. But then I said, this is my destiny, Angel and me together, so why worry about it?"

I groaned and let my head fall to my chest.

Gabi reappeared in the doorway. "Miss Jaymie, maybe you should think about Mike. Think about destiny, what I'm saying to you."

"Let's get to work, shall we?" I hopped off the sill. "I'm ready to get serious, and I need your advice."

Gabi looked at the wall dotted with cards, then looked back at me. "I'm all business, Miss Jaymie. But don't forget what I said."

A yellow and peach dawn unfolded over East Beach. I stood on the wharf and watched the show: the soft colors opened like origami, gradually revealing a fresh-faced sun.

The day promised to be another August scorcher. The dewy freshness would evaporate quickly, and the cheery sun would morph into a fiery single-minded orb.

I heard a vehicle approach, clunking along the timbers of the dock. A white delivery van turned a corner and pulled up at the back of the aquarium. *Tri-County Restaurant Supply* read the sign on the side, in bold red letters.

A stocky, silver-haired man in his late forties hopped down from the driver's side, went around to the back, and lifted the roll-up door. He wore khaki chinos and a navy blue golf shirt, and he moved with impatience, in spite of the early hour. I watched as he unloaded a stack of boxes, carried them over to the back door and set them on the ground, then punched in a code.

"Mr. Tactacquin?"

Caught by surprise, John Tactacquin spun around and glared at me just as the door chirped and clicked open.

"I'm Jaymie Zarlin." I stepped up to him. "Mind if we talk?"

"Talk? Who the hell are you?"

"I'm Jaymie Zarlin. A private investigator. I'd like to ask you one or two questions, if you don't mind."

He bent down, picked up the boxes, and started to back into the hall. "What about?"

"Skye Rasmussen."

"No way." He shoved through the door and let it fall shut. But not before I'd stuck my foot in the gap. I gave the heavy door a shove and stepped through, into the dimly lit space.

"You aren't supposed to be in here." Tactacquin continued on down the hall. I followed him through the entry foyer to the elevator. "You could get yourself into trouble, pushing your way in like that."

The man's hands were full. I stepped around him and pressed the button. "And you could get into some trouble too, Mr. Tactacquin. Since you aren't supposed to know the code. You got it from Delia, I suppose?"

He was silent as the elevator door slid open. He stepped in and I followed. The elevator was small, and John Tactacquin and I were standing close, eye-to-eye.

"So I get going early in the morning, so what? You seem to know a helluva lot. What do you want?"

I pressed the button to go up. "I want you to tell me where you were, between the hours of five and ten P.M. on the night Skye Rasmussen died."

He gave me a disgusted look. "You sound like an actor on TV. A rerun detective show."

"I'm not much of an actor. But I'd appreciate it if you'd answer the question." The door opened on the second floor.

"Sure, why not?" Tactacquin stepped out of the elevator and headed for the snack bar. He circled the rope closing off the space, went up to the counter, and set down the boxes.

"I started early like every day, knocked off around three. And then I went home."

"Can somebody at home vouch for that?" I wasn't going to tell him I knew Taryn. He'd find out soon enough.

He was quiet as he wrote on a pad attached to a clipboard. He ripped off the invoice and tucked it between two of the boxes. "My wife and daughter. Good enough for you?" His voice was careful now, controlled. Something told me John Tactacquin had just lied.

"I'll take your word for it, for now."

He slipped the clipboard and pad under his arm and looked at me, hard. "Who are you working for?"

"The Rasmussens. Melanie and Dave."

"Figures." He shook his head. "So you know all about the time I went by their place. You think I've got a motive, is that it? Suppose I do, in a way. Their son got my girl pregnant, then he bullied her into having an abortion. Yeah, I admit it. For a few weeks last fall, I could have murdered the kid."

"Those are strong words, Mr. Tactacquin."

He turned his back on me and started to walk away, then stopped. "Look. You're right, I'm not supposed to be in here before the aquarium opens. If you want to ask me anything else, it needs to be outside."

I squinted into the sun as we exited the gloomy interior, then followed Tactacquin to the rail at the edge of the dock.

"Listen, before you say anything." Tactacquin folded his arms across his chest and stared out along East Beach. "Believe it or not, I'm sorry about the kid. I heard how he suffered. And I'll tell you, my daughter is really broke up. If she cared that much about him, then he must have had a good side."

"What about the boy's grandfather? Do you think he has a good side?"

"What, Rod Steinbach? He's an asshole." He leaned over the rail and spat into the water.

"Steinbach seems to have rubbed a lot of people the wrong way."

"I don't know about that. But I do know he threatened to take away my contract when it comes up for renewal."

"Any reason?"

"Nope. No reason given. The jerk just wanted to light a fire under my ass. See me squirm."

I was quiet for a moment. I watched as three or four gleaming dolphins dashed parallel to the beach, cavorting in the surf.

"Here's the thing, Mr. Tactacquin. I'd like to believe you. But something tells me your alibi won't check out. You might as well tell me the truth. Save me bothering your daughter and wife."

"All right, all right. I *was* home . . . at eight." The words came out slowly. "Before that I was out in Goleta. Visiting a friend."

"A lady friend?"

He hesitated, a few beats too long. "Naw, a guy. We usually have a few beers after work, on Friday afternoons."

Oh sure, it was a guy. "Will this friend confirm what you've said?"

"If I ask him to. Which I'm not going to do. This is all bullshit."

"You might have to ask *him* to speak up, whether you want to or not."

"That enough? Done poking into my life?" He started to walk away. Then he turned back.

"I love my wife, all right? Our boy Kenny . . . he's in prison, it's a mess. Her life isn't easy right now."

Then quit cheating on her, I wanted to say.

But I didn't say it. Because it isn't my job to preach the truth.

My job is to try to uncover it.

That afternoon, my undercover agent reported in.

"The aquarium's cool," Claudia announced with an airy wave of her hand. "Me and Vanessa, we sneak out and smoke under the pier." She lay back on the couch and crossed her legs at the ankles. "Yeah, it's working out good."

Gabi peered around her computer. "You don't look like that when you go there, I hope?"

"Look like what?" Claudia smoothed her wife-beater shirt over her baggy shorts. "They think I'm tough." She pulled out her Smith & Wesson, popped the blade, and cleaned under a fingernail. "See, they heard how I carved up that prick Stellato with my knife a few months ago."

"Put that nasty thing away," Gabi snapped. "This is a place of—"

"Yeah, yeah, a place of busy-ness. And don't be callin' my dad's knife nasty." Claudia rolled her head to look at me. "Jaymie, can't just you an' me talk? I'm here to make my report."

I dropped into the hot seat. "Gabi's part of the operation, Claudia. You know that."

"Fuh. Then I'm outta here." She rolled over and hopped to her feet. "I'll make my report on the phone."

"No, tell me now. And please don't forget who's boss around here."

"Boss?" Claudia squealed. "I thought we were like, equal. I don't have no boss over me. I—"

"I, I, I." Gabi pushed back her chair. "I'm going out for my coffee break so I don't have to listen to this broken record."

"Record? What's that, somethin' from your childhood? Caveman times?"

"Sorry, Miss Jaymie. I gotta leave you alone with her. I just can't take it no more."

"Claudia, you cut it out. And Gabi, don't let this kid chase you off."

"Chase me off? I'm just thinking positively positive and taking care of myself!"

Claudia cackled. "What's with the 'positively positive' caca?"

"Positively Positive: Self-Talk-n-Walk Your Way to Fulfillment." Gabi picked up her bag and sat it on the desk. "It's a very important book. Maybe you should try it sometime."

"Sure. Leave it back in the bathroom, will you? You're just about out of toilet paper."

Gabi grabbed her bag and stormed out the door.

"Chased her off, didn't I!" Claudia tipped back her head and yipped like a coyote.

"Claudia, I wish you'd make an effort with Gabi." I put a hand to my mouth: I sounded just like a mom.

"I *do* make an effort, man. If I didn't, you'd know it. If I didn't—"

"Hey, back on topic. The aquarium—what's going on?"

"Hold on, it's too dark in here." Claudia went over to the side window and snapped up the blind, which Gabi had closed to keep out the withering heat. "Whoa, it's that bird!" She lifted the sash and Deadbeat, tethered to his outside perch, let out a god-awful scream.

Claudia turned to me with a grin. "Who owns that mofo?"

"The repo woman next door." I was beginning to understand just how Gabi felt.

"He's gonna be barbecued chicken out there in the sun." She screamed back at the parrot, then slammed the window shut.

"Claudia?" I tried again. "So, you're in with Vanessa."

"Yeah, I'm in. We do weird things when nobody's looking. Like, we gave Legs a jar of anchovies." She laughed. "You shoulda seen how fast that octopus opened that sucka."

"Don't get yourself kicked out, will you." Oops, there it was again: June Cleaver speaking out of my mouth.

"You don't get it, Jaymie. If I got kicked out of the aquarium, that'd be cool. It would just get me in better with the piñata party crowd."

"So there really is something called the Piñata Party?"

"Oh yeah there is, and that's what I want to tell you. I got invited. They're having a end-of-summer party, one last blast before most of them go away to college. It's Friday night, and I'm goin'. *Dale, dale, dale.*"

"Excellent work, but I'm not so sure you should go. What's it all about?"

"Don't know yet. I kinda asked, but Vannie—that's Vanessa—she said I'd find out on Friday. Bitch said, 'All will be clear to you.'" Claudia picked up the vase holding Gabi's most recent rose, an exquisite bloom called Blue Satin. "Somebody bringin' you flowers?"

"Not me. Gabi. She has a boyfriend."

"You're shittin' me," Claudia shrieked. "He must be one messed-up dude." She set the vase back on the desktop. "So, the piñata party. What am I looking for again?"

"Something happened there, back in January. Something involving Skye Rasmussen, maybe a fight. I want you to find out what it was all about."

"No worries. That it?"

"You need to be careful. The police called Skye's death an accident, but like I've told you, he was pushed. It could have been murder."

For a moment, Claudia didn't look so cocky. I knew she was thinking of her sister Lili, killed just three months earlier. I got up, walked over to the kid, and gave her shoulder a quick squeeze. "You OK?"

"I'm gonna help you catch the asshole who did it," she muttered.

"Good. But here's the thing: you're not staying past midnight. If you do, I'll come in after you."

"Tough lady, huh?"

"You've got that right. And if a problem comes up, anything at all, give me a ring. Understand?"

"It's a party, not World War Three." Claudia hitched up her baggy shorts. "One thing you don't gotta do, is worry about me."

Chapter Nine

I steered the rental car up the packed gravel road to Little Panoche Ranch. Outside my sealed-up windows, the air was blistering. The car's thermometer read 107.

Without warning, a stoplight-red farm bike shot out of the scrub, swerved in front of me, and careered up the drive. The dark-haired boy on the bike turned in the seat and waved.

I followed him in through the gate decorated with deer antlers and up to the sprawling one-story redwood ranch house. When I switched off the engine, fine dust rose in billows around the car.

The gangly kid climbed off the bike and walked over as I got out. My jaw dropped when I saw him up close. He was about fourteen, already six feet tall, and he looked exactly like Mike must have looked at that age. He was dark in complexion, and his eyes were narrow, his cheekbones high.

"Hi! Are you Uncle Mike's girlfriend?"

"Ah, no, you've got the wrong girl. Your uncle and I are just friends. I'm Jaymie Zarlin."

The kid grinned. "Yeah, you're the one. Grandpa says—" Then he looked embarrassed, probably realizing he was saying too much. "Anyway, I'm Tyler."

"Hey, Tyler." I smiled up at him. "You staying here at the ranch with your grandfather?"

"Yeah. We've been up here most of the summer. But school starts next week, so my mom said—"

"Don't listen to a word that boy says," Bill Dawson boomed down from the big wrap-around porch. "Jaymie, how are ya?" His voice was strong, but he held on to the rail with one hand and leaned on a cane with the other.

I slammed the car door and walked up the steps, Tyler in tow. "Fine, Bill. How about you?"

He extended a hand. I took it and he tightened his grip. "I'm doing all right. Feel that? Still strong. Not goin' anywhere in a hurry, don't care what those sawbones got to say."

"Glad to hear it, Bill."

"But what am I doing, blocking the doorway? Give your keys to the boy here. He'll park your car over there in the shade." He looked hard at his grandson. "Don't go takin' that car on a joy ride, son."

"No way," Tyler said with a grin.

We stepped into the dark, cool living room. Shep, Bill's old border collie, struggled up from his blanket in the corner and hobbled over for a pat.

"Hear that roar? Air-conditioning," Bill groused. "Damn thing's been runnin all summer long. Trudy had it installed. God-damn waste of money. Come on through, she's in the kitchen."

Trudy Freitas looked up from the chopping board. Again, I felt that frisson of recognition: she was nearly as tall as Mike, and had his gold-flecked brown eyes.

"Hi, Jaymie. Good to meet you. Welcome to my workstation." She laughed. "Ever since we came up to the ranch, I've hardly stepped out of the kitchen."

"That's where a woman belongs." Bill looked over at me and winked.

"Careful, Dad. I'll throw a ripe tomato at you." Trudy looked like Mike but she was different, I realized. Mike had a quietness about him, a holding-in. She bubbled up like a spring.

"Good to meet you, Trudy." Just then I heard a clatter of feet behind me on the oak floor. I turned to see two girls, both around eight years of age, framed in the doorway.

"Jaymie, meet the twins, Peggy and Perlina," Trudy said. "Girls, this is Ms. Zarlin."

"Just Jaymie," I corrected. "Hi, girls."

"Hi," they chimed.

"Peggy's named after their grandma, and Perry's named after their great-grandma," Bill explained.

"Are your eyes really two different colors?" the shorter one asked.

"Perry, for goodness' sake," Trudy scolded.

"It's fine." I smiled. "I don't mind one bit. Yes, one's kind of green and the other one's blue."

"Are you staying with us? Uncle Mike's coming up tonight," Peggy said. "We always make a campfire when he comes."

"Yeah, and cook s'mores," Perry added.

"Sorry. I have to be up in San Francisco at four."

"Are you sure? We'd love to have you," Trudy urged.

"Thanks, but I've got an appointment." Thank goodness. If I hadn't made that appointment with Steven Steinbach, I'd have had to invent something. S'mores with Mike under the stars was not something I felt I could handle just now.

"These two girls are big trouble, you better watch out for 'em." Bill eased himself into a kitchen chair. I could see how much effort it cost him, how weary he was. "What you two been doing upstairs, paintin' your toenails? You're too young for that."

One of the twins rolled her eyes. "Grandpa, we've been doing it for *years!*"

Tyler walked into the kitchen. He reached out and snagged a chunk of cheddar off the cutting board. "She's not Uncle Mike's girlfriend," he announced. "Jaymie said she's just his friend."

The talking stopped. Everyone looked at me. Everyone except Bill, who shook his head and studied the floor. "That's somethin' me and Jaymie are gonna discuss, after lunch."

"Jaymie, let's go talk in the office," Bill said as Trudy helped him up out of the dining chair and handed him his cane.

"That's quite some cane you've got there, Bill." I walked slowly beside him, ready to grab his arm if he stumbled.

"Think so?" He grinned. "Old buddy a mine sent it from Texas. Made from a bull's penis, believe it or not."

"Dad," Trudy called from the dining room. "That's enough about the cane." I heard the girls giggle.

The ranch office was located on the far side of the house. Bill eased himself in behind a carved oak desk, and motioned me to an old cracked leather chair. I looked around the room as Bill settled in.

A bookcase held a collection of volumes and manuals with sun-bleached spines. The topics ranged from ranch accounting to Hereford diseases. Two nicked and scarred file cabinets stood on either side of a big window looking out over the tawny burnt hills of Little Panoche.

"Nice view, isn't it. Never get tired of it," Bill observed. "Trudy don't know it yet, but I'm not going back down with her to San Luis." He said it the old-timers' way, "San Looey." "I don't want to die, but if I gotta, it's going to be right here. Right here, in the bed my wife died in. You understand?"

"I do, Bill. But that's not going to happen for a while yet."

"Maybe, maybe not." He began to cough, and pulled out a crumpled red bandanna. "Trudy's always after me to use Kleenex. I tell her I'm not gonna change my ways, not this late in the game." He coughed some more, then leaned back in the chair and stuffed the bandanna in his pocket. "Now. About Mike."

I'd been dreading this. I knew how much Bill wanted

us hitched. "I wish he'd told you, Bill. That we're not a couple anymore. The truth is, it's always been off and on with us. Now, it's off." I looked over at him. "Permanently, I'm afraid."

Bill waved a hand in the air, like he was swatting a fly. "I figured it out months ago, Jaymie. Mike didn't have to say nothin'. Whenever your name came up, he got real quiet. And it's none of my business why you dumped him. My boy can be damned stubborn and ornery, like me. He most likely deserved it."

"Bill?" I took in a breath and let it out. "Mike dumped me. Not the other way around."

"Then he's a goddamn fool."

"No. He broke up with me because I let him down."

I'd let Mike down, all right. I'd decided to move out of town, to run off without telling him or saying goodbye. It was a panicky thing to do, and implied I didn't give a damn about him—which wasn't true.

"We all got our problems." Bill shook his head. "I don't know you as well as I'd like, Jaymie, don't know what you been through in life. But now that I'm getting near the end, I'm trying to set things right. My boy Mike—there's something I gotta tell you about him. Hard to say it."

I didn't want to hear whatever secret Bill was about to reveal. But how to tell that to a dying man? I could only try to divert him.

"Mike has a new girlfriend now. Her name's Mandy. She's—she's nice. You'd like her, Bill."

"Fine, but she's not you. I see Mike every week or so, I can tell you one thing for sure: he's not in love with this new one." The old man placed both hands flat on the fuzzy blotter. "I was rough on him growing up. That's what I got to confess. I was a bad-tempered sonofabitch, and I took everything out on him." Bill was talking quickly now, breathing heavily.

"If there's one thing in my life I could do over, it would be how I raised that boy. It made him too hard. That's what I want you to know. Mike closed up some, the way I see it. And if he gets the rug yanked out from under him, like must of happened with you, well, he washes his hands of the situation, tout suite."

The room was too hot. I was prickly with sweat. "I don't know what I can—"

"But he's having a hard time washing his hands of you, Jaymie. I see it, I'm not makin' this up. I got no right to beg you to give him another chance, but I guess that's what I'm doin'."

There was a light knock on the door. It opened, and Perry stuck in her head. "Grandpa? Mom says you have to go take your nap."

"Come to this, has it?" He shook his head. "My own granddaughter tellin' me to go take a nap." Then he reached out a hand to the girl.

"Come here, sweetheart. Come and give your grandpa a hug."

When the girl wrapped her arms around her grandfather's neck, I had to look away. My eyes stung with tears.

I was out on the porch, saying my goodbyes to Trudy and the kids, when Mike's Silverado roared up the road and slammed to a halt.

"Uncle Mike! He's here!" the twins squealed. They raced down the porch steps. Tyler followed at a more leisurely pace, his hands stuffed in his jeans pockets.

"The main attraction has arrived." Trudy shook her head. "They won't leave him alone the whole time he's here." She looked over at me and smiled. "Guess you're staying for a while longer. Mike's blocked in your car."

I watched as he got out of the pickup and stretched. The girls were jumping around him and chattering away. Mike bent down and gave each girl a hug. Then he slapped Tyler on the back.

"He sure likes kids." Trudy shot me another glance. "Excuse me, will you? I need to get back to my post."

Mike waded through the welcoming throng and went around to the passenger's side to unload his old duffel bag. The girls grabbed it off him and carried it between them. Then they all paraded along the path and up the steps. So far Mike hadn't given me so much as a glance.

The kids were quiet now, all eyes, waiting to see how their uncle would react to me. I was kind of wondering, myself.

"Hey, Jaymie. How's it going?" Mike walked on past me. My heart dropped.

Then, as the girls screamed in delight, Mike spun around, grabbed me in a bear hug, and planted a big noisy kiss on my mouth.

"Mike!' I managed to gasp.

"Show's gotta go on," he said in my ear.

"Listen, you kids. Me and Jaymie gotta talk about some business. I'll be in pretty quick."

"What kind of business?" Perry shrieked. It looked like the excitement level was going to keep running high.

"Grown-up business, short stuff. Now go grill me a tomato and cheese sandwich, OK?"

"Kay. We already put some beer in the refrigerator for you, Uncle Mike."

"Good girls. Where's Grampa?"

"Mom made him go take a nap."

Mike still hadn't taken his arm away from my waist. "Tye, did you tune up that farm bike like I asked you?"

"Yeah, it runs real good."

"Great. I want to take Dad out in the morning, we'll all go for a ride. Now you kids buzz off."

"Why, do you want *privacy*?" Perry giggled.

"Uh-huh." Mike laughed. "And maybe some peace and quiet, if you don't mind."

He dropped his arm from my waist and took me by the elbow, steering me down the steps and around the southwest corner of the house. "Those two girls are going to be big trouble. Just give 'em four or five years."

"They're nice kids. You're lucky, you have a wonderful family, Mike."

"Yeah, I do. Thanks to my mom."

I stopped and turned to him. "Look, I can't stay. I've got an appointment in the city at four. What did you want to talk about?"

"It's too hot to talk out here. Let's go in the barn."

"Hot? It's brutal. How do the cattle survive?"

"Just fine, if the water tanks don't run dry and we feed them hay. We had a dry winter, so there's not much fodder left out there on the hills."

We approached the big two-story redwood barn. Mike lifted the hasp and shoved open one of the double doors. I stepped inside, and he closed the door after us.

Except for a half-floor at the back, the open space soared to the rafters. Bright strips of light gleamed through the gaps in the siding. It was like being in a church.

"Nothing like a barn," Mike said softly. "Something about that smell."

I breathed in deeply. It was a mix of horse hair, manure, hay, and machine oil. "But where are the horses?"

"Had to take them down to San Luis last spring. They're boarded down there. We have a ranch manager now, comes up three times a week. But we can't expect José to look after the cattle and the horses, too."

Mike dragged a hay bale down off a stack. "Here you go."

I sat down and watched Mike as he wandered around, checking on things: tack hanging on nails, a stack of empty gunny sacks. He walked back over and leaned against a post. "José's keeping it afloat, but a couple days a week just isn't enough."

"What will you do?" I didn't add, "when Bill dies." Mike would know what I meant.

"Not sure." He rubbed the edge of his boot against the layer of dirt on the concrete floor. "This is where I want to be, eventually. There are plenty of improvements I'd like to make. But—" He shrugged.

High above us, the corrugated iron roof cracked in the heat. "But what? You were made for this, Mike. It's your home."

"I hate to say it, but it's kind of lonely up here. I don't know . . . maybe I could put up another house, José could move up with his wife and kids."

But I knew that wasn't the answer. And I knew that Mike knew.

"The thing is, Dad—" Mike was quiet for a minute. When he spoke again, his voice was thick. "He won't be back, Jaymie. They're taking him down to San Luis to die."

I got up from the hay bale and went to him. When I put my arms around him, I started crying, too.

I don't know how to explain it. Human beings are odd ducks, I suppose. I can only say that one minute we were comforting each other, two old friends. But the barn was warm and dark and—*private*. And before long, my back was up against the rough plank wall.

We did it fully clothed, both of us a shade too rough. And fast, maybe because there wasn't a lock on the door, or maybe so we didn't have to think about it. I held back my cries.

"I miss you, Jaymie," Mike said as he pulled up his jeans. "I wish I didn't." He sounded almost angry, accusing.

I didn't say anything. I didn't know what to say, because I felt such a jumble of emotions.

I yanked the elastic band off my ponytail and smoothed my hair back, then snapped the band back on. "What did you want to talk to me about?"

"Nothing. I just wanted to get you on your own."

"Mission accomplished." I tried a laugh, but it sounded strained. "Move your truck, please. I need to go."

✦   ✦   ✦

I drove down the Salinas Valley through the summer heat, following the course of the ancient underground river toward the
sea. I'd have to step on it to get to San Francisco on time. My
usual MO was to arrive early for interviews, in order to catch
my subject off-guard. This time I'd be the frazzled one.

I didn't want to think about Mike. That chapter of my life
was closed. I'd made a mistake, and he'd moved on.

Oh, Mike wanted me, all right. But today I'd heard something else in his voice: he resented me, too.

I wanted to believe I'd moved on as well. But I hadn't, not
really. Even now, just thinking about the guy jabbed at me like
a yellow jacket.

And something else was jabbing at me.

I thought again about the note, which I'd slipped in a clear
plastic sleeve and tucked in my messenger bag. *Your brother did
not kill himself. What are you going to do about it?*

Do about it? I was doing nothing about it. In fact, I—Shit!
A horn shrieked in my ear.

I'd pulled into the center lane without looking in my rear-
view mirror. I gave a weak apologetic wave.

Shaken a little, I turned on the radio and scanned through
the stations till I found a mind-numbing oldies format. *Do ya
luv me, duh-duh-duh, do ya luv me, duh-duh-duh, now that I can
dance?*

I tried to keep my mind on autopilot all the way up through
Silicon Valley, the Peninsula, and into the great little city of San
Fran.

A cross-faced Steven Steinbach answered the door of the slick
postmodern three-story home. He wore baggy jeans and a rum-
pled T-shirt that read *Noe Valley Cooperative*. "You're late," he
complained.

"Sorry. The traffic . . ." Vaguely, I waved.

"Traffic's always bad. You have to allow time."

I was getting off on a defensive foot, and that wouldn't do. "Is it a problem, Mr. Steinbach?"

"I've got to go out later, that's all." He waved me in. "How long will this take?"

"Not long." The entry was low-ceilinged, almost uncomfortably so. I followed him through the tunnel-like hall, and stepped into a world of light. The room we'd entered, a kind of atrium, soared more than two stories to a massive skylight. Tropical plants wound and wriggled their way upward.

"Wow. This room—"

"Call it a space, not a room. Or better yet, call it an *environment*. That's what my partner insists on calling it. Say it's a room in front of Eugene, and he'll never forget what a pleb you are."

"An architect, huh?"

"And a snob."

Great timing. I seemed to have a penchant for arriving in the middle of family spats.

Steven led me through the jungle, then down another low-ceilinged hall to a room on the right. One long skinny window looked out to the neighboring building's brick wall, about two feet away.

He dropped onto a square black leather couch and pointed me to a leopard-print chair. It was uncomfortable, and I perched on the edge.

"Look, Mel called and asked me to meet with you again. Otherwise, I'd probably tell you to go take a hike."

I said nothing, though a few choice replies came to mind.

"Sorry," Steven said after a moment. "You've caught me on a bad day. Nothing personal."

"No problem. I'll get straight to the point, Mr. Steinbach, and leave you to your bad day."

To his credit, the guy laughed. "I'm a software designer, I work out of the house. Hard to leave work at the office when you work at home, know what I mean? Listen, call me Steven. Otherwise it sounds like you're talking to my dad."

I nodded. "All right, Steven. I'll just say it. We've uncovered evidence that suggests Skye was murdered."

"What?" His brow knitted tight. "Is this something I need to hear?"

"Don't you want to find out what happened to your nephew?"

"Skye's dead. It won't change a thing."

The man was like a goddamn seesaw, up one minute, down the next. "You sound resentful. Did he do something to earn your dislike?"

"I never disliked Skye. Never." Steven uncrossed his legs and leaned forward. "When that kid was little, I was his favorite. I used to take him everywhere. The merry-go-round down by the beach, the zoo. In the summers, whenever Mel needed a break, I took Skye to Leadbetter Beach. In fact, I was the one"—he stabbed himself in the chest with a finger—"I was the one who taught Skye how to surf."

"What changed?"

"You've met my dad. Can't you guess?"

I thought of Rod Steinbach, and the obvious pride he'd had in his grandson. And I thought about how single-minded Rod was, how strong-willed. "Your father took over. He pushed you aside and replaced you with Skye."

"Pretty much." He lifted a hand, let it fall in his lap. "Look. My father would say it's just fine that I'm gay. He's an old sixties radical, very PC. But underneath, when it comes right down to it, he despises me." Steven leaned back on the couch and shrugged. "Somewhere along the line Dad decided Skye was the chip off the block, not me. He even told Mel the genes had skipped a generation."

"So Skye was the golden-haired boy."

"Yes. But to be honest, Skye wasn't the first. Melanie and I, we're both wimps, I suppose. Anyway, that's how Dad saw us.

Growing up, we were basically ignored. Dad always had some favorite grad student who was going places. Later on, he focused on Skye. I guess I was kind of jealous of my nephew for a while. But I always knew it wasn't his fault." Steven looked over at me. "Got what you came for?"

"Not quite," I replied. "You were back in Santa Barbara for your sister's fortieth birthday, correct?"

He stared at me for a long moment. "Yes."

"And her party was that night, right? The night Skye died."

"Your point?"

"There is no point, Steven. I just want to know where you were that evening, between the hours of five and ten."

He flushed and opened his mouth. Then he turned pale. "You're asking me—you're asking *me*—"

A door slammed in the house. Then I heard two voices, one a child's, the other a man's. A commotion, the sound of scampering feet, and a call: "Daddy! Daddy, where are you?"

A pair of bright eyes peeked around the door. Then a little boy of around three, wearing a pair of striped overalls, slammed open the door and ran into the room with a whoop. He stopped and pointed at Steven. "I found you! Are you hiding, Daddy?"

Steven grinned. "Yeah, I was hiding. You found me, Luke."

The toddler whooped again, then ran over and climbed up on the divan. He threw an arm around Steven's neck and pointed at me. "Who is that lady?"

"That lady is Jaymie. Jaymie, this is Luke."

"Everything all right?" A thin balding man in his fifties appeared in the doorway. He wore a slight but permanently etched frown.

"Everything's fine, Eugene. This is Jaymie, a friend from Santa Barbara."

"Hi, Jaymie." The man fixed me with a brief penetrating look. "Well, I won't interrupt. I'm going upstairs to get some work done. Steven, I've asked you, please don't let Luke climb on the furniture." He didn't wait for an answer, but walked back out the door.

"Hey, little monkey." Steven plucked Luke off the divan and set him on the floor. "Go get your new toy, OK? Get the truck Grandma Alice sent you."

"Stay here, Daddy." The child ran out of the room.

Steven met my eyes. "You have to ask about that Friday night, I get it. I was the designated gofer, all right? Dave sent me out for some stuff he forgot for the party, plates and plastic utensils. Later on, I made a liquor run. Otherwise, I was at Mel's place." He shrugged. "That's all I can say."

No firm alibi there. But just maybe the truth. I decided to take a sidestep. "Your parents must adore Luke. He's the cutest thing ever."

"Mom drives up once a month, usually with Mel. But I never take Luke down to SB. I tried it once." He made a face of disgust. "Dad acted like his grandson didn't exist. Stared straight through Luke, like he wasn't there."

Chapter Ten

Call me a sentimental sop. Steven had motive, and his liquor-run alibi was weak as near beer. But as I waved goodbye to him and Luke, I found myself wanting to believe there was no way in the world a daddy like that would kill his nephew. No way in hell.

But I knew from experience that anything was possible. *Anybody* could kill.

I headed out of the city with the commute traffic, across the Bay Bridge. It was late, and I'd had enough drive time for the day. I turned off the freeway in Hayward and located the Sunset Motel, a cheap-looking establishment harking back to the fifties. The cheap-looking motel wasn't so cheap, as it turned out, but I was too worn out to look elsewhere.

Actually, I like a no-frills motel room. Maybe because everything is so simple? There's a Bible in the drawer, in case you have thoughts of killing yourself. And sometimes there's a motor to jiggle the bed. Other than that, there are no expectations.

I flopped down on the bed in Room 32 and stared up at the water-stained ceiling. I couldn't be certain Steven Steinbach hadn't killed his nephew, but I sincerely doubted it. Trouble was, that left me with the other guy I didn't want to suspect: John Tactacquin.

I felt bad for Taryn. A sweet kid. But her father had carried a grudge, and offered no actual alibi. What, he'd had a few beers with a bud, but wasn't prepared to reveal the guy's name? Give me a break. And there was more: as the Rasmussens had witnessed firsthand, Tactacquin had a short fuse.

True, I needed to know more about Vanessa and Porter. The piñata party was scheduled for tomorrow night, and by the following morning Claudia would have something to report. But did I seriously suspect either of the two teenagers of murder? I'd have to say no.

So I'd have to narrow the focus on Tactacquin. And let the chips fall.

I swung my legs over the edge of the bed and sat up. Time to go hunt for meat: a burger with fries. Across the room in my duffel bag, my cell rang. I wasn't in the mood to pick up. I let it ring itself to death. Just to nag me, it beeped as a message was left.

What the hell. I got up, rummaged in the bag till I located the phone, and called voice mail. My heart clip-clopped as I listened: the fixer had phoned.

Zave here. Listen, there's a guy you'll want to talk to. I hear he was working in the jail the night your brother died. I don't think he saw what happened, but he knows something, for sure. Call me for the contact, babe.

I waited a few minutes, till my heart rate calmed. Then I got a pad and pen from my bag, switched on a lamp, and propped myself up on the bed with the two skinny pillows. I dialed.

"Jaymie? Where are you?"

"Room 32. The Sunset Motel in Hayward. Not far from Oakland, where the infamous Zave Carbonel was born and raised."

"Hm. How did you get there?"

"Believe me, I didn't pedal up 101. I rented a car."

"So what are you doing?"

"I interviewed a guy in the city today, in connection with the aquarium case. What have you got for me?"

"I knew you wouldn't give up on that. Your pen at the ready?"

"It is."

"Guy's name is Thad Chaffee. He was a psych tech at the jail, on duty the night Brodie died. Doesn't work there anymore. I'm told by my source that Chaffee may know one or two things."

My hand trembled as I wrote down the name and details. "How do I contact him?"

"I've got his cell number. Jaymie, you need to keep your eyes open with this one. Chaffee's no choir boy."

"No surprise there." I took down the number. "Zave, is there a home address? Or a current workplace?"

"Chaffee lives and works at the same location: 758 Riven Rock Road."

"Fancy address." I knew better than to ask how Zave had learned all this. He frowned on such questions.

"Yeah, he's some kind of caregiver now. But listen, Jaymie. This business about your brother. I'm not so sure you should get involved. Just a sense I'm getting, you know?"

"All you're doing is encouraging me with that kind of talk."

"I knew you'd say something like that." Zave was quiet for a moment. Then his voice changed: he added some sugar. "Babe, when are you getting back? I got an itch."

"Right now I've got stuff on my mind. You'll need to scratch it yourself."

"Stuff? Bullshit. Know what I hear? I hear that old tone in your voice, the one that means you're thinking about the deputy. Sure you two aren't shackin' up at that Sunset Motel?"

"There's nobody here but me and the bedbugs." But Zave's antennae were fine-tuned. Mike wasn't present in the flesh, but I couldn't get him out of my mind.

✦   ✦   ✦

I got up with the sun the next morning and hit the road. I could snag coffee and maybe something to eat along the way. But as it turned out, I wasn't hungry. My mind was focused one hundred percent on a guy named Thad Chaffee, and what he might know.

By one o'clock I was barreling into Santa Barbara, fueled mainly by my churning thoughts. I left 101 and entered Montecito, forcing myself to slow down, and wound through lanes lined with the dense Victorian boxwood hedges that hid the massive estates from view.

Glimpses of 758 Riven Rock appeared through the shrubbery. It was an opulent property, a replica of a French château. I parked my car a hundred yards down the road, then shut my eyes for a moment to focus on the task at hand. I might have only one shot at Chaffee, and I didn't want to fumble it.

After a few minutes I climbed out and stretched my cramped muscles. Then I ambled up Riven Rock, assuming what I hoped was a nonchalant and entitled air.

The château reminded me of a giant wedding cake. The huge confection was peach-colored, embellished with dozens of white pillars and several hundred yards of lacy white trim. À la Provençal, the stately drive lined with olive trees swept through a field of lavender. The sweet, delicate odor sailed forth on the breeze.

I continued to circle the property, taking it in. I passed a pair of intricately wrought gates, art nouveau. And I noticed a second house set deep into the property, two-story but much smaller, built in a similar style. It was meant to look like a carriage house, I supposed. If I had a caregiver living on the property, that's where I'd stash him.

All very well. But how was a visitor like moi going to knock on the door? No doubt cameras were trained on the gate and the drive. No doubt a camera was trained on me at that very moment.

The caregiver couldn't stay home 24-7. Maybe I could discover a way to snare him outside the gates of his paradise.

My phone rang: Señorita Molina. "Claudia, hey."

"What up, dawg."

Dawg was a start. I'd instructed her not to call me bitch anymore.

"Are you ready for the party tonight?"

"That's what I want to tell you about. The party was last night, and it was badass!"

I stopped in my tracks. "Claudia, what are you talking about? You told me it was Friday."

"It's what they do, man. They change the day at the last minute, so they don't get busted. Smart, huh?"

"I wish you'd have let me know when you heard. Last night I was out of town. I wanted to be around in case anything went wrong."

"Hey, chill. Nothin' went wrong. Just wait till I tell you about it. I gotta say, those white kids can play. You at the office?"

"No, I'm not." I watched as a powerful Doberman galloped across the vast lawn of the pseudo-château, heading straight for me. Fortunately an eight-foot cyclone fence stood between us. Even so, I decided to mosey on down the road to my car.

"Listen, Claudia. Come by my place this afternoon, say around four. Twelve El Balcon. You probably haven't heard of the street, so I'll give you directions."

"What, is this the twentieth century or somethin'? I'll pull the address up on my cell."

I was struggling to single-handedly install a sunshade over my west-facing window when I heard Dexter out in front, barking his big dog bark. I climbed down off the ladder and walked around the corner.

There sat Detective Molina, frozen in position on a low-rider bicycle. The chrome fittings flashed like mirrors, and screaming orange and yellow flames licked along the frame.

"Jaymie! Get this three-legged thing offa me!"

"He won't bite. The most Dex will do is nip you on the back of your heels." I couldn't suppress a smile.

"Nip? I don't want no nip!" Claudia folded her arms across her chest and glared.

"Here, boy." Dex retreated to my side and flopped down, panting happily. "OK, Claudia. It's safe."

I watched as she dismounted and wheeled her bike over to the breezeway, keeping one wary eye on the cow dog all the while. "I thought you weren't afraid of anything," I said.

"I ain't afraid of that mutt. I just didn't wanna kick it in the teeth 'cause, you know, it's your dog."

Claudia trailed after Dexter and me, into the house. "Let's sit out on the back patio," I suggested. "It's too hot in here. How about a soda? Coke or Orange Crush."

"Orange Crush." Claudia plucked her wife-beater shirt from her chest and panted out some air. "It's hot all right. Why do you live up on this cliff?"

I opened the fridge and took out two cans of soda. "Nobody bothers me up here, for one thing. And for another thing, well, you'll see in a minute. Want a glass?"

"What for? You just gotta wash it."

"You're pretty cocky today." I handed her a can. "The piñata party must have gone well."

"You could say that." Claudia pressed the cold can to her cheek and smiled.

"Come on, party girl." I led her out back to the narrow strip of concrete I liked to refer to as the patio.

"Yeah, now I totally get it. That is a kickass view!"

I dropped down in one of the old redwood chairs. "I never get tired of it. Every day it's different." I looked out at the silvery islands, floating in a gold lamé sea. "So tell me about your big night out."

Claudia took a sip of her soda. "It was pretty amazing. The guy that died? He was the one who invented the whole thing."

"Skye Rasmussen?"

"Yeah. See, Vanessa told me all about it. It started up a year ago, last fall. They wanted to do something crazy and wild for their senior year, something totally new. And that kid Skye decided, let's do a piñata party. They all thought it was stupid at first. But then he explained." Her smile expanded to a wicked grin.

"*Dale, dale, dale.* See, Skye learned about piñatas in his ethnic studies class." Claudia shook her head in admiration. "I never knew this. But the piñata, the traditional one, has seven points. Each point stands for a sin. The seven deadly sins, get it? So when you whack the piñata, you're smashing your sins. Then you get rewarded for that, with the candy and favors."

"And if you lose your aim, you lose your way? That's interesting. But still, is it so wild and crazy, smashing a piñata? Sounds kinda childish."

"Ohh no, it ain't childish," Claudia said gleefully. "Trust me, it's strictly X-rated. See, they smash the piñata and the favors fly out all over the place, right? Gambling chips for avarice, condoms for lust, marijuana buds for sloth, and those little plastic liquor bottles for gluttony. Stuff like that. All the kids scramble around on the floor, fighting to get the ones they want. The condoms and the weed are the most popular."

"I'll bet they are." I wasn't liking the sound of this, not one bit.

"Then the fun starts. See, the party's in this old hotel that's closed down, right? Out near the ocean."

"The Miramar?" A public eyesore, the Miramar had been boarded up for years. No developer was willing to take on the renovation project, given the city's costly building requirements.

"Maybe. I don't know what it's called. But the security guy, they pay him and he lets them use it. It's perfect, see, because of all the empty rooms."

"The rooms?"

"Yeah." Probably without realizing what she was doing, Claudia reached down and rubbed Dex behind his ear.

"See, there's a room for every sin, right? And there's a guard at every door. They call the guard a Diablo. And the Diablo only lets you in if you've got the right favor for the room. If you wanna go in the sloth room, you gotta have that marijuana favor."

"It sounds very . . . organized." What I was actually thinking was, I shouldn't have sent a fourteen-year-old kid, cocky or not, to an orgy. "I hope you didn't—ah—participate."

"What? Course I did. I had to, they think I'm tough." She snuck a look at me. "I didn't pick up any of the condoms, though. And I'm not gonna. Don't need that shit, know what I mean?"

"Sure. But don't worry about it, Claudia. You're not going back."

"Oh, I gotta go back. They're having another one pretty soon. And Vannie and Port are starting to trust me. See, I only figured out part of it so far."

"Part of what?"

"It's just like you said, Jaymie. Something bad happened. This one girl I was talking to told me that Skye and some other kid got in a big fight at one of the parties back in January. And Skye stopped going after that."

Risking splinters, I slid forward in my chair. "Who was the other kid? What was it about?"

"All I heard is, it had something to do with a guy named BJ, but he wasn't the one who got in the fight." Dex now had a front paw on Claudia's knee and was gazing adoringly up at her. "That's why I gotta go back. I gotta find out the rest."

"How often do the kiddies hold these little play dates?"

"Sometimes it's two weekends in a row, sometimes a whole month goes by before they do it again. But the next one? Most of the kids are going away to college, so it's probably going to be pretty soon."

I was torn. I needed to know what had happened to Skye. But did I want to deliver this child into the arms of Satan? Claudia might think she was being careful, but I knew anything could happen in the heat of the moment.

"Listen. I don't think you—"

"Don't tell me not to go," Claudia said quickly. "You gave me a job and I'm gonna do it."

I knew it was useless to forbid her to attend. Claudia Molina was even more hardheaded than me, which was saying a lot. "Difficult though it may be, huh?"

"I really hate it." She snickered. "And don't forget, I'm getting paid for it."

"Yeah, isn't it great. You want me to pay you to party with kids who are three or four years older than you."

"Don't tell anybody how old I am," Claudia warned. "They think I'm sixteen. I told them I'm behind 'cause I was in juvie for nine months and the whole time I was there, I refused to do any schoolwork. They think that's totally cool."

"I'll try not to ruin your rep. But I am going to ask you for something."

"What?"

"Your knife."

She squealed like she'd been burned. "Ain't nobody touching my dad's knife!"

"You'll be safer without it," I insisted. "I don't want you getting tempted and using it, the way you did on the Stellato kid. Besides—not carrying a weapon is a condition of your probation, remember?"

I knew how impulsive Claudia could be. And she'd be in hot

water if she pulled her switchblade on one of the high-school kids.

"So I'll leave it at home." She stuck out her lower lip like a six-year-old.

"You'll leave it with me. I'll give it back when the gig's over."

"Shit." She took the knife from her pocket and handed it to me. "Don't go cuttin' yourself, girly-girl."

"No problem. I don't plan on using it."

Claudia bent forward and hugged the snaggletoothed Dex. "Know what? This dog's not so bad."

My heart softened. At that moment, the party girl looked about ten.

"Now remember, Cinderella, the same rule applies the next time around. When the clock strikes midnight, you're out of there. Agreed?"

"Sure, Jaymie. Whatever you say."

The aquarium was closed on Mondays, and the next morning I decided to take advantage of that. I wanted to talk again with Cheryl Kerr. She seemed like an introvert and lived with her mother, so I figured I'd find her at home on her day off.

It didn't take much searching to dig up the address: Modoc Road, near 101. I hopped on my Schwinn and coasted down El Balcon, then turned right onto Cliff. I ran through some facts in my mind as I pedaled along.

On the day of his death, Skye Rasmussen replied to a text from a friend at 5:17 P.M., before leaving his cell in his pickup. Skye's text said he had to stop by the aquarium, but that he'd get to Leadbetter Beach by 6:00.

Skye would have been in a hurry to feed the big jellyfish. His family planned to gather for his mom's birthday party at 7:30, so he didn't have much time to catch a few waves.

The aquarium closed to the public at 4:30, and the volunteers and staff members were usually gone by 5:00. Cheryl Kerr, however, left at around 5:10.

I'd no reason to suspect her of murdering Skye, even if she were physically capable of the act, which I doubted. Cheryl was so out of shape I wasn't even sure she could climb the stairs to the top of the tank. So the question was, who besides Skye had entered the aquarium between 5:10 and 5:45?

Of course, there was another possibility: someone could have entered earlier, hidden in the building, and emerged after Cheryl left. Either way, I wondered if Cheryl Kerr might have seen someone hanging around.

The small pre-WWII stucco house stood only a block from the freeway, and the roar of the traffic was heavy, oppressive. I sat on my bike for a moment and studied the faded paint, worn asphalt-tiled roof, and steel-framed windows.

Nothing had been done to the place in more than half a century. The yard was tidy but the lawn was thin, bare earth in spots. The property suffered from neglect.

I left my bike just inside the wooden picket fence, walked up the cracked concrete path, and ascended the three steps to the door. A dead azalea stood in a terra-cotta pot on the porch. The stiff, brittle branches seemed to beg for water.

When I pressed the bell, I heard it ring inside the house. I listened for footsteps, but the noise of the freeway filled my ears.

After a full minute or so, I rang again. Out of the corner of my eye I caught a movement in the window at my right. A finger hooked back a limp beige curtain, and a single bluish eye peered out at me. Then the curtain fell back into place.

Still I waited. At last the door crept open. "Hello?" Cheryl was wearing a fuzzy gray sweat suit. She looked upset.

"Hi, Cheryl. I'm sorry to bother you on your day off. But I need to speak with you again, if you don't mind." I waited, hoping she'd step aside and invite me in, or at least open the door further. Instead, it began to close.

"I'm sorry. It's not—not a good time."

I decided to try a pity plea. "OK. But I've ridden my bike a couple of miles, and I forgot to bring along my water bottle. Could you just spare me a glass of water? I don't need to come in, I can wait here on the step."

"Oh . . . all right." Cheryl probably wanted to close the door in my face, but she just couldn't bring herself to be that rude.

She disappeared, and after a moment I heard a querulous, haranguing voice call out. "Cheryl, what are you doing?"

I nudged open the door with the toe of my sneaker, and peered in. There wasn't much to see, just a narrow shotgun hall leading to a kitchen at the back. A collection of framed photos hung on one wall, but I stood at the wrong angle to make them out.

Cheryl stepped back into the hall, a glass of water in her hand. She noticed the door and gave me a sharp glance. "Here. I'm sorry, it's not very cold. Our refrigerator isn't keeping up with this heat."

"Cheryl," the voice whined. "Cheryl!"

I accepted the glass and took a sip. "It must be difficult, being a caregiver for your mom." It was low of me, using this tactic to get Cheryl Kerr to open up. But I'd run out of options.

"She's not good today." Cheryl shrugged. "I don't know why, her moods come out of nowhere."

"How do you manage while you're at work?"

"I come home on my lunch hour. And I have backup, a neighbor who checks in." Cheryl tucked a strand of iron-gray hair behind an ear. "So far it's worked out, but I don't think it will for much longer."

"It's not an easy life for you, I'm sure. All your spare time must be spent with your mom. How do you manage it—shopping and appointments, that kind of thing?"

Cheryl opened the door a little further. "My boss, Dr. Thompson? He's very good about letting me have time off when I need it."

I nodded and took another sip. "I can see why you'd be concerned about Rod Steinbach taking control. He's tightening everything up, isn't he?"

There it was, that same flash of anger I'd witnessed the other day. Cheryl opened her mouth to answer, but at that moment her mother gave a shout.

"Let me out! Cheryl, I said let me out of here!"

"I've—I've locked her in her bedroom." Cheryl looked down at the worn carpet under her feet. "I have to do it whenever I answer the phone or the door. I feel bad about it, but I don't have a choice."

My conscience got to me at last. "Look, I'm sorry for the intrusion. I just wanted to ask you again, are you sure there wasn't something you noticed that Friday Skye died? Maybe you saw somebody when you went to say goodbye to the octopus out on the wet deck."

"How do you know about Legs?" Cheryl had tensed. "Who's been talking about me?"

"Actually, you told me. The first time we met, remember?"

"Oh. Well, I didn't visit Legs that afternoon." She shook her head. "I don't always do it, you know. Sometimes it upsets me to see her."

"Why is that?"

"They need to release her. The tank is starting to drive her crazy, she's been banging her head on the glass. I told Dr. Thompson, but he—"

"Let me out!" Inside the house, something crashed.

"I'm sorry." Cheryl stepped back. "But you can hear how she is."

"I'll let you go. Just one other thing."

Her lower lip trembled. "What?"

"John Tactacquin may have visited the aquarium that afternoon, after closing. Are you sure you didn't see him? How about his van?"

"No. No, I already said. I didn't—"

"Cheryl!" her mother screamed. "Cheryl, come here this instant!"

"She won't give me a minute's peace!"

A sad pair of women, I thought as I walked back down the path to the wooden gate. How long had mother and daughter been locked in their painful embrace? Even in paradise, it seemed, there were pockets of hell.

The brash rose perched on the corner of the desk was flagrantly red. It seemed to pulse with desire.

I closed the office door behind me. "Good morning, Miss Gabriela. How was the hot date?"

"What?" Gabi's shocked—and slightly guilty—face shot out from the side of the computer. "How do you know?"

"How? The rose tells the tale." I dropped my messenger bag on the couch. "What's it called?"

"Passio-na-te," Gabi admitted.

"You've turned nearly as red as that rose." I couldn't resist the temptation to tease.

Like a tortoise, Gabi pulled her head back behind her computer. "It's private," she muttered.

"Angel's a nice guy and I'm glad it's working out."

"Miss Jaymie, this is a place of business. Personal lives don't belong here."

"I haven't noticed you mind talking about *my* personal life, Gabi. But now that it's *yours*—"

My cell jangled in my bag. I made a mental note to change the ring.

"Ms. Zarlin? Neil Thompson here."

"Dr. Thompson. How are you?" I eased myself down on the couch.

"Fine." His melodious voice sounded strained. "But we have a problem. I understand you visited Cheryl Kerr on the weekend? I have to tell you, she's very upset."

"There's no reason she should be." Not unless she was hiding something, of course.

"Reason or not, Ms. Zarlin, I have to ask you to stop harassing my employees."

Cheryl Kerr had the right to object to my visit. But I found it odd that Neil Thompson was so concerned for her feelings.

"What's changed, Dr. Thompson? Last I heard, you were happy to help out the Rasmussens in any way you could. My interviewing your employees and volunteers was fine by you."

"Maybe so. But now I'm asking you to stop." The tone of his voice told me something was going on. Something big was lurking below the surface, like a basking shark camouflaged on the ocean floor.

"Melanie and Dave Rasmussen are my clients, Dr. Thompson. I'll do what I judge to be in their best interests."

"The road you're going down won't bring the boy back. I'm saying, leave well enough alone. Let it go."

I've never left well enough alone in my life. Call it nosiness, obsessive-compulsiveness, or dedication. Whatever label you want to put on it, "leaving well enough alone" just isn't in my vocabulary.

And Neil Thompson had just convinced me to hold on tight.

Chapter Eleven

One hour later, the front door banged open without a knock. I leaned out from my chair in the kitchen as the imposing figure of Rod Steinbach filled the doorway. Without any hesitation, he strode straight into the office.

Gabi popped up at her desk. "May I help you?"

Steinbach looked at her for no longer than the blink of an eye. Then he turned and met my gaze. "I want to talk to you."

I pushed back my chair, stood, and walked into the main office. "Please take a seat." I managed a polite smile.

"I want to talk to you," he repeated. "Alone."

"Ms. Gutierrez and I work as a team."

"I don't care how you work. Tell her to go."

"Go yourself." No way in hell was this commandant going to order me around.

"I'm going, Miss Jaymie," Gabi said. "I need to move my car anyway, time's up."

"No. Dr. Steinbach here needs to learn a few manners." I was pissed. I was so mad my head felt like a teakettle coming to the boil.

Gabi froze. I could see her wavering back and forth: should she stay or should she go? I made eye contact with her, and she lowered herself back into her chair.

"Dr. Steinbach. You had something to say?" It was curious, actually. You couldn't tell if the man was angry or not, he was so self-controlled.

"Fine, have it your way. I'll condense it down for you. Keep away from everyone connected with my grandson's death. My family, the employees at the aquarium, Skye's friends. Stay away, understand?"

I understood him, all right. But Rod Steinbach didn't understand me. The more he pushed, the more I would stand my ground. "Your daughter and son-in-law don't feel that way. They want to know who killed their son."

"*Killed?* Are you trying to manufacture a murder case, Zarlin? What, for the money? That's low, and I won't let you get away with it!" His voice had roughened, and now he *was* angry. So what?

"Melanie and Dave want the truth. What parents wouldn't? I don't get it, Dr. Steinbach. Why would you deny them that comfort?"

"I think I know my own family. They want peace. And I'm going to see they get it."

"Once they have the truth, they'll find peace."

Rod Steinbach's expression changed. Oddly, it warped into something approximating friendliness. "Look. Maybe I'm going about this the wrong way."

He dropped down on the couch and crossed his legs at ankle and knee. "You know, it can't be easy, running a small agency like yours."

"We do fine," Gabi bridled.

I said nothing, just waited for what I knew was coming.

"I don't know what Melanie and Dave agreed to pay you." He fingered the sharp-edged cuff on his khakis. "But I'd be prepared to double it." He smiled. "Maybe I'd even go higher."

I faked a smile of my own. "What, for me to cease and desist?"

"If you want to put it that way."

"Why?"

"Why? I told you why. You're hurting people I care about."

"Altruism, Dr. Steinbach? That's admirable. Or is it just that I'm rocking your world?"

He shrugged. "What does it matter to you?"

"It doesn't. I was just curious. Either way, my answer's the same: no way in hell."

Rod Steinbach flushed. "Stubborn, aren't you. You'll get that attitude knocked out of you one of these days."

"Maybe so. But not by you."

I'd returned the rental car, and now I fantasized about the lost El Camino, much as a castaway might fantasize about a hamburger, as I climbed the hills of Montecito on my bike. I knew I should just forget about my brother's sweet little ride. I should break down, take out a loan, and get a grown-up's car.

But how could I do that? Forgetting about Brodie's Camino would be like forgetting about Brodie himself. I didn't plan on forgetting anything about my brother, not the cocky tilt of his chin or his crinkly-eyed laugh. And I'd never forget how he struggled with his mind during the last years of his life, and how he'd been forced to defend himself against the scum who take pleasure in tormenting those who are different. The scum that will always be with us, till the end of time.

In other words, I was in a lousy mood by the time I reached Riven Rock Road. I stashed my bike behind a dense stand of lemonade berry bushes and stepped out onto the asphalt.

What was it about these neighborhoods? They were spooky, somehow. Only the cleaners roamed through the vast mansions, and only the gardeners admired the roses as they formed buds, bloomed, and withered away. The owners themselves were uneasy ghosts, unable to remain in one place for long. They flitted from mansion to mansion, from Montecito to Maui to Santa Fe.

I strolled on down Riven Rock, pretending to be a Montecitan taking the air. Meanwhile I kept an eye on the grand château. The design, a fantasy originally dreamed up by an eighteenth-century Parisian architect, was now improbably brought to life here in coyote and wildfire country. Somehow the result was unattractive and sterile, like the progeny of a donkey and a horse.

I slipped into the shrubbery and lifted my pocket-sized binocs from my messenger bag. Thad Chaffee was most likely in the guest house, toiling away as a caregiver. No need to let him into the big house. Chaffee would be relegated to the guest quarters, to live out back with his inconvenient charge.

The guest house appeared to be divided into two apart-ments, upstairs and down. I wondered which portion was given over to Mr. Chaffee. Then I saw the steel cables barring the downstairs windows: they were dental-floss thin, almost invisi-ble. I'd only noticed them because they glinted in the sun.

"See something?"

I spun around. A pale young man with black hair stared back at me. He was tall and skinny, his Adam's apple pointed. But his hands were powerful looking. Somehow I'd expected the caregiver to be big and bear-like, but he looked more like an overgrown ferret.

"Mr. Chaffee?"

He stepped forward. I noticed black silky hairs on his up-per lip.

"Depends, lady. Who the fuck are you?"

Before I could answer, he raised the back of his hand to my face. A knife slid up from between his fingers, not six inches from my eyes.

I knew not to think much. As I ducked down I brought my fist up where I figured his balls had to be. I figured right: the ferret let out a thin scream.

He dropped the knife as he doubled over and crashed back

into the bushes. I scrambled for it, grabbed it, and spun around. But then, as Chaffee sucked in ragged breaths of air, I halted.

This was *so* screwed up.

I'd just messed with a potential informant, the guy I was counting on to tell me what had happened to my brother. Damn it to hell. Chaffee might have been the last person to have seen Brodie alive.

"Sorry," I called into the bushes. "I didn't mean to punch you so hard."

After a moment, the ferret slithered out of the thicket. If anything, Chaffee was paler than he'd been before. "Fuck, what kind of freak are you?" he snarled. "No girl can hit like that."

"Sorry," I repeated. "I'm Jaymie Zarlin. You're Thad, right?"

"Give me my knife, or I'll . . ." He dragged in a breath. "Just give me my knife."

I knew the boy needed his knife to change back to a man. And for the same reason, he needed me to act more like a girl.

Fine, whatever worked. I gritted my teeth. "Do you promise to put it away? You *scared* me with it."

"Give it the fuck back to me."

"OK." I was taking a risk. But if I didn't do this, I'd get nothing out of the snake. I closed the knife and held it out in my right hand.

His hand grabbed mine, and tightened. Just enough to show me how strong he was. Then he opened his hand and took the knife. "If you want me to talk, it'll cost you. You'll have to pay."

I wasn't too surprised Mr. Chaffee wanted to turn our conversation into a win-win. "I'll pay what I can."

"You'll need to pay *more* than you can. A body like yours, you won't have a problem."

Blech. "You don't even know what I'm here about, Thad."

"So tell me." He was relaxing now, imagining he was in control.

"What do you do here, exactly? The address seems a touch fancy for you."

"None of your fucking business."

"What if I told you I know you're a so-called caretaker? You keep an eye on whatever poor soul is locked away behind those bars." I nodded toward the carriage house. "You know, I'm not sure it's legal to lock a human being in a cage."

Why oh why couldn't I be nice? I needed something from the guy, yet apparently I couldn't resist the urge to grind him under my heel.

"I do what I'm hired to do." He curled his top lip, and I noticed several of his teeth were decayed. "Besides, plenty of people are better off locked up. Your brother was."

I nearly choked. Chaffee knew exactly who I was. And he knew about Brodie.

"Didn't think I knew, huh?" He adjusted the front of his pants. "Sure, I heard you were coming. Just didn't know what you'd look like. Didn't know—"

"Didn't know I could punch like a guy?"

He scowled. "Like I said. I talk if you pay."

Across the vast lawn I saw the Dobermans. They must have been dozing in the sun. Now they were awake, standing at rigid attention.

"Who told you I'd be coming to talk to you?"

"Nobody you need to know about." Now the beasts were loping across the emerald grass.

"You'll never be honest, Chaffee. I see that now that I've met you. So what would be the point of talking?"

The dogs had reached the fence. They were powerful animals, no doubt perfect specimens. They began to bark loudly at me, lunging at the fence.

"Shut it," Thad snapped. The dogs obeyed. One whined and dropped to the ground.

"There's one or two things I could tell you." He slipped the knife into the pocket of his baggy shorts. "One or two things you'd be interested in."

Dealing with this guy would be like entering a funhouse with mirrors. I'd never know when he was telling the truth and when he was lying. But I couldn't walk away.

"All right, Chaffee. I'll pay you a hundred dollars if you tell me everything you remember about my brother and the night he died."

"First off, I don't see no money." He ran a hand through his long stringy hair. "Second, a hundred's not enough." He looked at me, calculating what he thought he could get. "My bottom line is five hundred, cash. I figure most people would pay five hundred for their brother. Or—half in money, the other half on your back."

"In a minute you'll be on *your* back, Chaffee. With that knife at your throat."

He shrugged. "Take your pick."

The creep was sickening me. "All right, five hundred. But you better tell me everything you know, and not lie about it. Agreed?"

"Yeah. Yeah, get the money and I'll talk. Give me your cell number."

"I know where to find you." I glanced over at the château. "Who the hell owns this, anyway?"

"Guy who made a lot of money in the eighties. Bought it with cash."

Cocaine. According to my Realtor friend Tiffany Tang, a number of Montecito homes, priced in the tens of millions, were purchased with cash in the eighties.

"So the coke dealer locks up his son. What for?"

"Kid's autistic. They don't like having him around. Hard to keep under control."

"I'm sure you manage." I turned away and headed for my bike.

"Oh yeah, I manage," he called after me. "I got a few tricks up my sleeve."

◆   ◆   ◆

I was out playing catch with Dex early the next morning when I heard my cell ring back in the house. I decided to ignore the phone, because the morning was too delicious to abandon. Hummingbirds, tiny flares of burnished copper, chased one another through the big patch of Mexican sage, then shot away into a blue and white buttermilk sky.

The little heeler had never learned to fetch—he figured he was supposed to toss the ball, just like me. So I'd throw and he'd hobble after the thing on his three legs, pick it up in his mouth and fling it back. He was pretty darn good at it, too.

The ringing stopped. I tossed a high pop-up to Dex. Then the dratted phone started up again.

I walked slowly toward the doorway, willing the jangle to stop again. It did. And then, for the third time, it rang. Something was wrong.

"Jaymie . . . it's me." I'd never heard Claudia like this before, except around the time her sister had died. She sounded upset, on the verge of tears.

"Take it easy. Where are you?"

"At the aquarium. It's my day to—to—"

"Volunteer?"

"Yeah. To get things set up for the day. Jaymie, you gotta hurry. Come right now."

I glanced at the kitchen clock: 7:36. The aquarium wasn't scheduled to open for nearly an hour and a half.

"Claudia, what's going on?"

"Out on the wet deck. There's—*something*—snagged on the ladder that goes down into the hole."

"Something? What do you mean?"

"It's—it's a body."

"A body?" I stared through the open door, into the pristine blue morning. "Who is it?"

"I don't know, but I think it's a woman. They haven't lifted her out yet. Just hurry up, Jaymie! I'm not supposed to leave, nobody can. I'll let you in at the back—they've locked all the doors."

"Be there right away." I jammed the phone in my pocket and hurried out to the breezeway. Warning Dex to stay put, I hopped on my bike and tore down the hill.

I rode dangerously, skidding on the turn at the bottom of Cliff and nearly flying off. I braked with my feet, sacrificing the soles of my shoes, and sped up again. All the way there I thought about the wet deck, with its gaping hole to the ocean below. Who in God's name was hooked on the ladder?

I pumped hard over the timbers of the dock, then let my bike fall at the back of the aquarium. The door was open a crack. As I hurried toward it, it opened further, revealing a scared-looking Claudia.

"Jaymie—"

I slipped inside and closed the door. Then I grasped the girl by the elbow. "Claudia. Who's here right now?"

"Vanessa and Porter, and the lady who runs the snack bar upstairs. And Dr. Thompson."

"Have they called the police?"

"I don't know. Jaymie—"

"We'll talk later." I gave her a quick hug. "Wait for me in the foyer. You've seen enough."

I jogged down the hall. The front desk was unmanned and the gift shop dusky, its CLOSED sign in place. I hurried past the glowing tanks of the smaller fish and invertebrates.

I mentally steadied myself before entering the room holding the massive jellyfish tank. Without wanting to, I glanced at the tank as I jogged past. The box jellyfish was gone, and in its place a school of silvery herring veered through the softly lit water.

Telling myself to slow down, I took a deep breath before I pushed open the pair of doors at the end of the tank room. They swung open onto the wet deck.

The space was roughly circular, floored in boat decking. At the center of the space a large open cylinder rose about four feet up from the floor. The cover was folded back, and a net was drawn up out of the cylinder and draped over the side.

Neil Thompson and Porter Logsdon stood near each other, against a wall. Porter was smoking, his arms hugging his chest as if he were freezing. Neil's head was bent as he talked intently into his phone. Neither of them gave me a glance.

I walked over to the six-foot-diameter cylinder and looked down into the oily water.

It was a ghastly sight. A woman's body was hooked to the last rung of a narrow steel ladder riveted to the cylinder wall. Somehow, the sleeve of her pale mint-colored sweater had snagged as she fell.

I bent over the edge to get a better look, and let out a gasp. Cheryl Kerr's face floated like a moon in the black water, white and round. She'd apparently lost her glasses in the fall, and her pale blind eyes gazed upward. Opaque as pearls, they met my own.

I made myself look. And look and look, in case I didn't get another chance.

White froth bubbled from her gaping mouth. The wavelets lapped at her, and her body swayed back and forth.

Then I saw something so disturbing I could hardly breathe. I could only watch as a thick oily brown rope slipped up and onto her chest.

A rope that was alive.

The rope slid toward her open mouth. In spite of myself, I let out a sharp cry.

Thompson was beside me in an instant. "It's an eel," he muttered. "A goddamn eel."

I took a deep breath and let it out as the eel slipped back into the water. "Dr. Thompson, have you called the police?"

"I was just about to." But he hesitated.

"Forget about Steinbach," I snapped, regaining my presence of mind. "Call the police if you haven't already. Do it now."

"Wait, what are you doing here?" He was beginning to look confused. "You need—you need to go."

"I'm not going anywhere."

His cell rang like a wind chime, and Thompson slapped it to his ear. He glanced at me, then moved away to the opposite side of the room to talk.

I walked over to Porter Logsdon. He looked edgy, nearly as white as the corpse. "Porter? Who found the body?"

"Vannie." He took a deep drag on his cigarette. I was sure he wished he was smoking something else. "We were assigned to set up the wet deck this morning. Vannie, she rolled back the cover, and saw it." He was trying to sound cool, not succeeding at all.

"Where is Vanessa now?"

"The lady who runs the snack bar took her upstairs. Vannie freaked."

I nodded and turned away. I could go upstairs and talk to Vanessa and Delia, but first I needed to look around. It wouldn't be long before the cops arrived.

I circled the tank. Though the cover was folded back, it wasn't secured. Vanessa must have caught sight of the body before she completed the task.

Other than that, everything around the tank seemed in order. The trays that were used to hold specimens dredged up from the ocean floor were neatly stacked on a table. A variety of implements were arranged in rows. All very tidy. I circled again, in the opposite direction. And that's when I spotted it, on the floor.

A flower lay against the base of the tank. It was pressed flat, as if it had come off the bottom of a shoe. Carefully, I flipped it over with the toe of my sneaker. On the back side I could make out the color: burnt-orange, deep blue at the throat. Something tropical, maybe.

I fought the urge to pick up the squashed flower and slip it into my pocket. I was sorely tempted. But instead I pulled out my phone, crouched down, and snapped several shots. Then I turned it over again and snapped pictures of the other side. The side which, now that I looked more closely, did bear the partial imprint of the sole of a shoe.

"What's that?" Neil loomed over me. His thin ponytail fell forward over one shoulder.

"A dead flower. Probably nothing, but the police will want to take a look." I placed my hand on his arm as he reached down. "I wouldn't touch it. It could be evidence."

He shook off my hand and picked it up. "I'll make sure they get it."

And so would I. "Don't let it get lost in your pocket."

The blood rose like a tide, up Neil Thompson's scrawny neck to his hairline. He opened his mouth to answer, just as a dentist-drill of a voice pierced the air.

"Zarlin! What the hell are you doing here?"

I looked across the room and met Detective Krause's round baby-blues. I shrugged in reply.

"No, I mean it." Deirdre was at my elbow now, patting her fluffy blond hairdo as if it were a favorite pet. "I want to know exactly why you're here and then I want you to get the hell out."

"Anyone would think you'd be more welcoming, Deirdre. Since I solved your last case for you."

Her mouth pursed into a pout. "Showing off, that's all it was. Real police work is about attention to detail."

"Hm. And I thought it was about solving cases." Why was it, I wondered, that I could never keep my mouth shut around this woman?

"By the way, Zarlin. I heard it was Mike Dawson who dropped you, not the other way around. Can't say I was surprised."

My mind flipped back and forth between two equally juvenile options: to pop Deirdre Krause in the nose, or guffaw in her face.

"Cat got your tongue, Zarlin?"

"If only the cat would get yours."

She trilled her signature shrill-whistle laugh. "Now one more time. What are you doing here?"

I decided to answer. If I didn't, she'd hound me, and I wasn't sure I could stay cool. "Mr. and Mrs. Rasmussen are my clients. Remember, Deirdre? The parents of the boy who died here of an accidental fall. Sure are a lot of accidents around here."

Deirdre was uncharacteristically quiet for a moment. When she spoke, her words took me by surprise.

"Did it ever occur to you that maybe you're not the only one who wants to solve cases? It's easy for you, Zarlin. Try having a boss over you, or two or three."

Tongue-tied, I stared at the woman. I'd never heard her speak straight before. "Deirdre, I—"

As fast as it had disappeared, her pout returned. "Oh, never mind. I don't know why I'm bothering to talk to you. Just tell me, have you uncovered any actual info proving Skye Rasmussen's death wasn't an accident?"

Even though Deirdre had let slip and shown she was human, I knew from past experience that sharing with her was a bad idea, a one-way street. No good would come of telling her about Taryn's abortion or John Tactacquin's blowup at the Rasmussens'. Besides, I'd no intention of breaking my word to Taryn. But there was one thing I did want to make sure she knew.

"No. But I can tell you something about *this* case."

She actually tried to smile at me, and it was kind of scary. Like seeing a cat with a crocodile's grin. "What's that?"

"I found something on the floor just now, next to the tank." The smirk evaporated. "Hand it over."

"I haven't got it. Dr. Thompson's holding on to it for you."

"So I would have gotten it anyway. What else?"

"Nothing. That's it."

"Right. This is a crime scene." She held up a dimpled hand

and beckoned over the big officer who always seemed to follow her around.

"Troy? Make sure Ms. Zarlin locates the door."

"Jaymie, have you heard? The police arrested John Tactacquin last night." Melanie's voice was somber, dragged down. "They say he murdered a woman—and they're saying . . . Skye, too."

"Yes, I heard." I took a slow breath, and shifted the office phone to my left ear.

Cheryl had been dead for only two days, and her body hadn't even been autopsied yet. The cops had moved ultra fast, and who could blame them? Two deaths by drowning at the Santa Barbara Aquarium—the city's residents were on edge.

"Melanie. How do you feel about this—will it help bring closure to you and Dave?"

"I don't know how I feel. Not like I thought I would." She measured out her words one by one. "I'm just horribly sad. Sad for his daughter, too."

"Taryn's a nice girl."

"I know that our son . . ." Her voice broke. "I know Skye was fond of her."

"You could make contact with her. I think Taryn would like that."

"Maybe one day." She was silent for a time. I let the silence expand.

"Jaymie, I guess . . . we won't be needing you anymore."

"No, I guess not."

"Dave is *sure* it was Tactacquin!" Melanie blurted out. "But do you think they got the right one?"

"I'm sorry. I wish I could say yes. But no, I'm not sure."

I'd suspected Tactacquin, all right. I'd figured he might have killed Skye for revenge, revenge for hurting his daughter, revenge for pressuring her into an abortion and then dumping her. And he could have killed Cheryl, who might have seen or known too much.

After all, Tactacquin had the door code to let himself into the aquarium, and he couldn't come up with a solid alibi for either murder. Means, motive, no alibi: it all added up.

It added up, but somehow it didn't feel right.

Focus on the facts, I reminded myself. Feelings aren't good enough.

But that was part of the problem, wasn't it. Because the fact was, I was pretty sure John Tactacquin did have an alibi. He just didn't have one he was willing to reveal.

Chapter Twelve

"We met in high school. Santa Maria High." The slight, wispy-haired woman sat erect and still on the office couch. "John was a football star. I was in the band. I played the flute."

"That's nice," Gabi enthused. "He was your high-school sweetheart!" Gabi seemed to have forgotten that the high-school sweetheart was now accused of a double homicide.

"Yes." Donna Tactacquin smiled a little. "I thought John was quite a catch. Being in the band wasn't such a cool thing, you know."

"We can't all be cheerleaders," I said. "But I guess it didn't matter to John?"

"No, not at all. We had trouble, though. My dad didn't like it that John was Filipino. And when he found out John's dad was a field worker—" She shook her head. "I used to sneak out the window at night, John would pick me up out on the street."

"But you two got what you wanted in the end," Gabi observed. "That is true love."

"Yes, we did." Donna shrugged. "The usual way, I guess. My senior year, I was pregnant with Kenny, Taryn's brother. My dad, like I said, didn't like it that John wasn't white, and he didn't like it that I was pregnant and not married. But in the end he accepted it. And after a while, thanks to the grandkids, none of that mattered."

"That's how it is," Gabi said. "Grandkids—grandparents will do anything for them."

Donna looked over at Gabi and nodded. "Isn't that the truth?" She twisted the strap of her purse in her hands.

"I don't have no grandkids," Gabi continued. "But I have so many nieces and nephews. So many birthdays, I am telling you. I can't even—"

I cleared my throat. "Donna, how can we help you?"

"I want you to work for us. Gabi called and told me you aren't working for the Rasmussens anymore. I want you to prove my husband is innocent."

Gabi called? I gave my assistant a stony look. Chastisement would have to come later, after Donna was gone.

"I'm not sure what to say." I chose my words carefully. "I'm not the only PI in this town. Why me?"

"Taryn trusts you. So do I."

"You know there's evidence pointing to John's guilt."

"But," Gabi interjected, "Miss Jaymie goes for the truth. Only the truth, she don't care about no evidence."

"Ah—I wouldn't put it quite that way." I glanced at Donna, perched on the edge of the couch. She looked like a schoolgirl at that moment, all trust and hope. Why the hell did I have to be the one to stamp it out, to inform her that her beloved husband was most definitely a cheat? But maybe I didn't need to go quite that far.

"The thing is, Donna, your husband doesn't have an alibi for the evenings of the murders. He says he was out with a friend, but he won't reveal the friend's name. That's a big problem."

"Of course it is. But wait till you hear what I have to say about that." Donna pressed her hands to her cheeks for a moment, then folded them in her lap. "I know my husband is having an affair. And I'm sure that's where he was—with *her*. He won't say anything about it because he doesn't want to hurt me."

The schoolgirl had transformed into Joan of Arc. I had to hand it to the woman, she was sticking by her man.

"You impress me," I said. "Most women would kick their husband's butt out the door."

"Sometimes I feel that way. Maybe most of the time. But before all this happened, I was just too scared to bring it up, you know? Because I didn't want to lose him. And now, I don't want John to go to prison. No matter what happens, I don't want him to—to—" Her face blanched. "Could he *die?*"

Gabi got up from her desk and walked over to sit beside Donna on the couch. She took her hand in her own. "He's not gonna die. Miss Jaymie will look into it, she'll figure it out." She gave me an encouraging look.

"Let's take one step at a time." I studied the worn oak floorboards, searching for the right words. I didn't want to frighten Donna any further, but I had to be frank.

"There's no doubt about it, it would help a lot if you could convince John to tell the police where he was that night. But there are other problems, too."

"Do you mean the way he went over and yelled at that family? The Rasmussens. John told them how mad he was about the abortion." Her chin trembled. "Yes, he was angry, really angry. He was angry because Skye hurt Taryn, you know? She was so upset."

"I understand. But that shows motive on John's part, I'm afraid."

"But he would never *kill* anyone—never! I know him so well, he just wouldn't. He has a temper sometimes, but he's not what you'd call aggressive. Never once has he hit me or our kids. And what—they say he murdered the boy for revenge? And then he killed a woman because she knew something? It's just not him!"

Gabi put an arm around Donna and gave her shoulder a

squeeze. Then she looked at me expectantly. Apparently my PA thought I had an answer for everything.

Donna Tactacquin rose to her feet and hoisted her bag to her shoulder. "Please. Will you help us?" She looked spent, and I couldn't say no.

"It's like Gabi says, Donna. I'll go for the truth. If that's what you want, then I'll take on the job."

"That's what I want," she said without hesitation. "John is innocent, I know it. I'm not afraid of what you might find."

"All right then." I extended my hand, and she placed her own hand in mine.

When the door closed behind her, I groaned. "Gabi, what have I done?"

"The right thing, that's what you done. I'm happy you said yes, Miss Jaymie. She's a nice lady, and her daughter's nice too."

"Let's hope they don't get hurt. Let's hope I don't uncover something they'll wish they'd never known."

I leaned forward in the hard plastic chair. "Donna knows about your affair. She wants you to tell the police who you were with on those Friday nights."

"I know. She came to see me." John Tactacquin's hands were cuffed with zip ties. He cupped the black receiver in both hands.

"So it's time, right? There's no point in protecting your family anymore. Unless maybe you're protecting somebody else?"

"I told you. My family comes first." He stared hard at me through the thick glass. "You wouldn't understand."

"Maybe not." I shifted the cumbersome receiver to my other ear. "So help me understand. See, if Donna and Taryn are the ones you're protecting, but they already know—" I flicked open a hand. "Doesn't make sense."

He stared at me, mute. His mouth was pressed into a tight line.

"Oh. I get it." I sat back and stared at him. "It has to do with the woman's identity, doesn't it?" I nodded. "That's it. For some reason it will hurt Donna and Taryn to know who she is."

He let out a puff of air. "Something like that."

"Listen, John. I don't think you get it. The arraignment's tomorrow. You'll plead 'not guilty.' They'll set bail at an impossibly high amount. The wheels will start rolling right away. And in the end—look, I'm not here to scare you. But in the end you could roll right onto death row. Is that a price you're willing to pay?"

"I didn't do it!" he exploded into the phone. "Don't you get that? I'm innocent of all of it! Why the hell should I injure my family, maybe even destroy them, over this bullshit?" His nostrils flared. "Look. The cops will figure it all out in time. They'll find out who killed Cheryl Kerr, and the boy. And when they do, I want my family back. I want everything to be . . . to be . . ."

"The way it was before Skye and Cheryl were murdered? Don't count on it." I held his gaze. "By the way, the police aren't going to look for anyone else, not now. Why should they? You've got motive, no alibi. And you had access to the scene of the crimes."

"You don't believe me, do you." His shoulders drooped. "If you don't believe me, what the hell are you doing here?"

We stared at each other through the glass. I was about to say I was doing it for Taryn and Donna. But that wasn't entirely true.

There was a drive in me to uncover the killer, to not let him get the better of me. To show myself, and everyone else, that I had what it takes.

"Actually, John, I do believe you. But I'm pissed off at you. How can I help you if you refuse to help yourself?"

A deputy entered the cubicle and stepped behind John's chair. He said something I couldn't hear.

"I can't," John said into the phone. "I know what you want, but I just can't give it to you."

With both hands John Tactacquin hung the receiver on the wall, then heaved himself to his feet and shuffled out of the booth.

"Miss Jaymie, I tried to call you!" Gabi jumped up from her desk the instant I stepped in the door. "You should of been here."

"What, did you get tempted and polish off all the pastries?"

"Don't tease like that." She picked up a key ring and walked around the desk, dangling it out in front of her like a fishing lure. "Mike was here and he dropped something off. Something you lost."

Like a cat following a ball of string, I focused on the bobbing key. It was attached to a tarnished metal disc. Gabi pulled it away, just to tease. Then she relented and dropped it into my hand.

The disc was vintage—vintage Chevy. I'd never seen it before. "What's this?"

"Huh. I thought you were a detective." Gabi was trying hard to hold down a grin.

"The key—it feels familiar." I rubbed it between my thumb and finger. Light dawned.

Gabi clapped her hands together. "I knew you'd figure it out! Mike left it around the corner on Chapala. No parking places in front."

My mouth fell open, and she laughed. "Miss Jaymie? You're gonna catch flies."

"Wait, I gotta tell you one more thing," she said as I headed for the door. "Mike, when he walked in, he saw my rose." She touched the elegant purple bud with one finger. "And you know what? First he didn't look so happy. Then he looked real mad. And he said, 'Who sent the flower?' And when I said it was my boyfriend Angel"—Gabi pointed a triumphant finger at me—"he got a really big smile on his face! You should have seen him, Miss Jaymie."

I rested a hand on the doorknob. "Maybe he was happy for you."

"Sure. Mike's a nice guy. But that smile, it was way too big."

"I told you. Mike has a girlfriend. And she's young and cute."

Gabi waved a dismissive hand in the air. "Young and cute, who cares about that? Not Mike. No, he loves *you*. He don't care how old you are. And he don't care what you look like. And that is not gonna change."

"Thanks—I think." I hurried out the door, the key clutched in my hand.

As I jogged around the corner into Chapala, my heart prepared to burst into song. A row of cars extended up the block, but nothing blue caught my eye.

Something candy-apple red did, though. Shit!

That aging boomer down in LA, the one who'd purchased Blue Boy from the charity and renamed it Dudette, had apparently painted it *red*. Brodie would never have painted Blue Boy, and if he had, red would have been the last color he'd have picked.

Slowly, I walked down the block and stopped at the car. That is, I was pretty sure it was the one. The red El Camino was in such prime condition that it was hard to be certain. I walked around to the driver's door and slipped the key into the lock. Oh, yes. It turned like a knife in warm butter.

I opened the door. There was no metal-on-metal grating sound. I climbed in.

Dear God, the seats were resprung and reupholstered. I shut the door. My eyes pricked with tears.

It was Brodie's car, all right. And yet, it wasn't. There were no initials scratched into the dash. No bits of driftwood and sand underfoot. And I knew without looking: no dope tucked in the visor.

I turned the key in the ignition, and the engine purred sweetly to life.

There was a certain advantage to starting the first time, I

grudgingly admitted. And a renegade thought snuck into my mind. Brodie would have hated the red, but me . . . I kinda liked it.

"Forgive me, brother," I whispered.

I pulled out from the curb, turned a corner, and headed down to the beach.

I turned right at the bottom of Las Positas, passed Dog Shit Beach, and drove up the little palm-studded canyon leading to Yankee Farm Point. Then I pulled over at the top of the cliffs and drank in the view, one of the biggest and bluest in the world.

I was confused. How had Mike come by the Camino? And why? Sure, he knew how much my brother's car meant to me, and how I'd tried to buy it back after I'd donated it to charity. But why had he bought it for me, an ex-girlfriend? Didn't compute.

I relaxed down in the comfy seat, took out my cell, and made the call. "Mike?"

"Hi, Jaymie." His voice was friendly, laid-back. Very cool.

"I'm sitting here in Blue Boy. I can't believe it. What's . . . what's the story?"

"What's the story? It's a gift, Jaymie. From Dad to you. He had me trace the owner."

My heart swelled. "It's too much. Why?"

"You'll have to ask him." Mike paused. "You know he's always liked you. I have a feeling Dad's tying up loose ends."

"How is he doing?"

"His mood's pretty good. But physically . . . not so great. He's gone downhill since you saw him."

"But that was only a couple of weeks ago."

"Yeah. Well, they took him away from Little Panoche. He went kicking and screaming, but Trudy didn't have a choice. The kids had to start school, and she needed to go home. I thought about staying up there with him, but he needs Trudy now. And two hundred plus miles is a long way to commute."

"I'm really sorry. I know how much Bill wanted to stay up at the ranch."

"We don't always get what we want. Not even at the end."

"No, we don't." I gazed out into the channel. I thought I saw a whale spout, not too far off shore. "I'll phone your dad tonight. And I'll shoot up to San Luis to see him as soon as I can. After all, I need to take him for a spin in my snazzy new ride."

"He'd like that, Jaymie. If I were you, I wouldn't wait too long."

"Damn it's early." Claudia let the front office door slam behind her and stomped on through to the kitchenette. "Hi, Jaymie. What's in the fridge?"

Gabi turned from the counter, where she was filling the carafe at the sink. "Hey! Don't come in here and stick your head in our refrigerator like that. Ask first, like you would if—"

"Yeah, yeah." Claudia emerged with a soft-drink can in her hand, then slammed the refrigerator door. "Jaymie says we're a team. Right Jaymie? All equal, all the same."

"Do not close that door so hard," Gabi bristled. "When I was your age, if I acted like you, my mother tied me to a tree."

"Good idea. I see a tree for you outside the window. Jaymie, got any rope?"

"Both of you, stop." I turned from the whiteboard and glared. "Two innocent people have died. And a man's in jail, maybe on his way to death row, for crimes he may not have committed. Can we keep a focus on the big picture, for once?"

Both girl and woman avoided my eyes. Gabi spoke first. "Sorry. This kid here, she rubs me up the wrong way. But I gotta be professional, stay focused."

"I'm in a bad mood," Claudia muttered. "My mom wouldn't get out of bed this morning. She's probably still there."

We were all silent then. It had been just over a year since Lili Molina's murder, and we knew Teresa, Claudia's mom, was struggling with depression. She'd never gotten over the death of her elder daughter.

"Sorry, mija," Gabi said softly. "Sometimes I forget."

"I'm sorry too, Claudia," I said. "Maybe—I don't know. Maybe I'm asking too much. I'm not sure you should be involved in all this."

"No," Claudia said quickly. "I want to do it. It keeps me from thinking too much about stuff. And besides."

"Besides?"

"I decided I'm gonna be a detective."

"Investigator." I smiled. "You're making a good start."

"Oh yeah, I am. I got something important to tell you." She set the can down on the worktable.

"Claudia, hold that thought for a moment." I took the marker into my hand. "Let's work systematically here. These are the suspects we're looking at." I printed the names across the board: *Delia Foley, Steven Steinbach, Neil Thompson, Vanessa Hoague, Porter Logsdon, John Tactacquin.*

"Miss Jaymie?" Gabi lifted a finger. "I think you gotta add one more. That guy Dr. Steinbach. He was a jerk when he came in here. I got a bad feeling about him."

"Rod Steinbach is a jerk, and I don't trust him either. But I can tell you he was devastated when his grandson died. By all accounts, they had a close relationship. Plus, we know Steinbach has solid alibis. The evening Skye died, he was at a board meeting. After it finished he went directly to Melanie's birthday party."

"And what about when the gift shop lady died?" Gabi pressed.

"The Steinbachs and another couple were having tapas at the Figueroa Café."

Gabi looked disappointed. Her horse wasn't in the running. "Know what? I'm gonna double-check on that. My friend's primo is a waiter there."

"Good idea. Anyway, I'll jot down his name, just because

he's a sonofabitch." I wrote Rod's name at the end. "Now, let's go through them one at a time. Delia Foley."

Gabi firmly shook her head. "Delia is my cousin, my own prima's daughter. I don't know too much about her but I know she's a good mom to her kids."

"What kinda reason is that?" Claudia scoffed.

I hadn't told Gabi about the mean things Delia had said about her. Delia might be a good mom, but she was no generous soul. "Delia does have an alibi," I continued. "In fact, Delia and Neil share an alibi: they're lovers, and they were together the evening Skye died."

"She cheats on her husband?" Gabi looked surprised. "I guess she's not the kind of person I thought."

"Her husband beats her," I said. "Being with Neil, I think that's how she survives."

"Oh!" Gabi bit her lower lip. "You gotta try an' help her, Miss Jaymie. Even if she is a suspect."

"When all this is over, I'll talk to her. In the meantime, we've got two suspects, Neil and Delia, confirming each other's alibis. That's shaky in anyone's book."

"What about motive?" Gabi asked.

"In Delia's case, I don't see it. She seemed to like both Skye and Cheryl. She doesn't like Rod Steinbach, though. She says he threatened her job."

"But that's not enough, is it?" Claudia asked. "Not enough to make you actually kill a guy's grandson."

"I'd have to agree. Besides, Steinbach put other people through the wringer too, not just Delia. Cheryl Kerr and John Tactacquin, for example. He even leaned on some of the older volunteers."

"What about that Thompson guy?" Gabi asked. "Does he have any motive?"

"Not that I can tell. I suppose Neil Thompson's job performance could be under fire, because he does seem anxious about something. But he's tight with Rod Steinbach." I walked over to the open kitchen window and watched a hummingbird challenge a big carpenter bee plying a pink-flowering sage.

"It's *all* kinda shaky," Gabi observed.

"Uh-huh," I agreed. "Nothing adds up."

"Now it's time to talk about Vannie and Port," Claudia said. "Remember, I got some news."

"I know you do, Claudia." I turned back to the room. "But let's save the kiddies for last."

"OK, Steven Steinbach," Gabi continued. "You told me he's got a alibi like cheese."

"A cheesy alibi?" Claudia guffawed.

"Swiss cheese," I replied, "full of holes. He claims he was on a liquor run for his sister's birthday party at the time Skye died. The police could check the store's sales for that day, and the store camera—it's tricky for us to obtain that info. Anyway, Steven Steinbach had enough time to visit both the liquor store and the aquarium, too. And Skye would have let his uncle inside." I perched on the window frame, facing the room. "Steven resented the relationship between Skye and Rod, but he didn't seem to blame Skye for that. Again, I can't see a sufficient motive for murder."

Claudia walked up to the whiteboard, picked up the marker, and drew slashes through three names: Delia, Neil, and Steven. "I'm not erasing them. Just one line, so we can move on."

"Then draw a line through Rod Steinbach, too. He has no motive for murdering either Skye or Cheryl." I looked at Gabi. "Agreed?"

"One line is OK."

"This leads us to our client. The man we are trying to clear."

"It doesn't matter if he is our client," Gabi said. "We are trying to figure out the truth."

"Yes we are. Now, our client says he has an alibi, but he won't help us confirm it." I got to my feet and stuffed my hands in my pockets. "And I'm afraid John Tactacquin has motive, the way some people see it. That's two strikes against him right there."

"Yeah. Skye got Taryn pregnant, right? And then he told her he didn't want the kid, and she had to get an abortion," Claudia said. "When her dad found out, he went over to Skye's house and yelled at his parents."

"That's pretty much what happened." I studied the worn pattern in the old linoleum floor. "But I don't think Tactacquin's guilty."

"Besides why would Taryn's dad kill the gift shop lady?" Gabi looked puzzled. "Why would anybody kill her? I don't get that."

"Maybe Cheryl Kerr knew something about Skye's murder," I explained. "And the killer found out that she knew."

"I see what you are saying. I guess we better not draw a line through our client," Gabi said. "I'm sorry, 'cause Taryn and Donna are really nice."

I took my mug from the cupboard, the mug Brodie had given me not long before he'd died, and poured myself a cup of brew. "On to Porter and Vanessa. Claudia, you've got the floor."

"See, it's all about the Piñata Party Club." Claudia tossed back the last of her soda. "I figure there's only about thirty or forty kids in the club. It's really tight. If a kid starts talking, they get kicked out. And believe me, *nobody* wants to get kicked out. It's wild, totally wild." She managed to crush her empty soda can, but it took both of her small hands.

"Anyways. They do this thing where they bring in a special guest. And the guest gets like, trashed. Maybe they take the guest to the sloth room, you know? And then that kid has to do drugs all night till he's totally wasted. I saw this girl last time, they took her into the lust room. I didn't see what happened . . . but I saw her when she came out."

"That's it," I snapped. "You're done, you're not going back."

"Don't tell me what I can't do." Claudia glared at me. "I can take care of myself."

"You think." I glared right back. "I mean it, Claudia. Your membership in the Piñata Party Club is hereby revoked."

"What're you gonna do, Jaymie, put a ankle bracelet on me?"

"Now there's an idea."

Claudia growled. "Do you wanna hear my story or not?"

"You know I do."

"All right then. Back in January, they invited this kid named BJ to be the special guest. BJ Bonfiglio. BJ's kinda chunky. Not fat, just a little heavy, you know? He's nice."

"You know him?"

"I've seen him around. He's two years ahead of me in school. I didn't really know him till I contacted him. I wanted to find out directly, you know? What really happened that night."

I smiled to myself. This kid actually was a detective. How about that.

"Anyways, all I was hearing at the party club was, something happened to BJ back in January. Something nasty. And Skye Rasmussen made the other kids stop. He got in a big fight with Vanessa and Porter, then he grabbed BJ and left. He made them let BJ go."

"So that's when Skye quit the club? Good for him."

"Yeah. But I had to, you know, confirm it. Plus I wanted to know more. So BJ and me, we met at Alameda Park. We talked for a long time."

"Good work."

"Then . . . we met two more times. Three times in all." Claudia looked at me sideways.

"So you got quite a bit of info from Mr. Bonfiglio," I said in a neutral tone.

"Yeah, we talked about all kinds of stuff. But about that night. See, Skye and BJ already knew each other, before the party."

My ears twitched. "They already knew each other?"

"Uh-huh. Last fall they took a twentieth-century-history class together, where the teacher assigned these projects about the sixties. About the protest movement, the hippies, and all that. The teacher said who you had to work with. BJ and Skye, they were a team. BJ says it was kinda weird at first, cause Skye was Mr. Cool, and BJ—well, he gets laughed at a lot. But in the end, BJ said the project was fun."

"Interesting. So—what did BJ say happened that night?"

"Vanessa took BJ to the Chamber of Gluttony. It's full of junk food and liquor. They made him eat and drink, they forced him. And then somebody stuck something down his throat, made him puke. Then they made him eat more. BJ said he started to get scared he was gonna choke to death. He actually thought he was gonna die."

"Those—those bad spoiled kids," Gabi sputtered. "I wanna get my hands on them!"

"It's really messed up. But Skye heard what was going on, right? He came into the room, and sort of dragged and carried BJ outta there. Vanessa and Port tried to stop Skye, but he told them to go get fucked. Anyways, BJ passed out in Skye's car, and Skye took him to emergency. He maybe even saved BJ's life."

"And BJ never told anyone about this?"

"Not about the club. He just told his parents he was at some party, you know? Because Vanessa and Porter threatened him." Claudia looked over at me. "That's the thing, Jaymie. Vanessa told BJ they'd really hurt him if he ever told."

"So it's them!" Gabi jumped to her feet. "Those two kids are the killers. The girl and the boy, they both killed Skye because *he* was gonna tell. And the gift shop lady saw what they did to Skye, so they decided to kill her too!"

"It's possible, I suppose." I tipped the dregs from my cup down the sink and rinsed it at the tap. "That's a lot of killing, though, just to keep a secret like that."

The office phone rang in the other room, and Gabi started to raise herself out of the kitchen chair.

"Let it go, Gabi," I said. "The answering machine will pick it up, and I'll deal with it in a minute. I want to get to the end of this."

"We *are* at the end," Claudia replied. "Aren't we?"

"Pretty much. I just need to give you your marching orders. I'm going to talk with BJ myself. Do you want to arrange that, Claudia, or shall I?"

"I'll bring him here, to the office. Or we could go visit him at his place. I'd better call him. If you call instead of me, he might get upset."

Gabi and I exchanged glances. Claudia sounded a tad protective of her informant.

"Sure, that's fine. You contact BJ. I don't know about meeting him at his home, though. We don't want to involve his parents."

"Not a problem. BJ lives on his own. He doesn't have any parents."

"What do you mean, he doesn't have parents?"

"I just mean, they're never there. And I mean like, never. Right now I think they're in New Zealand. They're anthropologists or something like that."

Claudia seemed to know quite a lot about BJ Bonfiglio. But I wasn't going to get into that now. "Talk to BJ and let me know when and where. In the meantime, I need you to work your wizardry online."

"Sure. What do you want?"

I grabbed a scrap of paper, jotted down the so-called caregiver's name, and handed it to her. "This is a separate matter. I want to know everything you can discover about this guy."

"*Thad Chaffee.* I'm on it."

"And, Claudia? Don't leave a trail. This is one person I don't want visiting the office."

"Got it. Anything else?"

"One more thing." I sifted through the pile of papers on the table, found what I was after, and tacked it up on the wall.

"Huh?" Gabi squinted. "A picture of a squished flower—what does that mean?"

"I spotted that flower on the wet deck, the morning Cheryl's body was found. If you look close, you can see the marks from the sole of a shoe."

"So we're looking for a shoe?" Claudia asked. "Good luck."

"Maybe we're looking for a flower bush," Gabi said. "That flower don't look like one I ever saw."

"Just keep it in mind, both of you." I got to my feet and reached for my messenger bag.

"Where are you going, Miss Jaymie?" Gabi had given in to her urges at last, and was busy organizing the papers I'd scattered across the worktable.

"I'm going to see a man about an empty bucket. It's time I paid Neil Thompson a call."

Chapter Thirteen

Thompson's office door was open a crack. I gave it a nudge.

The man had drawn his desk chair up to the window and was staring out to the breakwater.

"Dr. Thompson?"

"I'm not a doctor, actually," he said without looking around. "Never quite finished my PhD. Never finished much of anything."

I walked in and invited myself to sit in the guest chair. "Having a piece of paper with your name on it isn't everything."

"I suppose not." He laughed shortly. "In the end, nothing matters." He swiveled his chair and faced me. "Two people have died here, under my so-called leadership. I suppose that doesn't matter much either, in the overall scheme of things. People die, don't they? That's what they do."

I wasn't joining the pity party. "Oh, it matters all right. And it matters that we catch the killer."

"The police have already done that." Thompson stared at me, unsmiling. The circles under his eyes were heavy and dark. "They've got Tactacquin. Didn't you know?"

"I can't prove it yet. But I think they've got the wrong man."

"Whatever you say." He reached over and picked up a smooth oval stone from his desktop. "Why are you here?"

I got to my feet, walked over and shut the door. "Look, Dr. Thompson. I don't think you're a killer. But I'm pretty sure you know something you're keeping to yourself."

"I *could* be a killer." He leaned forward. "Anybody could, even you. If you don't know that, you don't know anything."

He placed the stone in the center of the blotter. "Have you come here to ask me something specific?"

"Yes. The bucket at the top of the tank. You were the one, weren't you, who set it upright? You straightened up the crime scene, as a matter of fact."

His pale blue red-rimmed eyes bored into me. "Why would I do that?"

"Because you wanted to remove all signs of a struggle. You forgot to mop up the water, though."

"I didn't forget. I didn't have time to climb down and look for a mop." He rubbed his brow with both hands.

"All right. I straightened up. I didn't want Rod and Alice to see it the way it was. It looked like there'd been a struggle. Better for everyone, I thought, if Skye's death was an accident. Of course, that was before Cheryl died. Two fatal accidents—who would believe that?"

"You were sparing the Steinbachs' feelings? I find that hard to believe. Sure you and Skye didn't get in a fight? Maybe Cheryl saw you, and you had to shut her up."

"No!" His eyes blazed. "Now you're saying I killed them! I had nothing to do with their deaths, nothing at all."

Maybe Neil Thompson was telling the truth. But even if he was, things weren't adding up. I decided to try another tack. "You're close to Rod Steinbach, I understand."

"Close? I knew them in college, that's all. I've had nothing to do with the Steinbachs for decades, that's a fact."

"They—you went to school with *both* Rod and Alice?"

"We were at UCSB at the same time. That's all I meant."

"When was that?"

He hesitated again. And I wondered: what was I saying that was making him defensive?

"Late sixties," he muttered.

"Volatile time."

"I barely noticed. I was a student, into my work."

"But you left at some point? Didn't complete your PhD?"

He shrugged. "Lots of people were dropping out. I was one of them. I didn't like the political . . . atmosphere."

"Yet some students loved it."

"Sure. Some of them ate it up." He crossed his arms over his chest. "So now you know I tampered with evidence. Are you going to tell the police?"

"Not yet. I have a puzzle to put together first."

"Don't," he said sharply. "Don't keep—pushing. Just let it lie."

"A man's in jail, Dr. Thompson, for crimes he didn't commit. I'm not about to let anything lie."

Claudia hadn't taken long to uncover a few interesting facts about Thad Chaffee. He was born and raised in Vegas, the son of a woman who had a record for prostitution and possession. Father apparently unknown. He'd drifted into Santa Barbara half a dozen years ago and been arrested here twice, both times on drug-related charges. Hard to understand how Chaffee had gotten a job as a jail psych tech—but that was another story.

There was another curious thing about Thad: he had a rather surprising hobby. He was a skateboarder and had been featured in several online magazines. He seemed old for the gig, but I supposed skaters never die.

There was only one serious skate park in town, Skater's Point, located on the waterfront near the wharf. I'd moseyed by and asked after Thad. Apparently he usually showed up around four and skated till dark. I wondered what he did with his "client" while he was away.

It was nearly five in the afternoon when I rolled up to the

waterfront, dismounted, and leaned my bike against a towering old Mexican fan palm. I hung back, not wanting to call attention to myself.

Thad wasn't hard to spot. He was skating fast and hard, shirtless, without headgear and pads. And he was wickedly good. As he propelled himself out of a concrete curve, his tall skinny body tucked neatly into a flip.

Thad didn't look like he was having fun, though. He was hot, lathered in sweat. He skated like he hated it, like he was thrashing himself. Each leap was faster, each jump higher, till his board was banging so loud it seemed a miracle it didn't break.

I knew he wouldn't just stop. And then it happened: Thad corkscrewed in the air, missed the landing, and came down hard.

"Fu-uck!" he screamed. But then he got up laughing that high piercing laugh. He limped over to the far side, kicking his board in front of him. He'd scraped skin off his arm, and blood dripped to the concrete.

I waited a few minutes for the warrior to chill. He took a couple of long draughts from his water bottle. Then he got to his feet and looked around. That's when I made sure his gaze connected with mine.

Thad lifted the corner of his lip at me like a junkyard dog. A promising beginning to negotiations.

I ambled up to the enclosure and leaned on the steel fence. "Hey, Thad."

He glared at me. He wanted to tell me to piss off, but I could see he thought there might be money in it. "You think it over, lady?"

"Yeah, I thought it over. I'm going to pay you two hundred for what I want to know."

"Not enough. I said five."

"Oh, but that's not all I'm offering. See, I also promise not to rat on you. Social Services would be interested to hear about that kid you've got locked up." I planned on making a report anyway, as soon as I finished with Thad. There would be a brisk official knock on the doors of the château, before the end of the month.

But Thad didn't turn a hair. I'd have to sweeten the pot. "And your client's father might be interested to know how you spend your afternoons, don't you think? While he's paying you to watch his son."

He gave me a mean sour look. "Let's see the cash."

"Sure." I took the two hundred-dollar bills out of my pocket, held them up, then repocketed them. "Ready to chat?"

"Let's go for a walk on the beach. I don't want to talk here."

Oh, dear. Thad had a plan.

"Actually, Thad, I *do* want to talk here." I liked having bars between myself and this rabid weasel. "Now, you know what I'm after. I want to know what happened in the jail the night my brother died. I want to know everything you saw and heard." I shut up and waited.

"I knew Brodie. He was crazy, man."

I kept my cool. "So?"

Thad shrugged. I could smell him, and his sweat was rank. "They had him in isolation. Single cell, solid side walls instead of bars. I remember he was talking and talking, weird shit about panda bears on the beach or something. It was late, and people were yelling at him to shut up. But he just kept going, you know? Didn't bother me, I went to sleep in the nurse's office." Thad glared at me. "Don't try to run away without paying. You'll be sorry if you do."

"You'll get your money. What happened next?"

"Next thing I know I get woke up by this racket. Louder'n hell. Your brother's yelling, and some guys, more than one, are dragging him outta the cell."

My blood ran cold. "These guys, who were they? Did you get a look?"

"Didn't come my way." Chaffee's gaze slid sideways.

I noticed the tell but let it pass. "Then what?" My heart was pounding, as if it were all happening right now, in the present, as if I needed to run over to the jail to help Brodie. "Did you hear them bring him back to his cell?"

"Nope." He shrugged and wiped the sweat off his forehead. "Guess I went back to sleep. Next thing I know it's morning, real early, and more cops are swarming all over the place. That's when they found him dead, in his cell. Hung himself."

"Nobody told me he was removed from his cell during the night. It's not in any of the reports."

I liked it better when Thad didn't laugh. His laughter was eerie, giggly and high. "Believe what you want—who cares?"

I restrained myself. Because I wasn't done with the guy, not yet. "So what was the word? And don't tell me you didn't hear anything later."

Thad slipped his right hand inside his waistband and looked at me insolently. "You know, for an old lady you're kinda hot."

"Just answer my question, punk."

Again, that high laugh. "Some guys thought the cops strung him up. Other guys said no, the cops said some kinda shit to him that made him do it. They play with your mind that way. You gotta be hard."

"Did you see when they brought him back to his cell?" I asked again.

"I said no. That woulda been around three, maybe. When I was asleep." His face turned blank. "That's it, lady." He stuck out his hand.

I took the two bills out of my pocket. "Not quite. I think you recognized the guys who pulled my brother out of his cell, Chaffee. I want their names."

"They weren't the cops who worked in the jail. I didn't recognize them."

"So they definitely were cops."

He hesitated. "Yeah. They were cops, I could tell. But only a couple of 'em were wearing uniforms. Look, that's all I got to tell you. I'm done."

Off-duty cops? What the hell were they doing in the jail in the middle of the night?

I studied Chaffee. He wasn't smiling anymore. And in his eyes, I saw something that surprised me: a spark of fear. I knew that was all—for today.

I poked the money through the fence. Thad pulled the bills from my fingers, then pressed them to his lips. "Baby, that's sweet."

I slow-pedaled along Cabrillo, half hoping I'd spot the white van. Where the hell was Charlie? I needed to tell him about Brodie. When I talked to Charlie, things fell into place.

As I passed the dolphin statue at the entrance to the wharf, a long-haired kid leaned out the window of a beat-up old pickup. "Santa Barbara is *so* beautiful," he yelled.

An out-of-towner, of course. No resident would mock our little city. Most of us fought too damn hard to stay here for nothing *but* the beauty: the terra-cotta mountains, red-tiled buildings, and bright sparkling water. But beauty could be deceiving, it was true.

I stopped at West Beach and propped up my bike on its creaky old kickstand. I sat on the low wall bordering the sand and stared out at a blindingly white cruise ship, seemingly taller than it was long, anchored in the harbor. Cruise ships were frequent visitors to Santa Barbara these days, now that the drug wars had heated up in Mexico.

Charlie's absence was nagging at me. Something wasn't right. Maybe I should give Mike a call.

I pulled my phone from my messenger bag and tapped in the number I'd erased from my contacts, yet knew by heart.

"Hey, Jaymie. How's it going?" Mike's tone was impersonal, and I guessed he was with someone. Six o'clock on a Friday evening: my mind conjured up an image of Mike and Mandy, bumping heads over a plate of raw oysters.

"Fine. Can we talk?" Meaning, get up and walk outside, I have something to tell you.

"Can it wait? I'm busy right now."

"Don't bother." I pushed the button and ended the call.

Before I could get the phone back in my bag, it rang. "What, not so busy after all?" I snipped.

I heard an exasperated sigh. "Come on, Jaymie. You didn't say it was important. What's up."

"I wouldn't want to take you away from whatever you're—"

"Cut it out. I'm at work."

I was a tad ashamed, ashamed for being such a jealous tigress, and for asking for my ex's help yet again.

"It's about Charlie. Have you seen him around? His van hasn't been down at the beach, not for three or four weeks now."

"Can't say I've noticed. I've been working up in north county lately." A few seconds of silence rolled by. "Jaymie—I know you care about Charlie. But is something else going on?"

"Brodie," I admitted. "I learned something, Mike. Something not good."

"Hold on, I'm walking outside." I heard the sound of a heavy door slamming. "Now, what. You heard something about your brother?"

"Yeah. I talked to a guy who was working in the jail the night it happened. Mike, they messed with Brodie. Some off-duty cops, maybe plainclothes, dragged him out of his cell. Brodie was kicking up a fuss when they took him away. Later on, they carried him back. They could have beat him up, Mike. They could have hung him."

"Jesus, Jaymie, do you know what you're saying? Who is this guy, how did you find him?"

"Somebody I trust put me in touch with him. Somebody . . . reputable."

"Reputable? Bullshit. It was the shyster lawyer, am I right? Carbonel. What the hell did he go and do that for?" I could almost hear Mike's blood pressure roar up like Old Faithful.

"Zave did it because I need to know. Want to know! And since it sounds like half the PD might know my brother was dragged out of his cell in the middle of the night, I'd like to know how you *didn't* know!"

A long period of silence simmered between us. When Mike finally spoke, his voice was measured and quiet. "Jaymie, you need to listen to me. I work for the county sheriff, not the city police. I don't know everything that went on down there that night. But I do know one thing: Brodie hung himself. I wish to God it hadn't happened, but it did. Are you listening to me?"

"Yes, I'm listening. And all I'm hearing is you telling me to back off."

"Maybe I am. Maybe I'm telling you to let go, and start living your life like it matters. What are you after—*revenge?*"

Revenge. I let the word roll around in my mind. It sounded delicious, like a smooth cool drink for a parched tongue.

"What if I am? It's what people have wanted for thousands of years."

"It will eat you up, Jaymie. Your life will shrink down to nothing else." He paused. "Hell, you're halfway there."

I was livid, furious that he was judging me. "Yeah? Let me tell you what *I* think. I think you know something about this. I think you've hidden something from me all this time, ever since the morning you arrived on my doorstep to tell me Brodie was dead!"

"Knock it off. That's bullshit and you know it. I'm telling you for your own good, let it go."

Oh, how I wanted to punch off the phone. But I took a couple of deep breaths and swallowed my anger and pride. "What about Charlie?"

"I could look into it. What's his last name? Funny, I've been talking to him for years, but I never asked."

"It's Corrigan."

"Corrigan, huh? Tell you what, I'll check our records. Maybe I can trace his van, issue a bulletin. How's that?"

"Thanks," I said in a choked voice. "Thanks on Charlie's behalf."

The next morning I was pouring my second cuppa when the office phone rang. I jumped to answer it, sloshing hot coffee over my wrist. Cursing under my breath, I lifted the receiver. "Yeah?"

"Zarlin?"

I realized I detested Thad Chaffee's cunning voice. It seeped into my ears like a sickening syrup. "How the hell did you get my office number?"

"Get real. It's all over the net. Listen up, I got something to tell you."

I couldn't help it, I bit. "This better be good."

"Nothing like that. Just, don't come near me again. I don't have anything else for you, get it? So stay the fuck away."

"What, you're trying reverse psychology now?"

"What the fuck are you talking about?"

The creep was toying with me. My blood pressure screamed skyward. "Call me one more time, Chaffee, and I'll sic the cops on you." I slammed down the phone.

"Stop screwing around," I muttered aloud. "There's real work to be done."

I decided to start with the kids. I wanted to catch Vanessa Hoague unaware, and preferably alone.

"Vanessa? Hi. Jaymie Zarlin here."

"I'm really busy right now. Just a minute." There was a clunk, as if she'd tossed down the phone. I heard a distant voice speak, then Vanessa's reply. "No. I need that one in a size two. The size four is like really huge. And this one, the size is right, but I want to try it on in the blue. . . ."

After a minute she was back on the phone. "Like I said I'm *really* busy. What did you call for?"

"I've got something to tell you, something you'll want to hear," I lied prettily. "But it's not something I can talk about over the phone."

"I can't. Meet you, I mean. I'm going down to USC tomorrow, and I've got a ton of stuff to do first."

USC—Daddy must have bought her a place in the freshman class. Maybe not though, I reflected. Vanessa didn't impress me as much of a scholar, but she was plenty sharp.

"Sure. Why don't you just tell me where you're shopping. Macy's, Paseo Nuevo? I'll be there in a jiff."

"Macy's?" She sniffed. "I'm in Nordie's. So this is something really important, right?"

"Only if you think catching Skye's killer is important."

"What? Oh. OK, I'll be out in front in fifteen minutes. But I can't talk very long."

Chapter Fourteen

I skipped out of the office and jumped into the red El Camino. In no more than a minute I was cruising down State Street. The town was bustling with shoppers, women swinging labeled paper bags and chatting away with their shopaholic buds. Was the economy still struggling? If so, it was news on State.

I skimmed into the underground parking lot, hopped out, and took the escalator up to Paseo Nuevo. With its pseudo-adobe storefronts and concrete-cobbled walkways, the outdoor mall was meant to resemble the streets and shops of old Spanish California. But there was more than a whiff of Disney about it, and I suspected that was intentional. Shoppers were encouraged to forget that the cash in their pockets was real.

I joined the throng of women and men ambling along the passageways, chatting and laughing. Spending money, apparently, was not only child's play but an aphrodisiac. I'd never understood that. For me, spending my hard-earned dollars set off heart palpitations, and not the sexed-up kind.

I reached Nordstrom's steps and wasn't surprised to not find Vanessa. The Princess would make a late entrance. I noticed an empty bench and took a seat facing the department store's big plate-glass doors.

Vanessa stepped through the doors fifteen minutes later, a

bulging bag in each hand. She paused on the top step and looked around, then spotted me. The soon-to-be-queen of the USC freshman class scrunched her face in a frown. Then she tossed back her long blond hair and descended to my level.

"I haven't got much time. I'm getting my hair cut."

"Oh, you've decided to wear your hair short?" I said by way of conversation.

"Huh?" Vanessa looked at me like I was from some other planet. "I'm getting like one inch taken off." She sat down on the bench, placing her open bags between us. The bags pulsed out waves of perfume.

"What's this about?" She lifted her eyebrows, to inform me I would enjoy but a brief moment more of her time.

"Ever heard of BJ Bonfiglio?" I stopped talking then, content to observe the aftereffects of the bomb I'd just dropped.

"BJ . . . what? Who is that?" She succeeded in looking like a dumb confused blonde. Not a bad ploy.

"Who is that?" I let the moment draw out. "He's the guy you and Porter nearly killed. At one of your piñata parties, remember?"

"I *told* him!" Vanessa flushed. "I told that kid not to—" She stopped.

"What, not to talk? He hasn't. I've never spoken with the guy, never even laid eyes on him. This kind of gossip has legs, Vanessa. Know what I'm saying? It just gets around."

"I thought you had something important to tell me, something about Skye," she whined. "You lied. I should—"

"Stay right where you are," I growled. "This isn't a game, and I don't give a crap about your hair appointment. You and your friend tortured that kid. You could go to jail for it. Would you like that, Vannie? Maybe you could do your freshman year through correspondence, from the women's prison up in Chowchilla. One thing's for sure, you wouldn't have to worry about your hair."

"I didn't do anything!" Panic crept into her hazel eyes. "I swear, I didn't have anything to do with it."

"Are you blaming Porter? We'll do better here if you just tell the truth. Porter couldn't plan his way out of a paper bag. No, you devised BJ's torture. Just a game, an amusement, right? And Skye stopped it, he intervened. You must have been pissed."

"I—huh?" Her mouth fell open as she stared at me. "It sounds like you think I—" Her lower lip trembled. "I did not hurt Skye!"

Time to back off the bad cop. "Vanessa. Maybe you should just tell it like it was."

"I really, really liked Skye. How could you—I miss him!" she wailed.

"Make me buy that."

"OK. I'll tell you." She pressed the palms of her hands together and raised them to her chin. "I did think up the idea. But it was just a joke. That kid BJ wasn't supposed to really get hurt. I wasn't even in the room when Porter got going."

"But you were there at the beginning."

"All right, yes. But not when Port stuck his fingers down BJ's throat. I was somewhere else."

"Some other room?"

"Yeah." She glanced at me. "In the sloth room, actually. I was stoned. And plenty of kids were there with me. I can prove it if I have to."

"But you must have heard the commotion."

"I came out when Porter and Skye started fighting. Everybody did."

"What happened? Describe it to me."

"I saw Skye hit Porter hard. Port was drunk. He fell over, and sort of like couldn't get off the ground. He looked ridiculous, and people were staring at him. Then . . ." She shook her head. "I can't exactly remember. But Skye helped BJ get away."

I kept my eyes on Vanessa's mascara-smudged face. "What happened next?"

"Everybody was laughing after Skye and BJ left, you know? Laughing at Port."

"He must have been furious."

"Later, especially after he got sober. Yeah, later he got really mad."

"Mad enough to kill Skye?"

Vanessa frowned and leaned forward. "Port and Skye were friends, don't you get it? Besides, I know Port couldn't have killed Skye. I know it for sure."

"I'm listening."

"See, I know where Port really was when Skye, you know . . . died. Port wasn't surfing that afternoon. That wasn't true."

"What then? Why did he lie?"

"He was too embarrassed to tell you. See, Port's mom makes him go to therapy every single Friday at five o'clock. A psychologist, it's so lame. And after, his mom makes him come home and they're supposed to like, bond, and talk about his session. She's controlling, and it's kind of sick. Porter hates it, really *hates* it, you know?"

"And he was there that afternoon, with his therapist, and later on, he was with his mom? How do you know that for sure?"

"Because even though Porter hates it, he never ever skips it. See, his mom won't give him any money for the weekend if he does." She straightened. "I don't know the therapist's name, but she's in the San Marcos building downtown. You know, on the corner of State Street and Anapamu? One time I had to drop Port off there. It's easy to check—if you're really a detective, that is."

I smiled at the jab. "It sounds like you and Porter are close. But you aren't a couple, right?"

"God no." She flipped her hair over a shoulder. "We've been friends for ages, but Port isn't my type."

"Well, you two must have something in common. To be friends for so long, I mean."

"I guess." She stared down at her purple-black toenail polish. "We—well, both of us have divorced parents, you know? And for me, it's fine. Great, actually. I get everything I want. But for Porter . . . I don't know. . . ."

"His family life is difficult?"

"Yeah, it is. His dad left his mom when Port was around five. He married some other woman who worked in his office and they had three kids, all boys. Port—he's nothing to his dad, it's almost like he doesn't exist. His dad just buys him stuff, like skis and a car—Port got a new Mustang for graduation, a guilt gift, you know? But his dad didn't bother to come."

This was a side of Vanessa I hadn't seen before. "So your friendship's been important to him."

"I guess." She continued to stare at the pavement. I could see something was on her mind.

"Vanessa, anything else?"

"No . . . no."

But there was something. I decided to probe. "Are you sorry to be leaving Santa Barbara? I mean, USC's not all that far away. But still, it's going to be a change."

"Sorry?" Her head shot up. To my surprise, her expression was filled with pain. "No, I'm not sorry. I'm going down early. I'll be there the day they open the dorms."

She seemed to want me to ask why, and I obliged. "Is Santa Barbara that bad?"

"What I just said, about getting everything I want? Yeah. Yeah, I do. And I get stuff I don't want, too." Her face scrunched in anger, with the effort of keeping it down. "My stepdad. I hate him." Her words were half-choked.

"Vanessa, does he abuse you?"

"Oh, *not quite*, you know what I mean? He bumps into me in the hall and touches my breasts. Or he comes up behind me and pats my ass. That kind of thing, constantly. He's a lawyer, right? He never does anything he couldn't argue his way out of."

"I'm so sorry you've had to put up with that shit. Have you told your mom?"

"Believe me, she doesn't want to know." She gathered up her bags and stood. "I don't want to talk anymore. I just want to go away and never ever come back to this place."

I watched Vanessa hurry off. When she reached the corner, she stopped and looked back at me. I lifted my hand. For a moment, I thought she was going to wave too.

But she didn't. Vanessa stared a moment longer, then turned on her heel and was gone.

"Jaymie? We found Charlie's van. It was parked in the lot behind the Fishwife Restaurant, down on Cabrillo."

"That was quick." El Balcon was too steep for the kickstand, so I lowered my bike to the ground. "Mike, is he OK?"

"Not sure. The van was empty. I went in and talked to the manager at the Fishwife. He said the owner has a soft spot for Charlie, lets him park in the lot at night. Anyway, about three weeks ago, Charlie collapsed in a flower bed. They called an ambulance and he was transported to Cottage Hospital. They heard he made it, but that's the last they've seen of him."

"Charlie would have hated that. He can't stand hospitals." I spoke in a breezy tone, maybe to dispel my concern. "Three weeks ago—that's a long time to be hospitalized. Did you check with Cottage?"

"Thought I'd let you do that, Jaymie. Charlie would rather get a visit from you than me any day of the week."

I heard a sharp "yip!" and looked up. The three-legged member of my household was waiting at the brow of the hill, telling me I was late and to hurry along.

"Thanks, Mike." I paused, giving him a chance to say something more. But there was only silence. "Well, I gotta go."

"Let me know if I can help."

I wasn't over Mike, I admitted to myself as I picked up my

bike and wheeled it on up the road. And I needed to be over him, that was for sure.

Mike Dawson wanted a wife, and I didn't want to be one. Besides, he had Mandy now. The woman wore cute cotton skirts and styled her auburn hair in a bouncy bob.

Yep, Mandy Blaine was just Mike's type. And I wasn't. It was just that simple, wasn't it?

The following afternoon I drove up Carrillo and around the corner into Cliff. Three blocks along, I pulled up across the street from the Bonfiglio home.

Built in the 1920s, the dilapidated two-story Spanish colonial sang of dreamy romance. A gigantic purple-red bougainvillea climbed the wall and poured its molten fire across the second-story balcony grille work. The old clay roof tiles daubed a dark pattern of shade on the creamy stucco walls.

As I sat in the Camino admiring the house, a slight figure in a pair of bright red basketball shorts and a gleaming white wife beater stepped out onto the balcony and waved. "Hey, Jaymie! Come up!"

A second figure, a plump boy with dark wavy hair, stepped through the doorway. BJ Bonfiglio wore a mint green long-sleeved shirt and what looked like a pair of skinny-leg jeans. I couldn't really make him out, but there was something about the way the two of them stood there together . . . something that made them look like *a couple*. Could it be?

"What's the matter with you, are you deaf?" Claudia screamed. "The door's right down there!" She leaned over the rail and pointed. Then she turned to her companion and said something. The two of them disappeared back inside.

Ah, sweet life. Bursting with mysteries, large and small. I got out of the car, crossed Cliff, and walked up the short drive.

The front door sprang open. "Hey, Jaymie!" The lady of the

house was radiant, grinning from ear to ear. "This is BJ. Come in! We're making margaritas." Apparently I'd been invited to visit the Bonfiglio home at the cocktail hour.

I shook BJ's soft hand. His features were very Italian. In fact, his face looked as if it was lifted from a centuries-old portrait painted by a master. His skin was smooth and olive-colored, his nose classically curved, and his eyes liquid and round.

"Hi, Ms. Zarlin."

"Hi, BJ. Please call me Jaymie. I'm glad to meet you."

BJ smiled. "Me too. Claudia talks about you a lot."

"I'll bet she does." I felt a dash of sarcasm was warranted. But BJ just looked confused.

"I meant in a good way. She talks about all the people you help."

I smiled weakly, feeling mean-spirited. And a tad confused myself. This was definitely a new Claudia. I glanced over at her: I'd never seen her so happy.

"Come up to the kitchen, Jaymie. BJ's making some guac to go with the margaritas. His own special recipe."

I followed them to a wide staircase decorated with vintage tile risers. "I don't want to offend you guys. But aren't you a bit young for tequila? Not that it's any of my business."

"BJ doesn't drink," Claudia explained. "Not after what happened to him at the piñata party. Right, BJ?"

"Yeah. I pour my margarita before Claudia adds in the alcohol." BJ's voice was earnest. He seemed like a nice kid, and I mentally cringed when I thought of the abuse he'd suffered at the hands of his fellow classmates.

We climbed the staircase and entered a big old kitchen. It was tidy enough, but you could smell the drains. The counters were tiled, and the grout was missing in places.

Claudia went over to a blender set up next to the stained

porcelain sink. "Course, *I* drink tequila," she announced. "Who cares how old you're s'posed to be?"

I bit my tongue to keep quiet. At ninety pounds, a thimbleful of alcohol was probably about what this girl could handle.

"But," Claudia continued as she sloshed margarita mix into the blender over the ice cubes, "since you two pussies aren't gonna drink, I guess I won't either. I like company when I drink, you know?"

Very much the fifties housewife, Claudia continued to chat away as she finished the margaritas and poured the frothy mix into blue-rimmed glasses. I held open the balcony door as my hosts carried trays loaded with salsa, guacamole, chips, and margaritas out to the deck.

"Your place is wonderful, BJ. Your parents are out of the country?"

"New Zealand. They're both agricultural anthropologists. They have a dig site near Auckland."

I took a sip of the drink. It was so sweet it made my teeth ache. "So you get left by yourself a lot?"

"Yeah. I used to hate it. Really lonely, you know? But now—" He smiled at Claudia, who smiled back. "Now it's fun to hang here."

Their relationship was nice. Whatever it was.

I looked out over the roofs of the houses on Marine Terrace, to a strip of silver water glimmering under a mother-of-pearl sky. "BJ, I hate to bring up an unpleasant subject. But did Claudia explain why I'm here?"

"Course I did," Claudia answered. "BJ's cool, he can talk about it."

BJ nodded. "It's about that night, right? The piñata party."

"Yes. What I want to understand is the roles different people played."

BJ looked down at his hands, folded now on the pitted glass tabletop. "All right."

"Vanessa, Porter, and Skye. How did each of them figure into what happened?"

"Vanessa. . . ." He opened his hands and studied his palms. "I think she was the one who started it all. I think she, you know, decided ahead of time what they were going to do to me. And that's the only reason she invited me in the first place."

"What a sweetheart."

"A fuckin' *ho*," Claudia muttered.

"But after a while, she disappeared. And Porter . . . took charge." He bit his lower lip.

"He took charge of tormenting you, you mean."

"Pretty much. They forced me to drink all kinds of stuff. Porter was really drunk. He . . . he stuck these ice tongs down my throat and made me get sick. People were laughing." There was a tremor now in BJ's voice. "Then they held me down on the floor and he poured more vodka down my throat. That's when I really started to choke."

Claudia put a hand on BJ's arm. "Now tell her about Skye."

BJ nodded, twice. "I don't know where he came from, but all of a sudden, Skye was there. He pulled Porter away, and they started to fight. I think Porter hit his head on the ground. Anyway, I still couldn't stop choking. And Skye . . ."

BJ shut his eyes. "He helped me up and got me out of there, you know? It was all a blur, I couldn't really see. I heard some girl yelling at him, screaming, I think it was Vanessa. And then we were outside, heading for Skye's pickup. After that, I guess I passed out. The next thing I remember is waking up in emergency."

"What about your parents? Did the hospital get in touch with them?"

He gave me a sheepish look. "I lied and said they were away for a week, arriving back the next day. I couldn't tell them my parents were in New Zealand for six months. I was afraid if the school found out, there'd be trouble, you know? Like maybe they'd call Social Services or something."

"I understand. So Skye—he was a lifesaver."

"Yeah. Yeah, he was." BJ met my eyes. "And then—and then look what happened to him!" He tipped his head forward and covered his face with his hands.

Claudia rested her small hand on his shoulder. "It's OK, BJ."

But it wasn't OK, and we all knew it.

"Sorry. I need a tissue." BJ pushed back his patio chair and went into the house.

"BJ's afraid Skye got killed because of him," Claudia said in a husky whisper.

I nodded but said nothing. Now that I knew Porter and Vanessa had alibis, I doubted they'd had a hand in Skye Rasmussen's death, or Cheryl's, for that matter. But nothing was ever exactly as it seemed.

"Sorry about that." BJ stepped back through the door. "Skye was a really good person, you know?"

"That's what I hear." I waited until he'd seated himself again at the patio table. "Should we continue?"

"Yes, go ahead." BJ managed a weak smile. "I want to help."

"Good. Now, I understand you already knew Skye. Claudia said you worked on a school project with him?"

"Uh-huh. We wouldn't have ended up being study partners if it wasn't for Mrs. Sang. She drew names out of a box. A lot of kids didn't like that, but it worked out fine for me."

"Tell me about your project, what you guys did together."

"The assignment was to do a presentation on the sixties. Me and Skye, we decided to do the protest movement. It was real interesting, about Mario Savio up at Berkeley and stuff. But mainly we researched what happened here in Santa Barbara."

Santa Barbara in the sixties. I thought of Neil Thompson and the Steinbachs. "What did you find out?"

"Oh, there was a big protest here. The Bank of America got burned down in 1970, did you know that?"

"Yes, I've heard about that."

"Cool!" Claudia's eyes sparkled. "Nothin' like that ever happens here now."

"A lot of students got arrested," BJ continued. "Like Skye's grandfather."

The world slowed, and just for an instant, held still. I rested my hand on the glass tabletop. "BJ? Say that again."

"Skye's grandfather, Dr. Steinbach? He got arrested, a bunch of times. Skye and me, we went over to his house to interview him. He was like, a leader in the protest movement out at UC."

"Well, how about that." I got up and crossed the deck to the far railing, where a tall coral-flowered eucalyptus filtered the view of the ocean. "BJ, tell me what Rod Steinbach had to say. Tell me everything you can remember about your visit with him."

"Um, well—we didn't talk all that long, I remember that. They'd just moved back into town, and their furniture and stuff had just arrived, maybe the day before. There were lots of boxes in the rooms. First Skye and me helped him carry some stuff, because the movers put things in the wrong places." BJ looked at me to see how he was doing.

"All right. So the three of you chatted?"

"Uh-huh. We sat down in the living room. Skye asked Dr. Steinbach some questions, and he started telling us all about how it was in the sixties, the music and the drugs and the—the—" BJ glanced at Claudia and blushed. "And the girls."

"What else did he tell you?"

"Let's see . . . he said the hippies and the protesters, by 1968, they weren't the same people. I didn't know that. The protesters were real serious. Dr. Steinbach was a leader. He was important in—he called it *the movement.*"

Music, drugs, sex—and violence. "BJ, tell me something. Do you have any notes from your meeting? Or maybe you still have the report you handed in."

"It was a presentation, actually. PowerPoint. I put it together, but in the end, I think Skye kept the disc. But . . ."

"But?"

"I'm pretty sure I've got some of the stuff we used. Like copies of the pictures."

"Pictures of what?"

"People, mostly. Dr. Steinbach dug into some boxes that were stacked in his office. He found some old photos from back then. I remember he didn't want us to take anything away, so we set up his printer and made copies."

"Can we find those copies, BJ? I'd like to see them."

"Sure. I'll look for them." He relaxed in his seat.

"BJ," I said, "do you mind if we find those copies *now?*"

Both BJ and Claudia looked at me in surprise. "What are you looking for, Jaymie?" Claudia asked.

"I'm not sure exactly. I'll know it when I find it."

"OK," BJ said. "Let's go to my room. But I warn you, it's chaos up there."

BJ's room was only a moderate mess. The curtains were drawn, and the space was lighted by the glow from a big fish tank. Clothes were piled on the single bed.

BJ went to the window and pulled back the drape. Then he lifted the clothes and tossed them into a corner.

Claudia smoothed the bedspread and sat down, motioning for me to join her. But I walked over to the sparkling tank.

"Salt water. Beautiful. I've heard it's tricky to maintain." I watched a bevy of rainbow-colored fish undulate to and fro.

"It is till you get the hang of it." BJ was poking around in a closet. He emerged with a cardboard file box in his arms. "My parents don't like dogs very much. So the fish keep me company."

"Fish? How about me?"

I was so surprised at Claudia's coquettish tone that I laughed aloud.

"Sure, you too." BJ sounded embarrassed, but he grinned.

He set the cardboard box on a chair and lifted the lid. It was stuffed with papers and folders. "I'm pretty sure they're here." He rummaged around in the box and pulled out a dark blue file folder. "Yeah, I knew I kept this. I'm a pack rat, I never throw anything away."

I accepted the folder and opened it. There were maybe a dozen sheets of typing paper within, and each sheet was printed with a copy of a photograph. I studied them one by one.

A young Rod Steinbach featured in most of them: Rod on a speaking platform, commanding with his strong handsome features and long dark hair; Rod with a megaphone in hand, scowling like a pirate, clearly having the time of his life. And there were several photos of crowds, the young men shaggy, the women fresh-faced and girlish without makeup.

Two-thirds of the way in, I came on a photo of Rod sharing a bottle of vino with some friends. I caught my breath.

I set the folder down and took the photocopy over to the window.

"Jaymie? What did you find?"

I didn't answer Claudia right away. I was too intent on understanding the photo.

It was a snapshot of four people holding jam jars of what looked like red wine. They were surrounded by more people, a larger group. Yet you could see how these four formed their own knot, not apart from the others, but closer, tighter. Like seeds within an apple: Rod Steinbach, Alice Steinbach, a woman I didn't recognize, and a fourth—Neil Thompson.

Rod's left arm was draped around Neil's narrow shoulders. So Neil Thompson hadn't just "known" Rod and Alice from college days. They'd been close friends.

"Let me ask you guys a question. Come here for a minute." I held up the glossy black and white photo. "Look at these four. That's Dr. Steinbach, of course. Now tell me, do you think the four are just friends, or are they two couples?"

"Couples," Claudia said quickly. "See how that Asian woman's all over that guy with the blond hair? She's fucking him. And Dr. Steinbach? He's with this other woman here. Look, see where his hand is. He's probably grabbing her butt."

I wasn't so sure about the location of the hand. But I agreed with Claudia: Alice and Neil were close. "It's light red hair, actually, not blond. You can't tell because the picture's black and white. BJ, what do you think?"

"The same as Claudia. Two couples. And the four of them are friends."

Did this explain why Neil had tried to make Skye's death look like an accident? Maybe he still had feelings for Alice, and wanted to spare her the anguish of knowing her grandson was murdered. Actually, this explanation wasn't so far from what he'd claimed.

I shuffled the papers and slipped them back in the folder. "Can I take this? I'll get it back to you when I'm done."

"Sure. You can keep it if you want."

"Thanks, BJ. Now, I gotta run."

Well, I'll be damned: Neil Thompson and Alice. I thought about what I'd just learned as I headed back to the office.

Somewhere along the line, there'd been a swap.

Chapter Fifteen

I stayed late at the office, attempting to deal with paperwork. But in fact, I couldn't quit gnawing away at unanswered questions. I was still thinking about Neil and the Steinbachs as I pulled the Camino into the dark car shed and climbed out.

I stepped out to the yard and turned my face to the sky. The air was clear, and a scatter of stars quivered under the sleepy eye of a three-quarter moon.

Dexter scuttled out of the bushes. Low to the ground, he raced over to me as fast as three legs could take him.

"Dex? What are you doing out here?"

The cow dog wasn't so brave anymore. Not since last year, when he was lashed to the porch railing and partially butchered.

I looked over at the house. All seemed as usual: the porch light was on, the front door shut. Then, I glanced over at the studio.

"No," I breathed. "*No.*"

I never locked the studio door. Deep down, I suppose, I was still leaving it open for Brodie. Now the door yawned wide. I walked closer and saw their belongings strewn in the dirt. *Their* belongings: Brodie's, and Danny Armenta's.

Dex cowered beside me. "What is it, boy?" I whispered. "Is somebody still—" Just as I heard the sound of running feet, a figure dressed entirely in black appeared around the corner of the house and took off down the drive.

It took a moment for me to react. Then I was after him, running pell-mell down the steep slope. He rounded the bend on El Balcon. I sped up—and abruptly my feet slipped on the gravel. I was airborne for what seemed like an eternity—

—then came down front-first, scraping my right arm and cheek on the road. I lay there for a moment, stunned. What brought me to my senses was Dexter's warm tongue licking my neck.

I rose to all fours, then to my feet, testing my body. No broken bones, but the old injury to my knee twanged out a sharp warning. It wasn't till I started back up the hill, a concerned Dex at my side, that the pain in my right arm and cheek began to set in. The raw skin burned like a brand.

The heeler and I limped over to the studio. I felt sick: Brodie's Little League trophies were broken to bits, and Danny's high-school baseball cap lay in the dirt.

I walked up to the gaping doorway, reached just inside for the light switch, and groaned. The window in the back wall was smashed, and the studio was a shambles. Even the bed was upended, the blankets soaked. It took a moment for me to register the odor: urine. The asshole who'd done this had pissed on the bed.

Who—and why? Did it have something to do with the case? Rod Steinbach, maybe. He wouldn't have done this himself, but he could be behind it. Or Porter Logsdon—yes. It could have been him.

I picked my way through the chaos as I crossed the room. I peered through the broken window at the back, and saw daggers of glass in the dirt. The moon swabbed the shards in silvery light.

I turned back to the room. That's when I noticed the sheet of typing paper lying on the small kitchen table. I walked over, picked it up, and read the scrawled message:

BACK OFF OR THIS WILL BE YOU.

What the hell? I flipped the page over. And doubled over, as if I'd been kicked in the gut.

The paper fell to the floor, but not before the photo seared my retinas.

I only knew it was a picture of my brother because of the hair, the sun-bleached brown hair. It was Brodie, his face swollen beyond recognition, hanging by his neck from the bars of a cell.

Dexter hugged my heels as I left the studio and crossed the yard in the moonlight. My breath ran shallow and fast. I'd been wrong: this had nothing to do with the aquarium murders. Chaffee was written all over it. I would hunt down the bastard, tonight.

I unlocked the front door of the house and stared into my dark living room, half expecting the snake to uncoil himself from the couch. But no, Chaffee was gone, of course. He'd run off into the dark.

Back off or this will be you. Adrenaline scoured my arteries. I was focused on one burning goal.

Dex edged around me and trotted inside. I stepped into the hall and turned on the lights. The dog behaved normally now, wandering into the kitchen and lapping at his water dish. Chaffee hadn't entered the house. He could have broken in if he'd tried, but he hadn't bothered. He'd hit me where it hurt most.

Odd that he'd understood that. I'd underestimated the punk.

"All the better," I said aloud. All the better that Chaffee

understood. Because I wanted him to understand, when I ex-
acted revenge.

I went through to the kitchen and sat down at the table,
smoothed open the sheet of paper and stared at the words. I had
a job to do, but there was no rush. Chaffee might be anywhere
now. Hours would pass before I could be certain he'd be at
home in his bed.

When I glanced at my phone, I saw Taryn had called.
"Sorry," I said aloud. "I can't help you, not now." It was time for
me to take care of my own.

I fixed myself a pot of strong coffee. While it perked I
changed into a dark long-sleeved top, and replaced my red ten-
nies with my black ones. I wound my ponytail into a knot and
pinned it at the nape of my neck.

Then I collected some gear: a small flashlight, a few lock-
picking tools, and an old purplish raincoat. I slipped Claudia's
switchblade into my pocket. For a moment I wished I'd accepted the gun Mike had pressed on me awhile back. But no:
somehow it was better this way, more personal. The knife
would do.

I longed for revenge. But first, I needed to *know*. Chaffee was
going to tell me everything he'd seen or heard about Brodie's
death. Every last thing.

The kitchen clock read 11:00 P.M. I would pay the guy a visit
at four in the morning.

I stepped out into the flower-perfumed night. Insects
whirred, chirped. I looked up: the resident big white barn owl
swayed on her perch at the top of the cypress. She turned her
beautiful heart-shaped face down upon me.

The raptor was nothing like me. She was a coldhearted killer.
My own heart smoldered with revenge, like a red-hot star.

I set to work cleaning the studio to help pass the hours. For
the first time, I couldn't feel my brother's presence in the room.
I was alone: Brodie's spirit had fled.

* * *

As I backed the Camino out of the garage and coasted down the hill in the night, I thought of the Tactacquins. They were depending on me, and I was withdrawing my support. I knew I was letting them down.

But I felt no regret. Nothing and nobody mattered now, except my brother and all he'd endured.

Montecito was quiet and dark. No light pollution here. Oh, I didn't doubt infrared cameras recorded my passing. So what? I didn't care what anyone saw in the morning. I only required tonight. Tomorrow could bring whatever it would.

I parked a quarter mile away from the château, on Riven Rock, behind a stand of eucalyptus. I pressed the door shut with my hip, then cocked an ear and listened. No dogs barked. The sky had just begun to lighten to gray. The false dawn.

At first I walked along near the bushes at the side of the road. But my footsteps made loud crackling noises in the dry leaf litter, so I stepped over to the asphalt. Then I broke into a jog. In two or three minutes I'd arrived.

The mansion gleamed in the brightening sky like a glacé concoction, a storybook house made for children to nibble. I slipped inside the shrubbery and peered through the cyclone fence. Where were the guard dogs? Curled up in locked kennels, I hoped.

Dawn was breaking, but the outdoor lights still shone over the grand central staircase and at the corners of the château. I studied the guest house, where my quarry was tucked away in his den. It was set off to one side, toward the back of the big house. A battered old sedan was pulled up in front.

For a moment, I faltered. What if I failed? But I thought of the photograph of my brother. My desire for revenge reared up once more and roared through my veins like a freight train, drowning out any remnants of doubt.

I checked my pockets. Everything was in place.

I tied the sleeves of the jacket around my neck in a loose knot, shoved the toe of my shoe into the cyclone fencing, and started to climb. When I reached the top, I unknotted the jacket with one hand and laid it along the ridge of cut wire ends.

Then, just as I prepared to swing my body over, I heard a kind of chant. "Woo, woo-woo"—the strange keening notes rose and fell in the dawn air.

Still clinging to the fence, I peered through the wire. A thin young man wearing boxer shorts and a baggy T-shirt twirled on the lawn. He spun in awkward circles and lifted a tennis racquet to the sky. "Woo, woo-woo—"

Thad Chaffee, dressed in light-colored sweatpants and T-shirt, appeared in the open doorway of the guest house. He leaned against the doorframe and watched the boy's dance.

Arms stretched wide, the boy ran to Chaffee. He seemed to be imploring his caregiver. Chaffee disappeared inside the little house and the boy began to twirl in circles again. The notes of his song rose an octave.

I eased myself back down to the ground to observe the unfolding drama.

But there was no drama. Chaffee reemerged with a racquet of his own and a ball. The boy screamed with delight, and ran long. Chaffee waited, then hit the ball high and far. No longer awkward, the boy caught the ball on his racquet with perfect coordination, and returned it in a great looping arc.

I knew I was observing pure happiness, something precious and rare. What a time to learn Thad Chaffee had a decent streak in him.

Seeing this wouldn't make my job easier. But I'd no intention of turning away.

I scrambled back up the fence, swung first one leg over the jacket and then the other. I didn't try to hide myself as I dropped to the ground.

As I started across the plush lawn, Chaffee looked up and saw me. For a moment, he froze. Then he began to jog toward me. And at that moment, I realized something: Chaffee, who had the body of a whippet, was smaller than the guy I'd chased down El Balcon.

"What the fuck are you doing here? I told you to stay away from me, bitch!" He grabbed me by the arm.

This was not someone to reason with. I brought my right hand down hard on his wrist in a chop, and Chaffee gasped and bent forward.

"Fuck! What's wrong with you, freak? You broke my arm!"

"Don't lay a hand on me, Chaffee." Out of the corner of my eye I saw the boy take a step toward us. I spoke quickly. "Somebody trashed my place tonight. Was it you?" But I already knew I'd made a mistake. He wasn't the one.

"I don't want nothing to do with you, bitch! I already told you!" He cradled his wrist in his hand.

The boy was coming toward us now, trotting in a wide arc. He was tall and gangly, thin as a stalk of bamboo. Over and over, he made a noise: "Tha . . . Tha. . . ." He was saying Chaffee's name.

"Then why," I said. "Tell me why and I'll go."

"Why what!"

"I want to know why you changed your mind about dealing with me." I paused, watching him. "You were warned off, weren't you?"

He shook his head back and forth. Fear sparked in his eyes. Real fear, not the kind inspired by the likes of me.

"Don't know what you're talking about." He called over to the boy. "Mark, let's go."

I was about to lose him. I was about to lose my one chance at finding out what had happened to Brodie. I suspected Thad Chaffee knew too damn much, and he wouldn't be around forever. Somebody, sooner or later, was going to make certain of that.

"Listen up. If you don't talk to me, I'll go to the cops." A stab in the dark, it struck home.

"No!" Chaffee stopped and turned back. "No, don't do that!"

"So it *was* the cops who threatened you. What is it they don't want you to say?"

"If I talk to you, they'll kill me." Chaffee looked different now. His coiled-spring of a body had sagged. "I can't talk to you. Please—"

"If you don't talk to me, I'll talk to them. And you better believe I'll mention your name." I paused for that to sink in. "Tell me what you saw that night, Chaffee. I won't tell a soul where I heard it, and you won't see me again."

Mark was humming uneasily. He'd begun to sway from side to side.

"All right." Thad wiped a hand over his mouth. "They found out I was talking to you—that day at the skate park? Some drug cop, undercover, saw you give me the money. They hauled in my ass, 'cause they wanted to know why."

"So you told them all about it, I suppose?"

"They didn't leave me a choice."

"And they told you not to say anything else to me. Because there *is* more, isn't there."

"I told the cops I hardly told you anything," he stalled.

The gray light was warming now, bringing hints of color to the world. I glanced over at Mark. Red hair stuck up on his head like a bottlebrush flower.

"Say it now. Say it, and you won't hear from me again."

I could see him waver, trying to decide. I stepped into his space and leaned close, so close I could smell his sour morning breath. "This is my brother we're talking about, get it? I will *never* give up on this, *never*. So get it over with."

"I told you everything. All I didn't tell you was . . . I saw who was in the jail that night." He shot me a look.

"Who? Say it, damn you." Almost there.

He let out a long slow breath, as if his lungs had been punctured. "It was Wheeler. He was waiting when they brought your brother back to his cell."

"Wheeler. *Chief* Wheeler, you mean?" My tendons and muscles were tense as wound wire.

"Yeah. It was him."

I had what I'd come for. Yet I couldn't believe it. In the meantime, I could only shoot the messenger boy.

"You could have done something to help him. You were there as a medic, you prick." I shoved my hands in my pockets, to keep from scratching out his eyes.

The sun still hadn't raised its flaming head over the horizon, but the air was filled with golden light and birdsong. I climbed into the cab of the El Camino and shut the door. I just sat there for a while, staring at the peeling pink and green trunks of the eucalyptus trees.

All this time. For three long years I'd assumed Brodie had hanged himself, just as the coroner claimed. For three long years I'd blamed myself for neglecting my brother, and for aggravating the cops when Brodie wound up in jail. All this time I'd feared my badgering had caused someone to mess with Brodie, driving him to suicide.

But Brodie hadn't killed himself. He'd been murdered. And not because of me.

I roused myself, and turned the key in the ignition. Dexter needed his breakfast, and I needed a couple of hours of sleep. The engine started up, but still I just sat there.

"Brodie," I murmured. "You were dangerous to them." So dangerous they'd decided to shut him up forever. What secret had my brother known?

◆   ◆   ◆

The next morning was a Sunday, which Dexter knew perfectly well. He jumped into the driver's seat ahead of me, hoping for a leisurely spin around town. At first the little cow dog had done fine on his three pins. But he was aging, and arthritis was setting in. As his mobility had lessened, his passion for road trips had increased.

"All right. But shove over, bud, unless you've learned how to drive."

I backed out of the ramshackle lean-to of a garage, did a ninety-degree turn, and headed off down the hill.

"You know," I continued, "I once knew a poodle who lived in a semi. He learned how to get his owner out of a fast-food joint by leaning on the horn." I looked over at Dex. "A *toy* poodle," I said just to rile him. But the cow dog ignored me. He hung his head out the window, grinning into the breeze.

I circled through the streets around Cottage Hospital, search-ing for a park in the shade. "You owe me," I grumbled five minutes later, after finally locating a spot under a Hong Kong orchid tree. "Now do your job, will you? Guard the Camino with your life."

As I entered Cottage, a security guard motioned me toward a desk.

"May I help you?" an elderly volunteer asked.

"I'm here to see Charlie . . . Corrigan." I couldn't get used to using his last name. Charlie was just Charlie to me.

"Corrigan," the old lady trebled. "Let me see—" She bent close to read her screen, raising a finger to the glass. "You know, dear . . ." She looked up at me. "I'm afraid there is no 'Corrigan' here. None at all."

"Would you mind checking again? When I phoned they told me he was going to be here at least another week, and that was only two days ago."

"I'm a bionic woman, dear," she said tartly. "I had the lenses of my eyes replaced, cataracts, you know. I most likely see better than you."

"You probably do. But I don't understand."

"Why don't we have a member of the paid staff speak with you, dear? Put your mind at rest."

She was treating me like a confused child, but that was OK. I was confused, and worried as well. Charlie had been seriously ill, and . . . I didn't want to go there. "Yes, I'd appreciate that."

The young man who came around the corner to greet me was good at his job. He spoke to me in a conciliatory tone that was practiced and fake, yet calming all the same. "Hi there. I'm Jonathan Sanchez. You wanted to visit with Charles Corrigan?"

"Yes. I'm his only living relative, his niece." I'd already used that line on the phone, and found it worked well. "I called two days ago, and a nurse told me he had pneumonia. She said they were going to keep Uncle Charlie in for another week. But apparently he's not here."

"I'm afraid Charles Corrigan isn't with us anymore."

"What? Please don't—please don't tell me—"

"Oh, no. No—" The young man reached out and patted my arm. "Your uncle was very much alive when he left here." He made a small grimace. "*Very* much alive."

I burst into relieved laughter. "Sounds like Charlie. *Uncle* Charlie," I amended. "Alive and kicking, I suppose you mean?"

"Let's just say he made quite a fuss. He'd removed all the hookups and was nearly out the door in his hospital gown when we caught him."

I couldn't help but smile, thinking of what a sight Charlie must have been, masked and bare-assed. "So where is he now?"

"Actually, we had him transferred."

"Transferred? Where?" Something in the guy's expression set a fresh alarm bell tinging.

"I'm sorry. We can't give out that information."

I tried on a frown. "As I said, I'm his niece, Mr. Corrigan's only living relative. What, do you expect me to knock on the door of every medical facility in town?"

"Mr. Corrigan is an adult. He will contact you if he wants to. Now, excuse me—I've got to get back to work."

"Thanks. Thanks a lot." It was a feeble protest. Mr. Gatekeeper smiled kindly as he strode away.

Fuming, I stood there and ground my teeth. Bureaucrats were the curse of the planet.

"Miss," the volunteer said. "I couldn't help but overhear."

"What do I do now?" I raised my hands in frustration.

"I think I know who you're talking about. Is your uncle the man with the sack over his head?"

"Yes, that's Uncle Charlie. His face and scalp were badly burned in a fire."

"Oh, my. Well, I'm afraid your uncle did make quite a commotion. One of the nurses told me about it." The older lady beckoned me with an arthritic finger. "Perhaps I can help. Come closer, I don't want to shout."

I stepped up to the counter. "He needs me. I'm the only family he's got."

"I understand. And that's why I'm going to break the rules, dear, and tell you what I know. Your uncle was transferred to an awful place. It's called the Rose Garden Retirement Home. And believe me, it's anything but a rose garden." She shook her head. "It's for indigent people with dementia, you know? I've heard bad things happen to patients there, and then they get"—she raised a finger for emphasis—"*swept under the rug.*"

I broke out in a sweat. "The Rose Garden? Do you know where it is?"

"Somewhere in Noleta. You know, that area adjacent to

Santa Barbara, where the residents refused to become part of Goleta?" She nodded. "I'm telling you this because I'm on the side of your uncle. We silver panthers need to stick up for one another. Now, don't waste a minute more, dear. You young people think you have all the time in the world."

Chapter Sixteen

The Rose Garden Retirement Home was located on a small cul-de-sac not fifty yards from 101. The street was separated from the freeway by a towering concrete block wall. I pulled up in its shade, switched off the engine, and studied Charlie's new digs.

The facility appeared to consist of four run-down sixties tract houses surrounded by a sagging chain-link fence. The lawns were baked brown, and only a few shrubs struggled for survival in the adobe soil.

The gate, also of chain-link, was propped open with a tire. I got out of the vehicle and walked through. The house closest to the front had a sign taped to a window: DELIVERIES HERE.

The door was blistered and warped from the sun. I heard a television yapping away inside, and several voices. When I knocked on the door, the voices stopped.

A large woman with steel-gray hair hanging down to her shoulders opened the door and looked at me. She was tall, maybe six feet, and her shoulders were broad. "Yes?" she demanded.

I looked past the woman into a small living room. Three other people, two women and a man, sat facing a bulky old television set. A fourth person, a woman in a wheelchair, was pushed up with her face to a wall. Except for the woman in the wheelchair, they all appeared to be caregivers—so to speak.

"Yes?" the woman repeated.

"I'm here to visit my uncle. He was recently transferred from Cottage. Charles Corrigan." I smiled sweetly, with a smile that had endeared me to hardened criminals.

"Come back during visiting hours. Thursday, two to four."

"Oh." I put on my most disappointed face. "I've got to drive back to Bakersfield tonight. I work, you know? I can't come during the week."

"Sorry." She shrugged. "I don't make the rules."

The occupants of the room turned back to the TV, and someone amped up the volume.

I glanced over at the woman in the wheelchair. She had managed to twist her head around and was looking directly at me. Her mouth opened and her lips moved when our eyes met, but because of the TV, I couldn't hear what she was saying.

"I understand you don't make the rules," I said to the boss lady. "And of course your employer expects you to follow them. But . . . maybe you'll accept a donation? For the Rose Garden, of course."

"A donation?" The woman both tightened her mouth and smiled at the same time. The result was not pretty. "What did you have in mind?'

I didn't think twenty would swing it. "Oh, around forty."

"You'll have to give us a minute to—you know, clean him up for visitors."

I knew, all right. "Sure, no problem. I'll run around the corner to the bank, be right back."

"Christ, what a hellhole," I growled to Dex when I got back in the car. "Poor old Charlie."

In three minutes I was at the B of A, two minutes more and I'd withdrawn the cash. Another three minutes and I was back.

The door opened before I could knock, and the bulky gray-haired woman stepped out and shut it behind her. "He's over in S." She put out a hand.

Was she capable of stiffing me? Of course, but I didn't think she'd try it. That would cause trouble, and trouble she didn't want. I handed over two twenties.

"Follow me." We walked around the corner of the house, heading for the back of the property. Apparently Charlie hadn't even been placed in one of the ratty tract houses. I prepared myself for the worst, which was just as well. I pretty much got it.

"S" must have stood for shed, or maybe shack. A small run-down structure roofed in tar paper and walled in green asbestos siding cowered in the far corner of the lot.

I opened my mouth to tell the woman what I thought of her—then used my brains and shut up.

The guy I'd seen earlier in the TV room exited the shack and scurried past us. He met the woman's gaze and nodded. The cleanup man.

One thing was for certain: Charles Corrigan was checking out of the Rose Garden, *today*.

"We had to put him back here," the woman was saying. "He was freaking out all the patients, what with that creepy face of his."

"But Uncle Charlie wears a mask."

"He wouldn't keep it on, would he? Kept ripping it off, even when we put mitts on him." She pulled back the old screen door and unlocked a newer solid door. Then she pushed it open.

An elderly man in a filthy hospital gown lay flat on his back on an old army surplus cot. His face was turned to the wall.

"Charlie!"

"Jaymie? That you?" He covered his face with his hands. "Jaymie, don't you look."

"I'll be leaving you two. Like I said, I don't make the rules. Fifteen minutes is all that's allowed." The woman stepped back. "Talk some sense into him while you're at it, will you? Tell him we'll let him back in one of the houses if he'll promise to behave himself and keep that damn sack on his head."

I closed the door after her. Then I stood there for a moment, facing the shut plywood panel.

"Hi, Charlie." I fought to keep my voice steady. "I—"

"My mask, Jaymie. I hid it under the mattress. Stay right there, I'll just get it."

I continued to wait with my back to my friend.

"All right now, it's on. I hide it, ya see. I show 'em what's left of me to keep 'em away, the bastards. This face is good for somethin' after all."

"Charlie, why didn't you call me! What in God's name are you doing here?"

"Livin' out my golden years."

It hurt, but I laughed. "Look, we have to get you out of here right away. I've got the Camino out in front. Can you walk?"

"Walk? I could run a four-minute mile if it'd get me outta this dump." Charlie sat up and maneuvered himself to the edge of the bed. With one hand, he tried to close the back of his hospital gown. "But I ain't walkin' nowhere with my butt hangin' out, not with you."

"Forget your scrawny butt, Charlie. I'm not leaving you here."

"Ya know, Jaymie, I'm thinking. I ain't the only one trapped in this hole."

That stopped me. I thought of the woman in the wheelchair pushed up against the wall. "No, you're not. Maybe there's another way." I pulled my phone from my pocket. This time I didn't debate with myself, just made the call.

"Hey, Jaymie."

Mike's voice had never sounded so good. "Listen, Charlie and I need a knight in shining armor. Come with your badge, and bring a good camera."

When I'd finished explaining the situation and given Mike

the address, I slipped my phone back in my pocket and walked over to the bed. Charlie reached out and took my hand.

"Good for you. You called in the cavalry." His voice was raspy and weak. "Nothin' wrong with getting some help."

"It's not over yet, Charlie. You look like you need to go back to the hospital."

"I'm not lettin' another sawbones near me. One of the bastards sent me here."

"We'll have a talk with that doc. Maybe give him a chance to explain himself." I squeezed my friend's leathery hand. "If we don't like what we hear, I promise, he's toast."

I saw the anger rise up in Mike as his eyes adjusted to the gloom. He hid it well, but I knew he would keep it fresh, and use it.

"Why you sneaky old codger." Mike walked up to the bed and squeezed Charlie's shoulder. "You'd do goddamn anything to get a pretty girl alone with you and a bed."

"Ya caught me, pal." Charlie coughed hard, then tried to get up.

"No, don't move. Stay there for a minute while I take your picture," Mike said. "We want to nail these fuckers."

I was fighting back tears. The tears weren't for Charlie, though I felt bad for him. I think maybe I was crying for myself. Seeing Mike there—I hated to admit it, but I was relieved.

"I'm with ya, Mike," Charlie wheezed. "Listen, let's make it a good un. Look in that chest over there, top drawer. You'll find the rubber strips they use at night, to tie me to the bed."

The drama was over, at least for Charlie. Within an hour he was back in Cottage, propped up against a tall stack of pillows. A tube fed antibiotics into his skinny arm.

"Stay for a while, will you, Jaymie girl? Might as well confess, I got a god-awful fear of this place. Ever since I spent six months of my life in this torture chamber, getting my burned bits cut out."

I sat down in the bedside chair. "Sure. What shall we talk about?"

Charlie turned his head on the pillows. His eyes were bright through the holes in the sack. "Let's talk about you. 'Cause I get the feeling something's come up."

How the hell could he tell? "It's nothing, Charlie. Nothing that can't wait."

"Listen, I might not be here the next time you come lookin' for me. Better spit it out."

"Charlie, that's nonsense. The doctor said you'll be on the mend real soon."

"Ha, gotcha. I meant I might be down in Ensenada. There's a señorita I got a hankering to see. Now start talkin'."

I watched a clear fluid seep along Charlie's drip line. "It's about Brodie. I found out something."

My friend nodded and waited.

"That night in the jail? The cops hauled him out of his cell. When they brought him back, he was out cold."

"Goddamn sonofabitches."

I looked out the window. The mountains behind the city shimmered like mirages in the dry heated air. "Brodie didn't hang himself. It was the cops who did it. And it wasn't just the jailers who were there that night. There were other cops, too—and Wheeler, the chief."

"Jesus." Charlie gave a low whistle and struggled to sit up. "What hornet's nest did that boy get hisself into? He found out something he shouldn't of, that's for damn sure."

"Yeah. And I have to figure out what it was. *Have to*."

"I can see how you'd feel that way. Don't suppose I can convince you to back off?"

"Hah." I barked out a laugh.

Charlie fell back on the pillows. Neither of us spoke for a time.

"Tell me somethin', Jaymie. Aren't you working on a big case? The aquarium murders, I heard."

"That's right. I think a man's been falsely accused."

"What's new in the world?" Charlie stopped to cough. The rasping led to a series of gasps that seemed to go on forever. "You figure it out yet?"

"I'm getting there. But now the case doesn't seem all that important to me. I have to find out what happened to Brodie, and why. If I don't, nobody will."

"True enough. But maybe what happened to Brodie can wait. This fellow who's falsely accused, his family and whatnot—I bet they're depending on you."

I looked at Charlie in surprise. "I've never heard you give advice before. Why now?"

"Why now? 'Cause I almost took a trip south of the border, that's why. Makes ya kinda impatient. I'm going to say something, Jaymie, just in case I'm south of the border the next time you come around." Charlie tugged the sack down over his scarred neck.

"We only got what's right now, right in front of us. We ain't got the future and we ain't got the past, not really. Your brother can wait, but this fellow in jail? Maybe he can't."

I rubbed my temples with my thumbs. "I never figured you for a Zen master. But I understand what you're saying."

"Course you do. 'Cause I'm tellin' you somethin' you already know." Another bout of gasping and coughing ensued.

"I'm an old dog, Jaymie. In dog years, hell, I'm about five hundred years old. I forgot a helluva lot in that time, but I learned a few things, too. And one or two of 'em stuck."

Suddenly, I had a thought. "How old *are* you, Charlie? Are you about the right age to remember what happened in 1970, out at the university?"

"I'm about the right age to forget it." Charlie managed a cackle. "What do you want to know?"

"I want to know about the Bank of America fire."

"Oh, I ain't forgot that. One night the kids out in Isla Vista marched on the bank. We're talkin' about Santa Barbara now, not Berkeley, so they were making it into a party as usual, taking along wine bottles and such. The cops thought the wine bottles were Molotovs, which they wasn't. So they jumped on the kids, beat 'em up. That got the kids riled up. Some of 'em went off and made Molotovs after all."

"Were you living in Isla Vista at the time?"

"Nope, I was staying up in the hills, working on a big avocado ranch. But I was down in IV quite a bit. Annie was a student. See, Annie was younger'n me, around twenty-two. It was crazy times, Jaymie. Like they say, drugs, sex, rock 'n' roll. Not that Annie did any of that. No, she was just a real sweet girl."

I lifted my messenger bag to my knees, opened it, and took out one of the photocopies BJ had given me, the one showing Rod Steinbach and his friends. "Recognize any of these characters, Charlie?"

"Can't say I do. But I recognize the type. Drugs, sex, rock 'n' roll, all mixed in with savin' the world."

I slipped the photo back in my bag. "About the bank burning. Any arrests?"

"At least a hundred of 'em. Let 'em out the next day." Charlie flexed his left arm and winced. "Damn needle's buggin' me. I got a mind to rip the thing out."

"You said you'd behave."

"S'pose I did." He sighed and relaxed into the pillows. "About them protests. You know what happened a couple nights after the bank burned, right?"

"After? No, I don't."

"Boy was killed. Burned to death."

I lowered my bag to the floor. "I didn't know that. Tell me about it."

"Well. Those kids they let out of jail? Hoppin' mad. Needed somethin' to take it out on. It being IV and all, they turned on the rental agencies, you know? Winged bricks through windows, that kinda thing. But then, middle of the night, somebody threw Molotovs into one of the agencies. Burned it down to the ground."

"And someone was trapped inside."

"A student, if I remember right. He didn't die right away. They got him to the hospital . . ." His gravelly voice ground to a halt.

I realized that what had happened to the student had pretty much happened to Charlie, and to his beloved Annie, some ten or twelve years ago. Annie had died, mercifully, in the fire ignited by a camp stove that had engulfed their tent.

"Charlie, I'm sorry."

The sound of two women chatting out in the hall drifted in through the open doorway. I wanted to drop the whole subject, but I couldn't, not yet.

"You don't happen to remember the boy's name, do you?"

"No recollection."

"Did they ever find out who did it?"

"Don't think so. They had a list of suspects, if I remember right, but no evidence and no witnesses. Far as I know, they never caught the bastard." Charlie's eyelids flickered.

"Get some rest now, Unc." I walked around to the other side of the bed, picked up his untethered right hand, and gave it a squeeze.

"A local boy," Charlie murmured.

"What?" I bent close. His words were muffled.

"The boy that died. UC student, but I think he grew up around here."

"That's something to go on." I kissed his rough scar-bound

hand, and laid it down on the white sheet. "See you soon, Charlie."

"Jaymie, wait. Somethin' else I thought of to tell you."

"Still here."

"Slow dancing."

I wasn't sure I'd heard him right. "I thought you said—*slow dancing*."

"That's right. Annie and me, we used to love to slow dance, you know? Some song or other'd come on the radio, didn't matter where we was, we'd stand up and dance . . . you know how to slow dance, Jaymie?"

"I'm not a great dancer, but sure. Sure I do."

"You pull your partner in close, give em a hug. Then let 'em take a half-step away. Dance 'em loose. Easy does it, round and round. And that's what you gotta do with the dead, Jaymie, the ones you love that died."

I held very still. "If I let Brodie go, I'm afraid I'll forget him. I couldn't bear that."

"You'll never forget him, not ever." Charlie reached over and covered my hand with his own.

"You can't hold him too tight, sweetheart. Don't you see? The dead are the same as the living that way."

I was climbing into the El Camino when my cell rang.

"Miss Zarlin? You don't know me. But I'd like to meet with you." The masculine voice was pleasant enough, but unsure.

"Who are you?"

"Uh—Larry."

"Larry who?"

"I'll tell you my last name when we meet."

"What do you want to talk about?"

There was a long moment of silence. I was tempted to hang up on the guy, but something told me to stay on the line.

"A friend. John Tactacquin."

Now I was glad I hadn't hung up. "Where shall we meet?"

"Shoreline Park, near the steps down to the beach. Tomorrow afternoon, at four?"

"That'll work," I replied.

"I don't know what you look like. How will I know you?"

"I'll have my bike with me. It's an old Schwinn, blue."

"OK, then . . . OK."

"You sound undecided, Larry. Are you going to show?"

"I've made up my mind. I'll be there, you can count on that."

Chapter Seventeen

I would never give up my fight to uncover the truth about Brodie's death.

But Charlie was right: I'd have to put that mission aside. John Tactacquin's time bomb was ticking, and it was up to me to chop back the thicket of lies obscuring the truth about the murders.

The following afternoon was humid as Honolulu, hot as hell. Monsoon clouds lurked along the mountaintops as I pedaled through a half-deserted Shoreline Park.

An empty redwood picnic table stood near the steps down to the beach. I leaned my bike against it, climbed up on the bench and looked over the cliff's edge.

The tide was high, and the surf had swallowed the beach. The waves crashed against the base of the old sandstone bluff, eating it away in small steady bites.

"Uh—Miss Zarlin?"

I turned around. A good-looking guy in his fifties stood beside the picnic table. He wore workingman's clothes: a pair of faded and worn jeans, a wide leather belt, and a light tan work shirt. His Dodgers cap sat square on his head.

"Depends on who's asking." I smiled and stepped down off the bench.

"Sorry to be so secretive." He returned the smile, somewhat nervously. "Kind of silly, I guess. My name's Larry Millar."

I walked up to the guy and held out my hand. "Not necessarily silly. Depends on what it is you need to get off your chest."

"Yeah. Well." Larry Millar lifted his cap and ran a quick hand through his graying hair.

"Let's sit down, shall we?" I indicated the table. Larry was going to need a bit of coaxing to get under way.

He nodded, then slid into the attached bench. His cap was on, then off again, twisted and smoothed in his roughened hands.

"So I guess you've just come from work?"

"Yeah. I work for the city—tree pruning, nearly twenty-four years. Of course, I don't climb up in the trees anymore. That's what we've got the young guys for. I'm one of the old farts who tells them what to do."

I watched Larry Millar. He was more than just nervous. He looked downright scared.

"Hey, that's how it should be. So John Tactacquin's a friend of yours?"

I thought I'd said the right thing. But Larry dropped his head into his hands. "Yeah," he muttered. "Yeah, you could say that."

Behind Larry Millar, a squadron of seven or eight brown pelicans swept past, following the surf line. Their lives were so simple, I thought, so pared down and focused.

"Mr. Millar? Are you sure you want to talk?"

He placed his hands palms down on the weathered tabletop. "Yes. Yes, I do." He met my gaze. "John still hasn't given the police an alibi, right?"

"Right. Not for either of the murders. And I have to tell you, it makes him look guilty as hell."

"Of course it does." He drew in a deep breath. "He was with me, Ms. Zarlin. Both Friday nights. I was the one he was with."

"But I thought—I mean, I assumed—" I stumbled and started again. "I don't get it. I thought the whole reason John didn't want to talk was due to the fact he didn't want to hurt his family."

"That's pretty much true."

"But now you're telling me he was hanging out with you on those dates, at those times. What's so incriminating about that? What, were you guys at the Rhino Bar or something? Big deal." I felt a spark of anger. "John's risking his life. How is that not hurting his family? And besides, Donna loves him. She'd forgive him in a second for something like that."

"I know she would," Larry said. "Donna's a good woman. She'd probably forgive almost anything. Just like my ex-wife would've done for me."

"Mr. Millar." I released a sigh of frustration. "Are you prepared to give a sworn statement to the police?"

"Yes. I'd do anything for John."

I looked at him for a long minute. And then I realized that the heat, the goddamn August heat must be muddling my thinking, slowing me down.

"We've been together a long time, six years." Larry Millar's eyes moistened. "Know what? You're the first person I've told, ever. John didn't want me to tell you. But Jesus—to *die* for something like this?" In the quiet the surf boomed against the cliff below.

"But I still don't think I get it, Mr. Millar. It doesn't make sense. Why couldn't John just say you two were having a couple of beers?"

"Why? Because he knows what I think. I've been telling him for years he should tell Donna the truth." He grimaced. "John won't give you my name because he doesn't trust me to keep quiet about us. And you know what? He's right. I've told you, and now I'll tell anyone else who asks. I'm sick and tired of living a lie."

I thought of Donna and Taryn. Whatever else might happen, their lives were about to implode. But my job wasn't to protect them, I reminded myself. It was to solve the case.

"Larry. You need to contact John's lawyer, today." I pulled out my card and scribbled the name of the attorney on the back. "Your information may not be enough to halt the wheels of injustice, but it sure as hell can't hurt."

"You're wrong there, Miss Zarlin." He took the card and shook his head. "It's going to hurt. It's going to hurt some people a lot."

As I pedaled back through Shoreline, my phone rang. "Claudia. Hi."

"His name was Gary Hobson," the junior detective announced. "I found it on the net, how he died back in 1969. Somebody set fire to the La Playa Rental Agency. Hobson was asleep upstairs."

I braked, stepped off my bike, and straddled the frame. "Gary Hobson, huh? Was he a student?"

"A UC student and a night watchman. I guess that means security. He kept an eye on the building, and had a room above the office."

"Say where he was from? His hometown."

"He was from right here, Santa Barbara. And he was—let's see—twenty years old and a junior. That's about it."

"Anything about who might have set the fire?"

"Nope. But BJ and me, we could go out to UC and research it some more if you want."

"You and BJ?"

"Yeah. Got a problem with that?"

"Not at all. It's very sweet."

"Eff that shit," Claudia said happily. "I don't do sweet."

"No. No, I suppose you don't."

"Jaymie? Don't worry, we got it covered. BJ and me, we've got a plan."

"I swear, girl, I usually have to *drag* you out to lunch. And this time, you call me?" Tiffany Tang swirled her iced tea with a long clinking spoon. "That nasty case you're working on—I suppose you were just dying to get away from it for an hour."

"It's hard to think about anything else." I studied my friend. Everything about Tiff was perfect, as always: her plum lipstick, glossy black hair, turquoise and tangerine scarf. "How do you do it, Tiff? You look great—you're so put together. You make me jealous."

Tiff's laugh was always a surprise: low-pitched and naughty, it was one of the things I liked about her.

"What's put-together? I was late for an appointment this morning. I barely made it out the door."

"That scarf, for instance." I sipped my ice-cold pale ale. "How the hell do you tie a scarf? When I try, it comes out looking like a rat's nest."

"Dressing is like selling real estate, Jaymie. You rave about the view to draw the customer's attention away from the termite holes." Tiff fixed me with an appraising glance. "Let's take you, for instance. You're pretty, anyone can see that. But your eyes are two different colors."

"It confuses the enemy." I picked up a crunchy slice of sourdough and spread it with a pat of pale yellow butter. "Stay back, or I'll fix you with the evil eye."

"Of course, asymmetry isn't necessarily unattractive," Tiff mused. "Like tucking your hair behind one ear, or wearing one earring." She set the spoon on the edge of her bread plate. "Listen, sweetie. I can give you the name of a woman who will make you over. Jennifer's an artist, an absolute *artist*, I swear."

"Thanks but no thanks." I leaned back in my chair as the

waiter set a tossed salad in front of Tiffany and a tuna melt with fries in front of me. The aroma was to-die-for.

"How's work?" I asked, to change the subject.

"Work's fine, you know? But prices are still slightly depressed. Believe me, we can't climb out of this recession fast enough." She speared a curly leaf with her fork. It looked just like a weed growing in my yard.

"But my work is boring, Jaymie. I want to hear about yours. The Aquarium Murders, I hear they're calling them now. Were they committed for money or for love? It's got to be one of those two, right?"

"Not necessarily." I felt sorry for Tiff, having to munch away like a rabbit. My tuna melt was living up to its name, melting on my tongue.

"No? What else then?"

"Wounds and resentments." I dabbed at my mouth with my napkin. "Maybe revenge."

"Revenge? That's bad. 'If you embark on a journey to seek revenge, dig two graves.'"

"What?" I lowered my fork. "Who said that?"

"Confucius, sweetie. And he was usually right."

"Tiff, I know you practice tai chi. But Confucius? You don't seem like the type."

"Chinese school. Every Saturday for five years when I was a kid, Mandarin lessons at the Salinas Confucius Center in Chinatown. I can't speak more than a few words of Mandarin, but those sayings? Let's just say Confucius kind of sticks with you."

I sat back in the chair and stared at my half-eaten lunch. *I* wanted revenge. Revenge for my brother's death. According to Confucius, I was digging my own grave. And I didn't doubt what Tiffany had said: Confucius was usually right.

"Jaymie, I'm sorry." Tiff's gold bangle rang against the tabletop as she reached out to touch my wrist. "Did I say something to upset you?"

"No. I'm fine." I pasted on a smile. "Listen, can I show you something? I've got a photo I'd like you to take a look at. It's of a flower I can't identify." Before Tiff had transformed into a real estate agent, she'd owned a florist shop. I figured it was worth a shot.

"Oh, so that's why you called me for lunch! Sweetie, do you ever stop working?" Tiff took the phone from my hand and peered at the photo. "Something half dead, that's for sure. Kind of looks like a plumeria blossom." She touched her finger to the screen.

"But here, in the next photo, it looks like it's orange and blue. I've never seen a plumeria that color." She handed me back the phone. "Now you've got me curious. Hold on."

She pulled the latest iPad from her black patent bag, tapped away, and peered at the screen.

"Hm. How about that. 'Plumeria, *Eternal Flame*. Rare in cultivation. From Madagascar.'" She handed me her device. "Is it a clue?"

"It might be." I studied the picture. Sure enough, it looked like a match.

"This detective business is fun! Too bad there's no money in it." Tiff slipped her iPad into her purse and closed it with a loud snap. "I have to run in five, Jaymie. So tell me, how's that dishy boyfriend of yours?"

"Ex, Tiff. You know Mike's an ex."

"Whatever you say, sweetie. Whatever you say."

The next morning I gave a guilty glance to my trusty old Schwinn as I passed by the breezeway. I told myself I needed the El Camino today, especially as the afternoon would be hot. Truth was, I was getting soft.

The old redwood doors squealed on their hinges as I propped them back. Dex pushed in ahead of me when I opened the driver's-side door. This time, quick to accommodate, he zipped across to the passenger seat.

I backed out of the tight little garage and turned the Camino so that it pointed downhill. Then, just as I did every morning, I flipped down the visor and spoke to the snapshot of Brodie.

"Another day, brother. I'll make this one count."

Five minutes later I arrived at 101 West Mission. I found a spot right out in front, two cars down from Gabi's big old station wagon. I hopped out, then walked around and let Dex out at the curb. I had a lot to tell Gabi. Hopefully she'd stopped by the Rosarita Bakery on her way in.

Dex pushed into the shrubbery the minute we entered the overgrown courtyard. I heard him crashing around, but thankfully there was no yelping. I didn't need a trip to the vet's, not today. Dex felt it was his job to purge the courtyard of cats, and not all the feral felines chose to turn tail.

I walked around the stand of giant bird-of-paradise plants which hid Suite D from view. There was my business partner, bent over with a dustpan in one hand and a whisk broom in the other. The office wastebasket stood beside her.

"Morning, Gabi. How's the war on dirt coming along?"

She said nothing in reply, didn't straighten up or look at me. Not a good sign.

Gabi was sweeping up broken glass. Splashes of water darkened the tiled steps, and a squashed pink rosebud lay on the path. The flower looked as if someone had ground it under the heel of a shoe.

"Angel's latest offering? That's too bad. What knocked it over?"

Gabi looked up at me from the corner of her eye. "What knocked it over? My foot. My foot knocked it over on purpose."

I saw how furious she was. In fact, I'd never seen her so angry. I closed my mouth, nodded and waited.

"Broken glass is dangerous," she muttered. "So I guess I gotta pick it up."

Gabi swept up the remaining shards and emptied the dust-pan into the wastebasket. Then, she straightened.

"You want something, Miss Jaymie? 'Cause I'm really mad right now. You don't wanna talk to me."

"OK. For how long?" An angry Gabi was a force of nature. Best to go with the flow.

"Maybe a week, maybe more. Maybe a really long time."

"Whatever you say." Edging around her, I climbed the steps and entered the office. I deposited my messenger bag on the kitchen table and began to make coffee.

"I'm coming in now," Gabi yelled from the front porch. "You want this perro inside?"

"Yes, please. If you don't mind."

A moment later the screen door banged. Dex skittered into the kitchen and dove under the table. Dogs know forces of nature when they encounter them, too.

By this time, of course, I'd figured it out. Angel and Gabi were having a lovers' spat. And Gabi was experiencing a super hard bounce, having dropped from such an elevated pink cloud.

I'd reconciled myself to a week or more of towering silence when, ten minutes later, Gabi stomped into the kitchen. "No pastries. I am too mad to go to the bakery today."

"That's fine. We don't need pastries every morning."

"Why shouldn't we have them every morning!" she exploded. "Just 'cause I find out Angel's a liar, he's been lying to me all the time, why shouldn't we have some pastries? Huh, tell me that!"

"Fair enough, if you put it that way—"

"I'm gonna tell you, Miss Jaymie. I'm gonna tell you all about it, what he told me last night." She paused for dramatic effect. "That man, he told me he is a citizen."

Shit! Suddenly I wanted to be somewhere else, anywhere else.

"Gabi," I ventured, "is that so bad? Come on, you love the

guy. And if you two get married, well, then you could apply for—"

"Stop!" Gabi pressed her hands to her ears. "I told you, Miss Jaymie, I told you a long time ago. Just like I told *him* when I met him! I don't want no man who's a citizen. Angel will always think he gives me something important, you know? We won't be *equal*. But worse, way worse: he lied to me. OK, he didn't say 'Gabi, I got no papers.' No, he just kept quiet about it. That's still lying, Miss Jaymie! So how can I trust him, a man like that? I never can know if he is lying or telling the truth!"

Panting from exertion, Gabi paused for breath. Dexter took advantage of the moment of silence to creep out from under the table and dash into the front office.

I decided it was time to take my whipping. I pushed back my chair and rose to my feet. "Gabi, I have to apologize."

She narrowed her gaze. "Oh? Miss Jaymie, what did you do?"

"I told Angel he should tell you the truth. He wanted to tell you, but he was worried how you'd take it. Apparently with good reason," I added.

"No. I do not believe it." Gabi tilted her chin and drew herself up to her full height, five foot flat. "My business partner and my boyfriend, having a secret behind my back."

"Gabi, that's not—"

"I'm gonna go walk on the beach," she said with dignity. "I gotta think hard about this."

Head held high, she left the room. A minute later, the screen door slammed. Then it banged open.

"By the way, you gonna put some water in that coffeemaker, or do you wanna burn down the office?"

Only then did I noticed the smell of burning wire. As my hand reached for the Off switch, I heard a sharp *pop*.

The screen door slammed shut once more, and the office

was quiet. Except for a crackling sound from the coffeepot, everything was still.

Fueled by the fury of a woman scorned, Gabi must have caught a low tide and marched all the way from Butterfly Beach to Goleta. Three hours later, she still hadn't returned.

The office was getting me down. It was quiet, too quiet. For once, I was glad when my cell jangled in my pocket.

"Jaymie, it was *so* cool," Claudia effused into the phone. "BJ took me out to UC, to meet this administrator who knows BJ's parents. I told her I want to go there when I get out of high school. They need Hispanic students real bad—she almost wet her pants."

"I guess that means you aren't dropping out of school on your fifteenth birthday, like you planned?"

"Uh—maybe not. Just so you know, I didn't tell BJ about that idea."

"I won't mention it. Anyway, it sounds like your plans are changing. Glad to hear it."

"Hey, you know me. I always keep my options open."

I wasn't sure that spending a good part of her freshman year in juvie had been "keeping her options open." But the last thing I wanted to do was dampen the kid's enthusiasm.

"So tell me. Did you find out anything?"

"Yeah we did. BJ told this librarian we needed to do some research. Guess what, she gave him a special library pass cause his parents are professors. We looked through at least a hundred issues of old college newspapers, they've still got it all on microfiche."

"And?"

"And we read every article about the antiwar protests in the spring semester of 1970, I think there was around eighteen or twenty of them. A lot of it was repeat info, but we got some good stuff. See, we figured out the paper couldn't legally print the names of the students who were suspects in Hobson's death, because nobody was ever charged. But the paper published articles about the protest leaders, and then they put those articles right next to the ones about Hobson and the fire. BJ and me, we think the paper was kinda telling the readers who might have torched the rental office. Who was guilty, you know? And Jaymie, guess what."

"I can't imagine," I obliged. "You'll have to tell me."

"Skye's grandfather was one of the leaders. Actually, the main one."

I wasn't completely surprised, or even sure what it meant. But the news sent a shiver through me.

"Good detective work, huh?"

"Yeah, it is. Listen, did you copy everything?"

"Sure. Hey, are you at the office right now? Do you want me to drop the stuff by?"

"When do you get out of school?"

"Any time I want, woman. Ain't like the school's got bars or nothin'. I'm at the Hamburger Habit right now."

"I thought the high-school campus was closed during the lunch hour."

"I didn't see no CLOSED sign."

I knew I shouldn't contribute to the delinquency of this minor. But I felt frustrated and stalled, and I needed to move on with the case. Besides, I was starved. "Have any money on you?"

"Some. I'll have more after you pay me."

"I paid you three days ago, Claudia. Now order me a teriyaki burger, and get up here on the double."

Chapter Eighteen

Fifteen minutes later the screen door crashed back against the wall. I looked up from the kitchen table as Claudia wheeled her yellow and orange bike inside the office and leaned it against Gabi's desk.

"Hey, Jaymie. Where's the witch? Did you fire her like you shoulda done a long time ago?"

"Claudia. Maybe you should give Gabi a chance."

"What for? We're the opposite." Claudia swung her massive backpack off her narrow birdlike shoulders and carried it into the kitchenette. "She wants to Clorox the whole world. Me, I like it dirty."

"All right, grubby girl. Come in and show me what you've got."

"First, I got this." Claudia opened the pack, removed a wrapped burger, and tossed it over to me.

"Thanks. I owe you."

"Three-forty-nine. Got some tape? I'm gonna do what you do, Jaymie. Tape all my stuff to the wall."

I bit into the juicy burger and studied the grainy pictures and articles as they went up one by one. And I saw what Claudia meant: the university paper had paired half a dozen articles about the protest and its leaders with others about Gary Hobson's death and the rental agency fire.

I polished off the burger and rinsed my hands at the sink, then walked over and scanned the copies more closely. The young and handsome Rod Steinbach was oft-photographed and quoted. "We will keep pressing until our demands are met . . . the fascist university machine will have to deal with us sooner or later . . . the military-industrial complex includes the University of California. . . ." Then, as now, the man apparently loved to hear himself talk.

It wasn't until the final page went up on the wall that I spotted what I was looking for. It was a photocopy of six young women seated around an outdoor table. One of the women was Alice Steinbach. Another, seated in the center of the group, was the unidentified woman in BJ's photo: Rod's partner. The accompanying article was titled "Women in Protest."

"Bingo." I leaned close to read the caption. "Alice Tanaka, secretary. Rachel Berger, chair, Women's Committee. Yep. That's her."

"Her? Who's her?"

"The fourth person, the woman who was with Steinbach the night of the fire."

"Rachel Berger, huh? She looks kinda hot." Claudia turned to me. "So we did it, right? We figured out who she is."

"We're halfway there," I conceded. "We need to find out where Rachel Berger is now."

"That's a good job for me. Jaymie, can you switch on the computer? La Bruja won't give me the password."

It only took five minutes for Claudia to deliver the unwelcome news.

"I can tell you exactly where Berger is," she called from the front room. "Plot 34 North, six feet under. Fresno Cemetery."

"Damn!" Disappointment dropped like a lead sinker in my chest. "When did she die?"

Claudia entered the kitchenette with a printout in hand, and parked her tiny butt on the edge of my table. "About a year ago. She was *Dr.* Rachel Berger. Survived by a sister, a brother, and a shitload of nieces and nephews."

I wasn't ready to give up. "Does it say where the sister and brother live?"

She peered at the printout. "The brother, David Berger, lives in Boston. The sister lives in Fresno. Her name's Judith Rosenfeld."

I ran a fingernail along the wood grain of the desktop. "Tell you what. You get back to school. I'll pull up a phone number and address for Judith. Maybe Rachel confided in her about the past."

"I know what you're thinking." Claudia pulled the cord on her backpack and knotted it shut. "You're gonna try and prove Skye's grandfather set the fire back then. Maybe he did. But what does that have to do with the murders we're trying to solve?"

"I don't know how they're linked," I admitted. "Rod Steinbach had no apparent reason to kill Cheryl Kerr, and Skye was the last person in the world he'd have murdered. Still, something tells me there's a connection between the present and the past. At this point, all I know is Rod Steinbach's not the upstanding marine biologist and civic-minded fellow he seems."

Claudia hoisted the pack. "We're done, right? I'm takin' off. There's a movie at the Arlington I wanna see."

"No you don't. You're going back to school. We'll toss your bike in the Camino and I'll drop you off. I'm going down to Hard Body Gym."

"Hey, what are you gonna do at the gym? Maybe I'll tag along. Are you going to work out or maybe *pick up* a hard body? I'd like a hard body right now."

"You're too young for hard bodies, child." I reached for my messenger bag. "Besides, you're bluffing."

Just then the door squeaked open. "Miss Jaymie? It's me—"

Gabi appeared in the kitchenette doorway. "Miss Jaymie, I'm sorry. I—" Her eyes settled on Claudia, and she stopped.

"I'm outta here. I don't need no ride." Claudia hopped off the table. "See ya, Jaymie—good brainstorming session." She tilted her chin and looked over at Gabi. "You can go home, take a rest. Jaymie and me, we've practically got the case solved."

Gabi looked stricken. Her big purse fell to her side. She didn't even react as Claudia bumped her on her way out.

"Hi, Gabi! I hope you had a nice walk on the beach," I began.

"Mr. Thaw, he's having a party tomorrow. I shoulda cleaned him last week, I got way behind."

"Gabi, come on. Just now, what Claudia said—"

"Miss Jaymie? I gotta go clean." She hefted her heavy bag to her shoulder again, and walked back out the door.

I'd decided there was no point in approaching Rod Steinbach. Even if I were able to corner him, I'd never be able to extract anything out of the guy—he was too self-controlled. I didn't expect his wife to be a pushover either, but with Alice Steinbach, I figured I had a fighting chance.

Around 1:45 that afternoon I hopped in the Camino and headed downtown to Hard Body Gym. I found a park facing the front doors, rolled down all the windows and relaxed.

A steady trickle of gym rats flowed in and out of the portals to fitness. Maybe I should join, I mused, work on the old solar plexus. Yeah, I should. Just not today.

At 1:55 I slid down in my seat. Right on schedule, a newish gray Volvo had glided into the gym parking lot. Silver-haired Alice sat at the wheel.

I watched as she got out of the car and crossed the lot. Alice wore a charcoal and fuchsia tracksuit with matching gym shoes. With her smart geometric haircut and confident stride, she looked like a cover girl for *AARP Magazine*.

After a few minutes I tucked my phone in my jeans pocket, hopped out of the Camino, and set out after my quarry.

Hard Body wasn't messing around. Their security was tighter than a bank's.

"I'm interested in joining," I said to the pert young woman at the front desk. "Mind if I look around?"

"You'll need to sign in. And show me your ID. Would you like a tour?"

"I don't really have time. But I'll know if it's for me once I look. I just need to—ah—see what equipment you've got." I wasn't much of a gym person. I preferred to take my exercise in the great outdoors.

She studied my license and compared me with my picture, taking her time. "Hey, it's not the Pentagon," I quipped.

The young woman frowned. "Here's a map, and here's your temporary pass. Stick it somewhere on your top." Then she fake-smiled. "Enjoy!"

"Will do." I grimaced as I peeled the back off the fluorescent orange sticker and pressed it to my T-shirt. I love California—it's home. I just wish my fellow citizens would deep-six our state's nauseous motto: *enjoy.*

Now, where was Alice likely to go? I stepped away from the desk and studied the map. I noticed a space labeled *Women's Weight Room* and figured it was worth a shot. I pushed through a set of glass doors and headed down a tiled corridor.

Unlike several other rooms I passed, the women's weight room had no windows looking out to the hallway. A plaque on the door bore the image of a curvy female silhouette. Working out, apparently, would give you very large breasts.

Alice was walking rapidly on a treadmill set up on the far side of the room. She gave a start when our eyes connected. But she recovered, looked straight ahead, and strode on. I wove through the equipment, keeping my eyes on my prey.

"Hi, Mrs. Steinbach." I tried on a nice smile.

"Excuse me." Alice didn't miss a step. "I'm focusing, if you don't mind."

"Not at all. How funny to bump into you. I was just thinking we need to chat." I spoke loudly, raising my voice above the clatter of the treadmill in the concrete-walled room.

She glanced at my jeans. "You don't look like you're here to work out."

"Oh. Well, I didn't have my gym clothes with me, but I just got the urge." Did people still say "gym clothes," I wondered? I was pretty sure I'd last used those words in what we used to call junior high.

"You and I have nothing to 'chat' about." Alice kept on power walking. Her face was composed and her breathing was steady. Only a light beading of sweat on her forehead revealed her heart rate was up.

"Actually, we do." I opened my messenger bag and withdrew the photo I'd obtained from BJ. "I came across something, Mrs. Steinbach. An old picture of you."

"Please let me get on with my day. I don't—" I held it up in front of her eyes.

Alice stared at the picture. Then, she stumbled. I caught her elbow, and she righted herself on the belt.

"Mrs. Steinbach? Maybe you should switch that off for a minute."

Alice pushed a button and the machine ground to a halt. She reached over and snatched the copy from my hands. Her face was red.

"You—what—dug up some old photo, from college? You really are pathetic. Our grandson's killer has been caught. Go away, leave us alone."

"John Tactacquin didn't murder Skye. I know that for certain."

"I don't believe you." She held the photo out to me with two fingers, as if it were dirty. "Take it, go."

"Sure. But first, I have a question. You see, it's confusing. When I look at this photo, I see two obvious couples. But the curious thing is that you and Neil Thompson formed one of the couples, didn't you? And Rod, your husband, was with this other woman here."

"Mind your own business," she blazed.

"If you say so." I slipped the sheet of paper back into my bag. "Oh—you don't happen to remember the name of the woman, do you?"

"I have absolutely no idea who she was. Someone who had a crush on Rod, I suppose. It happened a lot."

"Not good enough, I'm afraid. You know perfectly well who Rachel Berger was, since she was Rod's lover at the time. No wife forgets something like that about her husband's past."

Her upper lip curled slightly as she stepped off the treadmill. She walked over to her bag and pulled out her phone. "I'm calling the front desk."

"No need. I'll go. But what are you hiding? That's what I want to know."

A burly security guard approached me out in the hall. "You come from the women's weight room?"

"Yeah, you better get on in there. Somebody's having a big hissy fit. They're fighting over whose turn it is on the Stair-Master."

"Girl fights. I hate them," he groaned.

The next morning Gabi arrived late. I watched as she rummaged around in her purse, removing a pound of bagged coffee and a small paper sack.

"I'm glad to see you. I've missed you, you know."

"Really? No, I don't think so."

"Hey, come on. This office is lonely without you."

Gabi looked at the wall crowded with papers, then met my gaze. "I was here yesterday, remember? I saw you got somebody else to help you now."

"Gabi, come on. Claudia's just pulling your chain."

"Huh? Pulling my what?"

"I just mean she's trying to get your goat."

"What are you talking about? I ain't got no goat, not in Santa Barbara. Don't you know nothing about goats, Miss Jaymie? You can't keep them in a backyard like a dog, you know."

I knew Gabi understood perfectly well this wasn't about goats, or chains either. She was in no mood for nonsense just now.

"Sit down." I pulled out a kitchen chair for her. "I'll make the coffee, for once. Guess what? Last night I bought a new pot."

Without a word of protest, Gabi did as I asked. She glanced once at the loose papers mounded on the tabletop, then looked away.

Five minutes later I set a steaming mug of coffee before her, and then a pastry oozing with chocolate. "Here, just the way you like it: three sugars, no cream."

Gabi frowned at the pastry as if it were poison.

"Just listen to me. Claudia is helpful. She knows her way around a computer. And I want to support her because of what happened to Lili." Gabi still said nothing, just bent her head to the mug and took a delicate sip.

"You and I know she won't be here forever. She'll move on in her life soon enough. This operation—we're the heart of it, you and I."

Gabi cradled the warm mug in her hands. "I . . . I know that."

"So is this really about Claudia? Or is it more about Angel?"

Gabi opened her mouth to speak, then closed it. Then she opened it again. "One time in my life! Just *one time* in my life I meet somebody, a man. And then he does that. You know, what he did."

"Angel didn't want to lose you, Gabi. He knew you didn't want a man with papers. But he wanted *you*, so he just kind of— hid the fact."

"Hid the fact?" She raised her face and looked at me. Her eyes were wet with tears. "I don't like it that Angel has papers, but I guess it's OK. What is not OK? He told me a lie."

"Lies are hard to take," I admitted.

"Especially for me. I guess I never told you this, 'cause it's personal and this is a place of business, you know? I had a good father, but he died when I was six. He fell off a horse and broke his neck. Then my mother, she married a borracho—you know, a drunk. He hit me every day, my brother Eddie and me. My mother, she always said we would leave him, but we never did. She had more kids. El Borracho never hit them—only Eddie and me. Every day he hit us, sometimes with a stick, sometimes with his fist. And every day our mother said we would run away soon. That went on for five years."

"I'm so sorry, Gabi." I reached down and gave her a hug, but Gabi didn't respond.

"That man, one day he fell down some steps and broke his neck. And I'm sorry to say this but thanks to God, three weeks later he died. And then we came to Santa Barbara, and that's another story." Gabi rose to her feet. "I'm just telling you, Miss Jaymie, that's all. I'm a strong woman, I don't feel sorry for myself."

"I know you don't, Gabi. And now I understand why you work so hard at being positive." I watched as she opened a cupboard, pulled out a canister of cleanser, and shook the white powder all over the spotless enamel sink.

"Look, Gabi. What you and Angel do is none of my business. But just so you know, this agency is chaos without you. You bring it order and peace."

Gabi stopped scrubbing and turned to look at me. "Are you just saying that, Miss Jaymie? 'Cause I don't want no more lies."

"I swear to you, Gabriela Martinez Gutierrez, I meant every word I just said."

"Gabriela *Rufina* Martinez Gutierrez," she corrected. "You know, it is important to get the little things right. I wanted to tell you, I was looking at the electricity bill, and I saw they made a mistake and charged us one dollar and seventy-nine cents too much. Now when I called them up they said . . ." She looked over at me and caught my smile.

"Gabi, I need you. Please don't ever forget."

"I know you do. Miss Jaymie? You and me, we make a good team."

The El Camino slipped down Highway 46 into the giant's skillet that is the southern San Joaquin Valley. I put my finger to the window, felt the blistering heat through the glass, and blessed the vehicle's interim owner for installing air-conditioning. Dexter was comfortably curled up on the floor on the passenger's side, cool as an Eskimo's dog under the vent.

Dex had once again jumped in at the last minute and refused to get out. Ever since the cow dog had lost a hind leg, I'd found it hard to say no. Naturally, he took full advantage of my weak-mindedness.

"It's going to be hot as hell in Fresno, Dex. I won't be able to leave you out in the car."

He lifted one round eyebrow and let it fall, as if to say, "So?"

"I'll tell you 'so.' I'm going to have to ask Judith Rosenfeld to let you inside. Let's just hope she likes dogs. If she does, you could be a plus. If she doesn't, having you along could mess up the interview."

We drove through the vast empty fields of burnt stubble. It was hard to believe all this had been lakes and marshes once upon a time, before the Yankees arrived and dammed the big rivers. Now the southern San Joaquin Valley was the essence of dryness, scorched earth.

The interim owner had also outfitted Dudette with a top-flight sound system. I switched on the only CD I owned, the

only one worth listening to, the Eagles' *Greatest Hits*. And for a
time I enjoyed myself as I cruised across the great state of California, listening to unmatchable music. Then that song came
on, the one Mike used to sing to me: *Des-per-ah-do* . . . I punched
the song off in midphrase, before I could get emotional.

We drove on in silence for a while, with the whir of the AC
for company. Ten minutes later, I got a call.

"Jaymie, what should we do?" Donna Tactacquin sounded
scared. "The trial's only two weeks away. And the lawyer we hired,
Mr. Gamboa? He thinks John did it. He doesn't come right out
and say it, but I can tell."

I hadn't told the police about John's alibi. I knew Larry Millar had contacted Gamboa, and I figured it was up to the attorney to do what he thought best with the information. Besides, I
kept thinking that if I could just identify the killer, John would
be set free. Then he could tell his wife about Larry Millar in his
own good time, or he could *not* tell her. Tactacquin's infidelity
was none of my business.

"I'm getting closer, Donna." I mentally crossed my fingers
to forgive myself for the fib. "It won't help to panic." Easy for
me to say.

"There's another thing, Jaymie. I'm worried about Taryn."

"Taryn? What do you mean?"

"She's really depressed. I'm having a hard time getting her
out of bed in the morning. And I just found out she's been cutting school."

"It's no surprise: she's been through a lot. You both have.
Hang in there, Donna. I'm putting together the puzzle, just a
few pieces left."

Bullshit, I admitted as I dropped the phone down on the
passenger seat. The truth was, the puzzle was a jumble. Lots of
loose pieces, and none seemed to fit.

Chapter Nineteen

Judith Rosenfeld lived in one of Fresno's old grande dames on Van Ness Avenue, a two-story pink-and-cream-colored Mediterranean-style house built in the 1920s. I curved up the drive through heavily irrigated lawns and flowering crepe myrtles, and parked just past the front door.

"Remember what I said about good behavior, Dex? Double underline that."

The heat slapped me in the face as I stepped out of the car. It was at least 108 in the shade, probably more. And to think I'd been complaining about a heat wave in Santa Barbara.

Dex and I walked up to the massive door set in the thick stuccoed walls. I raised my hand to lift the knocker and looked down at the heeler. "Sit," I suggested. "And pretend you're well-bred." He stared me down, then complied.

Judith Rosenfeld was younger than I expected, perhaps fifty-five. She wore a perfectly pressed blue linen pantsuit and old Taxco jewelry, turquoise mounted in darkened silver.

"Ms. Zarlin, hello. I'm Judith Rosenfeld." She extended a manicured hand.

"I'm pleased to meet you." And then, because her glance had moved on to Dex, I explained.

"I'm sorry, but it's so hot out. Do you have a cool corner

inside for my dog? Dexter's under orders to be on his best behavior."

Judith laughed, and the tight set of her jaw relaxed. "Oh, I'm not worried about that. He'll behave when he meets Ursula." She stepped to one side. "Come in, both of you. We'll get a bowl of water for Dexter. Would you like an iced tea?"

"That would be great. It was a long drive."

I followed Judith down the wide tiled hall to the back of the house. The interior was cool and dark. But when I stepped though a doorway into the kitchen area, I was met with a riot of color.

A wall of glass looked out on a garden lined with massive oleanders flowering in shades of pink and red. The blossoms glowed in the afternoon light. Here and there a white or pale yellow specimen offset the saturated color.

I heard a click-clack on the tiles. A bear of a dog, the offspring of a Saint Bernard crossed with something even furrier, ambled in from another part of the house. She stopped to examine Dex. Dex, no fool, didn't move a muscle.

"This is Ursula?"

"Yes, that's Ursula." Judith smiled. "We got her as a pup. At seven weeks we could already see what a monster she would become."

I watched as the two canines greeted each other. Dex was most certainly on his best behavior. Understandable, since Ursula's mouth looked bigger than his head.

Judith found a bowl in the cupboard, filled it with water at the sink, and put it down on the floor. "The only thing Ursula insists on is that no dog touch her bowl, not even her water bowl. I hope Dexter will oblige her."

"I'm pretty sure he'll cooperate." Dex was politely sniffing the mammoth canine. Ursula ignored him, flopped down on the tiled floor, and rested her massive head on her paws.

"Let's sit here in the nook. You know, we have this big old

house, but somehow we always crowd into this one little spot. Rachel always said—" She stopped and stared out the window.

"I still miss my big sister." Her mouth tightened again. "After the boys moved out and my husband died, Rachel moved in with me. We became close, closer than we ever were as children. She's been gone for just over a year now, and I still can't believe it."

We sat in comfy lounge chairs, facing each other. "I know how you feel," I replied. "My brother died three years ago. And after a while . . ." I searched for the right words, but failed to find them.

"I'm sorry about your brother. What were you going to say? I'd like to hear."

"It's just that after a while, I started to be afraid I wouldn't be able to remember him very well. It's the little things, you know?" I met her eyes. "They start to slip away."

"Yes, I know what you mean." Judith folded her hands in her lap and studied them. "I want to honor my sister's wishes, Miss Zarlin. That's why I agreed to see you. I'm not entirely sure why you want to see me, but I had the sense on the phone— well. I had the sense I could talk to you."

Judith was beautiful. Her light green eyes were wide-set, her cheekbones sculptured and high. I hadn't noticed her beauty at first, maybe because of her obvious tension.

"Please, call me Jaymie."

"And call me Judith. Just don't call me Judy, if you don't mind."

"I won't." I smiled at her, wondering how to begin. "As I explained on the phone, we recently had two related murders in Santa Barbara. Unfortunately, the wrong person was arrested. That's where I come in. It's a long story, but the family of the man arrested has hired me to find out the truth."

"The truth." She paused. "Some people like to be sophisticated and say there's no such thing as the truth. I don't agree." I could see Judith was choosing her words carefully. This wasn't a woman who spoke idly.

"Rachel—my sister—wouldn't have agreed either. She was a good, good woman, Jaymie. Before I say anything more, I want you to know that."

So Judith Rosenfeld did have something to tell me. Something difficult, something that might not put her sister in a good light.

"I'm sure she was. Rachel was a medical doctor?"

"Yes, an OB/GYN. She had a practice here in town, but from the very beginning, she donated a sizable portion of her time to the clinics for the field-workers, on the west side of the valley. She was dedicated, very giving." Judith laughed a little. "I told her she was lucky to be Jewish. Otherwise, she'd have become a nun." Abruptly, her smile disappeared. "Of course, there was a reason Rachel was like that."

She rose to her feet. "But I'm forgetting your iced tea. Sugared?"

"No, thanks. Just plain." I was about to tell her not to bother, but I stopped myself. Judith needed to tell her story at her own pace. Rushing the conversation wouldn't help.

She walked into the kitchen area to prepare the drink. A few minutes later she returned to the nook, handing me a tall glass of tea with a slice of lemon wedged on the lip. She slipped back into her chair.

"Did I interrupt you, Jaymie? I think you were talking about several murders in Santa Barbara."

I set down the drink on the coffee table between us. Then I withdrew a sheet of paper from my messenger bag. "I'd like you to take a look at this old snapshot."

"Ohh . . ." A funny little noise escaped from Judith's mouth as she stared at the photo. It sounded like a kind of giving in.

"I—I'm not surprised. When you called, I guessed this had something to do with what happened back then."

"I think you must know Rod Steinbach." I was careful to keep my voice level. "It looks like Rachel and he were a pair. Do you know the other two people in the photo?"

"Oh, yes. Neil Thompson and Alice Tanaka. They were going to be best man and bridesmaid for Rod and my sister." She bent closer over the photo, almost drinking it in.

"I was twelve at the time. Rod and Rachel had planned for a simple outdoor wedding, up in Yosemite. And I was part of the wedding party, a junior bridesmaid, you know? I was so excited." Judith looked up at me. Her expression changed.

"Tell me. These murders. Do they have something to do with Rod Steinbach?"

"I think they might."

Judith laid the photo on the coffee table. "Then it's time for me to talk—for Rachel's sake. You see, when my sister learned the cancer was terminal, she decided to speak out and tell the truth. But I'm afraid the end came more quickly than any of us expected."

I watched as Ursula, sensing her mistress's distress, lumbered over and pushed her big muzzle into Judith's delicate hands.

"After Rachel died, I decided I would keep her secret. I didn't want people to think badly of her, you know? But your phone call—it made me realize I have to carry out my sister's intentions, even if it tarnishes her name."

"You've given this some thought."

"Not as much as you might think, Jaymie. There was no need—it was clear." Judith smiled wistfully as she patted her dog. "Ursula knows I'm upset. Rachel was like that, too. She always tried to take care of me."

I knew I was about to hear something important. But I had no urge to rush the woman. A truth that had been hidden for nearly half a century could take its time to rise to the light.

"Well. It's time to tell Rachel's secret, and you're the person

to tell it to. Especially now that I've met you, I know it's right."
Judith rose to her feet again.

"Back in 1970 my sister was an activist against the Vietnam
War. She and Rod Steinbach shared political opinions—radical
opinions. Rachel was arrested, three times, for protesting. But
she was for nonviolence, always. I remember she and Rod argued about that. He thought the ends justified the means."

"Quite a few did, back then."

"Oh, violence was in the air. At any rate, their political dis-
agreements didn't seem to come between them. Rod was quite
handsome back then, and very persuasive. They became lovers.
And in the end Rachel agreed to help him firebomb a rental
agency office in Isla Vista. She told me it was the greatest mistake of her life. They did it at night, when the building was
empty—or so they thought."

"Gary Hobson," I said. "He was asleep upstairs."

"I'm afraid so. Rachel heard about the young man the next
morning. It was horrible, just horrible. He'd tried to get out, but
he only made it halfway down the stairs. And then—and then
my sister made another terrible mistake." Judith walked over to
the kitchen, turned around and paced back.

"Rachel wanted to turn herself in, but Rod wouldn't let her.
He said if she turned herself in she'd be implicating him too,
and also Neil and Alice, who were with them that night. He
argued Rachel had no right to do that."

"So she said nothing. Went on with her life."

Judith dropped into her chair. "Not at first. Rachel came
home to Fresno and worked in the canneries. I suppose you
could say she wanted to atone. Eventually she realized she could
help people if she went to medical school and doctored the
poor."

"And she dumped Rod, obviously."

"Immediately. He was unrepentant, you see—said the boy
was simply in the wrong place at the wrong time." She stroked

Ursula's ears. "Alice Tanaka took advantage of the vacancy and left Neil for Rod. Odd beginning for a marriage, but it seems to have worked out."

"Seems? What, have you had contact with them more recently?"

"Yes, I have. You see, when Rachel learned the cancer was terminal, she telephoned Neil and the Steinbachs. Rod and Alice made a special trip out to see her. Decent of them—they were living back East at the time. I think they were considering a move to California, but hadn't acted on it yet. And Neil came too, from Santa Barbara. They all visited with Rachel for over an hour."

I'd broken out in a sweat. "Judith, do you remember their visit?"

"Oh my, yes. I remember it clearly, because later that night, Rachel passed on. The oncologist had told us she had another four to six weeks, so it was a blow."

"Let me get this straight. The Steinbachs and Neil Thompson visited Rachel, and a few hours later she died?"

"Three or four hours later, I think. I wondered afterwards, was it a kind of letting-go?"

"Judith. Was Rachel on morphine?"

"Yes. The pain was—oh! Jaymie . . . what are you saying?"

"Was Rod Steinbach on his own with Rachel, at any point?" I tried to be gentle, but my voice sounded harsh.

"I don't know. I—I left them alone, the four of them. I thought it was best. Rachel had made up her mind to talk to the authorities about what happened back in 1970, and she wanted to explain her reasons. I thought . . . oh, God. He could have!"

"We can't know for sure."

"I went in to see her after they left, and Rachel was asleep, or so I thought. She never woke up. And some time in the night, she . . ."

I walked over and knelt beside Judith's chair. I wanted to

tell her it didn't matter, that Rachel would have suffered in the weeks left to her. That in a way Rod Steinbach had done her sister a favor, there were worse ways to go than overdosing on morphine. But the truth was, it did matter. Rachel Berger had been robbed of a precious month of her life.

I thought Judith would break into tears, but she didn't. Instead, she squeezed my hand.

Ten minutes later, Dex got up from the carpet and stretched. He somehow knew it was time to go.

"Just one more thing, Jaymie. I've been thinking since we talked on the phone." Judith went over to the kitchen island and picked up a pale blue envelope. "I'd like to hire you myself."

"Hire me? I'm afraid I'm pretty full up at the—"

"Wait. It's only a small matter—please, hear me out." She handed me the envelope. "Rachel didn't leave much money— she gave almost everything away to charities when she was alive. But as executor of her will, I've written out a check for the proceeds from the sale of her condo. Two hundred and twenty-three thousand dollars. I don't want to just mail it, you know? I'd like you to deliver it in person to Gary Hobson's heirs."

"So far I haven't—*Christ!*" There was a heavy knocking in my chest.

I'd glanced down at the envelope. And I'd read the names written there: *Helen Hobson*—and *Cheryl Hobson Kerr*.

I left the Eagles switched off on the drive home. I needed to think, and think hard.

My mind still whirled with the news: Gary Hobson's sister had been Cheryl Kerr. There was no doubt: Judith's attorney had researched the Hobson family before she'd drawn up the check.

I berated myself. I'd never wondered about Cheryl, whether she'd married, whether she'd once had another name. She'd seemed almost virginal, somehow.

I stared out the window. The flat landscape was empty,

unconscious as a surgical patient under the intense late-summer sun. Kind of like my brain lately.

Had Cheryl known Rod Steinbach was once a suspect in her brother's death? Probably the answer was yes. If so, how dismayed she must have been when Rod showed up, newly hired as a consultant at the aquarium. And how it must have infuriated her when he bore down hard, told her to lose weight and spruce herself up.

The highway twisted up out of the valley, heading into the San Andreas fault zone. Dexter whined and looked up imploringly from his spot under the vent.

"I know you hate the curves, Dex. Can't stop, though. Hold on and we'll be through this patch in a bit."

I hashed it all over again in my mind. And I wondered: had Cheryl threatened to reveal Rod's past? She'd been a timid woman, but even timid people can strike out when they're backed into a corner.

The phone rang, but I didn't look at it. A minute later a beep announced a message. I switched the phone off and pushed the distraction from my mind.

Yes. Rod could have shoved Cheryl over the side of the wet deck. But he hadn't killed his own grandson, surely. All the evidence suggested he'd loved Skye.

I stopped myself there. What the evidence showed was that Rod was proud of Skye, saw him as a chip off the old block. Narcissism wasn't love.

What if Skye had challenged his grandfather about the past, possibly armed with information received from Cheryl? Rod could have become furious, and he might have struck back.

Dexter was raking my trouser leg with his claws by the time we got to Cholame Junction.

I pulled in at the greasy spoon, switched off the ignition,

and braced myself. When I opened the door, the dry heat hit me like a board up the side of my head.

Dex didn't wait for me to lift him out. He tumbled to the ground, picked himself up and trotted over to the nearest Chinese Tree of Heaven. The gravel-strewn clearing was nearly surrounded by the weedy saplings.

I wandered over to the nearby James Dean Memorial. The actor had died a few hundred yards from here, wiped out on his motorcycle by a drunk driver. I sat down on an overturned cable spool in the sparse shade of a live oak, then switched on my phone.

The call I'd ignored was from Mike. His voice message was composed of four words: *Jaymie, please call me*. He didn't sound good.

Mike answered my call on the second ring. "Jaymie?"

"I got your message—what's up?"

"I'm in San Luis." I heard him draw in a breath. "Dad died an hour ago."

"But I—I was going to come up and see him again!"

Mike could have told me that was the dumbest and most self-centered thing he'd ever heard. But he was kind.

"Yesterday I told Dad you were thinking about him. He understood."

My throat constricted. I wanted to ask if Bill had suffered at the end, but I didn't. Best not to ask. "I'm so sorry, Mike. So, so sorry."

"I know. Me too." His voice was shaky. I could tell he'd been crying. "Jaymie, hold on a minute—"

I heard Trudy's voice in the background, Mike answering her.

"The undertaker's arrived. Jaymie—"

"Yes?"

"The funeral. Will you come up?"

I had questions I wanted to ask, like "What about Mandy,

won't she want to go?" Or even, "We aren't a couple anymore, do you think it's a good idea?" But this wasn't the time to ask stuff like that.

"Yes. Of course I'll be there. Your dad was so good to me."

We said goodbye. I walked over to the Camino, and retrieved Dexter's bowl from under the seat. I set it down in the strip of shade cast by the vehicle and poured half a bottle of water into it. I didn't have to call him over: Dex made a beeline.

A hot dry breeze stirred a nearby patch of rattlesnake grass. When Dexter finally stopped slurping, I could hear the rattle of the grass heads and the wind hissing in the saplings.

I tipped what water was left in the bowl onto the dry cracked ground. It was sucked up in an instant. A lizard skittered out of the grass, halted, and fixed me with a glittering eye.

The faint dark stain left by the water would be gone in a minute or less. Just about the length of time it took to be born, live out one's days, and die.

Chapter Twenty

I drove straight down to the marina when I got into town. It was late, and the sun had just plunged over the horizon's edge. The sunset was subdued, but a vast bronze mesh lay on the ocean.

The gate to the marina gaped wide open. A commercial fisherman pushed a plastic wheelbarrow down the narrow walk. It was loaded with small shiny fish, still twitching. The silver ellipses glistened in the twilight.

"Are you going to stand there all day?" The guy scowled.

Must have been a tough two hours before the mast. Dexter and I moved to one side.

Neil Thompson was washing down the *Lindy Sue*. He wore a dirty old canvas hat and black rubber boots, and held a thick hose in his hands. We studied each other for a moment, me on the dock, Thompson on the soaked deck. Finally he twisted a valve to close off the nozzle.

"I told you, I don't have anything else to say. Would you—well, would you just go away?"

"No," I called back. "No chance of that."

Thompson stared out to sea, then dropped the hose at his feet. He walked across the deck and up to me. We stood four feet apart, with a watery gap separating us. "You're harassing me," he tried. "I'm going to report you."

"Fine. But you might want to talk to me first."

"I've told you everything." Thompson's eyes were tinged red, maybe from the sun and salt air. "I'm sick of it all."

He wasn't the only one who was sick of this dance. I'd about had it up to here with Seaweed Man. "Look, let's cut the crap. I've just driven in from Fresno. You know who lives there? Judith Rosenfeld. And who is she? Rachel Berger's sister, that's who."

Neil hadn't expected this. His mouth flew open and he began to stammer. "N-nothing to—to do with me."

"Bullshit!" I was half pretending to be angry to rattle him, but on the other hand I was hot, bothered, and pissed off. "Rachel and Rod, you and Alice. Two couples, a sweet little foursome. But here's the bombshell, Neil. Ready for it? I know Cheryl Kerr was Cheryl Hobson. Gary Hobson, the young man who died in the fire? He was her brother."

But now it was my turn to be surprised. I saw the truth written in Neil Thompson's expression, heard it in his gasp: *this* he hadn't known.

"You're making it up. I don't believe you."

"It's a fact. What you believe doesn't matter."

Neil bent his head. The oily brim of his hat shaded his face from view. "I didn't want you to know about what happened back then. That part's true. Just didn't think it was any of your business. But, I swear to God. I never knew who Cheryl was."

"You worked with her for years. She never once mentioned her brother?"

"Never, I swear." He shook his head quickly, as if he had a fly in his face. "Cheryl never talked about anything personal. She mentioned her mother a few times, never said her name."

"Neil, listen to me." I made my voice friendly now, consoling. "I know Rod killed Gary Hobson all those years ago. He may not have intended to, but he did."

He kept his eyes on the deck. "That was never proved."

A powerboat ploughed through the water nearby. The wake hit the *Lindy Sue*, and she bobbed like a cork. Neil tottered.

"Why won't you leave me alone? Haven't you got anything better to do?"

"No, I don't. A double homicide has been committed under your watch—or hadn't you noticed? Skye and Cheryl's killer is at large."

"That's crap," Neil said stubbornly. "Tactacquin's guilty."

"I've got news for you. Someone's come forward. John Tactacquin has a solid alibi now, for both murders."

"Why should I believe you?"

"Don't. Like I said, what you decide to believe doesn't matter. And by the way, your little mop-up job at the scene of Skye's murder? Hardly an effort to spare the Steinbach's feelings, was it. No, it's looking more sinister now."

"I was just—just—"

A seagull swooped down and perched on the rail of the *Lindy Sue*. It let out the most god-awful, mocking squawk.

"Just what, trying to keep the hatches battened down?"

"All right! I didn't want the police to think Skye's death was anything but an accident. Don't you see? They would have focused on Rod, dredged it all up again. And not just Rod. They would have focused on all of us! What we did back then would have come out, been in the papers. It was an accident, that kid dying in the fire back in '70, but nobody would have seen it that way!"

"No. Oh, and besides: there's no statute of limitations for murder." I paused, then dropped the bomb.

"I'm not just talking about Hobson. I'm talking about Rachel's death, too."

"What? Rachel had cancer. Terminal. You—you—"

"Rachel had at least another month to live. You stole it from her. You dialed up the morphine, because she was going to tell the truth."

"Not me. I wouldn't!" His eyes brimmed with tears. "Maybe Rod. Rod and Alice, I left them alone with her."

"So maybe you didn't actually pull the trigger. But I think you knew."

Later that evening, I sank down in my old aluminum chaise and gazed out to the darkening water. The Channel Islands, ancient beasts of the sea, swam steadily north in the gathering dusk. The twinkling lights of the oil rigs lit their way.

I said a silent prayer for Bill Dawson, now gone from this world. Or maybe the prayer was for the rest of us, left behind.

I shut my eyes and let the night noises fill my ears. Insects clicked and sang, and a great horned owl boomed its loud yet velvety call. Now and then I could hear the high-pitched cheeps of tiny bats, not hunting but talking to one another.

I needed to phone Gabi, to let her know what I'd learned in Fresno. This was big, and she'd want to know.

I leaned back and slipped my hand in my pocket. *Uh-oh.* No phone.

I scrambled to my feet and checked all my pockets. Nada.

"Damn," I muttered aloud. I could go check in the Camino, and I would. But I was pretty sure I wouldn't find my cell there. I thought back to the last call I'd made. Mike. Mike, at Cholame Junction. When we'd finished I'd—well, shit. I'd set the phone down on the cable spool. Yep, and then I'd walked away.

I'd have to phone the Cholame greasy spoon in the morning, from the office. Transfer some cash, get them to retrieve my phone and send it along. In the meantime, the world would keep on spinning. Without a phone, I'd survive.

Gabi unlocked the door to her tiny apartment. She switched on the light, then shut and relocked the door.

She loved her apartment. She loved that it was all hers, hers alone. That was one good thing about not being with Angel anymore, she reminded herself. Now she'd get to stay in her own home forever, just like she wanted. And she wouldn't have to share it, either.

She dropped her heavy bag on the couch, went into the bedroom, and tugged off her tight pants. They kept shrinking in the dryer, and now they were so tight around the middle that she had to undo the top button whenever she sat down.

Gabi pulled her top over her head but didn't take off her bra, just in case a neighbor or somebody knocked on the door. It was late, but you never knew. She got her Hawaiian muumuu from the closet and slipped it on. She was tempted to lie down on the bed and relax. But thinking about Angel, even that little bit just now, made her feel depressed. So she decided to watch some TV.

Gabi had a bunch of telenovelas recorded and thought it would be good to watch one. All that drama and misery put her in a nice relaxed mood and made her forget her own problems. Soon, she would be ready for sleep.

She'd had dinner out, all alone, at Los Agaves. You had to treat yourself when you were sad. Her uncle's best friend worked there in the kitchen, and they always gave her almost double in amount, so she had food to bring home in a box for lunch the next day. This time she'd ordered the chiles rellenos, the best chiles rellenos this side of Guadalajara. That reminded her, the take-out box was still in her purse.

Gabi padded out to the living room, removed the food, and carried it to the refrigerator. The friendly little light came on when she opened the door, you could always count on it. Now she was getting in a happier mood. She wasn't hungry, but the pitcher of chilled sun tea caught her eye. She poured herself a glass, only small, so she wouldn't have to get up in the night.

It was late and she'd had a long day. Gabi had cleaned two big houses in the morning, one a two-story, so she'd had to lug the vac up and then back down, plus do the stairs. Then she worked at the office, making phone calls and paying bills. It was a good time to catch up, because Jaymie was away in Fresno.

And then, well, she hadn't wanted to quit. She felt bad whenever she thought about Angel, and work made her feel better. So Gabi had gone and cleaned one more house, the vacation rental on the Mesa. Lucky, the renters had left everything nice, washed the dishes and even vacuumed already. But even so, she was exhausted.

She dropped down on the couch and switched on the TV. In only ten minutes, her head lolled to one side. She pressed the off button on the remote and stretched out. Gabi knew she should get up and go to bed, but she was too tired to move. Another two or three minutes, and she was fast asleep.

A mariachi band woke her two hours later. It was playing near her feet, at the end of the couch. Confused, still half-asleep, she looked around for the radio . . . or maybe the TV was still on?

Then she realized the band was playing in her purse. She leaned down and reached inside it, blindly digging till her hand closed on her phone. "Hello? Who is this?"

"It's me," said a small faraway voice. "I can't talk loud."

"Claudia?" Of all the people who might have called her in the middle of the night, Claudia Molina was the least likely. "What did you wake me up for? Don't you know what time it is?"

"Jaymie. I gotta talk to Jaymie, I'm in trouble. But I called her number and nobody answered. I need help! I need help right away."

Now Gabi was wide awake. She stared at the blue light glowing on the DVD player. "Miss Jaymie went to Fresno this afternoon. She told me she was maybe gonna have to stay over night in a motel. Maybe she left her phone in the car, or—"

"Gabi." Now Claudia's voice was hoarse with fear. "I'm at the piñata party. They caught me listening, Vanessa and Port. Port said he's going to teach me a lesson. He's going to take me somewhere."

Claudia sounded terrified. And Gabi couldn't help it, her heart opened up. "Where are they gonna take you, mija. Tell me where."

"To the Chamber of Lust."

"The—the *what?*" Gabi's throat tightened.

"I don't have time to explain. I'm at the old Miramar Hotel."

"Shall I call the police?"

"No! I was in juvie for seven months! If they arrest me again, I'll—"

The phone went dead.

Gabi called the number back. It rang for two seconds, then stopped.

She sat there in the dark, focusing on the blue light. Thinking, thinking. The Chamber of Lust. Now she remembered how the piñata party worked. Yes she did. And there was no way she would let that girl, that girl who understood so little of life, be dragged into a room like that.

Miss Jaymie was still in Fresno. So that meant it was up to her. But she was fifty-one years old and five feet tall. Wherever she went in this town she got ignored. How was she gonna rescue Claudia? How was she even going to get into that room—that Chamber of Lust? She needed some kind of disguise.

She got to her feet, walked over and switched on the overhead light. That made the light in her brain come on too. She wasn't going to put on a costume. No, she was going to just be her usual invisible self.

Gabi knew exactly where the Miramar was. She used to work there years ago, before it closed down.

She steered her station wagon through the sagging gates of the abandoned resort. It was pitch black, no moon and two o'clock in the morning. Her headlights cut like Hollywood searchlights through the grounds.

The gardens, she noticed, were still kept up. But the buildings were dilapidated, spray-painted with graffiti. Sheets of plywood were nailed up over some of the windows and doors.

Gabi headed toward the ocean, winding through the maze. She turned a corner and came on the cars, maybe thirty of them, parked at the end of a cul-de-sac. She slowed down, trying to figure out the best place to leave the station wagon for a quick getaway.

She nearly had a heart attack a few seconds later, when a sharp rap sounded on her roof. She jammed on the brake and turned to see a face in her passenger's-side window. A mean man's face, not a kid's. The security guard.

"Open your window," he barked through the glass.

Gabi did as he ordered, the way any woman who cleaned for a living would do. She twisted away as a strong light slapped her in the face.

"This area's restricted. What are you doing here?"

She answered in Spanish, "I'm coming to clean."

"English," the man demanded. But he took the flashlight out of her face.

"Sorry my English is no good. Miss Vanessa call me to come and clean up a room."

"What, now?"

Gabi shrugged. "Yes Miss Vanessa said right away. She's gonna pay me extra, she said."

The guard shone his light through the back windows of the wagon. Gabi was confident her organized system of cleaning tools and supplies would impress.

"Park over there." The guard indicated a spot with his giant flashlight. "Take that walkway to the rooms at the back."

When Gabi got out of her car she could hear the sound of the waves at high tide, crashing against the cliffs. She opened the tailgate and took out just enough supplies to be convincing: a bucket on wheels and a mop, and, after a moment's careful thought, a spray bottle filled with industrial-strength ammonia.

To complete the picture, she tucked a rag into the waistband of her pants.

As she hurried along the stuccoed corridor, bucket in tow, she heard the noise. Drunken noise, crazy laughter, and something smashing. She couldn't hear the ocean now, even though she knew it was close, maybe only twenty or thirty yards away.

She turned a corner and there it was: the piñata party.

The old two-story "sea-view suites" wing ran along the edge of the cliff. Gabi counted five doors below and the same number at the upstairs level. More than enough rooms for seven deadly sins.

Windows were open and she could see and hear the partiers. But all the doors were shut, and several of the doors had guys standing in front, guarding access. Gabi felt like saying a prayer. But instead the song popped into her head:

> Dale, Dale, Dale.
> No pierdas el tino.

Gabi had a plan. And she would not lose her aim.

She straightened to her full height, stuck out her chin, and marched up to the line of hotel rooms. She scanned the faces of the entry guards, looking for the drunkest one.

He wasn't hard to find. A soft-looking boy in a pair of plaid Bermuda shorts with the fly hanging open. He was drinking from a big brown bottle, the kind you filled up at the brewery.

"Excuse me," she said. "I'm looking for the Chamber of Lust."

"You?" The kid burst into giggles and Gabi felt a spray of spittle hit her cheek.

"Hey," he called to another kid down the line, "she says she's looking for the Chamber of Lust!"

They both had a good laugh, and Gabi waited. When she had his attention again, she spoke politely but also very firmly, just the way she handled the rich kids in the houses she cleaned.

"Now you listen to me. Vanessa told me to go there. It's to clean up. What one is it?"

"Vannie said? Oh. It's—" and he craned his head, looking up. "It's that one up there, the one in the middle."

Gabi lugged the bucket, mop, and spray bottle up the rickety old stairs. She walked along the balcony, her heart in her throat.

The windows of the Chamber of Lust were boarded up. No one stood outside the door. But a rhythmic strobe light flashed through a gap at the threshold.

"*Dale, dale, dale*," Gabi murmured. Then she crossed herself. Because she wasn't sure what she was going to see.

She took a deep breath, and thumped on the door with the end of the mop. It opened immediately.

"No admittance—*huh?*" The boy blocking the door was having trouble focusing his eyes. "What do you want?"

"I'm coming in to clean. Miss Vanessa, she sent for me."

"Later, not now." And he started to shut the door.

"I'm sorry. Yes, now." Gabi dropped the mop, grabbed the spray bottle, stepped forward and sprayed the industrial-strength ammonia straight in his eyes.

As he screamed and fell back, she pushed her way in. And saw something she never wanted to see in her life, never ever again.

Claudia stood in the center of the room on a chair, surrounded by a dozen kids, boys and girls. And she was on her way to being totally naked. She had no shirt on and her jeans were pulled down around her ankles. Thank God she still had on a pair of boy's underpants. In the flash of the strobe light, Gabi saw steaks of tears on the girl's face.

The spray bottle was big, 32 ounces. Gabi walked up close and sprayed in the stupid drunk faces. Within thirty seconds everybody was screaming, clawing at their eyes. They were so drunk, most of them just fell down on the floor and squealed.

Claudia bent down and yanked up her jeans. Just as she stepped off the chair, a big guy with blond hair falling in his face caught her by the arm. Gabi stepped in and squirted him so many times it would have dropped an elephant. He staggered, reaching out blindly. "I'll kill you, bitch!" Gabi couldn't tell if he was yelling at Claudia or her.

Claudia grabbed Gabi's arm. "He means it," she cried.

Together they pushed their way out of the room. Gabi's trigger hand was at the ready, but the pandemonium was by now so great that no one paid them any attention.

"Let's get out of here," Claudia pleaded.

Together they raced down the steps. The occupants of the Chamber of Lust were staggering onto the balcony now, shouting and crying. Other doors were opening, the partygoers spilling out into the night.

Hand in hand, Gabi and Claudia ran through the passageway to the station wagon. They scrambled in and slammed the doors shut.

Gabi gripped the key. Her hands were shaking and she could barely fit it in the ignition. Finally she held her right hand with her left to steady it, slipped in the key, and started the car. She stepped on the gas too hard, and the engine roared.

The security guard started toward her, then thought better of it. That was a good decision, because Gabi wasn't stopping for anybody. The tires screeched as she peeled out of the cul-de-sac.

Three blocks away, Gabi pulled over to the side of the road. She reached over to the back, rummaged around, and located the old sweatshirt she wore when she was cleaning a really dirty house. "Here, mija. I know you hate pink, but put this on."

Claudia buried her face in her hands and sobbed.

Chapter Twenty-one

All the previous roses had arrived on the office steps in a variety of make-do containers: pickle jars, plastic water bottles, Styrofoam cups. This delicate beauty blossomed in a cut-glass vase. I'd never seen a rose quite like it: the petals shimmered with apricot fading to a creamy caramel center. An exquisite thing, somehow antique, it whispered of melancholy and loss.

It was already midmorning. Where was Gabi, I wondered. Maybe the vexed owner of Sparkleberry Cleaning Service was out on a job.

I picked up the vase and breathed in the perfume. It made me think of face powder, fox furs, and gardenias pressed between the pages of a book. Then I read the penciled label: *Farewell.*

I unlocked the door and carried the rose inside. I set the vase on the corner of Gabi's desk, and studied it.

My business partner had been so happy, so in love. And Angel was a good solid man, the perfect ballast for her energy and enthusiasm. *Farewell. . . .* Their breakup was a crying shame.

Of course, it was none of my business. None at all.

So when had that ever stopped me? I hesitated for only a moment, then sat down in Gabi's desk chair. Thank goodness Angel always used his carpenter's pencil.

The woman was nothing if not organized. In the center drawer, a variety of pencils, pens, and markers were arranged in a system I couldn't work out.

I selected a No. 2 pencil with a good eraser from Gabi's collection. Carefully, I erased the letters "arewell" on the label, leaving Angel's trademark, the scrolly capital letter "F."

Carefully, I wrote in "orever" after the "F." Who says you shouldn't play God?

Pleased with myself, I decided to fire up the coffeepot. I leaned against the kitchenette counter while I waited for my first cup of joe, and thought about what to do next.

First, I stopped off downtown to purchase a throwaway phone. Then I continued on to the Hobsons' home.

I would have to break in, and there was no point in leaving an eye-catching red El Camino parked right out in front. So I pulled up around the block and walked back to the tired little house.

As I stepped inside the wood picket fence, I glanced at the windows. The old beige curtains were tightly drawn.

I crossed the square of sparse lawn and walked around the side. The SBPD's calling card lay under a clump of calla lilies: a blue latex glove tossed in the dirt.

The backyard was as barren and neglected as the front. An old-fashioned clothesline, planted in a patch of rough concrete, raised its thin arms. A torn bag of clothespins hung from the crank.

The windows at the back were all covered with yellowing blinds. I climbed the three steps to the kitchen door. Of course it was locked, but I'd come prepared.

I withdrew my pick and a pair of gloves from my pocket, pulled on the gloves, and bent over the lock. It didn't take much: the door popped right open.

I turned to survey the yard again before stepping inside.

What I saw gave me a start. Someone was standing just behind the side fence, watching me.

It took me a moment to get over my surprise. I walked over to the disembodied head. "Hi, there. You're the Hobsons' neighbor, I guess?"

"Yeah. Wait, I'm going to walk around." The head dropped down. The guy must have been standing on a stepstool or something. This was one nosy neighbor.

A minute later, a man in his late sixties shambled into the yard. His body was slack-muscled, but his eyes were sharp. A tiny Chihuahua trotted along at his heels.

"You having a look inside?" He jutted his chin at the house. "I think she's in there, you know."

"What? Do you mean Mrs. Hobson?"

"Yeah, the old one. I know the young one got killed, I heard all about it. Too bad. She was all right, it's the old one drives you up the wall."

The Chihuahua minced over and sniffed at my shoe.

"Mrs. Hobson's not here," I corrected. "She has dementia, you know. The police would have seen to it that she got to a facility."

"Oh, they took her with them, kicking and screaming. And then they brought her right back the next day. Dementia, huh? I don't know about that."

"I visited here once. I heard her. She seemed very distraught."

"Distraught?" The man reached into his pants pocket and scratched himself. "They used to fight a lot, if that's what you mean. I know all about it, I saw things, you know?"

"If you witnessed abuse, you should have reported it."

"Naw, nothing like that. It was more like the old lady was nagging the young one to death. 'Do this, do that, get me this, get me that.'" He rubbed his chin. "The old girl killed my dog, you know. One before this one here. I found Tinker dead out in my backyard. Vet did an autopsy, guess what? Warfarin, that's what. Old lady tossed rat poison over the fence."

He knew things, all right. And if this nosy neighbor scratched his privates one more time in front of me, I was going to give him some hurt. "Excuse me. I've got work to do."

"Sure. Mind if I look inside while you're here?"

What made him assume I was a cop—the latex gloves? I saw no need to correct him. "It's against policy, sir."

"Thought you'd say that. Look, I always want to help the police. Maury Snyder. Knock on my door if you got any more questions."

He stuck out his hand, but I ignored it. No way was I going to touch that hand.

I slipped inside the back door and locked it behind me. Then I stood still in the kitchen for a moment, taking in what I'd just learned.

Snyder was a Peeping Tom. He knew plenty about the Hobsons, and it was possible he was right: Cheryl was bullied by her mother, not the other way around. Had Cheryl convinced herself Helen had dementia in order to keep from hating her?

Not everything would be answered. What those two women had thought and felt—that was most likely consigned to the past.

I surveyed the kitchen. Its contents were old and worn: a threadbare towel, now stiff, once spread on the counter to dry; a pair of pot mitts, stuffing protruding, hanging from a hook on the oven door. The sink had a bluish stain from the copper tap, where the water had dripped for years.

And there was a cereal bowl on the table. A spoon was glued to the bottom with half an inch of dried flakes and milk. Neighbor Snyder could be right: at some point Helen Hobson may have returned. But where was she now?

I walked through to the hall leading to the front door.

"Helen? Are you here?" I listened, but nothing stirred. All I could hear was the muted roar of the freeway.

One by one, I peered into the wretched rooms. The living room held a big old TV and a sun-faded lounge suite. What must have been Cheryl's bedroom, at the front of the house, contained a small double bed. The comforter was made from a shiny rayon fabric, little-girl pink dotted with pale green leaves.

The single bathroom possessed the universal odor of all neglected old bathrooms: mold laced with urine. The shower curtain was spotted black with mold, the chrome rings tarnished.

I opened the mirrored door of the medicine cabinet and sorted through its jumbled contents. The police never put anything back the way they found it. If there had been anything of interest in there, it was now gone.

I went back into the hall and walked down to the second bedroom. I twisted the knob, but it was locked.

"Mrs. Hobson? Helen, are you in there?" There was no reply.

I popped the lock with my pick. Then I opened the door— and put a hand to my mouth.

Helen Hobson, dressed in an old cotton nightgown, lay on the bed. Her head was turned sideways, and she stared straight at me. Her hand clawed at an old ivory-colored album, and a trickle of dried blood ran from her nose down her cheek.

I couldn't stop looking into the old woman's eyes. She'd been dead for maybe two days, yet she seemed about to speak.

I opened the door all the way, and made myself enter the room. It was stuffy, hot. The air smelled of feces and decay.

A tissue box, an empty water glass tipped on its side, and a lamp with a dusty cloth shade crowded a tiny nightstand. Three uncapped pill bottles lay on the old Afghan coverlet. A few pills were scattered about, but not many. Not many at all.

My eyes returned to the album. It looked like a scrapbook. I had to see what it contained.

Helen's thin arm was still somewhat rigid. Gently, I pulled the book out from under her hand, down to the foot of the bed.

The discolored covers were made of a heavy cardboard embossed to look like leather. They were laced to the pages with a faded brown cord. When I lifted the front cover, the book opened flat.

The first yellowed page was blank. The second bore an inscription written in an old-fashioned hand:

Dedicated to:
Gary Edward Hobson
1949–1970
Murdered, Never Avenged.

You might have expected a memorial, a loving tribute to Gary. But that's not what the book was.

Page after page, the scrapbook was filled with news articles about Gary's death, the fire, and the police investigation. There were dozens of photographs of possible suspects. Their names, addresses, and phone numbers were added to and erased over the years. And dominating the photos were those of Rod Steinbach.

It appeared Helen Hobson had kept track of Steinbach for decades. There was a brief article telling of his appointment to Brown University. And there was a wedding announcement: Rodney Allen Steinbach and Alice Keiko Tanaka, to wed in Santa Barbara, June 21, 1970.

When I'd turned the last page, I closed the book. Then I lifted Helen's thin, bony hand, and returned the album to its resting place.

There was no point in pretending I hadn't entered the house. Snyder would be only too happy to set the police straight on that score. But nobody needed to know I'd tampered with evidence. I rearranged the book and straightened Helen's nightgown. Then I walked out of the room and shut the door.

I stopped in the kitchen and pulled out my throwaway phone. Thank goodness I knew all Mike's numbers by heart. Because he was up in San Luis, I dialed the one in his office. It went straight to voice mail.

"Mike. I need to report a dead body. It's Helen Hobson. She's on her bed, in the room at the back of her house." I stared at a big black fly buzzing at the kitchen window. I must have let it in when I opened the door. "It looks like suicide, an overdose of prescription pain meds."

My conscience wouldn't allow me to leave Helen's body unreported. But in any way I could, I needed to slow things down. I was counting on Mike's habit of not checking his office messages while he was away. I needed to buy a little time before the long arm of the law reached out and grabbed me by the scruff of the neck.

I figured Mr. Peeper would be patrolling the back fence. I confirmed that the kitchen door was locked, then passed down the hall and let myself out through the front.

I was latching the gate when a Crown Vic slunk up to the curb. Why was I not surprised when Deirdre Krause bounced out of the driver's side? Troy, no doubt under orders to stay in the car, leaned out through the passenger window and fixed me with a bored stare.

"Breaking and entering. Thank goodness, a sharp-eyed member of the public caught you red-handed." Deirdre planted her hands on her hips. "If it was up to me, Zarlin, we'd slap an ankle bracelet on you."

I glanced over at the house next door. Snyder was standing beside his driveway, a dribbling hose in his hand. He hadn't thought I was police after all.

"Just doing my job, Deirdre. Unlike the PD, apparently."

"I take exception to that. I really do."

"Look inside. You'll find Helen Hobson's dead body. Your

people brought her back here and left her without any care. They dumped her and left her to die."

For a long moment, Deirdre had nothing to say. Her round face showed surprise, then annoyance. Annoyance to an extreme. Her fair skin blushed to the roots of her hair.

"Let's get this straight. You broke into this house. You found a dead body. And now, without reporting it, you're walking away?"

"I reported it. I phoned the sheriff's office."

Troy opened the car door. "Deirdre, do you want me to—"

"No," she snapped. "Stay where you are. Much as I'd like you to put a choke hold on Ms. Zarlin here, we've been told to go easy on her. The chief wants us to let her play her little games."

I stepped through the gate and pulled it closed behind me. "Go easy on me? Good to hear somebody likes me." But I knew that wasn't it.

Had Wheeler learned I'd been talking to Chaffee again? Maybe the police chief figured this case would distract me from finding out what had happened to my brother.

"Oh, the chief doesn't *like* you, Zarlin. Get over yourself." Deirdre patted a blond chunk of hair back into place. "He thinks you're harmless, as a matter of fact. What did he say, Troy? Something like, 'she's as fucked up as her brother.'"

It was good that I'd just seen Helen Hobson's dead body. That kind of thing sobers you up. Otherwise, I'd be in a different sort of mood. Otherwise I'd be lunging for Deirdre's milky white throat.

Chapter Twenty-two

The office courtyard drowsed in the midday heat. Through the screen door of Suite D I heard the murmur of female voices conversing in Spanish. I pushed open the door and stepped inside.

Soft rock flowed from the ancient clock radio on top of the bookcase. The apricot rose perched daintily on the corner of the desk, just as I'd left it.

Gabi and Claudia looked up at me. Confused, I looked back at them.

They seemed to be having a calm and intimate conversation. Gabi sat in the hot seat, her hands folded in her lap. Claudia sat—upright, for once—on the couch. She wore nice jeans and a short-sleeved white polo shirt. For the first time I noticed that the kid was actually pretty. She looked a lot like her sister Lili.

"Miss Jaymie," Gabi began. "Claudia and me, we been waiting for you."

This was all very nice, but I knew the truce could explode at any moment. I pulled the desk chair around and sat facing them. "My trip to Fresno was very useful. I learned one or two things."

"We learned some stuff too," Claudia said. "Last night."

"Last night?"

"Yeah. I . . . I went somewhere." Her voice trembled.

"Claudia?" I went over and sat beside her. I could see she was making an effort not to cry.

"Do you want me to tell Miss Jaymie?"

"Yeah," she said in a low voice. "Yeah, 'cause I—I don't wanna cry like a girl."

"Hey," I said. "Boys cry too."

Claudia managed a smile.

"Miss Jaymie, it was like this." Gabi leaned forward in the hot seat and cleared her throat. "You know how Claudia wants to be a detective? Well last night she decided to do it, you know? Be a detective."

"Ah." I turned on the couch to face the girl. "So you got into a little trouble."

Claudia nodded, but said nothing.

"Not a little trouble," Gabi corrected. "They had another piñata party, those kids. Claudia, she went there. And she listened to two of those kids when they were talking. She found out something important, Miss Jaymie, maybe really important. But"—Gabi glanced over at Claudia—"I don't know how much I should say."

I wanted to scold Claudia for going against my instructions. But something bad had happened, all right, and I figured this wasn't the time. I just hoped it wasn't as bad as I feared.

"You know what? I'm being a baby." Claudia tipped up her chin. "It was Port and Vanessa. I saw them talking together, you know? Out by where they'd parked all the cars. They were arguing, but trying to keep it quiet. So I snuck up behind a car to listen. And that's when I heard, Jaymie. I heard Vanessa tell Port she knew he didn't go to his therapy appointment the Friday afternoon Skye died."

My first thought was a resounding *no!* I was zeroing in on Rod Steinbach, and I didn't need to open yet another can of worms. But reason took over: what mattered was the truth. "Are you certain you understood her right?"

"Yes. Vanessa really pushed. She wanted to know where he went. And Port kept telling her to mind her own business."

"And then?"

"And then—" Her voice faded. "Then I sort of started coughing. I don't know why, I guess I was nervous. And they heard me." Claudia walked over to the screen door and looked out into the courtyard, her back to the room.

"Claudia? You need to tell me the rest."

"I don't want to talk about it, but I want you to know." Claudia turned back to face me, but kept her eyes on the floor. "Gabi saved me, maybe even my life."

"Do you want to go over to the bakery, mija?" Gabi said. "I think we could really use some pastries right now. And if it's OK with you, maybe me and Miss Jaymie will keep talking while you are gone."

"Yeah, that'd be all right."

"Claudia?" Something was bothering me, and I figured I might as well say it. "I'm sorry I took your knife away from you. Sounds like you could have used it last night."

"Maybe," she said in a low voice. "But there were a lot of them."

"I've got it at home. I'll bring it tomorrow."

The girl shook her head. "I'm gonna kinda lie low for a while, you know? Hang on to it, Jaymie. I'll tell you when I want it back."

It bothered me to see her like that. Defeated. I just hoped she hadn't been hurt too badly by her so-called friends.

"Anyways, the bakery. I'm broke. What do I use for money?"

"Petty cash," Gabi responded. "It's in the bottom drawer of the desk, the brown envelope inside the Kotex box. Only this one time, remember. Oh!" Her hand flew to her mouth. "I shouldn't have said that. I'm sorry."

"It's OK."

After the screen door closed, Gabi and I looked at each other.

"They dragged her off to one of the rooms," I guessed.

"The Chamber of Lust. She tried to call you, Miss Jaymie, but do you know your phone isn't working? I tried this morning too."

"I left it somewhere. Out in the boonies. Damn, that was bad luck." I felt guilty, responsible, even though I'd told Claudia not to go to the party. I should have known she'd ignore me.

"When you didn't answer the phone, she called me instead. I put on my cleaning clothes, Miss Jaymie. Nobody hardly noticed me—I walked right into that room. What worked real good was my spray bottle. It's full of super-strong ammonia. That bottle shoots good, right where you aim it."

"I'm proud of you, Gabi."

"I don't think they did the—the really bad thing to her. But they were going to, that's for sure. Her clothes were almost all off. You know, they were all really drunk. That's one reason nobody could stop me. Those kids, I think maybe they were too drunk to figure it out."

"You're a superhero. Thank God for you and that lethal weapon of yours!"

"I don't know nothing about no superhero. But maybe I can find that phone you lost. Do you have any ideas?"

"Pretty sure it's at Cholame Junction. Right outside the Cholame Junction Café. But I'll take care of that, Gabi. You don't need to worry."

"Who's worried?" She popped up from the chair. "That's exactly the kinda job a PA should do. I'm going to call this junction place right now and get things moving."

"I've missed you," I said.

Just as Claudia walked in through the door with the pastries, the office phone rang. Gabi was back in the kitchenette making coffee, so I picked up.

"Jaymie? It's Donna Tactacquin."

"Donna, how are you?"

"To tell you the truth, I'm afraid. Last night somebody smashed our living room window with a rock. Taryn was in there, watching TV. It could have injured her, Jaymie. Glass was everywhere."

"That's terrible! I'll come right over."

"We're all right for now." Donna took an audible breath. "We boarded it up, and a glass installer should be here this afternoon. I called a security company too, for an alarm system. But what good is that going to do? People know all about Johnny. Everybody knows. An alarm system won't stop a rock. Or rotten eggs."

"So this isn't the first time."

"Three days ago my car got plastered with eggs. And—didn't Taryn tell you? She lost her summer job."

I cursed myself for not staying in touch. Taryn and Donna were isolated—besieged—and for over a week I'd barely given them a thought. "Taryn was fired because her dad's in jail? That's illegal. We can do something—"

"Jaymie." Donna paused. "Jaymie, what about Johnny?"

"We've had some good news." I cleared my throat. "Good news for your husband's case."

"But—why didn't you call me right away? Never mind. What is it?"

I stepped out on the tightrope. "Someone came forward. A—person—who will supply an alibi for Johnny." I was working hard to avoid using a pronoun. "That person agreed to contact Johnny's lawyer. Gamboa should have informed the police by now."

"But that—that is good news! Thank heavens."

"On its own, it's not enough. But it's good news, yes."

I heard a sob. Donna Tactacquin was a strong woman, but the stress had to be tough to bear.

"Thank you, Jaymie. Taryn said you wouldn't give up."

"The DA's office still isn't looking at anyone but John," I cautioned.

"You'll get there. I know you will." She hesitated. "I understand why you didn't want to tell me about John's alibi. You were afraid I'd be furious at my husband."

"Maybe something like that," I said in a weak voice.

"You don't need to worry. Like I told you, I love John, and I forgive him." Her own voice was firm now. "I'm not saying I'm happy he had an affair, but we'll move beyond it and be a couple again. Can you tell me her name?"

I opened my mouth and closed it again. After a long moment I found a few words to fill the strained silence. "I'm sorry, Donna. That's got to be between you and John."

"OK, I understand. It probably wouldn't be ethical for you to tell me. Anyway, I don't want to upset him. When all this is over, I'll ask him then."

That evening I poured myself a glass of chilled wine and went out to sit on the low wall separating my concrete patio from the edge of the cliff. The evening sky was a soft funereal purple, the channel waters a solemn blue gray. Santa Cruz Island, dark and still, stretched along the horizon.

I thought about time. Heavy, grinding, unstoppable, time crushed everything in its path. And in spite of Larry Millar and the alibi, I feared time would crush John Tactacquin soon, if I couldn't find a way to solve the case. As so often happens in this world, a killer would go free.

A coil of worry tightened in my chest. I didn't want to admit it, but I knew I had a problem. My money was on Rod Steinbach, but was Porter Logsdon somehow involved? I couldn't see how he fit in the picture. But what Claudia had overheard at the piñata party had me thinking.

I hopped off the wall and reached into my pocket for the throwaway phone. My first thought was Mike. But no, that was out of the question. Mike was up in San Luis with Trudy and her family. They were mourning Bill's death.

I thought of Charlie. Somehow, in a few words, Charlie always managed to set me straight. But his pneumonia had proved to be tough to cure, and he was still languishing in Cottage, sorely trying the patience of the staff. I could visit Charlie tomorrow, but I didn't want to bother him now. It was too late.

Then I thought of Zave. He was a night owl. I picked up the phone and dialed his cell. I was surprised at just how disappointed I was when there was no answer. But the deep velvety recorded voice encouraged me to leave a message.

"Zave, I need to see you tonight. Sorry I didn't make an advance appointment, consigliere. I'm in need of advice. Call me back at this number. I'm using a temporary phone."

The minutes crept by. Dexter stood and stretched, as best as a three-legged dog could. I knew Zave kept his phone close, was sure he'd see that I'd called. Why wasn't he getting back to me?

When the phone rang some twenty minutes later, I grabbed for it, and it tumbled out of my hand. Thank goodness, it only fell on the patio and not down the steep bank. Zave was leaving a message by the time I managed to reply.

"Hey, Jaymie." Immediately, his voice calmed me. Zave was purring tonight. "How can I help?"

"It's the aquarium murders. I think I know who the killer is, but I don't have enough evidence. And besides, something's not right."

He hesitated. "Can it wait till the morning?"

It was bedtime, and Zave was asking me to come tomorrow? That should have alerted me, but I was too frazzled to think straight.

"No, but never mind. If you don't want to help me, that's—"

"Jaymie, stop it. Give me thirty minutes. The gate will be open, just drive on through."

◆   ◆   ◆

The moon, strong as a searchlight, illuminated every pebble and blade of grass as I crossed the yard. I slipped into the narrow car shed, climbed into the El Camino and inserted the key in the ignition. The engine responded with its new throaty *grr*.

I drifted down El Balcon and through the Mesa, driving slow. I'd be arriving early at Zave's, so there was no need to rush. I switched on the fancy new CD player, relaxed and listened to music—the Eagles, of course: *There's a hole in the world tonight.*

I turned off Carrillo, into the Lower West Side. Here and there women chatted under porch lights, and young men joked on the corners. A couple of kids tossed a glow-in-the-dark Frisbee. The day had been long and hot, stifling. No doubt the little stucco-and-wood-frame houses still retained the heat of the sun, like ovens. Outside, the temperature was refreshing, cool.

The road began to rise up from the flats. Streetlights disappeared. I watched for the rutted alley leading to Zave's place. At the last moment, my headlights illuminated the entrance. I backed up, then entered the overgrown track.

No rain had fallen for months. I could smell the dust and dirt in the jungle of ivy, and the sharp odor of rotting citrus.

Another bend in the alley and I came to Zave's beautiful Spanish colonial, La Casa de la Boca del Cañón. As the man had promised, the security gate was open. But there was a car I didn't recognize in the drive.

The Mercedes was silver and sleek. And the dark-skinned woman descending the steps, bathed in Zave's Klieg lights, was sleek and beautiful too. Her clingy dress enhanced her stunning figure, and her impossibly high heels caused her to prance like a filly. She turned back to the doorway and gave an airy wave.

The woman was all class. I hated her. I was tempted to ram the Mercedes as it moved out through the gate.

I couldn't do that—but I wouldn't move out of the way. The beautiful one was forced to steer a few feet off the road. She slowed and came to a stop when our windows aligned.

Out of the corner of my eye I saw her window slide down. "'Scuse me?" she said in a voice as warm and smooth as Zave's favorite cognac. "Girl, I'm talking to you."

I turned my head and met her sparkling eyes. I willed her to age quickly, and to gain fifty or sixty pounds. But she'd still be beautiful in either event, I supposed. "What? Something to say?"

"Uh-huh. Just want to let you know, honey, you might as well go on home. Man's in a funk."

As I was searching my brain for something smart to answer her with, anything at all, she smiled. Not sweetly, but broadly, revealing a crooked front tooth. Suddenly she wasn't perfect. But now the lady was human, and beautiful in another, more genuine way. I saw I couldn't win.

She laughed, then drove on. I thought of turning around and leaving too. But when I glanced up at the house, I saw Zave looking down at me. His door was wide open, and it threw gold light all around him. The worst of it was, Zave was wearing his plush velour robe, the crimson robe I thought of as "ours."

No way would I let him see me run off.

I pulled in through the gate, switched off the engine, and got out. "You should have told me you had company," I snarled.

"Come in, baby." He stepped forward and held out a hand, but he wasn't smiling. "You're early, you know."

I ignored his hand and mounted the steps. "If this isn't a good time, I'll go."

"It's a good time. She had no intention of staying." He took me by the elbow and steered me toward the open doorway. "Let's go fix us something to eat."

I sat at the counter chair and watched as Zave selected ingredients from his massive stainless-steel fridge.

"I'm gonna make you the fanciest damn omelet you ever had

in your life." When I didn't answer, he stopped what he was doing and looked over at me.

"What the hell, Jaymie? You jealous or something?"

I stared at the speckled granite countertop. "Your private life is none of my business."

Zave set the green onions and sausage down on the counter and walked around to where I sat slumped in the chair. He put his arms around me and held me tight. "I get it. It hurts."

I wanted to just let go and cry on his shoulder. But I smelled *her* perfume on his robe, so I leaned away from the embrace. "She's beautiful. Perfect for you. I feel like a skinny little white girl, I guess."

Zave tipped back his head and laughed. My heart softened in spite of myself. I loved it when the guy laughed, when his eyes narrowed to glittering slivers.

"I knew you'd cheer me up, girl. But I'm not talkin' about that woman to you." Zave cupped my chin in one hand. "I just want to say something about you and me."

I nodded, dumbly. He held me in thrall, caressing my cheek with his thumb.

"Love," he said softly, "is a many-splendored thing. There's all kinds of love. And some kinds, like this one you and me have, don't have a name."

I noticed he'd gripped the edge of the counter with his right hand. "Zave, tell me. Who is she?"

He looked at me for a moment. I'd never seen him like this: vulnerable, exposed. "Name's Tonayah. Tonayah Carbonel."

"Carbonel? So you have a sister." A tsunami of relief flooded over me.

"Sister? She better not be. Tonayah's my wife."

The wave of relief sucked back off the shore. "Your *wife*? But you never said you were married! And all this time—" I stared at him. "My God, Zave. You love her, don't you. You love her for real."

Zave pulled a paring knife from the block and began to chop the onions. His big hands moved like an artist's, deft and precise. "Guilty as charged. Let's leave it at that."

After supper we moved into the living room. Zave handed me a glass of dry sherry. I wanted to ask him more about Tonayah, but I knew I wouldn't get anywhere. He'd steered me away from that subject and shut the door.

"All right, Jaymie. You said on the phone you've pinpointed the killer, but something's not right. Fill me in."

Chapter Twenty-three

I began at the beginning, and told Zave everything I'd learned.

"Tactacquin's attorney is Louis Gamboa," he said after hearing me out. "Gamboa's not bad, but he doesn't stand a chance against the DA. And the guy coming forward to support the alibi? That's a two-edged sword."

"But why? Millar's a law-abiding man, hardworking—"

"Hey." Zave brushed a hand in the air. "Millar's gay, but he lived most of his adult life with a woman, as a married man. The alibi will reveal that Tactacquin has done the same—hidden his secret life from his partner. Once the jury hears that, they won't trust either one."

"Still, the alibi shows Tactacquin wasn't there at the time of the murders." I folded my arms across my chest. "That's got to count for something."

Zave dismissed this with a shrug. "Look, let's forget Tactacquin for a minute. I like Steinbach for it, I admit. But the way I hear you tell it, you've got a complication. The kid."

"Porter Logsdon." I took a sip of the tawny golden elixir, felt its warmth trickle down my throat. "Claudia heard Vanessa practically accuse him of killing Skye."

"And you're sure Vanessa was right about Logsdon's alibi being false?"

"Yes. I phoned the psych doc's office pretending to be Porter's mom, and asked about the billing. Porter didn't show for his therapy session the afternoon Skye died."

Zave braided his hands behind his head, leaned back and studied me. "Motive?"

"How about good old-fashioned jealousy? Skye was going places, Porter wasn't. Porter likes to think of himself as a superjock, but Skye was the better athlete. And then there's the desirable Vanessa. She doted on Skye and regarded Porter as just a friend."

"Mm." Zave leaned forward and opened a hand-tooled leather box on the coffee table. "Cigar?"

I wrinkled my nose. "Do I look like a chimney?"

"My dear, 'tis a pity you're not a man." He lit the cigar with a silver lighter, puffed several times, and set the lighter back on the table. "Want to know what I think?"

"You know I do."

"I think you're just about out of time. Proving Tactacquin's innocence—or disproving his guilt—won't get you anywhere, not fast enough. Even a good alibi won't help at this point. Too little, too late."

I jumped up from the chair. "There's got to be something I can do!"

"Focus on Steinbach. Forget about Tactacquin. Forget about the kid's involvement. Prove Steinbach's guilt."

I circled the room. "How the hell do I do that?"

Zave let out a long slow puff of smoke. "How stiff are Steinbach's alibis?"

"Pretty stiff," I admitted. "Steinbach was at the aquarium board meeting when Skye was killed. And he was having tapas at the Figueroa Café with his wife and some friends when Cheryl Hobson died. Gabi checked up on that one—she knows one of the waiters and he looked through the receipts. Steinbach footed the bill."

"Have you got any physical evidence?"

"No. No, I—wait a minute. Maybe I do." I took out my phone, opened it to photos, and handed it to him. "There's this."

"What am I looking at here? A squashed flower?"

"A flower tracked into the aquarium on the bottom of a sneaker. It's somewhat rare, a plumeria blossom called *Eternal Flame*. I spotted it on the wet deck when I went to look at Cheryl Kerr's body."

"It could have been tracked in at any time."

"Over a period of about twenty hours," I corrected. "The wet deck's swabbed down once a day."

"I suppose you could check the Steinbachs' garden. If the plant's rare, as you say, and it's growing there, you might have an argument."

"I drove by his place on the Riviera. I didn't see anything that looked like a plumeria out in front. But there's a garden around the back."

He shrugged and handed me my phone. "Something's not adding up."

"I know." I walked over to the old fireplace, and ran my hand along the painted Mexican tiles.

"Two murders," Zave mused. "Two drownings in the same unlikely location."

A chill crept through my veins. Time slowed as I reached out to the fireplace to steady myself. "Zave. Say that again."

He looked at me. "Two murders. Two drownings in the same unlikely location."

"Two murders . . . *that's it*." I sucked in my breath. "The aquarium setting—the circumstances surrounding the drownings—the murders were so similar, and so bizarre! I assumed both crimes were committed by the same person . . . but maybe . . . just maybe not."

"Hold on." Zave stubbed out his cigar in the ashtray and got to his feet. I could see he was excited, too. "Two different killers. It's possible. But who?"

"Don't you see?" My heart began to rat-tat like a nail gun. "Rod Steinbach and Porter Logsdon. Porter must have killed Skye. I'll bet they got in a fight at the top of the jellyfish tank." I'd broken out in a sweat.

"By God, you could be right. Logsdon killed Skye. And Steinbach—"

"Yes. Rod Steinbach killed Cheryl Kerr."

"What, do you think Steinbach suspected her of killing his grandson?"

"Maybe. Or Cheryl challenged him, spoke out about the death of her brother all those years ago. Steinbach's a strong man in spite of his age. He could have shoved her over the wet deck, no problem at all."

"Jaymie, you clever girl!"

Was I really so clever? It had damn sure taken me awhile.

Together we walked through the front door and onto the porch. I turned to him. "Zave? It can't be the same between us, not anymore."

He put his hands on my shoulders. "Because I'm married?"

"Because you love her. I think you love Tonayah more than anything. How did you hide it so well, how come I never sensed it?"

"Maybe I needed to hide it from myself." He leaned forward and kissed me on the forehead. "Still friends?"

"Sure, same as always." I managed a smile.

I got up at the crack of dawn, then forced myself to wait till nine before I hopped on my Schwinn and coasted down Cabrillo Boulevard toward East Beach. I wanted to arrive at Porter Logsdon's place on Channel Drive after his mother went off to work.

Porter and his mom lived in a modest town house complex wedged between the cemetery and Tye Warner's sublime oceanfront estate. I pedaled through the condos, orienting myself. Once I'd delivered my message to Port, I'd little doubt he'd make a run for it. I wanted to make sure he wouldn't get far.

The Logsdons' unit, 10B, was located away from the street. I moseyed over to the nearest carport and located the kid's new Mustang, parked at an odd angle. A quick look around, and I bent to my task: stabbing toothpicks into each of his door locks, breaking them off, and jamming them home with an awl. Then I squirted in a few shots of Krazy Glue, just for insurance.

Satisfied with my handiwork, I returned to 10B. I took note of a side door, and a slider at the back. Then I rode around to the front.

The drapes were drawn wide open, and I could see into the Logsdons' living room. There was Port, lounging in a big nest-shaped chair, watching a baseball game on TV. I dismounted and dropped the bike down on the small patch of lawn. When I looked up, Porter was staring straight at me.

As our eyes connected, his expression changed. One minute his mind was caught up in the game. The next, he looked lost, frightened and alone.

Porter stared at me a moment longer. Then, he bolted. He was off the couch and out of the room in a flash. I wheeled my bike around to the back.

His car keys must have been in his bedroom upstairs, because it took a minute before he raced out the slider.

I watched Porter sprint over to the carport, and followed at a leisurely pace.

"You bitch! Fucking asshole!" Porter shouted as he yanked on the door handles and repeatedly pressed the beeping remote. Then he kicked the shiny red Mustang. The kick left a sizable dent.

Porter turned toward me, and I could see him debate. Go for my throat, or run? Lucky for me, he chose to take off.

He tore through the complex and out into the lane. I followed on my bike. Porter was fast and strong, but he was a big kid, carrying a lot of weight. I figured it wouldn't be long before I ran him to the ground.

It happened sooner than either of us expected. He tore into the cemetery, racing for the far corner where the grounds met the Delaney estate. I had to give him credit, it was a plan. But he didn't watch his feet.

Porter must have stepped in a sprinkler hole, because he tripped and went down hard. I stopped a few yards away and watched as he got to his feet and tried to stumble on. Then, with a scream of frustration, he collapsed among the headstones.

I dropped my bike and approached him. "Porter. Listen to me."

"No." He covered his ears with his hands. "Go away!"

I stopped beside a Monterey cypress and rested a hand on the shaggy bark. And I waited, as reality trickled into Porter Logsdon's terrified brain.

"I didn't mean to," he said at last. "It was his fault, not mine."

I walked up to him. "Hurt your ankle?"

"Broke it last year in football. Feels like I broke it again." He looked up at me, his face white with pain. "We got in a fight. Up there at the top of the tank."

I nodded. "You got in a fight. You were bigger than Skye, stronger. So you pushed him over the edge, into the water."

"It wasn't like that!" Porter's face contorted. "I—he fell."

"I know you didn't think about the jellyfish. You didn't mean to kill your best friend. But Skye didn't just fall. You shoved him, right?"

Porter covered his eyes with both hands. "I shoved him," he echoed. "The jellyfish, it came out of nowhere—so fast. I should of—I should of—"

"You should have helped Skye get out."

"It happened so fast! I couldn't think straight—and then that—that *thing* grabbed him—" He began to weep.

The cemetery was still. I could hear the waves crashing below.

"Let's take it from the beginning, Porter. So, you went to the aquarium after it closed." I spoke quietly now. "How did you get in?"

"I had the code. Skye gave it to Vanessa. She gave it to me. Vanessa and me, sometimes we went in there to smoke."

"Why did you go that afternoon?"

"To talk to Skye! To fix it between us. I saw his pickup out on the street and I knew he was there. I thought, what the hell, Skye and Vanessa made up. Why shouldn't Skye and me be friends? All the shit that came between us, none of it mattered. But Skye, oh no. He didn't see it that way."

"Skye didn't want to be friends with you."

"He said he didn't want to hang with me anymore. He was too good for me, you know? That's what he thought!" Porter was crying now, his voice a racked sob. "He made me mad, the fucker. It was all his own fault, he deserved what he got!"

"I see what you're getting at, Porter. Skye was too good for you all of a sudden. He couldn't be bothered with you anymore . . . kind of like your dad."

"Fuck you!" He started to rise, gave out a sharp gasp, and collapsed back on the grass. "What's—what's going to happen now?"

"You're going to turn yourself in to the police. It will be to your benefit if you do. I'll give you one hour, before I phone them myself." It was the best I could do for him. I turned and walked toward my bike.

"My ankle—how the fuck am I going to get out of here?"

"One hour," I repeated. Then I climbed on my bike and pedaled away, heading down to Cabrillo. I figured it was time Porter Logsdon started working things out for himself.

"Congratulations, Miss Jaymie!" Gabi handed me an ice cold bottle of Pacifico as I walked in the door. Before I could say anything, she'd ushered me into the kitchen. "You and me, we're gonna celebrate."

I saw that my table was organized, the mound of papers arranged into discreet stacks. Each stack was labeled with a fluorescent green Post-it note.

"Now sit down." Gabi went to the refrigerator and removed bowls of guacamole, red and green salsa, refries, and a cheese dip. She set them on the table, added a big basket of homemade tortilla chips, and stood back to admire. "For you, Miss Jaymie. Cause you proved you are a real detective. This wasn't no accident: only you solved the case."

I looked at her out of the corner of my eye as I tipped back la cerveza. Then I set the bottle on the table. "Gabi? There's no reason to celebrate. Let's just call this lunch."

"What are you talking about? Oh, no." She raised a warning finger. "Don't say it—*please* don't. The police arrested that boy Porter. He confessed. And they said Cheryl's murder was an accident, she fell in while she was dropping the octopus over the side. They let Taryn's father out of jail! It's over. I am begging you—"

"What, let it go?" I stabbed the refries with a chip. "No. I won't and I can't. Thank God they released John Tactacquin. But Cheryl's death was no accident, Gabi. She didn't just tumble in. She wasn't a tall woman, and the wall surrounding the wet deck came up to her waist."

Gabi set her bottle of Pacifico on the table and her hands on her hips. "Remember, I'm not just your PA. I am your partner. Miss Jaymie, please. You gotta move on."

The office phone rang out in the main room. Gabi went to pick up.

I washed the tortilla chip down with a swallow of beer, and stared out the window at the scorching afternoon. I heard Gabi say something, then give a sharp cry.

A second later she appeared in the doorway. "Miss Jaymie. That was Donna! You gotta go to their house real quick. It's about Taryn—she has a knife, she says she's gonna cut open her arms!"

Chapter Twenty-four

I gunned the Camino up the narrow streets of the Riviera. Each corner I turned presented a sparkling view of the Santa Barbara Channel, blue tinged in gold. For the first time ever, I resented the flamboyant show.

I should have been paying attention. Damn it to hell. I should have known.

I slowed to a stop in front of the modest Craftsman. The Tactacquin home looked peaceful. The shades were drawn, and a tuxedo cat was curled up on a mat outside the front door.

I got out and shut the door quietly. Then I eased the latch on the redwood gate, stepped into the front garden, and closed the gate behind me. The black and white cat jumped up and strode down the steps, meowing in a demanding tone.

"Ssh, kitty. Ssh." I bent down and stroked the cat, and he arched his back under my hand.

I half expected the door to be opened by John Tactacquin. But it was Donna who peered through the gap, then lifted the chain.

"Jaymie, thank God you're here." She grabbed my sleeve and pulled me inside.

"Donna, is Taryn all right?"

"No, she's not. She's out in the garden house. She has a knife. Jaymie, I don't understand it. She won't tell me why. She says she'll really do it this time if I don't stay away from her. And she warned me not to call the police. There was no one to call except you."

"What do you mean, she'll really do it this time? Has Taryn done this before?"

"Three days ago. The day they let John out of jail, she slit her wrists. Only the skin, not—not the veins. They called it a cry for help."

"I wish you'd phoned me. I would have come by."

"You couldn't have made any difference. They put her in the psych ward at Cottage, on a seventy-two-hour hold. No visitors." Donna wrapped her arms across her stomach.

"She was only released a few hours ago. John went and got her, and dropped her off. She won't talk to me, won't say a word. They said she didn't talk to anyone, the whole time she was in the hospital. Taryn—my little chatterbox!" She buried her face in her hands.

I felt so bad for Donna. "Is John here now?"

"John?" Donna looked up. A flash of anger showed in her eyes. "I sent him packing. Didn't you know, Jaymie? My husband of twenty-two years is gay. He's been gay all along, but he never bothered to tell me."

"I know. I didn't think it was my place to tell you."

"I understand." She shrugged. "You know, I was so ready to forgive him for having a lover . . . then I learned our marriage was nothing, a fake. All these years I've been providing cover for him, that's all."

"I'd tar and feather the guy for lying to me," I admitted. "But John does love you, Donna. He told me so, and he meant it."

"Yes. Like a sister. But what does it matter? Right now it's Taryn I'm worried about."

The time had come. I couldn't delay any longer. "The garden room's out in the back?"

"Through the kitchen door and down the side. I'll watch through the blinds in the bedroom. I can't go with you, Jaymie. Every time Taryn sees me, she holds the knife to her wrist."

The side yard was picture-perfect. A red-leaf Japanese maple branched under a tall wispy stand of Mexican bamboo. Against the fence, a Cecile Brunner rose ambled over a trellis.

The cat followed me, coiling his tail around my ankle as I descended a short flight of steps and followed the gravel path around to the back. He meowed, demanding attention. I shushed him and he glared at me, narrowing his green eyes.

The yard sloped away at the back. The garden house stood below, in the far corner. It was constructed of redwood timbers, screening, and lath. All the materials had weathered to a silvery gray.

Through the screen door I could see Taryn slouched in an old wicker chair. Strips of sunlight fell through the lath and crossed her body. A small heap of bandages, glowing white in the gloom, lay at her feet.

I crunched over the decomposed granite, following the path as it zigzagged down the slope through a phalanx of bottlebrush trees. I stopped at the top of the last flight of sandstone steps. The garden house lay directly below.

"Taryn," I called. "It's Jaymie. Just me." I shaded my eyes from the sun.

Her still body was slumped sideways. In her lap, the thin edge of a butcher's knife shone.

For a long second I feared Taryn Tactacquin had made good on her threat. But then she straightened. I prepared to descend, and looked down at my feet.

That's when I saw them.

My fear was confirmed. Dozens of orange and blue flowers, dead and dying, lay scattered over the steps.

On the day Cheryl died, John was in jail. And Donna, I knew, was visiting their son up at Avenal Prison.

That left one possibility. Only one.

I'd checked Taryn's alibi for the night Skye died. But I'd never bothered to verify that she'd also babysat on the evening Cheryl drowned. And I'd never asked Taryn if she knew the combination to the aquarium door. I'd slipped.

I liked Taryn Tactacquin, and maybe I hadn't wanted her to be guilty. I knew one thing for certain: I would never make that mistake again.

I tipped back my head and looked up: the rare plumeria, planted beside one of the redwood posts supporting the garden house, arched over the path. All along the branches, flowers blossomed in tongues of flame.

When I lowered my gaze, Taryn's eyes met my own. She let out a strangled cry.

I descended the steps and lifted my hand to the screen door.

"Stay back!" Taryn raised the knife. "I'll do it, I swear!"

"I won't come in. But please, while we're talking, just put down the knife."

She lowered the weapon, but didn't let go. "I wanted to be close to Skye after he died, any way I could! So I went to the aquarium. I missed him so bad!"

"But it was shut. How did you get in?"

She rested her bare arms on her thighs. I saw the practice cuts—they weren't as superficial as I'd expected.

"Skye gave me the code to the back door. We used to meet in there to be alone . . . usually I got there first."

"It was your special place."

"Yes. We'd go to the wet deck. There's a bench with cushions—" Her voice trailed off.

"So you went there that afternoon to think about Skye. And she was there, right? On the wet deck. Cheryl Kerr."

"Yes. Throwing an octopus into the water." Taryn bent forward, as if she were going to be sick.

"Releasing it?"

"I guess. She asked me what I was doing there, and I tried to explain. I said I didn't want to get into trouble, I just wanted to be there when nobody else was around. I told her I missed Skye so much, and I was his girlfriend. I told her we were in love."

"How did Cheryl react?"

"I thought she'd be nice. But she got real mad. She said horrible stuff. Like Skye deserved to be dead, and she was happy about it! Because Dr. Steinbach killed her own brother." Taryn jumped to her feet. "An eye for an eye—that's what she said."

"That must have made you furious."

"Yes. Yes, and I pushed her!" Her face contorted. "I did it, I killed her. I pushed her over the edge."

Taryn raised the knife to her throat. I slammed the door open and launched myself at her, grabbing for the knife. She went down hard: I heard the air puff out of her. The knife clattered, skidding away on the concrete floor.

Then there was blood, lots of it, sticky and slick. Thank God, it was my own.

A love ballad, crooned in soulful Spanish, streamed through the open doorway of 101 West Mission, Suite D.

I could hear Gabi tapping away at the keys behind the computer screen. And I heard something else: laughter, coming from the kitchenette.

I stepped up to the threshold and looked in.

A triumphant yellow and pink rose flared in the crystal vase. I knew it was "Peace."

I stepped into the room, and Gabi popped up. "Miss Jaymie, our hero!"

"There's nothing to celebrate. This time around, nobody won."

A purple-haired Claudia appeared in the kitchen doorway. "Come on, you're the best." An ear-to-ear grin filled her face.

"You're looking very suave, Miss Molina."

"Think so?" She pirouetted to show off her hip black jacket and slacks and merlot T-shirt, purchased in the men's department. No, correct that: at size zero, she'd shopped in the boys'.

"How about him?" Claudia stepped through the doorway, turned back and presented BJ with a flourish.

BJ's hair was also purple, though of a more subdued shade than his partner's. He also wore a black suit. A pantsuit, actually—he'd crossed the department store aisle too, heading in the opposite direction from Claudia. His russet-colored top had a silky sheen. "For the homecoming dance," he announced. "What do you think?"

"I think maybe you should trade those outfits," Gabi began. "See, Claudia should wear yours, and you—"

"What do you know about clothes?" Claudia started up. "You're gonna bust outta those sweatpants any day now, and all that pink and purple shit—"

Ah, back to normal. I raised my hands, calming the waters. "Claudia, you and BJ look amazing together."

"Not bad, huh?" She beamed.

"And Gabi? I adore your new rose."

"Me too. Oh Miss Jaymie, it's so good you are home!"

"I'm glad to be back. Did you pick up some pastries?"

"Naturalmente. They're right here in my bag."

"I'll make the coffee," BJ volunteered.

As I headed for the kitchenette, Gabi called after me. "Miss Jaymie? There's just one more thing I gotta say."

I turned back to look at her.

"If you wanna use one of my pencils, sure, I got no problem with that." A corner of her mouth twitched. "But don't forget to put it back where you found it, OK?"

An hour later I climbed into Mike's pickup for the ride up to San Luis Obispo. I'd argued a lift wasn't necessary, I could drive myself up to Bill's funeral just fine. But he'd insisted on coming down from San Luis to get me.

"Jaymie? Those scrapes on your face don't look so good." Then he nodded at the bulky bandage wrapped around my upper arm. "How about that, is it healing?"

"Sure. The scrapes got infected, they're nothing. The stab wound is going to take awhile. Twenty-eight stitches in all."

"You're lucky the knife missed an artery."

As Mike pulled onto the freeway heading north, I rested a hand on his knee. "It's going to be a tough day."

"Yeah. Everybody keeps telling me Dad had a good long life, like that should make it OK. Somehow it doesn't."

"I know what you mean." On our left, the wide-open ocean flashed under the ascending sun.

"Another hot one. Too hot for the cattle. Dad would have cursed this weather."

"Those monsoon clouds." I pointed to the big fluffy masses skimming the nearby mountaintops. "They look full of rain, but all they ever do is tease."

"Uh-huh. What we really need never comes."

"I need Brodie back," I blurted out. "I feel like I've lost him all over again. Always chasing revenge—somehow that helped me keep him alive."

"But did it?" Mike reached over and took my hand in his own.

"Seemed to. Sometimes—" I stared straight ahead through the windshield.

"Sometimes?"

"Sometimes I can't remember my brother's face."

We entered the Nojoque rocks. The contorted columns towered over us. Mike turned in to the rest stop and pulled up beside a stand of California sycamore trees.

"Jaymie, there's something I want to say to you." He switched off the engine. "You may never know what happened to Brodie."

"No. I can't accept that." I unclipped my seat belt and faced him. "I don't feel like I've got to get revenge, not anymore. But now that I know Chief Wheeler was involved in Brodie's death, I can't give up."

"How is that going to help Brodie now? I think it's time for you to let it all go."

Mike was being absurd. Did he really think I was going to

just walk away? "Don't forget, there's the note. Somebody sent it—somebody out there wants to talk."

"About that note." Mike cleared his throat. "I wasn't going to tell you, but I think maybe I should. All that stuff I was spouting, about the note being a joke? I was just trying to point you in the wrong direction."

"What?" Shocked, I pulled back. "You did that? But why?"

"I'm sorry, Jaymie. See, I found out who sent it. And I didn't want you to know."

"You have to tell me!" I clamped a hand on his arm. "I have a right."

"Yeah, you do. It was Mandy, actually. Mandy Blaine."

Mandy? No, this was impossible. "I don't believe it. If Mandy knew something, why didn't she just—"

"That's the thing. She knows nothing, all right? Mandy heard you were trying to find out what happened to Brodie, that's all."

"I still don't get it. Why send the note?" I stared hard at him: there had to be more.

"She just wanted to—aw, shit." He cleared his throat. "Mandy knew you and I were talking again. What she wanted was to throw a monkey wrench between us. She figured the note would sidetrack you, and she figured right."

I was speechless. Almost. "You've got to be kidding me. How did you figure out it was her?"

"Hey. You're not the only one who can do some detecting. When you showed me the note I recognized the paper, that thick fluffy stuff?" He covered my hand with his own again. "Don't get mad, but she sent me a few love letters on that paper."

"Me? I'm not mad, don't flatter yourself."

Mike smiled. "Anyway, I went back to the office and looked through her desk. Sure enough, I found a box of the paper. That's when Mandy and I had a talk."

He took my chin in his hand. "So that's it then, right? You can let it all go."

But something in his tone caught my attention. Something a shade too urgent, maybe, something I couldn't quite name.

"They killed him, Mike. I know that now. They dragged Brodie out of his cell—"

"Jaymie, please." Mike pulled me close and held me tight. "I only want what's best for you. Trust me on that."

I was pretty sure Mike knew more than he was saying. But I gave in and stopped talking. Because at that moment, I needed to trust him. I needed his arms around me, more than anything in the world.

"This is ridiculous," I blubbered. "We're on our way to your dad's funeral. I should be comforting you."

"You are." He squeezed me harder and didn't let go.

We sat like that in the cab for five minutes or more. Then three things happened, in quick succession.

First, the sky darkened.

Next, a wind sprang up, twisting the leaves on the sycamores.

And then a few fat drops of water plopped in the hood.

The few drops became many. "I'll be damned." Mike's voice was almost a whisper. "August rain."

A van pulled up next to us, and two little kids piled out. They began to dance in the rain shower, their faces tipped to the sky.

"Look at them," I said wistfully. "Not a care in the world."

"Come on." Mike opened his door and stepped out. He reached in, caught me by my good arm, and pulled me across the seat.

"Hey!"

"Protest all you want." He grabbed me around the waist and half lifted, half dragged me out of the truck.

I laughed in spite of myself. I couldn't stop laughing. And then I was crying, then laughing again. We held each other and started dancing, right there in the mud.

I closed my eyes, and Mike disappeared. Brodie was there.

I held my brother effortlessly. We were so light and easy together: one-two-three, one-two-three, one-two-three.

When I opened my arms he smiled at me, and danced away.